THE
FALL
GIRL

MARCIA
CLARK

ALSO BY MARCIA CLARK

Novels

Guilt by Degrees

Blood Defense

Killer Ambition

Guilt by Association

The Competition

Moral Defense

Snap Judgment

Final Judgment

Nonfiction

Without a Doubt

THE FALL GIRL

MARCIA CLARK

RARE BIRD
LOS ANGELES, CALIF.

RARE BIRD

THIS IS A GENUINE RARE BIRD BOOK

Rare Bird Books
6044 North Figueroa Street
Los Angeles, CA 90042
rarebirdbooks.com

FIRST HARDCOVER EDITION

Set in Dante
Printed in the United States

10 9 8 7 6 5 4 3 2 1

Library of Congress Cataloging-in-Publication Data

Names: Clark, Marcia, author.
Title: The fall girl / by Marcia Clark.
Description: First Hardcover Edition. | Los Angeles, Calif. : Rare Bird, [2022]
Identifiers: LCCN 2021058162 | ISBN 9781644282656 (hardcover)
Subjects: GSAFD: Mystery fiction. | Suspense fiction.
Classification: LCC PS3603.L3653 F35 2022 | DDC 813/.6—dc23

LC record available at https://lccn.loc.gov/2021058162

CHAPTER ONE

I EMPTIED THE LAST bag into the pit and stared down at the tangled heap. The pale pink cashmere sweater, the engraved leather briefcase, the cowskin pillows—every gift he'd given me, and everything I'd worn, read, or shared when we were together.

Together. The word itself filled me with pain and self-loathing.

I poured the whole can of Kingsford lighter fluid onto the pile and tossed it into the pit. Then I pulled the box of kitchen matches out of my pocket, struck one, and dropped it.

The heat seared my nostrils as I watched the fire swallow up my old life. I held the last two items in my hand: my driver's license and my ID from the Chicago Public Defender's office.

Do I really want to do this?

But the truth was, I didn't have a choice. If he found me, he'd kill me. And although I wasn't one hundred percent sure I deserved to live, I wasn't ready to accept that fate…yet. A fist squeezed my heart as I threw my IDs onto the flaming pile.

Goodbye, Lauren Claybourne.

No one would miss her. Certainly not her family, who'd cut her out of their lives like a festering tumor. Not that I blamed them—not after what'd happened.

I waited until all that was left were smoldering embers. Then I went to my car, opened the glove box, and pulled out my new driver's license. It was my face…but it wasn't. Amazing what a pair of blue contacts and blonde hair dye can do. I stared down at the name and repeated it out loud: "Charlotte Blair. Charlotte…Charlie—Blair. Charlie Blair."

Driving off, I felt like an astronaut whose tether had been cut, like I was floating out into space. I had no idea I was driving straight down the collision course that would lead me to the Hansen case—and the very peril I'd hoped to escape.

CHAPTER TWO

Three Months Later

Erika leaned back in her chair and watched the piece-of-shit defendant yuck it up with his lawyers, his sneering arrogance on full display. It was a view the jurors never got to see, thanks to some very intense coaching by his team. Unlike so many other defendants, he was smart enough to go along with it. Blake Steers was a sociopath, but he was no dummy.

Erika gave a quiet snort of disgust and whispered to her lead detective, Skip Arneson, "I hope his lawyers are bleeding him dry."

Skip glanced at Steers, then at the quartet of bespoke suits that flanked him. "If they don't, it won't be for lack of trying."

It was small consolation, but given what they'd been through for the past month, she'd take it. The case had been an uphill battle from the start. Not because the evidence wasn't there, but because the hideousness of the murder didn't jibe with the charming golden boy the jury saw at counsel table every day.

Erika glanced down at the coroner's photos on the table in front of her. Beautiful young Natalie Hemingsworth was almost unrecognizable. The bloated face, the wire around her neck embedded so deeply it was barely visible, the bruises on her breasts and stomach in the shape of the lead pipe used to beat her.

She glanced at Blake Steers again. Handsome, charismatic, a highly successful and adored celebrity chef. Erika knew the jury was having a hard time squaring one set of images with the other.

But her biggest problem was that another man in Natalie's life—T. Rayne, a notoriously degenerate DJ—fit the bill perfectly. When Steers' lead lawyer held up T. Rayne's photo during opening statements, showing him mid-snarl, his pierced nose and earrings glowing red in the colored stage lights, Erika could practically hear the jurors thinking, *Yeah, that's more like it.*

It didn't matter that there was no physical evidence linking T. Rayne to the murder or that they had plenty on Blake: his prints on the lead pipe, his DNA in the bathroom sink. He had motive, too; Natalie had just broken up with him, and both the housekeeper and Blake's assistant had been there to see him go berserk. He'd thrown a marble bookend at Natalie. If his aim had been better, it might've killed her then and there. When she ran out the door, he trashed the living room. And days later, when he found out she was seeing T. Rayne, he'd "gone postal," according to his trainer. Correction: former trainer.

No, evidence wasn't the problem. The problem was the optics. Blake didn't look the part. T. Rayne did. Stories of his raucous parties, of trashed hotel rooms across the country, of confrontations he'd ended with his fists—with both men and women—were legion.

But what almost no one knew was that glittery wunderkind Blake Steers was every bit as abusive—and then some. Natalie's closest friend, Jennifer, had told the jury about the physical and emotional abuse Blake had inflicted on Natalie. But Jennifer had been the only one who could testify to it because Natalie—embarrassed that she'd let herself be treated that way—had sworn her to secrecy.

Unfortunately, that made it easy for the defense to dismiss Jennifer as biased and unreliable on cross-examination. Erika had seen a few of the jurors frown when the lawyer got Jennifer to admit that she hadn't told anyone about the abuse until a month after Natalie had died.

At first, Erika had assumed Natalie was one of those women who gravitated to violent men. But ironically, by all accounts, T. Rayne had been good to her. And according to Jennifer, Steers was the only man who'd ever assaulted Natalie. It seemed she'd simply had a thing for big personalities.

But playing right into the hands of the defense, T. Rayne had no alibi. He'd been home alone on the night of the murder. Erika's interview with him was still fresh in her mind. It'd been like pounding on a brick wall—a hostile, heartless brick wall. Multiply pierced and grotesquely tattooed, T. Rayne hadn't so much sat as sprawled in the chair in front of her desk, his legs stretched out, bare feet crossed at the ankle. "What do you want, Ms. Prosecutor?" His smirk reeked of misogyny, condescension—and weed.

Erika had known he'd be an ass. Skip had warned her. But this was worse than she'd expected. Still, she kept her voice calm. "I need you to tell me every move you made that night."

"What the fuck difference does it make?" He nodded at Skip, who was sitting next to him. "I told your guy I was chillin' at home. How long is this gonna take?" He glanced at his cell phone. "I've got shit to do."

Erika gritted her teeth. "Right. But you were alone, so we need to prove it. The question is, what were you *doing* while you were at home alone?"

His lip curled—that familiar sneer. "Probably got high, watched some porn, jerked off." He glanced at Skip. "Same as you. Right, my man?"

Erika wanted to slap the leering grin off his face. But she needed something—anything—that would corroborate his alibi. They'd checked the surveillance cameras in his neighborhood, his cell phone records, and canvassed the houses near his, hoping someone had spotted him through his living room window. Nada. "What channel were you watching?"

T. Rayne blew a raspberry. "What channel? The fuck should I know?"

"Listen, the defense is trying to hang you for Natalie's murder. You might think that's funny now, but if people buy their bullshit, they might start canceling your gigs."

He shrugged. "Nuthin' I can do about what people think. Long as y'all know I didn't kill her, I'm golden."

Erika stared at him, disgusted. "You've been claiming you loved Natalie. At least, that's what you told the tabs. Or was that just for publicity?"

He looked away, his voice—finally—somber. "Yeah, sure. I cared about her. She was a doll."

Erika could tell he meant it. "Then how come you don't seem to give a shit about getting her killer?"

His expression hardened; the brief window of humanity slammed shut. "Look, lady, she's like…dead. Right? Gotta move on."

His callousness had left Erika breathless. She shook her head at the ugly memory. No, no point talking to that pig again.

She felt a sharp pain in her palms and stared down at her hands, perplexed. She'd been clenching her fists so tightly she'd drawn blood. What was going on with her? Self-absorbed assholes like T. Rayne were nothing new. She'd dealt with dozens like him over the years. They'd never gotten to her this way before.

But ever since she'd picked up the Steers case, she'd felt a constantly simmering anger that would flare up into a full boil without warning. Like the buried embers of an old campfire, the rage would begin to smolder—often for no apparent reason—then burst into flame and spread through her body, leaving her shaking and nearly blind with fury.

This case, this entitled, pretty-boy murderer who was pulling the wool over the jury's eyes, was smashing all her buttons. It wasn't news to her that the worst people got away with so much, used their privilege to run roughshod over the powerless, so she didn't understand the level of outrage it incited in her, though she was fairly sure it'd pass once Steers got convicted.

If Steers got convicted. If he didn't…

Erika forced herself to take deep breaths. She had a more immediate problem on her hands. That morning, Tracy Conlin, a key witness who'd been sure she'd seen Blake Steers leaving Natalie's house on the night of the murder, had buckled on cross-examination. It'd taken the defense lawyer just ten minutes to get her to admit that she might have been wrong, that it might not have been Steers. That it might even have been T. Rayne.

In any other case, it would've been a bump in the road. In this case, it was a head-on collision with a Peterbilt.

Natalie's parents hadn't been there to witness the debacle—a first since Erika had been assigned to the case. She'd warned them that the coroner was due to testify and advised them not to come. The photos and testimony would be hideously painful for them. Phillip and Rochelle had decided to take the day off, certain that Tracy would be as solid in court as she'd been in her previous interview.

And the reason they knew Tracy had done well during that interview was because they'd been there, just as they had for her and every other witness since Erika got the case. They'd read every report, sat in on every strategy session, even weighed in on exhibit preparation. Phillip, the senior partner at Hemingsworth, Struck, & Wagner, a prestigious corporate and civil litigation law firm with offices around the world, had pronounced on day one that there was no move they could make that wouldn't benefit from his input. And his new best friend, District Attorney John Harrier—who just happened to be up for reelection in six months—heartily agreed.

Not only did Phillip insist on overseeing every inch of the case, but he also monitored public reaction, watching the news coverage and commentary on every outlet. Erika knew the press would trumpet the Tracy Conlin stumble as "another bad day for the prosecution," which meant she and Skip had to get to the Hemingsworths first, warn them not to believe the spin. Phillip went ballistic at the slightest blip—and Tracy Conlin was more than just a blip.

She whispered to Skip, "Did you talk to Phillip and Rochelle yet?"

Skip sighed. "Not yet. I figured I'd go while you have the coroner on the stand."

"Good idea." The coroner was entering the courtroom now. As they exchanged nods, Erika saw the new prosecutor, Charlie...something, in the courtroom—sitting, as usual, in the back row. Erika had seen her there several times over the course of the trial, but she'd never said a word to Erika. Odd. When Erika had first joined the office, she'd done it too—watched the veteran prosecutors in action. But she'd always made it a point to say, "nice job with that witness," or "you really nailed that argument." She supposed Charlie might just be shy, but somehow Charlie didn't strike her as the shy type.

"Time to go," she whispered to Skip.

He pushed back from counsel table. "Okay. But if I kill the bastard, you have to back me up."

"Don't worry. No one's going to convict you for killing a lawyer." She patted him on the arm. "Maybe leave your gun in my desk, though."

Skip gave her a side-eyed look. "I'd rather strangle him, anyway."

She suppressed a laugh as he headed for the door. She and Skip had been an unofficial team for the past ten years, and in that time they'd become real friends, an old married work couple. Except Skip was gay and had a partner, Carson, probably the funniest—and best-looking—paramedic to ever ride in an ambulance.

The coroner, Indira Tolle, an East Indian woman and one of the few ME's that was really good on the witness stand, sat down next to Erika and pulled a manila envelope out of her briefcase. "I have some new photos, closeups." She laid the eight-by-ten blowups on the table. "See how deeply the wire cut into her neck? This took a great deal of strength—and time. Should be good for premeditation."

The photos were so graphic even Erika had a hard time looking at them. Maybe this would sober up that damn jury.

"Thanks, Indira. Did you bring extras for the defense?"

"Of course." She handed four copies to Erika.

Indira was such a pro. Erika smiled and took the photos to the other end of counsel table, where Steers had the defense attorneys laughing at something—probably another humble-brag story about a famous client and a rare mushroom.

She handed the photos to the lead lawyer. "The coroner just brought these in."

A look of shock flashed across his face—a rare moment of honesty—before he remembered to cover with a nonchalant, "Thanks."

Blake Steers glanced over his lawyer's shoulder at the photos. Then he looked up at Erika and sniffed the air, deliberately raking his eyes up and down her body. "Love your perfume, counsel. What're you wearing?"

Fury shot through her like a ball of fire. For a brief second, Erika literally saw red. It took all she had to ignore him and walk away.

Focus, she told herself. *Don't let him get to you.* The best revenge was about to take the witness stand. Indira was going to bury him.

And she did. Her calm, singsong voice, an eerie counterpoint to the descriptions of Natalie's gruesome injuries, somehow made them sound even more horrific. As Indira pointed to the photos on the monitor, Erika snuck glances at the jury. Their stunned expressions gratified her. But whether that would convince them Steers was guilty or make it even harder to believe the fair-haired boy sitting in front of them had done it, she couldn't say.

Whatever the impact, the testimony went well. When Erika headed upstairs at the end of the day, she was in a pretty good mood—until she saw Phillip and Rochelle waiting for her in her office with Skip.

"Phillip, Rochelle, I'm glad you're here. The cor—"

Phillip's cheeks flamed bright pink. "What the hell happened with Tracy Conlin? How could you let the defense get to her?"

She had to bite back the *fuck you* that wanted to fly out of her mouth. "She did identify Steers on direct examination. And I got her to repeat it on redirect. It's just a bit of a setback. Don't worry."

He gripped the arms of his chair. "A bit of a *setback*? What do you call a tsunami? A bit of a wave? She killed us!"

With an effort, Erika kept her voice calm. "Tracy's only one witness. We've got many more to go. And the coroner's testimony went really well. She had the jurors in the palm of her hand. By the time she got off the stand, I'm sure they'd forgotten all about Tracy."

Phillip was still agitated. Out of the corner of her eye, Erika caught Rochelle's apologetic expression. But Rochelle, ever the calm one, the counterpoint to her husband's explosive temper, never actually interceded. Erika supposed she'd learned over the years to let his rage play itself out. But today Erika didn't have the time—or frankly, the energy—for that. The only other way to slow Phillip's roll was to give him something else to think about.

"Let me tell you what's coming up."

She spent the next half hour outlining the testimony she planned to present that week while Phillip peppered her with questions. Phillip wasn't tall or buff—in fact, he was downright slender. But his mane of white hair and piercing blue eyes were classic patriarch material. When he walked into a room, he filled it and then some. It was no mystery why his daughter had been attracted to men who blocked out the sun.

Though Rochelle was just a few years behind him at fifty, she looked twenty years younger; no doubt thanks to some excellent plastic surgery. Erika could see Natalie's blue eyes, delicate mouth, and slightly crooked nose in both their features.

But if Rochelle owed her unlined face to a great doctor, her near-perfect body was all on her, the result of good genes and hard work. Between her younger years with the rowing team and on the tennis court, and likely thanks to a high-priced trainer, she wasn't just fit, she was strong. She practically glided when she walked. If Erika could manage to rock sleeveless shirts half as well in her fifties, she'd die happy.

And both Phillip and Rochelle had the kind of smooth, relaxed confidence that came from being born into a life of nearly inexhaustible wealth.

Erika had no idea what that might be like. She and her little brother had been abandoned by their parents at a truck stop motel when she was six and he was four. Her first experience with security—or any kind of power over her life—hadn't come until she was eighteen, when she'd managed to score a full-ride scholarship to Stanford. Phillip and Rochelle were a window into a world she could never have imagined, and she viewed it with a mixture of awe and envy.

As she finished describing the upcoming testimony, Skip glanced at his watch and gave Phillip a warm smile. "Seven o'clock already? I didn't realize we'd kept you so long."

Erika breathed an inward sigh of relief. *God bless Skip.*

Rochelle picked up on the cue. "Neither did I. Thank you both."

Phillip stood, held out a hand to his wife, and glanced at Erika. "By the way, we're meeting John for dinner."

Erika knew her smile was strained. All Phillip would have to do was snap his fingers and her boss, the district attorney, would throw her out on her ass. "How nice."

He moved to the door and paused. "What'd be nice is if you'd convict that son of a bitch."

Erika's stomach churned, but she put on a confident smile. "We will. I promise."

Hard as he was to deal with, Erika did sympathize. The loss of a child under any circumstances was the worst tragedy a parent could suffer. But to lose a child, an only child, at the hands of a brutal monster like Blake Steers had to be excruciating.

She held onto her plastic smile until the door closed behind them, then sank back in her chair, depleted.

Skip gave her a puzzled look. "You 'promise'?"

They never promised a win. Never. It was asking for trouble. "I know," Erika said. "But I had to get him out of here. I'm wiped." The previous night, she'd woken up almost every hour on the hour in a panic about how to save the case.

Skip studied her. "If you don't take your foot off the pedal, you're going to stroke out."

Erika gave him a wan smile. "Pull the plug if I do. I don't want to be a drooling rutabaga."

"I promise I *won't* pull the plug. It'll be the only time I ever get to win an argument." He stood up. "Come on, I'll walk you to your car." As he moved toward the door, he added, "I might have a new witness for you tomorrow."

Erika shook her head. "I need to get some more work done. But I could use the good news. Are we talking about an alibi witness?"

"I don't know yet. A uni who works the Beach Flats area just left me a message saying that a man had something to tell us about the case. She didn't seem to know what it was."

Erika tried to push down the surge of hope, but it flooded through her anyway, like rain in a parched desert. "Okay, let me know."

"Will do." He gave her a serious look. "And get some sleep. I mean it."

She gave him a mock salute.

One minute after he'd left, the intercom on her landline buzzed. It was Marta, the receptionist. "A woman just called. She said she wants to see you tonight—alone. I told her the office is closed, but she said it was about the Blake Steers case."

Alone. Erika frowned. It was dangerous to talk to a witness without a detective in the room. If the witness decided to go south on the stand, she'd need someone to testify to what they'd said before. And Erika—the lawyer on the case—couldn't do that. "Did she give you a name?"

"I asked, but she wouldn't say. She seemed awfully nervous."

Very mysterious. And maybe trouble. But Erika couldn't afford to say no.

×××

WITH HER LONG BLONDE hair, cornflower blue eyes, and slender build, Melody Newman could've been Natalie's sister. It seemed Steers, too, had a type.

But that was where the resemblance ended. By all accounts, Natalie, who'd founded GirlPower, a headhunter company for women, was a high-octane extrovert. Melody was so shy and soft-spoken, Erika had to lean forward to hear her.

"I...um," Melody tucked her hair behind her ear and whispered, "heard you told Jennifer that if any other women were abused by Blake, they should come see you."

Erika felt her flagging spirits soar. This might be the break she'd been hoping for. "I'm so glad you're here, Melody. Were you...with Blake?"

Melody nodded and blinked rapidly. "We were dating before he met Natalie. He...um...broke up with me right after he met her."

That was a worry. If it looked like Melody had an axe to grind, it'd pose a real credibility problem. "How did you feel about that?"

Melody closed her eyes and exhaled. "So relieved. I'd been wanting to end it with him, but I was too scared."

Perfect, and obviously true. There was no faking that reaction. "Why? What was going on?"

Melody gazed over Erika's shoulder. "At first, it was just that he was so controlling. Like, every time I told him I needed to go anywhere for more than a day, he'd find a way to stop me. When I said I wanted to go visit my sister in Paris or go to Colorado to help my parents move into a new condo, he went crazy."

"Crazy, how?"

"He accused me of lying, said I was making up an excuse to leave town so I could cheat on him. He...he threatened to kill me." She stared down at the floor. "The last time, when I wanted to go see my grandmother in Albuquerque, he hid my driver's license and all my credit cards." Melody took a deep breath. "I was just totally, like, trapped."

Erika's chest tightened. It sounded like absolute hell. "Did he ever... hurt you?"

Melody bit her lip. "Not in the beginning. He'd hit the wall next to me, pound the table I was sitting at. Stuff like that. But then, after about a month, he…yes. He hit me. He'd punch me, or twist my arm behind my back, or drag me around by the hair. Once, he kicked me so hard he broke a rib."

Melody's breathing had become fast and shallow. When she spoke again, her voice was a fragile whisper. "And sometimes he…he'd…rape me. From behind."

"You mean anally?"

Melody nodded.

"Did you ever see a doctor?"

She shook her head. "I was too ashamed. And scared. If he found out that I'd gone to a doctor, I—I don't know what he'd have done to me."

"Did he ever give you a black eye?" If he had, and Melody had photos of it, that'd be all Erika needed to corroborate her testimony.

Melody shook her head. "He never hit my face."

So Steers had been careful not to inflict visible injuries. The fact that he could exert that much control made it even worse. Erika remembered a story Jennifer had told her and asked, "Did he ever drug you?"

Melody looked away. "Near the end, after I said that maybe we should take a break. He roofied me and…and raped me."

Just talking about it was making Melody tremble. Erika felt her resolve strengthen; she had to put this monster away.

"Melody, I need you to testify at the trial."

She'd been sitting hunched over, eyes downcast. Now she jerked up in her seat, her eyes wide. "No! I can't! He'll kill me!"

Erika leaned in and looked her in the eye. "Not if he's in prison. And if you testify, he will be. Your story is so powerful. It'll prove beyond all possible doubt that Blake raped and murdered Natalie. And he'll never get out. You'll be safe, forever. Testifying is the best insurance policy you can get."

But Melody was shaking her head, her soft voice stretched tight with anxiety. "No. I'm sorry, but I can't do it. I won't."

Erika understood her fear—and she knew part of it was the shame of having to tell her story in public. But Melody's testimony was a game changer. "Please, Melody. If you can't do it for yourself, do it for all the other women he'll abuse—maybe even kill—if he gets acquitted."

Melody began to sob. "I'm sorry! I know you think I'm a weak, terrible person. And you're right. I should do it. But I just...can't." She raised a tearful face to Erika. "And please, please don't tell anyone what I told you. I'm begging you."

Erika could force Melody to take the stand. But she'd just clam up, deny she'd said anything—and make Erika look like a desperate bully. And truthfully, she couldn't bring herself to traumatize this poor woman any further. "Okay, Melody. I won't."

Melody gave Erika a pleading look. "Promise me. Please."

Erika nodded and handed her a box of Kleenex. "I promise."

Which meant she couldn't even risk telling Skip. He'd be obligated to write up a report, and she couldn't be sure it wouldn't get leaked. When it came to media cases, neither her office nor the police department could be trusted.

As for telling Natalie's parents, Phillip Hemingsworth would drag Melody into court by the hair.

"But if you didn't want to testify, then why tell me?"

"Because I wanted you to know how important it is to put him away."

As if she needed to be told. "Have you ever talked to anyone else about what he did to you?"

"No. I...I c-couldn't. There was no one..." Melody pulled out a tissue and wiped her tears.

Erika understood. Melody had needed to tell someone who wouldn't judge her, who'd believe her—and who could be trusted to keep it quiet. So often women who'd been abused wound up being victimized twice: once at the hands of their abuser; a second time by the callous skepticism of the people to whom they reported the abuse. "I understand."

Melody stood up. "I have to go. I'm sorry I can't...help you. But I hope you get him."

Heart sinking, Erika watched her go. Her best chance to put Steers in prison had just walked out the door.

CHAPTER THREE

One week later

I SLIPPED INTO COURT and sat in the back row. Every chance I got, I'd been popping in to watch our "Trial of the Century," the case against Blake Steers. Closing arguments were supposed to start today, and I wanted to see Erika in action.

Erika Lorman was a legend in the Santa Cruz DA's office. From my very first day, I'd been hearing war stories about her brilliance. Her track record was almost perfect—two losses in fifteen years. And it wasn't just her stellar strategic moves and command of the law. It was her seemingly magical touch with juries. They loved her. More than that, they believed her. You can't teach that in law school. You've either got it or you don't.

Back in Chicago, people had said Lauren Claybourne had it. But after I left the public defender's office three months ago and moved to Santa Cruz to join the DA's office…I didn't know anymore. Charlie Blair was just a name to me. I wasn't sure who she was. More than that, I had no idea who I wanted her to be.

And then I'd met Erika. I'd expected her to be an ego-driven bragger who sucked all the oxygen out of the room. So many big-name lawyers were. But Erika was none of those things. True, she was a strong presence, the kind of person you noticed immediately. She seemed to radiate power. But she wasn't trying to impress. She was just…being Erika. And when she told war stories, it wasn't the type of self-fellating, attention-grabbing show that gives me the dry heaves. The opposite, in fact. She told her stories with a rueful emphasis on her mistakes and fumbles.

But it was the way Erika talked about the victims that really struck me. She was so deeply committed to them; it was as though they were her family. Until I fled Chicago, I'd spent my entire career on the defense side. While I usually did sympathize with the victims to a degree, put practically, I also saw them as obstacles to overcome. Hearing Erika talk about their pain and loss was an inspiration. To me, she embodied all that a prosecutor should be. I'd found a role model for Charlie Blair.

And now that I'd seen her in trial, I knew the stories of her courtroom prowess were legit. Smooth on direct examination, quick and incisive on cross—impressive all the way around. She made it look easy—though I knew it wasn't. I'd thought I was pretty good, but now I found myself copying the way she emphasized a witness's good answer with a pause and a thoughtful nod—a subtle way to signal to the jury that they'd just heard something important.

The plan I'd made when I fled Chicago was simple: if I had to be a stranger in a strange land, it might as well be a land of sunshine. I've heard people who leave the Midwest miss the seasons, but I was happy to give them up if it meant not having to slog through another Chicago winter.

I still wanted to practice criminal law, but I needed to change as much of my identity as possible. I couldn't stomach the idea of doing more defense work, and the thought of civil practice bored me silly. The only thing worse than writing contracts—where the most exciting issue is "How many zeroes can I add after the 'three'?"—were divorce cases. Those make the ugliest, most gruesome murder trials look like an episode of *Sesame Street*.

That left me with only one real choice: becoming a prosecutor—a hundred-and-eighty-degree career turn. Would I be able to handle it? I had no idea, but there was only one way to find out.

Knowing I needed to bury myself in a small town, I'd applied to the DA's offices in every Podunk county I could find. Crime being a universal constant, I figured I'd have my choice of jobs.

But as one office after another said they weren't hiring, I got more and more anxious. I'd been hiding out in a hotel, but I couldn't afford to keep paying for that, and I had to get out of Chicago if I wanted to stay alive.

All too late, I realized the flaw in my plan: small towns didn't have much crime—ergo, they didn't need many prosecutors—and the few prosecutors they did have stayed put until their grandkids had grandkids.

Desperate, I'd decided to just pick a city in California and figure out what else I could do with a law degree when I got the letter from the Santa Cruz DA's office. Not as small a town as I'd have liked, but a hell of a lot better than LA or San Francisco. And when I checked it out on Wikipedia, it looked beautiful—all seasides and redwood forests. Another plus: the DA's office was a ten-minute walk from the beach and the Boardwalk.

Santa Cruz it was. I just had to ace the interview.

On the day I met with the hiring supervisor, I was so wound up I had to pop a Xanax to keep my hands from shaking. I almost never did that during the day. Xanax was for bedtime. That, and a tumbler of vodka…or scotch… or tequila. It didn't really matter. It wasn't a taste thing.

But even so, I felt the sweat trickle down into my bra as I waited to be called in. My résumé *looked* solid, thanks to a very dear—and, more importantly, trustworthy—friend in Chicago with his own law firm. He let me list him as my boss for the past six years and even told me to put in a quote saying I'd been a superstar.

But while I thought I'd done a decent job covering my tracks, I knew there was no such thing as perfect. And if the Santa Cruz DA investigators had looked hard enough, they might've figured out it was all BS.

Maybe they had. Maybe this wasn't an interview after all. Maybe it was a ruse to get me in so they could confront me and report me to the State Bar—or the police.

Given my state of mind, I didn't exactly burst out of the gate. For the first ten minutes, the only words I managed to choke out were "yes" and "I think so." But as the interview wore on, I realized the interviewer had no idea. Knowing I was safe—for now—I managed to relax enough to string together complete sentences and even smile at one of his jokes. By the time we shook hands, I felt like I just might've pulled it off.

Sure enough, two days later, I got the call saying I was hired. I'd told the supervisor I could start in two weeks—purposely giving myself a lot less time than I needed. I had to keep busy. Too busy to think.

That meant I landed in Santa Cruz with just ten days to find a place, move in, buy furniture, stock the refrigerator—and install a home security camera. I wasn't picky about housing. As long as it had a refrigerator and wasn't on the ground level, I was good to go. In the end, I rented the first apartment I saw—a one bedroom on the second floor that was really a glorified studio. The realtor had euphemistically described it as "open concept." Kind of like calling a janitor a hygiene engineer.

The apartment's one saving grace was a big picture window in the living room. I had a view of the ocean and a sliver of the Santa Cruz Boardwalk. It made me think of my little sister, Hannah. She loved the ocean. I wished I could send her a photo of that view.

Of all my family members, Hannah was the one I missed most. I'd known we'd be close from the day my mother brought her home from the hospital, a sweet-smelling pink doll with a fringe of white blonde hair. Now that hair had turned brown, like mine had been before I'd had to dye it. Hannah was ten years younger than me, but if we'd been closer in age, people would've thought we were twins.

Would I ever see her again? Or anyone else in my family?

Probably not. I pushed the painful thought away.

Those ten days were an endless blur of errands and trips to Ikea and Home Depot. At night, I was so tired all I could do was punch down my drink-and-Xanax cocktail and spiral into bed. But that didn't stop the nightmares, surreal dreamscapes wrapped around too-real images of Hannah, or my parents, bleeding out as I tried—futilely—to staunch the flow with my hands. I woke up every time with my heart pounding, my face wet with tears.

Still, I kept up the pace. By the night before my first day at the DA's office, I'd managed to get myself set up. I'd been dreading that first day all along, but now the thought of it made me break out in a sweat. Would I blow it by not answering to my new name? Had the DA investigators found me out yet? I was a wreck. But I couldn't risk my usual cocktail. Showing up sloggy and hungover on my first day was a no go. I mean, I had to save *something* for day two.

The problem was, I'd lost the ability to fall asleep without a tumbler of vodka under my belt. The night gave me too much time to think—about all

I'd done wrong, all the misery I'd caused—and the tragedy I might still have set in motion. I took a double dose of melatonin I'd bought at Trader Joe's, then put myself to bed. Given my anxiety level, though, I wasn't optimistic.

Sure enough, I lay there, wide awake, listening for any stray sounds. Every creak and scrape made me bolt up—*What was that?*—and grab my phone to look at my Ring app.

By the time morning came, it felt like the night had been thirty hours long, and I was a mess. My hair was going in all different directions, and my eyes were so red and gritty I had to douse them with two kinds of drops to get my blue contacts in. I picked up my hair dryer with shaking hands and did what I could to pull my look together, then gripped the sides of the sink and stared at my face in the mirror as I repeated the mantra I'd kept running in my head since leaving Chicago: "I'm Charlotte Blair. Call me Charlie. I'm Charlotte Blair. Call me Charlie."

And then, I headed out to start Charlie Blair's new life.

× × ×

MY ENTIRE FIRST DAY, I kept waiting for someone to come up behind me, put a hand on my shoulder, and say, *"Ms. Claybourne, you need to come with us."* I didn't realize I'd been holding my breath all day until I got home.

That night, I lay on the couch, tequila in hand, and closed my eyes. I remembered a fox-faced prosecutor named Patty…Brockman. Right. Patty, who was dressed in jeans and black boots, had given my navy blue skirt suit and white silk blouse a skeptical look, circled a finger in the air, and said, "You can take it easy with the lawyer cosplay. We're pretty militant about the trés casual thing here."

Funny—but dangerous. Patty obviously didn't believe in boundaries. *Keep your distance.*

In general, though, they were nice—and fun. The kind of people Lauren Claybourne would've liked to hang out with once upon a time. Whether Charlie Blair could risk it was another matter. It'd be dangerous if someone got too close, asked too many questions.

With that in mind, I'd begged off on all lunch and Happy Hour invitations. But after a month, I'd started to feel a little safer—and a lot lonelier. When Suzanne, whose office was next door to mine, invited me to join a bunch of them for drinks at Blinky's, the sports bar across the street, I decided to break down and give it a try. I'd be in a crowd where everyone just wanted to party. No danger I'd have to face any prying questions. It seemed safe enough.

The bar—festooned in Christmas lights and filled with dozens of plastic good luck cats in an array of colors—was noisy as hell. Eighties pop music blasted from a jukebox; a soccer match was playing on two televisions. We commandeered two tables at the back, and before anyone could place an order, the waitress brought three pitchers of beer.

I raised an eyebrow as I said to Suzanne, "She's one hell of a mind reader."

She smiled and shrugged. "Yeah, we're regulars. Boringly consistent regulars."

Eva, a freckled redhead, filled her glass and launched into a long complaint about a visiting judge who'd scared the defendant out of taking a plea bargain. The spate of shop talk that followed ranged from speculation about Harrier's chances of winning another term as DA to the hot new public defender in Department Twelve. It was just the kind of camaraderie I'd been missing since I'd left Chicago, and as I joined in, I found myself relaxing. For a change, I wasn't obsessively checking the Ring app on my phone—or reaching into my purse to make sure the can of Mace was still there.

Eddie—dark-eyed, intense, his tie always askew—was managing the pitcher of beer closest to me. As I held out my glass for a refill, he asked, "So, you missing Chicago?"

My stomach clenched. "Not really. Nothing beats having an office five min- utes from the beach." Eager to deflect, I added, "Is this your first lawyer gig?"

"First and last," he said. "I'm a lifer."

Lance, who was in his forties and a little older than the rest of us, gave him a skeptical look. "You say that now, my friend. But just wait. Trial work will wear you down."

And with that, the group fell into a heated discussion about the pluses and minuses of being a prosecutor. Crisis averted.

Or so I thought.

At the end of the evening, just as we'd finished paying the tab, the cherubic-faced Tommy declared, "Group selfie! Say guilty!"

He whipped out his cell phone and snapped the photo before I had a chance to turn away. I inwardly gasped, trying to keep the note of hysteria out of my voice, said, "You're not going to post that, are you?"

If he put it up on Instagram or Facebook...

"Gotta keep my followers happy." He grinned. "All twelve of 'em."

My heart began to pound. "Would you mind...could you please delete that?"

He stared at me. "Why?"

I stammered. "I—uh, I look like shit."

He rolled his eyes. "C'mon, Charlie. You look great."

I felt sick as I watched him pocket his phone. I knew, on a rational level, that the odds of that photo getting any farther than Tommy's little group were virtually nil. But it was the internet. Anything could go anywhere.

That night, I was a complete and total wreck. Too panicked to fall asleep, I paced the living room, cell phone in hand, watching my Ring app for any sign of movement. I needed a drink, but I knew I wouldn't be able to stop at one, and I didn't dare get drunk. Eventually, I dozed off on the couch. But it was a windy night, and every time the tree branches blew against the window, I jerked awake, my heart in my throat, sure he'd finally found me.

I learned my lesson that night. No more Happy Hours or birthdays or lunches or...anything. My world would consist of a population of one: Me.

The upside? I was incredibly productive. Because I had nothing to do but work, I hit the ground running and chewed through my stack of cases like a thresher. My supervisor, Mike Brannigan, a former Marine so comically gruff the prosecutors called him Deputy Dogg, had had his reservations about hiring a former defense attorney. But seeing me churn out one trial after another earned me some Deputy Dogg love. All to the good. Unlike his less favored prosecutors, whom he rode like Preakness ponies, he left me alone.

That meant I could sneak out every now and then to watch Erika do her thing.

There was an air of mystery about her. For all the admiration and respect she inspired, no one seemed to know much about her personal life. I'd never heard a single mention of a spouse, boyfriend, or girlfriend. I'd heard she had a younger brother. But nothing about parents, aunts, or uncles. The only person she seemed to hang out with on a regular basis was a detective, Skip Arneson.

Oddly, that made me feel better. Like me, she wasn't part of an office "lunch bunch." According to breakroom gossip, in her fifteen years in the office, she'd only gone to a handful of after-hours get-togethers. It kind of puzzled me. I knew why I was so solitary, but why was she?

In the courtroom, Judge Butler took the bench and called for the Steers jury, and I snapped back to the present. The defense had identified a plausible straw man as the "real murderer," a DJ/asshole named T. Rayne who'd been seeing the victim and was with her the night before the murder. For the first time, other deputy DAs were privately making dire predictions about Erika's chances.

And the victim's parents were breathing down her neck. Two weeks ago—the day Erika had finished her case in chief—I'd bumped into the Hemingsworths in the breakroom. I'd introduced myself and offered them coffee. "It's not Starbucks," I said, smiling, "but it's safe."

Phillip's eyes had flicked toward me, then back to his cell phone. "No, we'll be leaving soon. I just want to have a word with Erika before we go."

Uh, you're welcome.

But I wasn't surprised. We'd all heard his voice—peremptory and imperious—booming out from behind Erika's closed door morning and night.

As I poured myself a cup, Erika walked in. Without so much as a hello, Phillip pounced. "Why didn't you put that housekeeper on the stand? She saw how Steers went crazy when Natalie left!"

Erika sat down, her tone patient. "Because she would've fallen apart like a cheap suit. If you'll recall, she said she didn't want to testify. I practically had to use a crowbar to pry that statement out of her."

"So what? If she tried to recant, you could've impeached her!"

I knew Erika had to be reining herself in. But it sure didn't show.

"She'd just say we pushed her into giving us that statement. Did you want to risk ending our case in chief on a note like that?"

Phillip didn't answer, but he still looked dissatisfied. Rochelle put a hand on his arm. "She has a point, Phillip. And we're going to be late for dinner."

Erika stood up. "I'll walk you out."

I watched them leave, thinking we didn't get paid enough to put up with shit like that. I had to hand it to Erika, though. She'd managed him like a pro. Knowing me, I'd have told him to fuck off long ago.

Now, I watched Erika stand and move to the podium as the judge told her she could start her closing argument. She put two photos on the monitor. One showed a smiling, beautiful Natalie Hemingsworth. The other showed Natalie lying dead on the bedroom floor—her face blue, her blackened, swollen tongue protruding. The angry bruises on her body stood out in high relief against her pale skin.

I glanced at the defendant. Steers wore a sad, dejected look—but it was a look that said none of this had anything to do with him. He knew how to put on an act, I'd give him that. But in my old life, I'd sat next to my fair share of sociopaths, and Blake Steers was definitely one of them.

×××

THAT EVENING, AS I PACKED up to go home, I felt my stomach rumble. "Lunch" had consisted of five Saltine crackers. I'd taken things a little— okay, a lot—too far the night before, and paid for it with a monster headache and a bad stomach. Hardly the first time and definitely not the last. But now I was hungry, and I didn't feel like cooking.

My favorite taco stand, I decided. It was down in Lower Ocean, just a short hop from the Boardwalk, one of Santa Cruz's big attractions and featured in *The Lost Boys*, a cult movie I'd watched at least ten times in high school. Hot male vampires with a snarky sense of humor living in a beautiful beach town. For a kid growing up in a quiet Chicago suburb, it was edgy, sexy, and weirdly glamorous.

But the Boardwalk and Lower Ocean—for all their physical proximity— might as well have been on different planets. Police patrolled the shit out of the Boardwalk. Families played in the arcades, rode the roller coasters, and walked along the ocean day and night. *The Lost Boys* made it seem intriguing and dark; in reality, it was a sweet, PG place for the whole wholesome family. Pretty much a snore.

But on the streets of Lower Ocean, gangbangers mixed with hookers and drug dealers, and cops were in short supply. Tourists were warned to stay out of the area at night and to give the motels down there a pass.

Which meant those poor tourists would never experience the almost mystical pleasure of Lupe's Tacos. They were a thing of beauty. A crunchy shell, savory ground beef, and just the right amount of lettuce, tomato, cheese, and sour cream.

I'd found Lupe's by accident. Having sworn off all socializing after that disastrous Happy Hour at Blinky's, I'd needed a place to unwind. Bouncing between my office and my tiny apartment day in and day out was making me crazy. But it had to be a place where I could be anonymous, where no one from the office would go. And it had to be far enough from my neighborhood that *he* wouldn't be able to find me, even if he did figure out where I lived.

Lower Ocean fit the bill. So, I'd gone exploring—as always, with a wary eye in the rearview and a can of Mace close at hand—and found a dive bar, the Buck Nail. From the look of the place, I assumed all the nails were probably buck. Battered wooden bar stools; ugly plastic booths that'd been stabbed and scratched to hell; and a heavy smell of old smoke, sweat, and cheap booze. But the bartender, Pete, gave a good pour—my highest priority. I gave the place two thumbs up.

The only downside was that after just one tequila on the rocks, I needed something in my stomach before I got behind the wheel. When I stepped outside, there was Lupe's, a block away. It was meant to be.

Now, as I pulled up to the taco stand, I saw a group of heavily tatted bangers hanging out in the parking lot. The tallest guy looked up as I got out of the car and nudged the chubby one standing next to him. They leered at me, gold teeth shining. As I passed by, one of them gave a low growl. *Wow, hot.* I considered telling him what I thought of his mating call, but I was hungry and didn't want to waste the time.

When I got to the order window, the tall one came over to me. "Hey, mama. I got a fiver if you got the time."

"Even for the ten seconds it'll take, that's a lousy deal. Pass." I tapped the bell on the counter.

"Fuck you, bitch." He stepped in closer, his eyes burning. "You don' wanna mess with—"

Lupe appeared at the window and glared at him. "*Callate!* Get outta here! Go! Find somewheres else to do your business."

My admirer gave her a narrow-eyed look before sauntering off. But he didn't fool her—or me. Everyone knew Lupe packed heat under the counter. I turned back to her and gave my usual order: two beef tacos with rice.

She shook her head, exasperated. "Chica, you keep pushin' your luck. One day it's gonna run out. You know this ain't no place for you."

I shrugged. "Your tacos are worth it."

Lupe muttered to herself about the *estupida gringa* as she went to put my meal together. I stared down the street at the Buck Nail. A couple of hookers—one black, wearing thigh-high patent leather boots, the other white, wearing glittery green platform sandals—were standing in front of the bar's darkened window, smoking. It was a weeknight, so I knew from past experience I'd probably have the place to myself. And if I only had half a vodka soda, I'd be safe enough to drive.

I'd just started to head down the street, when Lupe called out. "Hey!" She pushed a bag through the window. "Now get out of here. I don't need you dyin' on my block tonight."

No Buck Nail, then. I paid her, took the food, and headed home, where I wolfed down my tacos and poured myself a double shot of Ketel One.

As I drank, I thought about Erika's closing argument. It'd been powerful. A dramatic summary of the evidence with just the right touch of emotion. The emotion was the tricky part, especially for the prosecution. Show too much and it comes off as biased; show too little and it comes off as uncaring, or worse—unsure. Erika'd hit it right in the sweet spot.

Still, as she'd argued, I'd watched the jurors glance at Blake Steers with expressions that said, *Really? Him?* It worried the hell out of me.

Jurors believe what they want to believe. And no matter how hard we try to convince them that murderers come in all stripes and sizes, that you can't tell whether someone's a killer by the way they look or act in court, jurors still—consciously or subconsciously—want to believe they can. It makes them feel safer. Today, I could tell these jurors *really* didn't want to believe Blake Steers could be the monster who'd so brutally murdered Natalie Hemingsworth.

But he was.

And Erika had to get him.

CHAPTER FOUR

ERIKA PACED, HER ARMS folded around her aching stomach. It'd been three days since the jury had retired to deliberate, and they hadn't heard a peep. That couldn't be good.

Frantic, she'd bribed the bailiff with a six-pack of his favorite beer to tell her whether he'd heard any yelling. Not a sound. Not even laughter. That felt ominous, too.

Thankfully, Phillip and Rochelle had left to get some air. Phillip was wound up so tight he could barely speak—a first, in her experience. Probably in his, too. And though Erika could see that Rochelle was trying to keep it together, she couldn't stop asking questions. What was taking the jury so long? What did it mean? Had her other cases taken this long?

Erika had tried to reassure them, but she couldn't have been that convincing because she wasn't convinced herself.

There was a knock on the door, and Skip stepped in. "Hey, how're you doing?" He took in her appearance. "Never mind. I can see."

Erika threw him an irritable look, then noticed his uncharacteristically formal suit jacket. "You think they're coming back today."

He shrugged. "Just a feeling."

He hadn't offered to bet on the verdict—something they always did. But then, neither had she. "Your feeling tell you what they're gonna do?"

Skip's expression was tense. "No."

"How about how long it'll take Phillip to get me fired?"

His tone was sympathetic. "No."

Erika resumed pacing. Harrier wouldn't put up with such a high-profile loss. He'd fire her, and that'd be the end of her career. No other DA's office would want someone who'd been dumped after losing a case this big.

What would she do? The DA's office was her life, her mission, her everything. And on a deeper level, being a prosecutor had given her the security she'd always craved. It was home. A place she belonged. Something she'd never had.

She'd never forgive herself if the jury let Steers go. Natalie. Sweet, trusting Natalie. And Melody. And all the others who were too scared and traumatized to talk—not to mention the many more who were sure to come.

"If they acquit, I'll spend the rest of my life looking for a way to get that bastard."

"From what I've seen, we won't have to wait long. He's an arrogant fuck-up with zero impulse control. He'll blow it again."

Erika stared at him. "Is that supposed to be good news?"

He sighed. "We haven't lost yet."

The intercom on her phone buzzed. Erika stopped mid-stride, threw a worried look at Skip, then reached across the desk. "Yes?" She listened for a second. "Okay, thanks."

She dropped the receiver back in its cradle, feeling like she might faint. "Good thing you wore a tie. They have a verdict."

Skip went to her and put a hand on her shoulder. "You okay?"

Erika nodded. They had to tell Phillip and Rochelle, but she didn't trust her voice. "Can you call them?"

Skip pulled out his cell. As he spoke, Erika could hear his nervousness. He ended the call and buttoned his blazer. "They'll meet us there."

"Good." She didn't have it in her to give any more pep talks. It was the biggest—and possibly the last—case of her career. And Steers, one of the most dangerous, vicious criminals she'd ever prosecuted, might well walk out the door.

×××

NEWS VANS CROWDED THE courthouse parking lot. As expected, every seat in the gallery was full. When Erika walked up the aisle to counsel table, she could feel the eyes following her.

The court clerk, Letitia, flashed her a quick smile. As Erika nodded back, the bailiff called the court to order.

The jurors filed in, and Erika searched their faces for a sign. Their expressions gave nothing away. She'd always wondered whether they pulled that deadpan act because they enjoyed this moment of power, everyone in the courtroom waiting to hear what they'd decided.

The bailiff took the manila folder from the foreman, a retired teacher, and handed it to Judge Butler. Erika focused on him now, but his face was impassive. As he handed the folder to Letitia, Erika clasped her hands together so no one would see them shaking.

Letitia opened the folder and read. "In the matter of the People of the State of California versus Blake Steers, the jury finds the defendant, Blake Steers…guilty of murder in the first degree, as charged in count one."

Erika, light-headed from holding her breath, began to sway. As Skip put out a steadying hand, she whispered into his ear, "Did she say 'guilty'? Did I hear that right?"

He whispered back. "She sure did."

The clerk went on. "As to the charge of rape, we the jury find the defendant, Blake Steers, guilty. And we further find that the murder charged in count one was committed in the course of that rape."

A clean sweep. Not just the murder, but the special circumstance of rape-murder. Blake Steers would never be paroled. Blake Steers would die in prison.

Erika felt tears sting her eyes. She blinked them back and whispered to Skip, "We did it, Skip. We got him."

Skip nodded and swallowed hard. Erika knew he was feeling unusually emotional, too. Natalie was such an innocent victim. Steers was such a dangerous, remorseless sack of shit. And they'd come so close to losing.

Erika drew what felt like the first full breath she'd taken since she'd filed the case and watched the jurors scurry out the back door. She'd hoped to talk to them, to thank them. But they probably didn't want to get attacked by the press. She couldn't blame them.

She leaned toward Skip. "We need to get out of here. Harrier doesn't want us talking to any reporters." It was Harrier's SOP to make sure he—and *only* he—was front and center when it was time to take credit for a win.

Skip gave her a knowing smile. "Of course not."

Erika moved to the gallery, where Phillip and Rochelle were sitting in the front row. Another thing to be grateful for. She didn't want to think about the public ass-kicking Phillip would've given her if they'd lost.

She smiled at Skip over Rochelle's shoulder as they hugged. Erika wasn't much of a hugger by nature. She hated when people insisted on it with the excuse, "I'm a hugger." Well, today, so was she. A big hugger.

She told Phillip and Rochelle she had to go straight up to her office. "But you're free to talk to the reporters if you like," she added.

Rochelle wiped away tears. "Phillip will want to give them a statement, but we'll meet you in your office after."

Phillip nodded, his eyes red. His voice broke as he said, "I'm very, very grateful for all you've done, Erika. And you, Skip."

The Hemingsworths left, and Skip ushered Erika out. He put his body between her and the crowds as they moved swiftly toward the freight elevator, where no public was allowed. Inside, with the doors closed, they both leaned back against the wall and took deep breaths.

"You did an amazing job, Skip. As always."

Skip smiled at her. "You don't suck either."

×××

"GOD, I HOPE THEY GET here soon," Erika said, as she flopped down in one of the chairs in front of her desk. "I just want to go to bed and pull the covers over my head. I feel like I could sleep for a month."

Skip loosened his tie as he leaned back in the chair next to hers. "Or two."

Ten minutes later, Phillip and Rochelle arrived. They were generous with their praise, exultant and relieved that the jury had done the right thing.

"I want to thank you both for all your support," Skip told them, and Erika bit the inside of her cheek to keep from laughing. Their "support" had drained her and Skip, body and soul. But not to be outdone, she added a lie of her own.

"Yes, you two have been wonderful."

Rochelle dipped her head, a royal nod. "We appreciate how much time you managed to spend with us. You've been a great source of comfort under very trying circumstances."

"It was our pleasure," Skip said as he moved to the door. "I'm sorry, but I've got to get back to the station." He shook hands with Phillip and Rochelle. "See you at the sentencing."

After he left, Phillip asked, "When *will* Steers be sentenced? I can't imagine there'll be much to talk about."

"Right," Erika said. By law, since the jury had convicted Steers of special circumstance murder—and the office hadn't sought the death penalty—he had to be sentenced to life without the possibility of parole. "But the defense will bring a couple of motions. A motion for a new trial, for sure."

Phillip frowned. Being a corporate lawyer, he didn't know the ins and outs of criminal law. "Is that common?"

"Yes, very. And they'll definitely lose. After that, the defense will ask the judge to strike the special circumstance. They'll lose that, too."

Phillip reached for Rochelle's hand and held it as they exchanged a weary smile. It was the only show of affection Erika had ever seen between them.

"Then I guess we'll head back up to the city. But we'll be here for the new trial motion." He looked Erika in the eye. "In the meantime, I'd like you to consider something. I could use a trial lawyer with your talent. I'd like to bring you in as a junior partner."

Erika stared at him, stunned. Junior partner? At a mega-firm like that, she'd make a hundred times the money she was making now. She'd never liked the idea of corporate law—or private practice, for that matter. But she knew she should let it breathe before turning him down. She'd never get an offer like this again.

"Thank you, Phillip. I'm really honored. But I'm going to need to give it some thought. It's a big decision."

Phillip nodded, but the fleeting look of displeasure showed that wasn't the answer he'd expected. "How much time do you need?"

"I couldn't leave until I've handled the motion for a new trial," Erika said. "So...a month, maybe two."

Phillip stood and gazed down at Erika. "A word of advice: You're not going to want to keep doing these monster trials forever. And you're single. It's going to get more and more important to make decent money. Just keep that in mind."

For Christ's sake, she was forty-one, not eighty-one. And her marital status was none of his damn business. But she just said, "I'll do that, Phillip."

And then she smiled as she swore to herself she'd never work for that overbearing asshole.

CHAPTER FIVE

W ITH THE STEERS TRIAL over, the media decamped and life in the office got back to normal. Busy, but not terribly exciting. Santa Cruz had a fair amount of crime for a small-ish city, but it was mostly a mix of drugs, burglaries, robberies, and assaults. When it came to murder cases, Chicago—tragically—had it beat. Or so I thought.

Two weeks later, I found out I was wrong. Very wrong.

I was leaning against the kitchen sink, gulping down my third cup of coffee. That, plus three aspirin and a gallon of water, was my foolproof remedy for the hangover twirlies. It'd been a rough night. I'd had the nightmare again—this time it was my mother's blood that covered my arms up to the elbows—when a thump had shaken my bed. I'd screamed and jumped up, still so dizzy with sleep I had to grab the nightstand to keep from falling. Was it him?!

Heart pounding, I'd turned on the light and looked around the room. iPad on my desk, where I'd left it, check. Basket of unfolded laundry in front of my dresser, check. The suit I planned to wear on the back of my chair where I'd put it, check.

Then I saw I'd gotten a notification from the NextDoor app: *Did anyone else feel that? I heard it was a 3.4.* An earthquake. The thump had been an earthquake. I got back under the covers, my heart beating way too fast. But by the time I managed to go back to sleep, it was 5:00 a.m.

As I poured myself a fourth cup of coffee, I heard the TV news anchor saying, "…the shockingly brutal murder of bail bonds woman, Shelly Hansen."

A female bail bondsman? That was a first. I turned up the volume and saw police tape blocking off the driveway of a large, ranch-style home on what looked like a quiet residential street. The reporter said the victim, whose body had been found by her eighteen-year-old daughter, Mia Hansen, appeared to have been stabbed to death. According to an anonymous source, the crime scene was a blood bath.

A photo of Shelly standing arm in arm with Mia went up on the screen. I squinted, forcing my eyes to focus. Shelly, a pretty brunette, had on a blazer and slacks, her hair styled in a chic bob. She was in great shape, a little shorter than her daughter. Her wide smile made me think she'd been fun to hang with. Mia had the same high cheekbones and thick brown hair—though Mia wore hers long, well past her shoulders. But her smile was lopsided, half there, half not. A teenage "I'm-too-cool" smile.

But I couldn't hang around to get more of the story. I had a full calendar, and I was in front of a judge who liked to start early. I put on my sunglasses to ward off the sting of daylight, picked up my super-sized water bottle, and hurried out the door.

×××

BY THE TIME I GOT to court, my side of counsel table was packed with lawyers waiting to wheedle me for deals. I sat down, head throbbing, and dived in. I didn't finish the morning calendar until past noon, when the judge declared a recess for lunch. He looked down at me and pointed his gavel at the gallery. "I believe you've got a guest."

When I turned, I saw the District Attorney's second-in-command, Fred Summers, standing at the back of the courtroom, his arms folded. That was weird. Fred never came to court. Glad I'd had enough time to even out from my hangover, I gathered my files and walked over to him.

"Is something wrong?"

"I need you to come to John's office with me."

John Harrier? The District Attorney? Shit! Had they figured out my résumé was a lie? I tried to play it cool as I asked, "What's going on?"

He'd already turned and headed for the door. "You'll know in about five minutes."

Four and a half minutes later, I walked into a spacious office with a panoramic view of the ocean. Harrier had the best seat in the house. What a waste. The man did nothing but glad-hand rich guys and cozy up to reporters, and he got a palace. The people who did all the work were stuck in offices the size of a shoebox.

I noticed he had a telescope set up on a tripod in front of the window. Sure, why not?

Then I registered something else: Erika, sitting in front of Harrier's desk. She turned and smiled. "Hi, Charlie."

I returned her smile. "Hey, Erika." Seeing her there was good news. If Harrier had planned to bust me, he wouldn't have called her in. So what *did* he want?

Harrier gestured for me to take the chair next to Erika's. "I imagine you've heard about the Shelly Hansen homicide." When I nodded, he said, "I've decided to assign the case to Erika."

I stole a glance at her. She looked so tired. It seemed crazy for her to tackle another big case after what she'd just been through. But I knew some lawyers needed the constant action. "No rest for the weary, huh?"

Harrier gave me a sharp look. "I don't run a sweat shop. Erika asked for the case. But she's just been through a lengthy trial, so we've decided to give her a second chair for this one."

I looked from Erika to Harrier to Fred, who nodded. "Ready for the big leagues?"

He didn't know I'd been in the big leagues for years back in Chicago. Or that the big leagues were *not* where I wanted to be. The press was already chasing this case. The brutal murder of a successful businesswoman and mother in an upper-middle-class suburban neighborhood? There'd be cameras everywhere.

Harrier took in my hesitation and frowned. "Erika's the lead. You're just the spear carrier. You can handle it."

Of course I could handle it—with or without Erika. But I desperately didn't want to. I found myself stuttering, "I—I appreciate the opportunity and all. But I really don't—"

Harrier interrupted. "This isn't an invitation. It's an order. I'm assigning you as second chair."

×××

ERIKA TOOK ME TO her office and gave me her copy of the murder book, the binder that held all the reports on the case. "Get this organized and make a copy for yourself. We'll put together our To-Do list tomorrow." She gave me a curious look. "It's a real show of confidence that they're already giving you a high-profile case. I'd have thought you'd be thrilled."

I knew my reaction had registered as more than a little bizarre. I couldn't think of a single prosecutor who wouldn't jump at the chance to work a big case like this.

"I'm just not a fan of the way the press screws things up," I said weakly.

Erika rolled her eyes. "No argument there." She went to her desk and turned on her computer. "But I don't know that it'll get a ton of coverage. The victim isn't famous. It'll probably just be a local news story."

True. It's not like Shelly Hansen was a *celebrity* bail bondsman. But the possibility of any press made me nervous. Very nervous.

Fortunately, since Erika was the lead lawyer, I'd be able to stay in the background. "Yeah, well…just know I'm totally good with you being the face of the case."

She nodded. "Duly noted."

I started to leave, then turned back. "I've been meaning to tell you, I watched some of the Steers trial. You really crushed it."

"Thanks," she said, her tone somber.

"Gotta admit, I was a little worried. Your jury didn't want to believe what an asshole he was, you could tell."

"I think they would've been a lot more receptive if…" She paused, then looked me in the eye. "Can I trust you to keep this to yourself?" I nodded. "A woman who'd been with Steers before he started seeing Natalie came to me during the trial. She told me how he'd abused her." Erika shook her head. "It was hideous. Some of the worst I've heard."

I hadn't heard about other victims. It must have put even *more* pressure on Erika to nail that asshole. Very few people I knew could've handled that kind of stress, let alone brought in a win. It made me admire her all the more.

"What happened to her?"

Erika's lips stretched into a tight line. "She refused to testify. She was too scared and…embarrassed."

"Poor thing. And poor you." It was impossibly painful to lose a witness that crucial, especially given what Erika had been up against. "You must've been pulling your hair out."

She gave a grim nod. "To put it mildly."

"Well, thank God, you got him."

She sighed, "Yeah, thank God."

Back in my office, I got to work. There wasn't much to the murder book yet, but I carefully sorted the reports we had into the appropriate sections. Although the thought of media attention worried me sick, I was glad for the chance to work with Erika. Getting to see how she built a case from the ground up was the opportunity of a lifetime.

The crime scene photos showed a bloodbath. It looked like Shelly had been stabbed over a dozen times. Which meant the case would attract its share of crime junkies—a phenomenon I was painfully, and very personally, familiar with.

Hard to believe Erika's prediction that it'd only get local press. But she'd been handling high profile cases out here for years, so I just had to hope she was right. If we got national attention, my face would be splashed all over TV sets across the country. That'd be the end of Charlie Blair—*and* Lauren Claybourne.

CHAPTER SIX

Skip had barely closed Erika's office door when she blurted out, "Goddamn it! I told him I didn't need any help. Why the hell is he making me take her on?"

He raised an eyebrow. "Do you need to ask? You're wiped out. And so am I."

Erika didn't care. "The last thing we need is some newbie sticking her nose into everything." She drilled him with a dark look. "You're sure the killer couldn't be…?"

But she didn't dare say the name out loud.

Skip's voice was firm. "I am."

"Good." But not all the way good. The more time prying eyes had to look into Shelly's murder, the more likely they'd see the connection to the Steers case—and the more likely Steers' conviction would get thrown out. "We need to shut this down fast."

"I know." His tone was worried. "Can't you keep the new girl busy with the chickenshit stuff?"

"I can try. But she'll want to prove herself, get hip deep in everything." It's what Erika would've done—what she *had* done when she'd been second chair a hundred years ago.

Skip ran a hand across his forehead. "You'll have to find a way to stop her." He paused, then added, "It might not be that hard. From what you said, Harrier had to force her to take the case. Doesn't sound to me like she's dying to prove anything."

Erika frowned. "Yeah, true."

But that almost worried her more. It was so...strange. In fact, there were a lot of strange things about Charlie. She didn't seem to have—or want—any friends. And if she had family out here, Erika sure hadn't heard about it. She had lunch alone in her office every day, and when she'd gone to court to watch the Steers trial, she'd never so much as said hello. Charlie was a cypher. And Erika didn't trust her.

Skip's cell phone buzzed with a text. "They're bringing the daughter in now."

Erika had read the first officer's report. He'd found Mia sitting on the neighbor's porch, her head on her knees. She'd claimed she'd been at a party all night, had found her dead mother lying on the bedroom floor when she got home. The officer had noted her pupils seemed to be dilated. "So she's willing to talk?"

"Apparently." He gestured to Erika's iPad. "Did you check out the crime scene photos?"

Erika nodded. "Looks like a total frenzy killing. It's got to be someone who knew her." She couldn't imagine the pain Mia must be feeling. Skip always said Erika identified with the victims a little too much. But having suffered her share of loss and injustice for most of her younger years, doing so was baked into her psyche. "You talk to Mia at the scene?"

"Not personally. I just got a look at her when she was with the uni."

Mia would probably be a wreck, but it was important to get to her as soon as possible—before she started to forget the little details that could make all the difference. "What'd you think of her?"

Skip frowned. "First impression? Spoiled party girl. Still pretty high when I saw her but not nearly as freaked as I would've expected."

Erika blinked, surprised. But then, she didn't read much into people's first reactions. She'd seen the gamut from primal wailing to utterly mute. Everyone—guilty or innocent—dealt with trauma differently.

"I heard Shelly was divorced." Skip nodded. "Where was Mia's father?"

"Dead," Skip said. "Five years ago."

Damn. She crossed him off her mental suspect list. "Past boyfriends?"

"None in the past six months, as far as we know. I'm going to hunt down Shelly's girlfriends, see if they have any more info."

"She might've been seeing someone on the down low." Maybe Mia could help on that score. "This can't turn into a cluster, Skip."

He held up a hand. "I've got this. Don't worry."

She wouldn't worry. She'd agonize. "How about the door knocking in the neighborhood? Anything?"

Skip shook his head. "Not yet. But you know how that goes."

Unfortunately, she did. Some people wouldn't even answer the door, didn't want to get involved. And those who did might not remember everything until the second or third go-round. Normally, that wasn't a big deal. But they couldn't afford that kind of time suck. Not with the Steers dilemma hanging over their heads.

He glanced at his watch. "Mia's probably already down at the station. Should we invite your new best friend?"

Erika shot him a glare. "Remember this: Charlie will be doing as little as possible." She swung on her jacket. "She can read the report *if* I think it's necessary."

Skip gave a wary nod, then followed her out.

×××

ERIKA STUDIED THE GIRL who sat across from her, slumped down in her chair. She'd heard that Mia'd vomited in the back seat of the uni's car. She believed it.

Angry, irritable, and obviously still high, Mia Hansen looked like hell. Her skin was ghostly pale, her eyes fiery red and smeared with dark circles of eyeliner and mascara. Lank strands of striped neon green and black hair were plastered to her sweaty face and neck. As she put an elbow on the table to rest her head in her hand, her cluster of metallic bracelets jangled like tinny windchimes.

And the way she was glaring at Erika…Erika usually had a good rapport with victims. She wasn't sure why Mia's reaction was so hostile, but given her attitude, it was probably best to let Skip take the lead. When she nodded to him, he asked what had happened when Mia'd gotten home from the party.

Mia rolled her eyes. "I already told that cop…Jason. I told him everything. Can't you just go ask him what I said?"

Skip spoke quietly, his voice warm. "I understand. It's a drag to have to go over stuff again and again. But sometimes you remember new things the second time around. So, you said you got home and found the front door locked with the deadbolt. Then what?"

Mia's features screwed up with the effort to focus. "I...ah...I went around to the back to see if there was a window open." She rubbed her eyes, then stared at the black makeup smudges on her fingers.

"And then?" Skip asked.

A panicked look crossed her face. "That's when I saw...my bedroom window. It was broken. Someone smashed it in."

Skip's brow knitted. "Mia, we found your hoodie wrapped around a rock just inside the window—it was lying on your bed. *You* broke the window."

Her head popped up. "No! That's not true! It was already broken when I got home."

Erika had seen the photos. Why was she arguing? "Mia, we don't want to put words in your mouth, but your hoodie was covered in broken glass. *You* broke that window."

Mia glared at Erika as she sat back and folded her arms. "I did not."

Erika scrolled on her iPad and pointed to a photo of Mia's bed, which showed a red hoodie, partially wrapped around a melon-sized rock, laying under the broken window. "That's the rock you used, right?" She scrolled down again and pointed to another photo of Mia's bed. "And that's your jacket?"

Mia stared at the photo. "I...don't remember doing any of that. But maybe...I mean, I was pretty out of it." She swallowed.

"Why did you break the window?" Erika asked. "Why not just open it?"

"Because..." Mia rubbed her temples. "It—it was locked."

"No, Mia," Skip said. "It wasn't."

Mia looked at him for a moment, then frowned as her gaze slid away. "Yes, it was. It's always locked."

Erika blinked, perplexed. Was Mia too high to remember, or was she lying? "Always?"

Mia licked her dry lips. After a long beat, she said, "Um...maybe not always. But usually."

Erika took in that shift. Mia had clearly realized someone could contradict her if she insisted the window was always locked. So she wasn't *that* high. "Why not just call your mom and ask her to open the door?"

Mia gave Erika a piercing, angry look, then dropped her gaze back to the table. "I don't know. I was kind of confused. She doesn't usually lock the door with the deadbolt. I guess I was just kind of…messed up."

"If your mother didn't usually use the deadbolt," Skip asked, "didn't you think that was a sign something was wrong?"

Mia gave him a sullen look. "No. I thought it was because I was out so late. After I knocked and all, and she didn't answer, I figured it was payback."

Erika felt the anger rolling off Mia even now. "You must've been pretty pissed off."

Mia glared at her through hooded eyes, then shrugged. "No. Not really."

Erika was careful to keep her expression neutral as she registered the obvious lie. Something here wasn't adding up—or rather, it *was*. "You and your mother fight a lot?"

"Not a lot. But sometimes." Mia fidgeted with the zipper on her jacket. "She never lets me do anything, and she hates my friends," she blurted. "She pretty much hates everything I do."

"She let you go to that party, didn't she?"

"No. I snuck out."

Erika took in Mia's affect. No tears. No sadness. Anger, yes. Irritation too. But no sorrow. "What time did you leave the party?"

Mia rested her head on her hand again, her expression weary. "Um…I don't know. Late."

Skip glanced at the reports on the table. "Everyone at the party said the last time they saw you was around midnight or twelve thirty."

"No. It had to be later than that." Mia slumped lower in her chair. "Like I told that cop, I went to the guest bedroom to lie down for a minute and fell asleep. By the time I woke up, everyone was gone. And fucking Axel was passed out on the living room floor."

Mia was sweating, Erika noticed. Probably from all that booze—and God knows how many drugs. "Axel's your boyfriend, right? And he was supposed to be your ride?" Mia gave a sulky nod. "Then how did you get home?"

Mia pushed up her sleeves and lifted her hair off her neck. "I walked home. Or...no, wait. I was going to walk home, but then I decided to hitchhike."

But Erika's gaze was locked on Mia's arms. Deep red scratches were gouged between her wrists and elbows. She pointed to them. "How'd that happen?"

Mia looked at her forearms. For the first time, she seemed scared. "I guess maybe the bushes outside the window...when I was trying to climb through it?"

Erika opened her iPad and scrolled to the photos of the bushes. "I don't see how. Those bushes would've been below your waist."

Mia stared at the photos, then turned away. "I...don't remember."

A female deputy knocked and poked her head in the door. "Detective? I've got something you need to see." She handed Skip a manila file folder.

As he took it, he nodded to Erika. "Keep going."

Erika nodded. "What happened after you got inside the house?"

Mia was distracted as she watched Skip open the file. "What?"

She seemed less and less high, Erika thought, and more and more worried. "I asked you what you did after you got inside?"

Mia's gaze drifted to the wall behind Erika. "I...nothing. I thought she was going to come to my room and start screaming at me. But she didn't." Mia closed her eyes. "It was just...quiet."

What she said next would be critical. "Then what?" Erika asked.

"I—I thought that was weird. So I went to my Mom's bedroom, and..." Mia took a deep breath. "I saw her...lying there. It was horrible."

She squeezed her eyes shut, then put her hands over her face. But when she lowered them, her eyes were dry.

Erika had seen the crime scene photos, and she agreed. It *was* horrible. But Mia's voice was flat. And it looked like she'd tried—and failed—to make herself cry. "Did you go into her bedroom?"

Mia shook her head. "Just...like, one step."

"You didn't go over to her, try to see if she was still breathing?"

"No," Mia said. "I could tell she was...wasn't breathing."

"What did you do next?"

She swallowed. "I got out of there and ran to the neighbor's house."

Erika needed to nail this point down. But she didn't want to tip off Mia. She asked softly, "You're sure you didn't touch her?"

Mia frowned at her. "Yeah, I'm sure. I think I puked in the neighbor's yard." She leaned back in her chair. "Are we almost done?"

Skip looked up from the file. "Just about. You said you hitchhiked home. Do you remember anything about the person who picked you up?"

She squinted, then sat forward. "I just remembered…I know how I got those scratches. It was when I was walking home. I got dizzy. I tripped and fell down this little hill. That's how I ended up on Bakers Road, where that guy stopped for me." She paused. "Jack…something. He gave me a ride home."

Skip pulled a report out of the folder and slid it over to her. "Right. But according to Jack, he picked you up around one a.m." He waited for her to meet his gaze. "And when they asked Jack to describe you, he didn't mention any scratches on your arms."

Mia gripped the edge of the table as the import appeared to sink in. Then she spoke fast, her words tumbling out on top of each other. "That's bullshit!" She took in Skip's stare and lowered her voice. "Or maybe he just didn't see. It was dark in the car."

Skip went on, "Jack told us that you seemed angry. When he asked if you were okay, you told him your mother was going to," Skip pointed to the report, "quote 'kill you' for going out after she'd told you not to."

Mia was breathing hard. "I never said that! He's lying!"

Erika asked, "Why would he lie?"

Mia looked frantic. "I don't know."

Skip was watching Mia closely. "Jack said that when he dropped you off, he didn't see you knock on the door or ring the bell. You just stood there. He thought it seemed like you were waiting for him to leave."

"I was just…moving slow, that's all." Mia raked her fingers through her hair, her eyes darting from Skip to Erika. Then she burst out, "No, I can prove the deadbolt was locked! I texted Axel when that Jack guy dropped me off. I told him my mom locked me out. I asked if I could crash at his place."

If she *had* sent that text, Erika thought, then Shelly had to have been dead already. Otherwise, the noise of the window breaking would surely have woken her. And Erika couldn't imagine that Mia—in her drunken, drug-hazed state—would've been able to get the jump on Shelly if she were awake. "Great. Let's see your phone."

Mia slumped back in her chair. "I…I lost it."

Erika shrugged. "That's okay. If you sent Axel a text, it'll show up on his phone. And we can check your cell phone records, too."

If that text existed, Erika wanted to find it sooner rather than later so they could forget about Mia and move on.

Skip said, "Let's take a little break. If you don't mind, I'd like to send in one of our techs to do a swab of your arms. It'll only take a minute."

Mia blinked rapidly. "What for?"

Skip spoke softly. "Just DNA."

Mia's eyes widened. When she spoke, her voice was breathless. "No." She gripped the edge of the table. "I—I want a lawyer."

Skip gave Mia his kindest, most fatherly look. "Are you sure? If you get a lawyer, you won't be able to talk to us anymore."

Mia was shaking. She shoved her chair back, voice rising. "I don't want to talk to you! You're fucking assholes—you're trying to make me say I did it! Get me a lawyer!"

Erika and Skip exchanged a look. Erika stood up. "Okay, Mia."

They walked out.

CHAPTER SEVEN

I'll DRIVE," ERIKA SAID. When they needed to talk in privacy, they always took a short trip to the beach.

As Skip got in and fastened his seat belt, he said, "So what do you think?"

"She's not what I expected."

"Me either." Skip stared out the window. "Pretty feisty for a girl who just found her mother all sliced up."

"I agree. Though she *was* still high, and I guess she might've been in shock." Erika mentally replayed the interview. "But…I don't know. Trying to claim someone else broke in through the window?" She shook her head. "She wasn't *that* high."

"No. And she looked pissed off when she said her mother locked her out on purpose."

That reaction had bothered Erika, too. "I was imagining her standing out there in the cold, knowing her mom was doing this to punish her. Yeah, I'll bet she was mad as hell."

"But she insisted she wasn't." Skip gave Erika a meaningful look. "And her story about how she got those scratches kept changing."

Erika pictured Mia's arms. "They looked bad. Could be defensive wounds." Most likely inflicted by Shelly as she fought back.

"I'm sorry. I really blew that." Skip's tone was aggravated. "I should've asked to swab her the minute we saw them. We'll never get anything off her now."

Erika waved a hand. "She just would've lawyered up that much sooner."

"But that makes her look even more guilty to me. If she's innocent, why refuse?"

"If I were her lawyer, I'd say she just freaked out. But, yeah, she definitely didn't help herself." Again, Erika pictured the scratches. Most of them were on Mia's right arm. "See if you can find out whether she's right-handed."

"Good idea," Skip said. "What do you think about that guy, Jack?"

Erika stared out at the choppy ocean, trying to focus. The wind had picked up, and the tossing palm tree fronds looked like a woman's long hair flying in the breeze. A couple huddled together as they walked along the beach. She wished she could join them. The fatigue that'd built up during the Steers trial had only grown worse; Erika felt like she'd be tired for the rest of her life.

"It's interesting that he didn't notice any scratches on her. Did he say what she was wearing?"

"A really tight sleeveless top and a hoodie tied around her waist."

"Probably the one she used to break the window," Erika said. "That bit about the deadbolt being locked…she said when she left the house, she ran out through the front door."

"Right," Skip said. "The only way to know if it was locked is that text she said she sent the boyfriend, Axel."

"Anyone talk to him yet?"

"He gave a preliminary statement to one of the unis." Skip stared out at the rolling waves. "But I think we should talk to him ourselves. We'll be able to get a lot more out of him." He pulled out his phone. "I'll take care of that right now."

"We should talk to the other kids who were tight with her, too."

"Already on the list."

Erika shook her head. "Assuming she told the truth about the deadbolt being locked, and it really can't be opened from the outside—"

"I'll get the crime scene techs to check on that," Skip said.

"Then I'd guess the killer locked it to keep visitors away and climbed out through a window. Were any of them locked?"

"All of them," Skip said. "Except Mia's."

That was another thing. "So why break the window and lie about it? And if she did lie about the deadbolt being locked, why?"

Skip shrugged. "If the deadbolt's locked, then the killer would have to break in, right?" Erika nodded. "So, Mia smashes the window."

"With her own hoodie, and leaves it there?" Erika said. "Pretty lame."

"It is. But it's about what you'd expected from someone that loaded. This obviously wasn't a planned murder. She had to come up with something on the fly, and she's not exactly a criminal mastermind."

Erika pictured the crime scene again. "True. And it had to be personal. All those stab wounds—"

"And no ransacking. A rage killing all the way."

"Any visible blood on Mia?"

Skip shook his head. "I'm guessing she cleaned up. I told the crime scene techs to swab the drains and check the windows for prints, fibers. They already told me they got some prints off a couple of windows, but..."

Erika sighed and nodded. There was no way to tell *when* prints had been left on a surface. So even if they found foreign fingerprints on the windows, unless they matched someone who was already in the criminal database, it wouldn't mean much. They could've come from anywhere: the company that'd moved Shelly in, a house painter—even the family who'd lived there before. And it'd mean absolutely nothing if they found Mia's prints on the windows. She lived there. Her prints would be all over the place.

Erika said, "Well, Axel's phone should give us at least one answer. If it shows Mia did text him, we can put her on the back burner. I assume they're checking her mother's clothing for prints—"

"And hairs and fibers. The whole nine yards."

"What's the word on the murder weapon?" Erika had read that they'd found a knife block in the kitchen with one empty slot.

"Coroner confirmed the missing carving knife is about the right size. But we still haven't found it."

The empty slot in the knife block was such a cliché. But clichés are clichés because they're true, Erika thought. A big, sharp knife, ready at hand on a kitchen counter, was so often the weapon of choice in an impulsive murder. And it was more evidence that Shelly's murder hadn't been planned. More evidence that it was personal. More evidence that pointed to Mia.

And yet... "I've never had a case where a daughter killed her mother."

"Me either. It's pretty rare." Skip's phone *pinged* with a text. "The unis talked to Shelly's friends. They didn't know of any ex-boyfriends who had it out for her. I'll follow up, but I'm not optimistic."

"Do what you can. If there *is* some guy who looks good for it, we need to go after him now. I don't want to get blindsided once we go down the road with Mia." It could be a real credibility killer with a jury if they had to change suspects midstream.

Erika sighed. She wished Skip *could* find a vengeful ex. He'd be an easier target. Getting a jury to buy the idea that an eighteen-year-old girl had stabbed her mother to death was going to be tough.

On the other hand, the girl she'd seen in that interview room wouldn't win any hearts and minds. Mia clearly had serious issues with her mother. And Erika wondered whether there might be another motive in play.

"Does Shelly have a will?"

"We're checking. We found the number for a civil lawyer on her cell. Richard Sheldon. Heard of him?"

"Maybe." Erika tapped the steering wheel as she tried to remember. "Text me the number. I'll give him a call."

As Skip flipped through his notepad, his cell phone pinged. "Axel's coming in at five o'clock."

Erika looked at her watch. It was almost 4:30, and she wanted to go over the statement Axel had given the uni before she talked to him. "We'd better head straight to the office."

"Not a problem. You can drop me at the station when we're done." He texted her the lawyer's phone number. "You going to let Charlie sit in on this one?"

Erika drove out of the parking lot and turned onto Ocean Street. "I can't keep her out of everything." It'd look bad—not to mention awkward—to bring a key witness into the office and not even let her observe.

"I agree." Skip sighed. "What've you got her doing?"

"Putting together a witness list with contact information. Organizing the murder books, going through the evidence reports—that sort of thing. Basically, secretarial work. Think she'll complain?"

"I'd let her do a little more if I were you," he said. "We need to keep her happy enough to leave us alone."

"It's weird, you know." Erika frowned. "She doesn't seem like the timid type."

"You don't have to be shy to want to stay out of the spotlight. Some people just don't like it."

"That's true."

As she parked the car, she could feel the wet, icy wind through the window—the kind that sliced through a body like a razor. She grabbed her puffer coat from the back seat. "I'm gonna make a run for it."

Erika took off at a gallop, and Skip followed. By the time they got to her office, they were both out of breath. She pulled up Axel's statement on her computer. There wasn't much to it, but that was okay. The fewer details, the fewer inconsistencies a defense lawyer could play with.

When she looked up, she saw Charlie in the doorway, a sheaf of papers in her hand. "Hey, good timing. Mia's boyfriend's coming in."

"Great." Charlie handed her the pages. "The witness list with contact info." She pointed to a binder on the table next to the wall. "And your copy of the murder book."

"Thanks." Erika's intercom buzzed. It was the receptionist, saying Axel was there.

Skip stood up. "I'll go get him."

A minute later, Skip returned with a shaggy-haired guy in a down vest and Timberland boots. He had sad-dog brown eyes that made him look vulnerable and sensitive—a look that didn't mesh with his cultivated five o'clock shadow.

Erika stood up. "Hi Axel. Thanks for coming in." She introduced him to everyone and shook his hand—which was unappealingly limp.

Skip gestured to one of the chairs in front of Erika's desk. "Make yourself comfortable."

Axel took in the three of them as he sat down. His expression said "comfortable" was not going to happen. He said, "I already told that cop everything I know."

If only Erika had a dollar for every witness who'd said that. "We just have a few more questions. Let's start with the timing. Did you see Mia leave the party?"

It was a throwaway. But his answer would give her some idea of how cooperative he was going to be.

He cleared his throat. "No. I just know I didn't see her after, like, midnight or twelve thirty."

"She says that when she left, you were passed out on the living room floor."

Erika saw him bristle. He shifted in his seat, irritated. "I didn't 'pass out.'" He made air quotes around the words. "I was tired. I may have closed my eyes for a few minutes."

Erika hadn't intended to make him turn on Mia, but it seemed she had—which was good. Maybe he'd be more willing to spill. "What kind of mood was Mia in that night?"

He gave a weary sigh. "Bitched out. She'd gotten into it with her mom. As usual."

His tone said Mia's combative relationship with Shelly was common knowledge. "So they fought a lot?"

"Seemed like constantly."

Erika asked, "What about?"

He looked away, uneasy. "I don't want to dump on her. I mean, my sister gets into it with my mom all the time."

She needed to pull back. Axel might not be madly in love, but he didn't like being a snitch, either. "I was only wondering if you knew what their particular issues were. Not a big deal."

He sighed. "It was just...her mom wouldn't let her do anything, always hassled her about money, and she was always giving her shit about how she dressed, where she went, who she was with, her grades, curfew...hanging out with me. That kind of thing."

Erika gave him an understanding look. "Typical stuff." Axel nodded. "And did she say her mom told her not to go to the party that night?"

He rolled his eyes. "Yeah. I mean, that's the thing. She'd bitch about her mom not letting her do anything, and then she'd just do it anyway."

"Did Mia talk to anyone else about her mom that night?"

Axel started to shake his head, then paused. "Wait...yeah." He looked up at the ceiling. "Jenna? No. Maybe Larissa. But I'm not sure."

Skip flipped through his notepad. "Would that be Larissa Bronson?"

Axel nodded.

Erika asked, "Did Mia and her mom ever physically fight?"

He pressed his lips together. "Sometimes."

The hostility ran deep, then. Erika leaned forward. "How serious were those fights? Did anyone wind up in the hospital?"

"Not that I know of," Axel said. "I mean, I never saw Mia with a black eye or anything."

Out of the corner of her eye, Erika saw Charlie leaning back in her chair, her posture casual. But Erika could tell she was taking in every detail. It was a smart way to help a witness relax—and a reminder that Charlie wasn't just some baby lawyer.

"What about Shelly?" she went on. "Ever see her looking beat up?"

"Nah. But I hardly saw her—period. She worked a lot. And I wasn't her favorite person."

Erika glanced at Skip to see if he had anything else to ask. He shook his head. Time to get to the big-ticket item.

"Do you happen to have your phone on you, Axel?" There was no way he didn't. No one—especially no one under the age of thirty—even left a room without their phone. Erika was going to get it from him if she had to grab him by the ankles, turn him upside down, and shake him.

He frowned. "Yeah. Why?"

Erika kept her voice level. "Can you check it and see if Mia texted you that night?"

As Axel pulled his phone out of his pocket, Erika thought, *the case against Mia might be about to disappear.* That'd put them back at Square One. More time lost—time that would only increase the risk of the Steers conviction going south. Her stomach clenched.

He scrolled through his messages, then stopped. "Yeah. She did. Once."

"Can I see it?" Erika held out her hand, and Axel reluctantly gave her the phone.

Mia's text had been sent at ten minutes after midnight: *Can we go home? I'm fried.* She'd still been at the party.

Axel had answered: *I'm staying. Uber.*

Apparently, Axel was where chivalry went to die.

"Mind if I see if there are any other texts from Mia that night?" She held her hand up. "Promise I'll only look at that night."

Axel glanced from Erika to Skip. He clearly didn't like the idea. "I'd, uh… rather not."

Erika raised an eyebrow. "Fine. I'll get a search warrant. But you'd better buy a new phone. We'll be hanging on to this for a while."

The truth was, Erika would have to seize the phone anyway. But she couldn't afford to wait. She needed to see what was—and wasn't—on that phone right now.

Axel frowned, then sighed and waved a hand at her. "Whatever."

Erika scrolled through all the texts he'd gotten that night. He was right. Mia had only sent him the one she'd read. She nodded at Skip, who reached across her desk for the phone. "Sorry, Axel. I'm going to have to take this after all."

Axel sat up, alarmed. "Hey! What the…? I need that for work!"

Erika gave him a sympathetic look. "We'll be fast. Buy yourself a burner in the meantime. I'll get you reimbursed."

She'd check Mia's cell phone records just to be sure. But it seemed pretty clear: Mia had lied. And if she'd lied about texting Axel, then the door *hadn't* been deadbolted. And she *hadn't* thought she needed to break in through the window.

In which case, the broken window was just a lame coverup to make it look like Shelly was already dead when Mia got home.

And Mia was the killer.

CHAPTER EIGHT

THE TEXT ON AXEL'S phone must not have jived with what Mia had told them. But I wasn't sure, because I hadn't been invited to join the party when they'd questioned her.

I should've been there. Not to do the questioning. That was Skip's—and if he chose to let her, Erika's—gig. But I should've been there to observe, to be another pair of eyes and maybe catch something in Mia's answers they'd missed. If I had to be stuck with the case, I wanted to be part of the team, not some glorified law clerk.

"So, what did Mia say you'd find on his phone?" It took everything I had to keep the irritation out of my voice.

Erika filled me in and showed me the single text Mia had sent.

I frowned. "Why would she lie? She had to know we'd check her phone."

"She said she lost it. The unis are searching, but so far, nothing."

I looked from Erika to Skip. "You think she got rid of it?"

Skip shrugged. "Maybe."

It still made no sense to me. "Okay, but how could she not know you'd get the cell records and check Axel's phone?"

Erika glanced at Skip. "She was pretty out of it. I don't think the wheels were turning all that well." She paused. "Which fits with the murder. It clearly wasn't premeditated. This was a messy, sloppy rage killing."

I knew all about rage, and being messed up was my forte. "And she tried to cover it up by claiming someone else broke into the house?"

"That's what I'm thinking." Erika said. "When she finally admitted she was the one who broke the window, she claimed it was locked—also not true. It was actually the only window in the house that *wasn't* locked."

It could've been a coverup. But I wasn't sure that was the only explanation. "She might've just forgotten her window was unlocked. You said she was pretty fucked up."

"I'd agree if that was the only thing that was…off." Erika told me about the scratches on Mia's arms, her refusal to let Skip take a DNA swab, her obvious fury with her mother. Taken together, it did seem like a coverup, albeit a pretty pathetic one.

"You video her interview?" I wanted to get a look at this drunken, fucked-up, eighteen-year-old girl who might've stabbed her mother to death.

Skip nodded. "I'll get you a copy."

"That'd be great. Thanks." I *thought* I'd kept the note of sarcasm out of my voice. But given the way Erika was looking at me, I might not have succeeded.

"Anyway, I was thinking there might be a more concrete motive in play," she said.

A front runner immediately came to mind. "Money."

"Right. Skip found the number for a civil lawyer on Shelly's cell. He might've drawn up Shelly's will. Want to give him a call, see if he'll cooperate?"

I knew she was throwing me a bone. An easy, boring bone. But it was better than more grunt work. "Sure."

Skip tore a page out of his notepad. "Here's his name and number. If he gives you a hard time, we'll go see him in person."

I took the page and glanced at my watch. Almost six o'clock. "He might be gone for the day, but I'll give him a try." I stood up. "What about Larissa Bronson?"

"I'll set it up," Skip said.

I noticed he didn't say whether I'd be invited to that dance. "Anything else I can do?"

Erika smiled. "That's it for today. I'm sure there'll be more tomorrow."

Yeah, but more what?

I was an experienced trial lawyer and a damned good one. Erika had me doing the kind of bonehead work you dumped on interns in their first year of law school. Which, by the way, I had hated even then.

I guess I was disappointed, too. I'd hoped to show her I had chops, but she wasn't even giving me a chance. I got that she might not be used to delegating, though it felt like more than that. Like she was deliberately keeping me on the sidelines.

I closed the door to my office and dialed the lawyer's number. Surprisingly, he answered. When I told him who I was and why I was calling, he said he'd call me right back. One minute later, my intercom buzzed. Marta, the receptionist, told me a Richard Sheldon was asking for me.

"You were checking to make sure I was really a DA, weren't you?"

His voice had a slight southern drawl. "Never hurts to be careful. What can I do for you?"

"We wanted to know whether you drew up Shelly Hansen's will." I decided to add one more item to the agenda. "And whether she had any lawsuits pending."

If she was suing or being sued by someone, that person might've decided to settle out of court—with a knife.

"No lawsuits that I'm aware of. But I'm not the only lawyer in town, so you might want to dig a little to make sure. I did do her will, though. Awful thing, what happened to her. She was a nice woman, had a big heart. Donated to battered women's shelters, homeless shelters."

I'd never know Shelly, but she did sound like a good person, and I certainly agreed with him about the awfulness of it all. "I guess you'll be filing it in probate court?" And when he did, it'd become public record: i.e., there'd be no need for me to issue a subpoena to see it.

"Yeah." His tone was lightly sarcastic. "I'm going to play psychic and guess you're about to say that I might as well tell you who stands to inherit, because you'll find out anyway."

"Something like that." Maybe it was the accent, or his playful tone, but I liked him.

He took a beat before answering. "Can't really see the harm. Her daughter Mia's going to get seventy-five percent. Shelly's sister, Georgia, will get the other twenty-five."

"And what's the estate worth?"

"If you count the house, total value is roughly ten million."

Holy shit. That was about as concrete a motive as it got. "I never knew the bail bonds business was that lucrative."

Bail bondsmen do okay—but not *that* okay. They charge ten percent of whatever amount the judge sets for your bail. In return, you get to go home instead of awaiting trial in a shitty, smelly cell with a bunch of junkies, drunks, and car thieves. It's not a bad living, but I've never heard of anyone making millions at it.

Richard chuckled. "Six million of that came from Mia's father, Shelly's ex, who's now deceased. That's separate from the rest of the estate. By the terms of his will, Shelly and Mia were supposed to split that money when Mia turned twenty-one."

"What happens now that Shelly's gone?"

He cleared his throat. "I don't know how old Mia is now, but the will states that if she's at least eighteen years of age, she gets it all."

I did the math in my head. "So Mia gets the whole six million plus seventy-five percent of Shelly's estate?"

"Right. For a total of about nine million."

Nine million. For an eighteen-year-old kid. "Are Shelly's parents alive?"

"No. Far as I know, her only living first-degree relative is her sister." He paused. "Believe her last name is Traynor. She lives in town. But I'm not sure I have her most recent contact info. When you get it, would you shoot it over to me?"

"Be happy to." I had one more question. "Did Mia know what was in Shelly's will?"

"As I recall, Mia's father told her. He wanted her to know she'd be taken care of in case..." his voice trailed off.

In case anything happened to him or Shelly. And now it had. To both of them. "Richard, I may have to call you back, but I think that's all for now. Thanks for your help."

"Not a problem. Just do me a favor. Get the son of a bitch who killed her. Shelly was good people."

I told him I'd do my best.

If the evidence kept stacking up against Mia, we sure weren't going to have a problem proving motive. I went to Erika's office to report in, but her door was closed, and I got no answer when I knocked.

With a sigh, I bundled up in my down coat and heavy wool scarf and headed out into the windy evening. I'd have thought all the years of freezing Chicago winters would make California weather seem like a joke, but apparently the construction companies here didn't believe in insulation. Being inside wasn't much warmer than being outside. But the wind did push the clouds out of the way. Above me, the deep oranges and reds of the setting sun spread across the sky.

The minute I got home, I poured myself three fingers of scotch, no rocks—and kept my coat on. I sighed as the liquid warmth slid down my throat and smoothed out the rough edges. I needed to eat something, but I didn't want to ruin my buzz. I gave myself a refill instead.

In the living room, as I reached for the remote to turn on the TV, my cell phone rang. Sure that it had to be a telemarketer, I gave the screen a quick glance—and recognized the number. My heart gave a painful thump.

"Hello?"

"Lauren?"

It was the soft, sweet voice of my little sister, Hannah. Tears sprang to my eyes. I'd given her my new number when I left Chicago but had little hope she'd ever call. Now that she had, terror swept through me. I barely managed to choke out, "Are you okay? Did something happen to Mom and Dad?"

A beat. "N-no. we're all okay. I—I just wanted to tell you. Mom and Dad decided to stay in Hilton Head, make it permanent. They bought out their time share."

"Oh...good." I bent over, head spinning from the sudden adrenaline drop. South Carolina was far enough away from Chicago to keep them safe. I hoped.

Throat tight with anguish, I asked, "How are they doing?"

Hannah sighed, "You know Dad. He always finds something to bitch about. But, honestly, they seem fine. They always said they were going to move there at some point."

"Just not at this point," I said, my voice bitter. "What about you? How've you been? How's your new school?"

She'd only had a year to go at Loyola University, but like everyone else in my family, she'd had to get out of Chicago. In the end, she'd quietly transferred to George Washington University in DC.

Racked with guilt, the tears I'd been holding back began to roll down my cheeks.

Her voice brightened. "I really like it. The dorms are way better, and my roommates are pretty chill."

"But you must be missing Lisa and Sandy...and what about Tom?" They'd just started dating when she'd been forced to leave. My voice trembled as I said, "Please don't sugarcoat it for me."

"I'm not! I swear!" she said in a rush. "It was scary at first. But now, I think it was a good thing? Time to get out of the nest, see new places, meet new people."

Her words brought on a fresh surge of fear. "You have to be careful, though. Remember what the detectives said. Don't go out alone at night, don't—"

"I know all the 'don'ts,' Lauren," she said, cutting me off. "I'm not a little kid anymore. I'm twenty-two. And trust me, I'm being careful." She added, in a softer voice, "Honestly, I've been worried about *you*. All alone out... wherever you are."

"Please don't worry about me." My voice caught, and I had to swallow. I pictured her sitting on a bed in a dorm room I'd never seen, her long brown hair spilling over one shoulder, covering the side of her face. I squeezed back another wave of tears. I wanted her back in my life. I could only hope this call meant she wanted to be back in mine.

"It's so good to talk to you. I...I miss you." I held my breath. If she hung up now, I'd know it was really over. Forever.

A beat. Another. Then, "I miss you, too. So much."

I held a Kleenex to my eyes. "I'm so sorry, Hannah. I—I don't expect you or anyone to forgive me. Ever. And I'll never forgive myself."

Hannah's voice was shaky. "I do, though. You didn't know—" She stopped as she began to cry. "I kept trying to tell them, Mom and Dad. But they're so...closed off."

More like blinded by grief and rage. I heard her sniffling.

"Are...are we okay, though?" I asked, my heart in my throat.

"Y-yes." After a few heavy breaths, she continued. "Can we talk tomorrow?"

Tomorrow and every day. Forever. "Of course." I told her I'd be home by nine o'clock her time and added, "I love you, H."

She sniffed. "Love you back, L."

We ended the call, and I slumped down on the couch, spent. My little sister had forgiven me. The thought lifted my heart, even as it ached with the awareness that I didn't deserve it.

I reached for my bottle of Xanax, swallowed a couple of pills with a sip of scotch and thought about how it all started—the defining moment of the downward spiral that landed me here, alone and in hiding.

The day I met Roman Stiler.

×××

ROMAN WAS A SUCCESSFUL photographer who owned a studio across the street from the Northwestern University campus, where I'd been asked to do a Career Day presentation about the joys (using that term loosely) of being a public defender. He'd been asked to photograph the event, and after my appearance, he offered me free copies of my photos. "And maybe coffee?"

Warmth and fun sparkled in his green eyes. I was more than a little wary. The easy charm, the sexy smile and tastefully buff body all said *Warning!* in flashing red lights. *Hit-and-run artist, serial cheater, liar!* No way someone that hot could be good news.

"Uh, no thanks. I don't need to see any more of myself than necessary."

He gave me a puzzled look, running a hand through his curly dark hair. "Self-deprecating. I like that. But in this case, it borders on delusional."

I rolled my eyes. "Does that line ever work?"

He laughed. "I love a challenge. Have coffee with me, and I'll help you get in touch with reality." He saw my reluctant expression. "Come on, it's just coffee."

It *was* just coffee. I told myself I could enjoy the view, then be on my way.

But almost from the moment we sat down in a cozy corner of the diner across the street, I felt an excitement—a sense that something special was about to happen. It took less than ten minutes for the usual small talk to give way to the kind of intimate discussions I'd never had with men I'd known for months let alone one I'd just met.

"I know—or at least I *hope*—you're joking about not liking the way you look," Roman told me. "But I get the impression you're pretty hard on yourself in general." He lifted his eyebrows. "Am I right? Be honest."

He had a point. I'd been told more than once by close friends—and even my elementary-school counselor—that I was too unforgiving, too self-critical. I didn't understand how this man, a complete stranger, could already know so much about me. And it was kind of scary, the way I already felt so connected to him.

"Maybe." I smiled. "I've heard it's older sibling syndrome. We're the only game in town for our parents, so we get too much attention—which translates to a lot of pressure to achieve."

He nodded. "And the more time you spend as the only child, the greater the pressure. I'd bet you're at least six or seven years older than your..."

"Sister. Hannah. Yep, ten years older." I tilted my head. "And I'd bet you're the younger sibling."

Roman chuckled. "Guilty. But, hey, it wasn't all unicorns and rainbows. Us younger sibs had to learn how to share from day one."

"Yeah, you babies had a tough ride," I teased.

"Scarred me for life," he said, and laughed. Then he looked into my eyes and added, softly, "You know what? I'm going to find a way to let you know how perfect you are, every single day."

I laughed. "Oh, Lord. Stop it, Hugh Grant."

He smiled, but his voice was firm. "I'm serious. You'll see."

It was so over-the-top it was ridiculous. And yet.

It was such a change from all the guys I'd been seeing, who acted like paying a compliment was a sign of weakness.

And Roman *was* serious. We talked or texted almost daily, and he always found a way to slip in something sweet. By the next weekend, I was spending the night at his condo.

I considered keeping our relationship quiet until I was sure we had a chance of going the distance. I'd woken up next to more than one guy after the red-hot, eat-you-alive phase passed, only to realize that all we really had in common was a love of vodka martinis and *Breaking Bad*.

But with Roman, it just kept getting better. I looked forward to the weekends and dreaded Mondays. Don't get me wrong, I loved being a public defender; I didn't mind the long hours and hard work. But I liked to play, too. And it'd been the major league drag in my life—and a major league disappointment for my parents, with their clichéd husband-and-kid expectations—that I hadn't been able to find anyone I wanted to play with for the long term.

Until Roman. Until Chinese food dinners in bed, luxurious baths in his oversized tub, day-long strolls on the Riverwalk—even a hot air balloon ride. It was like something out of a rom-com, so sweet it made your teeth ache.

Prince Charming was real. Happily ever after was my life. I couldn't keep the news to myself. My parents were thrilled, Hannah was delighted, and my friends ("All that and pretty, too!") were impressed.

I drifted off to sleep to those memories of happier times and woke up on the couch in the middle of the night, my empty glass on the floor. Stumbling toward the bedroom, one hand braced against the wall, I prayed that sleep would come fast.

Before my brain could call up memories of the hell that followed those two perfect months.

CHAPTER NINE

ERIKA PUT HER FORK down. The fish was great, but she couldn't force another bite. She took a sip of wine instead, and asked, "How's development on the app coming?"

"Pretty well." Danny polished off the last of his trout almandine and glanced at Erika's nearly untouched plate. "What's going on?"

"Nothing. It's just...these late nights are hard for me, Danny." She loved her little brother, but his vampiric hours had always been problematic. He never got up before four in the afternoon, and he usually wouldn't answer the phone—let alone go out—before seven. That was fine with his tech company bosses. They didn't need coders, especially the uber-geniuses like Danny, who did his best work after midnight, to show up at the office.

But it was a killer schedule for Erika, who got up at 6:30 a.m. even on the weekends. She'd tried to get him to understand, to compromise, but that wasn't Danny's way. Her brother was what he was, take it or leave it—and he was okay with the fact that it meant just about everyone chose to leave it.

Danny had always lived alone, and the few women he'd dated hadn't lasted more than a few months. It wasn't for lack of interest—he was handsome, with big brown eyes, eyelashes that were so long and curly it was unfair, and a charming smile. But his rigid habits and other...quirks made him a tough bet for the long haul, and at thirty-eight years old, it was starting to look like he'd be a bachelor for life. He'd managed to hang onto the two male friends he'd met in college, but they weren't local—one in San Diego, the other in Portland—and they seldom saw each other in person.

Not that her social life was much better, Erika admitted to herself as she pushed her plate away. She'd dated sporadically—men she met online—but had never been tempted to take it much further than the third dinner. In the past two years, she hadn't even had enough interest to do that.

The truth was, Danny had always been Erika's mainstay, and she'd been his. Neither of them had ever been able to trust anyone else. Skip was the one exception, and Erika was hard-pressed to explain how or why he'd managed to get past her defenses. But from the start, he'd made her feel safe, protected, and even valued.

Danny gave her an impatient look. "Come on, Grandma. It's only eight o'clock." He studied Erika as she toyed with her wineglass. "What's wrong? Is it the new case?"

Erika wished he didn't know her so well. But a shared childhood of misery, abuse, and abandonment had left them finely attuned to one another. "No, it's going okay, so far. I guess I'm just still thrashed after that last one."

"Yeah, I've never seen a case take it out of you that way." He paused. "Can that girl—what's her name—take over?"

"Charlie Blair. And I can't do that."

She wished he'd let it go. But that was one of Danny's *things*. If there was something he didn't understand, he'd push and push, trying to get an answer. And sometimes there wasn't one.

Like why their asshole foster father had chosen to make Erika his punching bag. Handsome, smooth-talking Vincent Brogan had known just how to charm the Children's Services workers. To them, he was the perfect foster parent: kind, warm-hearted, good with kids. They had no idea—and never would've believed—that the man they so admired got drunk, dragged Erika into his bedroom, locked the door, and beat her until he was tired.

Erika had tried to keep the abuse from Danny. Partly because she'd wanted to protect him, partly because she'd been so ashamed. But his closet shared a wall with Brogan's bedroom, and one night, Danny went and put his ear to the wall. He'd heard everything: the slap of the leather belt hitting flesh, Erika's cries of pain, her muffled whimpers after Brogan left.

Afterward, Danny confronted her. *Why was Brogan doing this? Why hadn't she told him? Why didn't she call the cops?* Erika had tried to deny it. But Danny pointed to the long pants she always wore—even in the heat of summer. When he'd yanked up her T-shirt, the angry red welts on her body left no room for denial.

She'd pushed him away, told him that she didn't want to talk about it. That he should let it go, be grateful they got to be together. Lots of brothers and sisters wound up separated. Especially when they were as young as Erika and Danny; he'd been just two years old, and Erika five, when their drug-addict parents abandoned them.

But Danny kept after her with his *whys?* and *how comes?* He didn't understand that the questions were almost as painful as the beatings. Because the only answer her child brain could find was that she deserved it. As she got older, she realized that wasn't true—on a rational level. But deep down, there was still a part of Erika that believed she'd done *something*. And now she knew she'd have to give Danny some kind of answer, or he'd just keep asking what was going on with her.

To be fair, a lot of Danny's probing came from genuine concern. But it was also his obsessive-compulsive disorder. He couldn't let *anything* go. If he'd just take the meds his shrink, Julia—who was as much a mother figure as a psychiatrist—had prescribed, it'd probably ratchet down a few levels. But Danny hated meds, said they made him feel like a zombie. Even when he took them, he undermedicated.

"Don't worry, Danny," Erika said in a firm voice. "I can handle it. When this one's over, I'll take a break. A long one."

Danny tried another tactic. "So...this Charlie. What do you think of her?"

Erika didn't want to go *there*, either, but at least it got him off the subject of what was wrong with her. "She's smart. Used to be a defense attorney."

An image of Charlie's frustrated face came to her. It was dangerous to keep pushing her off. If she complained to Summers or Harrier, they might decide to keep a closer eye on the case. And Erika couldn't let that happen.

"I don't know much about her yet. She pretty much keeps to herself."

Danny flashed her a sardonic smile. "You guys'll be perfect together."

Erika grinned back. "Maybe. We'll see. So, how much longer before you finish the app?"

He sighed and patted his mouth with the napkin. "Should be done next month—if that idiot Greg doesn't throw another one of his stupid roadblocks in my way."

Erika sipped her wine, relieved to be off the hotseat—and, as always, happy to escape into Danny's world.

×××

ERIKA WOKE UP AT four the next morning, bleary-eyed, with a killer headache. She'd fallen asleep only to be jolted awake an hour later—eyes wide open, pulse racing—as though someone had fired a shot through her bedroom window. Unable to get back to sleep, she'd lain in bed for hours, agonizing about how it might all go wrong. How the Hansen case could start toppling the dominos that would knock down Steers' conviction. How so many women would suffer if that happened.

Not to mention the ruinous consequences for herself and Skip.

Hoping the hot water would work out the kinks, Erika stood under the shower spray for as long as she could, letting it beat down on her knotted neck and shoulders. That—and some yoga—helped. By the time she'd finished getting ready, she was feeling better. Tired, frazzled, but better.

She drove up the onramp to the freeway, mentally reviewing her plans for the day. She wanted to talk to the neighbors who lived near Shelly. Maybe she'd have Charlie come along, let her do some of the interviews.

Traffic ground to a halt, and Erika had to stomp on the brakes to keep from barreling into the Acura in front of her. *Damn it!* She hit the steering wheel in frustration. This was a bad day to be late.

Without warning, her heart began to pound fast and hard. Her breath caught in her throat; sweat sprang out on her scalp and palms; her vision blurred, and she bent forward, feeling like she was going to faint.

What's happening? Am I having a heart attack? She looked around for a place to pull over, but she was boxed in, cars all around. There was nowhere to go. Her heartbeat like it was going to explode.

Oh my God! I'm going to die.

Barely breathing, sweat running down the sides of her face, she held the steering wheel in a death grip. Maybe if she rolled down the window. She pushed the button, but as the air rushed in, the smell of exhaust hit her like a fist, and she began to choke.

Her eyes swept the lanes on either side of her, frantic, trying to find an opening. But there were just inches between the cars. Her breath was ragged; her throat felt like it'd been scraped raw. She gasped for air as tears filled her eyes. *What the hell is happening?!*

Ahead—finally—the cars began to move. Erika's heart slowed, and she managed to draw one full, clean breath. Then another. She made it to work, her whole body trembling, and sat in her car, stunned and frightened.

What *was* that? Erika noticed she was still shivering, saw that her blouse was damp with sweat. She put on her jacket and laid her head down on the steering wheel.

She'd been terrified, sure she was about to die. But the moment traffic loosened, it'd all gone away—so fast it was almost as though it'd never happened.

As she grew calmer, she dimly remembered reading about panic attacks. Was that what that was? Would they keep happening every time she got in the car? *Oh, God, no.* The thought of losing control like that again was unbearable. There had to be a way to make it stop.

At her computer, Erika pulled up articles about panic attacks, expecting to find helpful tips on how to make them stop or what kind of meds to take—a drastic measure for her; she hated drugs—but as she scrolled, her heart sank. There was no real cure. Apparently having panic attacks while driving wasn't uncommon. Certain shrinks specialized in the area. They'd ride in the car while their patients drove and try to talk them through it. Erika had no time for that. And judging by the comments section, the success rate wasn't impressive.

The only other suggested fix was "imaging," i.e., recreating the feeling of relief she'd experienced when the cars had started to move. She'd try that on the way home. *Please let it work.*

At 9:15 a.m., she called Charlie and told her the plan for the day. "Do you mind driving? I'm a little low on gas. Forgot to fill up yesterday."

"No problem. Meet you out front."

✕✕✕

As CHARLIE DROVE, ERIKA glanced through the reports of the neighbors' statements. The folks who lived closest to Shelly and Mia seemed well aware that the two were frequently at war, though the statements they'd given the unis didn't provide any specifics. Hopefully, she'd be able to pry some out of them now.

Significantly, no one had suggested another possible suspect.

When Charlie turned on Shelly's street, Erika pointed to an open space on the curb outside the small stucco house. "You can park there. Want to take the first one?"

"Sure. But don't we need to wait for Skip?"

"Not for these guys. They're basically already on the record. If anyone comes up with something radically different, I'll get a uni to come out and take a new statement."

The sky was clear and sunshine bathed the neighborhood in a golden glow, but Erika noticed dark clouds gathering to the south. It looked like rain, and she hoped they could finish the interviews before the bad weather moved in.

As they walked up the driveway to the house next door to Mia's, Charlie asked, "Do you always re-do the door knocks?"

Erika nodded. "There's no such thing as too careful."

It'd driven some detectives crazy, the way she checked and re-checked everything, but she needed to be sure she'd done everything she could to get justice for the victims. If that pissed off a few alpha male detectives, so be it.

That was probably one of the reasons she'd gotten along so well with Skip. With her, he'd never been that kind of "I call the shots" macho man.

The first neighbor—Shane Margos, a heavyset man in his sixties who lived in the house to the left of Shelly's—was less than thrilled to see them. "For God's sake, when is this going to end? We've had cops swarming all over the place for the past week."

"I get it," Charlie said. "But do you want a thorough investigation or a fast one?"

His tone was peevish. "Both. Go ahead, ask your questions. But let's move this along. I've got things to do."

Erika liked the way Charlie stood up to him. But it didn't surprise her. From what she'd seen, Charlie was no pushover.

"Did you see anyone in the area that night who looked suspicious?" Charlie asked. "Or anyone you didn't recognize?"

"No. Or I would've said so when I gave the cops my statement. Don't you people talk to each other?"

Charlie didn't take the bait. "Did you hear the sound of glass breaking?"

"Yeah. Around one thirty in the morning. Actually thought about calling the cops then." He frowned. "Probably should have."

Erika wanted to chase that down. "Why didn't you?"

"There was always so much…drama in that house. Seemed like those two were constantly fighting, especially the last year or so."

That was useful, and credible. As far as Erika could see, he didn't have any skin in the game. "Do you remember any fights in particular?"

He leaned against the doorframe. "Not offhand. They all seemed about the same to me. Lots of screeching and door slamming, and the girl running off like a bat out of hell."

Erika didn't love his condescending attitude, but the picture he painted of Mia as an out-of-control, hot-tempered, wild child, was coming into focus.

"How about the night of the murder?" Charlie asked. "Did you hear any fighting? Any arguments?"

"No. But," he added, "I didn't get home until ten thirty, so I don't know what happened before then."

"Do you remember seeing Mia after you heard the sound of glass breaking that night?"

He nodded.

"How long after?"

He stared at the floor. "I'd say it was about ten minutes later." He pointed to the front porch of Mia's house. "Saw her come busting out the door and head over to Jerry's. That's when I thought something must really be wrong."

Charlie asked, "Did you see her again after that?"

Margos said he hadn't, and after a few unsuccessful attempts to get more information, Charlie wrapped up the interview. They headed to the house on the other side of Shelly's—the house Mia had run to that night.

"Nice work," Erika said as they walked.

"Thanks. But do you think it was really ten minutes? Seems like a long time."

Erika shrugged. "It's consistent with what he told the unis, and he sounded pretty solid to me. You're right, though, he might be off. Still, any longer than two minutes would be weird."

"The cops didn't see any blood on Mia, right?" Erika shook her head. "What do you think? Was she hiding the knife? Cleaning herself up?"

"Maybe both. They swabbed the drains. If we get lucky, we might find blood." Erika made a mental note to push the lab to move faster. "Since you're on a roll, why don't you take the next one too?"

According to the unis, Jerry Tonsing had backed up Margos' statement that it'd taken Mia a while to come to his door after he heard the window break. He'd let her in and called 9-1-1. Not much there, Erika thought. Safe to let Charlie handle it.

Unlike Margos, Jerry invited them inside. Tall and rail-thin, with a fringe of white hair, he'd been retired for over twenty years, and he lived alone. Erika thought he was probably glad to have some company—even cops and prosecutors.

"I don't know what you've heard, but Shelly was one great lady," Jerry said. "Couple of years ago, a teenaged boy who lived up the street went missing. Shelly made fliers and helped the family put them up all over town. Even set up a hotline for tips."

"Nice," Charlie said. "Was the kid ever found?"

"Sure was." Jerry shook his head, his expression disapproving. "Turned out he'd just run off to be with his girlfriend."

The more Erika learned about Shelly, the sadder she felt about her loss. She wished the jury could hear that story, but there was no way it'd get into evidence.

Charlie asked, "How well did you know Shelly?"

"Unfortunately, I didn't have much contact with her." Jerry said that between Shelly's business and her daughter, she hadn't had a lot of time to socialize.

Charlie moved on to the preliminary questions, then asked, "You said you heard the sound of glass breaking at Mia's house that night?"

"Yes. And then, it seemed like two seconds later, she was pounding on my door." He nodded to underscore his answer.

What? How the hell had he come up with two seconds? Erika kept her expression as neutral as she could. But that answer eliminated the possibility that Mia had cleaned up and gotten rid of the murder weapon. She had to back him off.

She held up a hand to Charlie and gave Jerry her warmest smile. "How did you know it was that fast?"

Out of the corner of her eye, she saw Charlie looking at her. As a matter of protocol, you didn't take over someone else's interview. But Erika had no choice. She had to fix this.

"I mean, it all happened like that." He snapped his fingers. "I heard the glass break and *boom*—she was at my door." He nodded again. That nodding was irritating as hell.

But Erika kept her smile going. "You were in bed asleep when you heard the glass break, I assume?" He nodded. "But you didn't get out of bed at that point, right?"

"No. I didn't."

"Is it possible you went back to sleep after hearing the glass break, and you woke up when Mia knocked on your door? And maybe it seemed like she came right over when in fact, it might've been closer to ten minutes later?"

Jerry frowned. "It's…it's possible. I guess."

Gently, Erika said, "So you really can't be sure how much time passed between the glass breaking and Mia showing up at your door? It could've been as much as ten minutes?"

Jerry scratched his head. "You know, you're probably right. Probably *was* more like ten minutes after I heard glass breaking."

Erika asked a few more innocuous questions, then thanked him and ended the interview. As they walked outside, out of the corner of her eye, she saw Charlie's disapproving look.

This was bad. Not only had she elbowed Charlie out of the way, she'd wrestled Jerry into submission. That kind of witness coaching was unethical—it posed a serious risk of twisting the truth into a falsehood. But Erika had had to straighten him out before he got too attached to his timeline. Everything was pointing to Mia as the killer. The less ammunition she gave the defense, the better.

Charlie said, "Don't you think…"

"What?"

Charlie shook her head. "Nothing. Never mind."

Erika wasn't sure what to make of that, but she didn't want to encourage any criticism. "He was confused. I helped him get back on track. End of story." She took out her cell phone. "Hold on. I've got to tell Skip to get a uni out and take his statement." After she sent the text, she decided she'd better try to mollify Charlie. "You can take the rest of them."

That shouldn't be a problem. The other neighbors didn't live close enough to have seen or heard much of anything.

And fortunately, Erika was right. The interviews went as expected. Though they hadn't seen or heard anything unusual that night, most of the neighbors were aware of the fights Mia and Shelly had had over the years. Especially the past year. The overall opinion on the block was that Mia was spinning further and further out of control.

If Erika didn't get any more nasty surprises like Jerry, all she'd need was a little physical evidence, and she'd be able to file the case.

They'd finished the last interview and were heading back to the car when a woman in brown velour joggers and a matching hoodie came out of a house across the street. She waved to them. "Hi! Are you guys from the DA's office?"

Wary, Erika waved back. What had this woman all fired up? "Yeah," she called, feeling her pulse quicken. "We tried your door, but you didn't answer."

The woman walked down the driveway and put out her hand. "I'm Beverly Watkins."

Erika made the introductions. But this time, she took over. "Have you given a statement to any of the officers yet?"

A hank of Beverly's corkscrew hair blew across her face. "Whew! This damn wind." She pushed it back and pulled the hood of her jacket over her head. "No, I wasn't home when the officers came around. And you probably caught me in the shower when you came by earlier. Lucky thing

I happened to call Shane and ask for help with my garage door opener. He told me you were here."

Erika wasn't so sure it was lucky. She braced herself as she asked, "What did you want to tell us?"

Beverly hunched over, folding her arms across her chest. "I probably should've called this in right away, but they were always fighting, so at the time it didn't seem all that important. Now…"

"When you say 'they,' you mean Shelly and Mia?" Erika asked.

Beverly nodded. "It was the day before Shelly…died. They were in the driveway, and Shelly was yelling at Mia, saying she was spending money like it was water. And then Mia hollered back, saying, 'It's not *your* money! It's mine!'"

Erika took that in. Still *more* motive for Mia. She told Beverly a police officer would contact her to take a formal statement, and added, "Thanks for your time."

Beverly stared across the street at the Hansen house, her expression troubled. "Shelly was such a sweetheart. She'd give you the shirt off her back if you said you liked it. Did you know she volunteered at Monarch on the weekends?"

"Monarch Services?" Charlie asked. "The battered women's shelter?"

Beverly nodded. "She was amazing. But that daughter…she was out of control. And after the divorce, she was a total mess."

"The divorce from Mia's father?" Erika asked.

"Yeah. Shelly felt guilty about it because Mia and her dad were so close. That's why she let her get away with…" The word "murder" hung in the air. Beverly bit her lip. After a deep breath, she added, "I told her not to blame herself. Merrick was a good dad, but he was a lousy husband."

This was the first Erika had heard about Mia's father. "How so?"

Beverly frowned. "To be fair, I didn't know him that well. He just wasn't around much, and I got the impression he wasn't super responsible." She paused and looked across the street again. "I always thought Shelly deserved better—from him *and* her daughter." She sighed. "Anyway, I hope to God it wasn't Mia. Shelly loved her so much."

Maybe too much, Erika thought.

As she'd predicted, by the time they got back to the car, the dark clouds had moved in. The first heavy drops of rain splattered the windshield as they opened the car doors.

"That was one hell of a fight," Erika said.

"On the day before the murder no less. If we file, Beverly'll make a good witness." After a brief pause, Charlie added, "Can't imagine what it was like to live in that house. All that fighting and…craziness."

Erika *could* imagine it—and a whole lot worse—but she just said, "No kidding."

Charlie seemed better now. Less frosty. Erika hoped it was a sign she was going to be cool about what she'd seen. But she was such an unknown quantity. Of all the damn times to be saddled with a wild card…

Erika's cell phone rang. It was Skip. "Hey, Charlie and I just finished the neighborhood."

"Then my timing's perfect. We got some DNA results. Those dark hairs in Shelly's bedroom? Came back to Mia. Solid match."

Not a shock. Mia lived there. "*Where* in the bedroom?"

Skip took a beat before answering. "Under the body."

"Perfect!"

If those hairs had been almost anywhere else, it wouldn't have proved much. But under the body? Hairs get vacuumed up, stepped on, and swept away. The odds of Mia having shed hair in that exact spot at any time before the murder were pretty low. And based on the crime scene photos, Shelly'd kept the place immaculate.

"I'm thinking it's time to get an arrest warrant."

"Hell yeah. Go for it. Mind if I come along when you serve it?

"Shouldn't be a problem. I doubt she's armed and dangerous."

Relief spread through Erika's body. They'd have this case wrapped up in no time—provided Charlie didn't get in the way.

CHAPTER TEN

THANKS TO THE RAIN, the air in The Buck Nail was wet and heavy, the smell even more pungent than usual. As my eyes adjusted to the dim lighting, I saw that the place was almost empty. Two men wearing long-sleeved flannel shirts and work boots were drinking beer at the end of the bar, and a miserable-looking couple hunched over a table filled with an impressive array of empty shot glasses.

I took a stool on the end and nodded at the bartender, who was wiping down the sink. "Hey, Pete."

He sauntered over with his usual deadpan expression. I'd never seen him smile. "Hey, Charlie. What'll it be tonight?"

I decided to splurge. "Patron Silver. Make it a double."

Pete lifted an eyebrow. "You get a raise or something?"

I shrugged. "Just feel like treating myself."

As Pete went to get my drink, one of the construction workers called out, "Hey, honey, you look like you could use some company."

I picked up my cell phone and opened my email. "I'll be sure and tell my husband you said so."

"Yeah?" His voice was loud, sloppy. "How come he ain't here?"

I ignored him, thinking maybe he'd stop. But the big mouth kept at it. "Hey! I asked you a question."

Pete—who was six foot four of lean muscle—came back with my tequila and turned to the jerk. "Give it a rest. She's not interested. So leave her alone or leave. Got it?"

The jerk muttered something to his buddy, but he seemed to get the message. "Thanks," I told Pete. For the help *and* the drink, which looked more like a triple.

Pete said in a low voice, "I'm not saying you should be hanging out in one of those fruity mixologist bars, but I don't need to tell you this isn't a great place for a woman alone."

Actually, for reasons he'd never know, it was probably one of the safest places I could be. Out of the corner of my eye, I glanced at the idiot who'd been hassling me and said, "Mr. Smooth doesn't exactly strike me as the homicidal type."

Pete sighed and shook his head. "Whatever." He moved to the sink and went back to scrubbing.

As I sipped my drink, I thought about the identification of Mia's hairs under Shelly's body. Erika had been stoked, and I couldn't argue with her decision to make the arrest, but I didn't think it was a slam-dunk. If Shelly hadn't vacuumed her bedroom in the last day or two, Mia's hairs would naturally be there. Was it a heck of a coincidence that they'd landed in that exact spot? Sure. Still, it was possible. And if I were Mia's lawyer, that's what I'd argue.

But what really bugged me was the way Erika had arm-twisted Jerry. Was this how she'd won all those cases? By mind-fucking the witnesses? It was a masterful combination of gaslighting and cross-examination, I had to admit. But it was unethical as hell. Exactly the kind of thing I'd always deplored regardless of who did it, defense or prosecution. The truth matters. To me, anyway.

Beyond that, I didn't understand *why* Erika had done it. I doubted Jerry's testimony would've made much of a difference. Neither he nor Margos knew exactly how much time had passed between Mia breaking the window and running from the house. It might've been ten minutes or it might've been two seconds. They were just estimates made in the middle of the night by witnesses who were half-asleep. Even the most boneheaded defense attorney would be able to shred that testimony. A new, inexperienced prosecutor might not realize that, but Erika knew better. And that bugged me even more.

Still, there wasn't much I could do about it. The only thing complaining would get me was an invitation to apply to the public defender's office. But I told myself that if I saw any more shady shit, I'd revisit the issue. It wasn't fair to railroad this train wreck of a girl—even if she had killed her mother.

In the months I'd been with the DA's office, I'd heard a lot about Erika but never anything negative. My only source of intel was other prosecutors, though. I needed to know what the defense lawyers had to say. Problem was, she might be friendly with some of them. They might tell her I was asking around.

And then I had it.

The perfect—and safest—person to ask: Letitia Sandoval, Judge Butler's clerk. Judge Butler handled all the big homicide cases, which meant Erika had done most of her trials, including the Steers trial, in his court. I'd had a few trials with him, too, because he sometimes took lower-level felonies to help other courts with their backlogs. In the process, I'd gotten friendly with Letitia.

Tomorrow, I'd get her to talk about Erika.

As I thought about how I'd pry out the information, I saw that my glass was empty. I was already feeling blurry, knew I should probably call it a night. But what the hell. Maybe just a short dog. I raised my glass.

"Hey, Pete. How about a single for the road?"

He peered at me. "You sure?"

I gave him a thumbs up. "Yeah, I'm good. But make it Cuervo Gold this time." No use wasting money on the good stuff. I wouldn't be able to tell the difference.

He gave me a look as he poured. "If you get killed, I'm gonna be so pissed."

×××

IT HAD STOPPED RAINING. Putting my hand on the can of Mace in my purse, I took a moment to breathe in the cold night air and clear my head. I'd forgotten where I'd parked my car. I scanned the area carefully and finally spotted it down the block, near a doorway where a couple of homeless guys were tucked into sleeping bags.

As I peered at them, my heart started to beat faster. Could *he* be one of them? Would he go that far? Pretend to be homeless, lie outside in the rain...?

I clutched my can of Mace and kept one eye on the two men as I moved toward my car. My balance wasn't great, and the split focus didn't help matters. Stumbling a bit, I stepped off the sidewalk so I could get to the driver's side without passing too close. I was about thirty feet away when one of the men got up and started to head toward me.

Was that *him*? It was so dark I couldn't tell. I had to do something and fast. Maybe hit the panic button on my key and hope the noise would scare him off. But which one was it? If I lost sight of him while I looked for it...

I began to run as I pushed the button to unlock the doors and saw the trunk fly open. Shit!

But it startled him. He stopped, and I saw that he really was just a homeless man. That didn't mean he wouldn't come for me, though. I was shaking all over as I hit the unlock button, slammed the trunk closed, and hopped into my car. Gunning the engine, I pulled out and oversteered, heading straight for a giant oak tree in the median. A few feet away, I managed to yank the steering wheel to the right. And overdid it *again*. I was about to nail a parked car! I stomped on the brakes inches from the rear bumper and sat still, heart pounding as I gasped for air.

I put the window down and cranked up the air conditioning. The freezing blast did the trick. I made it home. But as I climbed the stairs to my apartment I thought, *If you don't stop doing this shit, you're going to die—or kill someone else.*

I was still shaky as I pulled out my phone and checked the footage on my Ring camera. Thankfully, there was nothing, just neighbors going about their business. Hopefully that meant he hadn't found me.

But what about my parents? What about Hannah? I felt the ever-present knot of anxiety tighten in my chest. I made myself a drink, thinking I could only hope he'd come for me instead. It was the best protection I could give them.

×××

THE NEXT MORNING, I TRIED to remember my genius ideas for getting Letitia to talk about Erika. Nothing came to mind. As usual. I sighed. I always got great ideas over a drink or two, and they always disappeared by morning.

But I sure hadn't forgotten my near-disastrous ride home. I couldn't let that happen again. I had to knock it off with the drinking and driving. I might try to dial back my nightcaps, too, but that'd be a heavier lift. Alone at night, the punishing weight of guilt and the constant fear made it hard to breathe. Alcohol gave me my only respite. I fished aspirin out of my glovebox and washed them down with water and a long pull of coffee from my travel cup.

I wanted to catch Letitia alone, so I waited until lunch. At ten minutes to twelve, I headed to her courtroom and made my way up the aisle through the fleeing lawyers. She was squinting at her monitor, her fingers flying over the keyboard.

"You know, you could just break down and get glasses."

She gave me a dirty look. "Glasses are for old people." She hit a key, then sat back. "I hear you're second chair on that Hansen murder. Always knew you were going to be a star."

"Then you know a lot more than I do." A star. God forbid. "But I'm pretty sure we'll wind up doing the trial here, so I'll be hanging around a bunch."

She folded her arms. "Just remember to bring me those churros in the morning, and I'll keep you at the top of my list."

"Happily." I love a clerk who's easily bribed.

"So what's it like working with Erika?"

I couldn't ask for a better opening. "Great. She's a national treasure."

Letitia laughed. "Yeah, she's pretty well liked around here."

"How does the defense bar get along with her? Just trying to get an idea of what to expect in the way of fireworks at trial."

Letitia shrugged. "There've been some, of course. These murder cases are high-pressure, high stakes. But no one's ever had a serious issue with Erika. You should have a pretty sane time of it."

Erika had either hidden her tracks too well to get caught—and no one's that good, especially after fifteen years—or this was the first time.

So why now? Why take that kind of risk? Erika didn't know me, not really. For all she knew I could be some kind of ethics kamikaze willing to take us all down.

I would've stayed to chat with Letitia, but Erika texted: *Larissa Bronson is coming in at one o'clock.*

She'd let me talk to the neighbors, and now she was letting me sit in on Larissa's interview. A good sign? I smiled at Letitia and said, "Gotta run. But those churros will be coming by the bagful, starting soon."

Letitia grinned and patted her stomach. "I hear elastic waistbands are making a comeback."

×××

Larissa Bronson and a woman who had to be her mother sat in front of Erika's desk. Not only did they have the same dark eyes and straight black hair, they wore the same heavy black eyeliner, false lashes, and pale pink lipstick. And both had on tight, black, low-cut sweaters and skinny jeans. On Larissa, the look came off as teenage with a soupçon of slutty. On her mother, it came off as Elvira, Mistress of the Dark. And also slutty, but in a sad way.

Erika jumped right in. "I hear you were hanging with Mia at the party."

Larissa crossed her legs. "Yeah, for a little while."

From her tone, I could tell that she wasn't happy to be here. Whether that was out of loyalty to Mia or just teenage disdain for "the man," I couldn't tell. But it did strike me that neither Larissa nor Axel seemed terribly intimidated by us. They were children of privilege. They knew Mommy and Daddy would always be there to take their side, to shell out money, to shove them to the head of every line. Nauseating as it was, I felt a little sorry for them. They'd get one hell of a wake-up call when Mommy and Daddy weren't around to clear the way.

Erika's voice was casual as she asked, "Did she say anything to you about her mother?"

Larissa looked at her own mom, then back at Erika, her expression sullen. "Um, not that I remember."

"Axel said she did. That you told him she was complaining to you about her mother that night."

Not exactly true. Axel only said Mia had complained to *him*. But it was a fair tactic—as long as Erika didn't get too heavy-handed about it.

Larissa made a face. "Axel doesn't know shit."

Her mother tapped her arm. "Don't talk like that. It makes you sound like trash."

Larissa snorted, "Takes one…"

Jeez. What a pair. Erika cut in, "Maybe so. But he's not the only one who told me that."

Which was an outright lie. Why was she pushing this girl so hard? She wasn't exactly a critical witness. Just another in what was clearly going to be a long line of people saying Mia and her mother had a lousy relationship.

Larissa was getting agitated. "Who else told you that? Cause they're full of shit, and I'll tell them right to their fucking face!"

"I can't say, Larissa." Erika drilled her with a look. "But it's not just dumb to lie to me. It's a crime. It's obstruction of justice."

For God's sake. Now she was threatening her with a *felony*? I was about to say something, when Larissa spoke up.

"Her mother called and told her to come home."

"And what did Mia say to her?"

Larissa's expression hardened. "Told her to fuck off."

"And then what?"

"Mia hung up and said her mother was a fucking bitch, and she hated her."

Erika pressed her. "Did she say anything else?"

Larissa hesitated. When she spoke, her tone was reluctant. "She said her mother threatened to cut her off if she didn't get her ass home."

"What else did she say?"

She glared at Erika. "That was it. I told her to chill. We were there to party."

"And then?"

"And then nothing! My boyfriend got there, and we went outside."

Erika continued, unfazed. "Did you see her again after that?"

"No." Larissa edged forward in her chair. "I just remember seeing Axel passed out on the floor. Can I go now?"

Erika glanced at Skip, who shook his head. She tilted her head at me, which I appreciated.

I held up a hand. "I'm good."

She turned back to the girl. "Yes, you can go. Thanks for your time, Larissa."

As Larissa and her mother moved to the door, Larissa turned back to us. "Do you really think she did it?"

"Yes. We do," Erika said.

I figured it was safe for me to chime in now that the interview was over. "Are you planning to visit Mia if she gets arrested?"

Larissa looked down. "Uh…no. Probably not."

I found that curious. Weren't they friends?

"What about Axel? Do you think he'll visit her?"

She shook her head "I don't think anyone's going to."

Some crew Mia had.

But my more pressing issue was with Erika. She'd managed to squeeze more evidence of motive out of Larissa. But we already had so much, I didn't see the point in getting badge heavy with the girl. And angry witnesses can be vindictive. All Larissa had to do was insist Mia "always said shit like that," and claim Erika had twisted her words. That'd tank her testimony *and* make Erika look bad.

What got me was—once again—Erika knew better. There was something off-kilter about her, a kind of sweaty desperation in the way she was acting. Not at all the way she'd been during the Steers trial—a much more high-profile case. She'd been stressed, yes. Exhausted and worried, of course. But I'd never seen her be this brittle, this nervous. She was definitely acting strangely.

I just didn't know why.

CHAPTER ELEVEN

STORM CLOUDS HAD GATHERED again by the time Skip pulled to the curb in front of Georgia's house. Erika eyed the loose, Buck rain gutter, the peeling paint and cracks in the driveway. Georgia lived a very different life than her sister.

"Has Mia been staying here all along?"

Skip nodded. "Aunt Georgia told the unis she left the house a few minutes ago. But she can't be far. She doesn't have a car and none of her friends have been coming around."

Erika made a face. "No surprise there."

Skip sighed. "Yeah. You want to wait in the car until we find her?"

"No, I'll come with."

Based on what they'd seen during the interview, she expected Mia to throw a major league fit and cuss them all out when they told her she was under arrest. If only she'd just say, "You got me," and confess, Erika thought. But that seemed unlikely.

It *was* possible she'd accidentally pop out an incriminating comment. The trauma of getting arrested can make people say and do stupid things. Erika had seen it happen before.

The darkness of the sky gave the run-down house an ominous air. Like one of those shacks in the movies where a serial killer tortures his victims. Erika and Skip walked around to the backyard, a small patch of weeds and dirt surrounded by a chain link fence. Beyond it, Erika saw an open field.

Skip's radio crackled with static-y voices. "They've got eyes on her. Let's go!"

He pointed to a hole in the fence, and Erika raced behind him as he ran through it. She spotted Mia at the far end of the field, just as one of the unis called out, "Stop! Police! You're under arrest!"

Mia whirled around, a look of panic on her face. Then she twisted away and looked back over her shoulder. Was she going to run? If she did, this arrest could get out of control fast. Erika held her breath as she silently pleaded, *Don't do it!*

Fortunately, one of the younger, faster unis got to her before she could move. He pulled Mia's arms behind her back and snapped on a pair of handcuffs. "Mia Hansen, you're under arrest for the murder of Shelly Hansen. You have the right to remain silent…"

Mia fell to the ground, dropping like a rag doll. The uni called out, "She fainted!"

Skip yelled, "Get me some water!" He hurried over to Mia and knelt down. One of the unis gave him a bottle of water, which he poured into his hands and used to pat her cheeks.

Her eyes flew open. With her face now bare of makeup, Mia looked so young, so vulnerable that Erika couldn't help but feel sorry for her. She drew closer. "Is she okay?"

"Yeah. She'll be fine." Skip looked down at her. "Remember me? Skip?" Mia gave a little nod. "Think you can stand up?"

Mia ran her tongue over her dry lips. "I—I don't know."

He held out the water bottle. "Want a sip?" She nodded, and he lifted her head, put the bottle to her mouth, then helped her to her feet. Erika watched him lead her to the patrol car. She looked dazed. This hadn't gone as Erika had expected—or hoped. But Mia was, after all, just an eighteen-year-old girl. Her only brush with law enforcement had been a curfew violation in junior high. It stood to reason she'd be frightened and overwhelmed.

Still, it worried Erika. That scared teenager was the girl the jury would see. This wasn't going to be easy.

×××

THE WEATHER COOPERATED JUST long enough for Erika to get into her car, but as she headed home, it began to hail. Icy chunks pounded down on the roof so fast and hard it sounded like machine gun fire.

She eyed the traffic as she drove up the onramp to the freeway. It didn't seem to be jammed. If it stayed that way, she'd hopefully be okay. She hit the gas and steered into the fast lane.

Then, without warning, it started again. Her heart, beating out of control. Her lungs, closing up. *I have to get out of here.*

Erika put on her blinker, looked to her right, and saw a white SUV next to her. She was trapped between it and the dividing wall. Her breathing got fast and shallow; her vision pulsing in sync with her racing heartbeat. She screamed at the SUV, "Move! Get out of the way!" and slowed to let it pass. The Mercedes behind her leaned on his horn, the blast making her jump in her seat.

Frantic, she looked to her right again. The SUV was gone, and she moved across the freeway to the slow lane. A sign said it was one mile to the next offramp. Her whole body was shaking, and her head felt like it was clamped in a vise.

Just one mile. Come on, you can make it! Erika gritted her teeth and squeezed the steering wheel to keep from screaming. She had to force herself to keep her foot on the gas. She made it to the offramp...

And just like the last time, it all stopped. Her pulse slowed; her vision cleared. She could breathe again, but she was limp with exhaustion. She took surface streets the rest of the way home, dropped her briefcase and purse on the coffee table, and collapsed on her bed. She'd only meant to rest, but the panic attack had so drained her; she fell asleep.

When she woke up an hour later, she actually felt hungry—a rare thing nowadays. She made herself a turkey and swiss sandwich, but after two bites, nausea twisted her stomach. She wrapped it up and promised herself to try and finish it later.

On TV, an old rerun of *Friends* was playing. For some reason, Erika found it soothing. Maybe it was just that—other than Phoebe—everyone had such normal lives. It was a galaxy away from Erika's world. And never more so than now. She'd prayed the panic attacks would go away, but clearly, that wasn't going to happen. She'd have to live with the constant fear of knowing an attack was coming, but never knowing when.

Erika couldn't bear to think about it. She turned up the volume and dove into the latest fight between Rachel and Ross. After a few episodes, she decided it was late enough to call Danny. Skip had invited them over for dinner on Saturday.

She tried his landline, which he preferred. No answer. Erika frowned at the phone. He should be up by now. Probably doing errands. At this hour that could only be grocery shopping—or the twenty-four-hour pharmacy. Something always seemed to be bothering Danny—his head, his stomach, his back, his feet. Erika was never sure how much was real and how much was imagined. She suspected that a lot of his problems were just excuses to have physical contact with someone. The thought made her heart ache.

She tried his cell phone. No answer. She started to pace.

Another hour passed. Erika tried his landline again. Still no answer. Hands shaking, she re-dialed his cell.

This time, he answered, his voice a bare whisper. "Hey, Erika."

"Hi. How're you doing?"

"I—I'm good. What's up?"

"I can barely hear you. Are you okay?"

He raised the decibel slightly, but his voice was still low. "Yeah, I'm fine."

No. He wasn't. Erika could hear the note of tension. "Where are you?"

A long beat of silence. "I'm...I'm at home."

But she'd just called his landline, and he hadn't answered. Something was wrong. She kept her tone light. "How about if I come over? I'll bring a bottle of that wine I told you about. The one Skip turned me on to."

His voice was even softer now. "Um...I'm not sure."

He was in trouble. No room for discussion. "Good. I'm on my way."

She ended the call, grabbed the wine, and hurried out. Fortunately, Danny's house was just a few miles away. She could take surface streets.

As she drove, she realized with a sinking feeling that this was going to have to be her work-around for the foreseeable future. It'd take her forever to get anywhere—especially the office. But if leaving earlier meant no more horrifying panic attacks, it was worth it. It wasn't as though she ever slept past 5:30 a.m. anyway.

×××

ERIKA TEXTED DANNY FROM his doorstep. He never answered the door unless he was expecting someone, and he hadn't exactly invited her over. Would he even let her in?

But finally, she heard the slide of the security chain and the turn of the deadbolt. He cracked the door and peeked out at her. "Erika. You're here?"

She held up the bottle of wine. "Me and my tasty friend."

He opened the door a little further, poked his head out, and looked up and down the street. "Come in."

He was still speaking with unnatural softness as he closed and locked the door behind her. Erika walked into the kitchen and found the wine opener, but Danny was eyeing the bottle. "I don't want any," he said.

She put down the opener and gestured to the kitchen table. "Let's talk."

He gave a wary glance out the window, then took a seat. Erika sat down across from him. Her stomach tightened as she asked, "What's going on, Danny?"

He glanced out the window again. "The assholes are back."

Oh, God. Not again. Erika's heart sank.

Back when he'd lived in Pasatiempo, Danny'd complained about his neighbors tormenting him. She'd believed him at first, had even advised him to call the police. But when his complaints escalated to claims that his neighbors were walking around on his roof and dangling boomboxes down his chimney to blast him with Napalm Death songs, she'd realized it wasn't real. It was delusional.

She'd spent a few nights at his house, hoping to show him it was just his imagination. But he'd said, "Of course, they're not going to do it when *you're* here."

Erika had suggested he come stay with her, but he'd refused. Danny liked his privacy, and he needed his own space, his particular routines. So Erika persuaded him to move away, hoping that might solve the problem. And for the past three years, it seemed like it had.

Now, it was all she could do to keep from crying. She couldn't bear to see him suffer this way. Though she feared it was pointless to try and reason with him, she had to give it a shot. "Danny, you didn't tell anyone where you were moving. How could they have found you?"

He gave her an impatient look. "Well, obviously they followed the moving truck."

"But why would they wait until now? You've been here for three years already."

He put a hand to his forehead. "Why would they do any of the shit they do? They're crazy."

What could make him feel better? Erika wracked her brain. "Do you still have those motion detectors?" At Skip's suggestion, Danny'd put them all over his property in Pasatiempo, and for a while, they seemed to help. Danny'd said the lights had scared "them" off—until they didn't.

He brightened a little. "No, but I can get some more pretty quick."

"Good. And you know you can come and stay with me, right?"

"Thanks, sis." He gave her a grateful look. "But I'll be okay. Don't worry."

She thought he seemed more relaxed. Hopefully, he *would* be okay. In any case, there was nothing else she could do for him right now, other than keep him company. "So, you binging anything good?"

He threw another wary glance at the window, but said, "Not really, but we can go see what's on."

Erika followed him into the living room, and when she saw the TV screen, she froze. The lead lawyer for Blake Steers' defense team on some talk show, crowing about how they'd developed "compelling new leads" for the new trial motion.

"We're going to toss out that sham of a conviction and make Blake Steers a free man!" the lawyer boasted.

Erika clenched her fists, shaking with anger. "Bull*shit*! You fucking liar!"

Danny turned to her, brow furrowed. "Well...duh. They're all liars. Why're you so upset?"

Erika glanced at Danny, then away, embarrassed. Why *was* she so upset?

Her brother turned off the TV, and said in a soft voice, "Erika, doesn't Blake Steers remind you of someone?"

She frowned. "Not really."

He tilted his head. "No? How about Vincent Brogan?"

Erika stared at him, stunned, as the pieces fell into place. Vincent Brogan, her violent drunk of a foster father, who'd fooled the world into believing he was a great guy. The shock of recognition left her speechless. Danny was right.

A memory flashed in her brain. A week after she and Danny had moved in with Brogan and his wife, they were having dinner—meatballs and spaghetti. Danny, just two years old at the time, was struggling with his knife and fork. As he tried to cut the meatball, his knife slipped, and a piece flew off the plate and hit Brogan on the chin. Erika—only six years old herself—laughed.

With a look of cold fury, Brogan slowly wiped his face, stood up, grabbed her by the arm, and yanked her out of her seat. He dragged her into her bedroom, her feet barely touching the floor, threw her down and locked the door. In a calm, soft voice, he said, "You think that's funny?"

Erika had stared up at him, shaking with fear. "No! I'm sorry!"

"Sorry?" His lip curled in an ugly smile. "I'm afraid that's not good enough."

He took off his belt, folded it in half, then grabbed her by the hair and shoved her face into the floor. As Erika began to cry, as he whipped her with a savage ferocity, she could hear his voice: "How about now? You think this is funny?"

Erika wailed in agony, curled up in a ball, her head in her arms, afraid she was about to die. She cried so hard, she started to choke. As she gasped for air, she begged, "Please, oh please."

Finally, he stopped. She didn't dare move until she heard the door close behind him.

The memory was so vivid, Erika could still feel the burning sting of leather against her skin. She touched her ribcage, where the most painful welts had been.

When the Family Services counselor came to the house later that week, Brogan was just this side of Santa—warm, even jovial, as he joked with self-deprecating humor. The counselor was charmed, completely taken in.

Erika remembered how she'd laughed and told him he was her "favorite foster dad."

Just like Blake Steers. It was so obvious. Erika had done her best to bury the memory of Brogan. The thought of how powerless, how vulnerable she'd been—even now it enraged her. She'd never be able to make him pay for what he'd done. He was dead.

But Steers. Him she *could* make pay.

She understood now why the Steers case had infuriated her from the very start—and why she'd done…what she'd done to get him convicted. But that didn't make her feel any better. In fact, it made her feel worse. In spite of all her efforts to put those years of abuse behind her, she'd failed. Badly.

She gazed down at the table, defeated. "You're right."

"I'm sorry." Danny reached out and touched her hand. Something he rarely did. "Do you want to talk about it?"

No. She never wanted to talk—or think about—that time in her life. The time when she was a weak, defenseless victim. She squeezed his hand. "Thanks, Danny. But there's really nothing to say."

×××

ERIKA PULLED UP THE zipper of her navy blue skirt and buttoned her jacket. Today was Mia's arraignment and bail hearing. The ball was rolling. It felt good.

She left half an hour early and drove surface streets all the way to work; didn't even try to take the freeway. It was a long drive, but it was worth it—much as she hated to give in to the craziness. She had a feeling the panic attacks would just keep coming until the Hansen case was done—and Steers had lost the new trial motion. At least she'd found a doable solution in the meantime.

At the office, she checked the mirror to make sure she was camera ready. The view wasn't great. Her face was pinched and drawn, but concealer hid most of the dark shadows under her eyes. It'd have to do.

She called Charlie. "Ready?"

Charlie was silent for a beat. "Do you need me there? It's just an arraignment."

So odd, the way Charlie hated the press. Erika didn't love reporters, but Charlie's attitude was downright phobic. "You're second chair, you should be there."

Charlie sighed. "Okay. On my way."

As Erika had expected, the spectator gallery in the courtroom was only half-full, and the press was all local. She looked across counsel table at Mia's lawyer, Tyler Messing. Skip had heard he'd transferred to Santa Cruz from San Francisco six months ago. He'd clearly just had a haircut, and his suit was typical "public defender chic," i.e., barely serviceable. But that could garner jury sympathy. And she was sure he'd capitalize on that by making Mia look like an angel.

Erika leaned over and whispered to Charlie. "You ever try a case with him?"

Charlie shook her head. "You?"

"No." Charlie seemed awfully edgy. Erika opened her mouth to ask what was wrong, then stopped. A sheriff's deputy was bringing Mia out of lockup. In her long sleeved, high-necked white blouse, her hair gathered up in a ponytail, Mia looked like a cherub. No makeup, no earrings, no piercings—it must've taken hours to get them all out.

As soon as Mia was settled, the bailiff called the court to order and Judge Butler came striding out, black robes flowing behind him. Impatient, brilliant, and a devotee of swift justice, he had no compunction about cutting off lawyers on either side if he thought they were grandstanding, repeating themselves, or stating the obvious. He looked down from the bench at Erika, then at Tyler.

"This is the time and place for arraignment. Your client is charged with first degree murder. How does she plead?"

Tyler motioned for Mia to stand up and face the judge. In a soft, shaky voice, she said, "Not guilty, Your Honor."

A perfect performance. If it were allowed, Erika would've slow-clapped.

The judge nodded. "I assume, Mr. Messing, you intend to ask me to lower her bail."

"Yes, I do, Your Honor." He gestured to Mia. "Mia has no criminal record, and no means to flee. Given her young age and background, jail will be particularly dangerous for her. She should be allowed to go home with an ankle monitor."

He'd called her "Mia." Another smart move, Erika thought. But she'd been expecting his pitch, and she was prepared to fight it to the death. If Mia got bail, this case could drag on for months. No way was she going to let that happen.

Erika stood up. "Your Honor, Ms. Hansen stands accused of a heinous murder, and the evidence of her guilt is overwhelming. I'd also point out that her mother was a bail bondsman with a lot of connections, one of whom might be able to help Ms. Hansen flee—"

"Objection!" Tyler threw a glare at Erika. "There's no evidence whatsoever that Shelly Hanson had any such—"

Judge Butler held up a hand. "Agree. Sustained." He turned to Erika. "We don't speculate in my courtroom, Ms. Lorman. You know that. Stick to the facts."

Erika nodded. "I apologize, Your Honor. The defendant has a severe drug and alcohol abuse problem. Given her current circumstances, I don't think it's much of a stretch to predict that problem will get a lot worse if she's released. She'll pose a danger to herself and others. We submit that bail should remain at two million dollars."

The judge looked at Tyler and raised an eyebrow. "I assume you'll say Ms. Hansen has family who'll make sure she stays sober, and that the evidence is far from overwhelming. Anything to add to that?"

The attorney shook his head. "No, Your Honor."

Erika gave him credit. He'd picked up on Judge Butler's style pretty quick.

The judge nodded. "Request to lower bail is denied. Let's set a date for the preliminary hearing."

Tyler cleared his throat. "Uh, Your Honor, we'd like to skip the preliminary hearing. My client wants to get this case before a jury as soon as possible, so we won't be waiving time."

The judge leaned back, his expression surprised. "Far be it from me to impede the wheels of justice." He turned to Erika. "What's the earliest date you can be ready, Ms. Lorman?"

Erika had not seen that coming. They didn't have all their lab results in yet, and a short timeframe would seriously limit the possibility of finding new witnesses. But she wasn't about to object. "We can be ready three weeks from today."

"That'd mean starting on a Wednesday. You're both okay with that?" Tyler and Erika nodded. "Then that'll be the date. But I'm warning you both: I'm going to hold you to it, and I won't take kindly to last-minute requests for more time." He picked up his gavel. "Defendant is remanded to custody. Court is adjourned."

As he rapped his gavel and left the bench, Erika saw that Charlie seemed concerned. "What's wrong?"

"Can we really be ready that fast?" Her expression said she doubted it.

"Absolutely." Erika nodded toward the door. "Come on. Time to meet the hounds of hell."

An odd look flashed across Charlie's face.

"Are you okay?" Erika asked.

"Yeah, sure."

Erika turned and walked down the aisle, then noticed Charlie wasn't behind her. Glancing back, Erika saw her fiddling with the clasp on her briefcase. "Hey, you coming?"

Charlie looked up. "Be right there."

But as Erika reached the door, she saw Charlie walk over to Letitia's desk. She sighed and moved out into the hallway as a gaggle of reporters surrounded her.

CHAPTER TWELVE

I couldn't get my key into the lock on my office door—then I looked down and realized how hard my hand was shaking.

Being in court with all those reporters was a nightmare. Afraid to breathe, I'd tried to keep my back to the gallery so they couldn't get a clear shot of my face. Even if Erika was right about it just being local media, that didn't mean some national news outlet wouldn't pick up the story at some point. And if they did, he'd spot me in a heartbeat.

Luckily, I had an escape route from the courtroom, an exit at the far end of the hallway, where reporters wouldn't notice me. But that wouldn't always work. And I was sure Erika was wondering why I'd disappeared after the arraignment.

I leaned against the wall, my heart thumping. A wave of anger surged through my body, and before I could stop myself, I hurled my briefcase across the room. It hit the wall and burst open, sending folders flying. *Goddamn* this fucking case—a case I never wanted that had stuck me with a prosecutor pulling one dirty trick after another.

Frustrated, angry, and scared, I reached into my purse for my emergency stash of Xanax. And, *of course*, it was empty. I'd forgotten to refill it.

A wave of bile rose up in my throat. I dug into the bottom drawer of my desk for my box of saltines—and saw my reflection in my little makeup mirror. The skin under my eyes sagged, and my face was a pale, puffy mess. I looked like shit. If I kept going like this, I wouldn't have to worry about anyone recognizing me. They'd never connect this bagged-out hag with Lauren Claybourne.

Great. I'd found a silver lining.

I took a few deep breaths, then turned on my computer and opened the file marked "Forensics." Since the discovery of Mia's hairs under Shelly's body, we hadn't gotten anything of great value. The techs had dusted for latent prints on the inside of Mia's window, looking for any that didn't belong to Mia or Shelly. Erika had been worried about those results. If the techs found foreign prints, it'd give the defense a chance to claim someone else could've killed Shelly and climbed out through the window before Mia got home. Not a great theory, Erika and I agreed, but I'd seen weaker arguments sway juries. Hell, in my past life, *I'd* argued weaker theories.

In any case, the techs hadn't been able to lift anything recognizable— not even prints that matched Mia's. But after lunch, I got a call from our DNA expert, Leo Gold. He'd just finished the testing on some touch DNA at the crime scene.

The labs were getting better at touch DNA. It had its flaws, contamination by crime scene techs being one of them. But because it only required a small amount of DNA to get a result, it could put a suspect at a crime scene with just a few skin cells.

"Where'd you find it?" I asked

"The doorframe of the mother's bedroom." Papers shuffled on his end of the line. "Didn't match either your victim or your defendant."

Interesting, but again, not earthshattering. A housekeeper, one of Shelly's boyfriends, or one of Mia's friends might've left it. We'd have to try and get swabs from as many of them as we could. But we couldn't force them, so this might well be a dead end. "That it?"

"So far, yes. I'll get back to you when we have more."

"The defense is jamming us for time, so we're going to need to move a lot faster than usual."

He sighed. "I'll do what I can."

I went to Erika's office and knocked on her door. When she told me to come in, I saw that she was on her cell phone—and she looked stressed.

"So you'll get them today?" She listened. "Great."

"Everything okay?" I asked, sitting down.

She nodded. "Just had to get an electrician out to replace a couple of dead outlets. What's going on?"

Somehow, her expression said it was more than bad wiring. But I let it go.

"Finally got some test results on the DNA." I told her about the foreign touch DNA on the bedroom doorframe, and she sat up with a look of alarm.

"Who did the testing? I hope it wasn't some rookie."

What? "Leo did it himself. But it's no big deal. Probably just the housekeeper or a friend of Shelly's."

Erika knew better than anyone that crime scene techs always found random evidence that had nothing to do with the case. She'd argued that very point *ad nauseum* in the Steers case.

"I'm getting it retested." She picked up the phone. "Is that it?"

I nodded.

"You can go, then."

Wow. *Sir, yes sir.* What the hell was wrong with her? Maybe she was dealing with some personal thing. But Erika seemed to get bent out of shape when *anything*, no matter how inconsequential, threatened to put a dent in the case against Mia. I'd seen her manage obstacles in the Steers case that were ten times bigger without batting an eye. Something strange was going on.

Still, I had to admit, Mia was looking pretty guilty, and no other suspects had appeared on the horizon. Maybe I was reading too much into things, leaning too hard into my public defender roots. If Erika didn't make any other dicey moves, I'd chalk up her behavior to pretrial jitters and let it go.

×××

WHEN I GOT BACK TO my computer, the coroner's report had come in. I opened the file and read the analysis of Shelly's injuries. The description of all those stab wounds—fourteen, to be exact—was stomach-turning. And yet, based on what we'd learned so far, that kind of rage killing might well be in Mia's wheelhouse.

I checked out the section on evidence collection. Everything seemed to be in order. DNA swabs, hair samples, stomach contents...fingernail scrapings.

Shit. I'd been waiting for the test results on Shelly's scrapings, but the lab still hadn't sent them. Which was weird. They were a critical piece of evidence for us and should've been a high priority.

In a murder case, the medical examiner always collects scrapings from under a victim's fingernails. It can be some of the best evidence, because if those scrapings turn out to have the killer's DNA, it's virtually unbeatable proof of guilt. In our case, Mia had had gnarly scratches on her arms the night of the murder, and several witnesses—the guy, Jack, who'd given her a ride; the kids at the party—had said they weren't there earlier in the evening. If the DNA from Shelly's fingernail scrapings matched Mia, it'd be a slam dunk.

I didn't think there was any way I'd overlooked the test results, but just to make sure, I searched through every report we'd received from the lab so far. Nada. Had they run into some problem with the testing? God, I hoped not.

For now, I decided not to tell Erika. After seeing her lose her shit over something as small as the touch DNA, I was afraid she'd stroke out. I'd handle this myself.

Speak of the devil: as I picked up my phone to contact the lab, Erika called.

"Leo refused to retest. Said he didn't want to risk contamination. Go ahead and send his report to the defense."

"Got it." I took a shot at reassuring her. "The case is looking pretty strong. This won't be a big deal."

"Sure." She ended the call.

But maybe she was right to worry. One hour later, Tyler filed a motion asking to set an "emergency discovery hearing" for tomorrow morning.

I called Erika. "What the hell is an 'emergency discovery hearing'?"

"No clue. Probably an excuse to put the touch DNA report on blast to the press. Do me a favor. Go through all the reports and make sure we've turned everything over."

"I'm on it."

I spent the rest of the day and into the evening checking our discovery. We were up to speed. At last, I stood, stretched, and went to the window. Yesterday's storm had dropped so much rain, the parking lot was filled with puddles. The leaves on some of the trees were still dripping. But my car was the cleanest it'd been in a month.

Looking at the moody sky, I felt my vision blur. When I'd taken the job in the Santa Cruz DA's office, I hadn't bargained for the Hansen case. Today's appearance in court had shown me that a new identity and a new city might not be enough to keep me safe. And now it raised the memory of what had put me in such danger to begin with.

It had started with a panicked text from Roman.

I need your help. Detectives at my studio. Asking about that girl who got killed on campus. I don't know what to do.

The case had been all over the Chicago local news. Six days before, Angela Morelli, a young co-ed at the university, had been raped and strangled, her nude body found by the school security guard in the science building lab. There were no suspects, no angry ex-boyfriends, no crazed stalkers. Police were theorizing they might have a serial killer on their hands, which had the whole campus, not to mention the students' families, worked up to a fever pitch.

But I didn't understand why Roman seemed so upset. His studio was right across the street from the campus. The cops were looking for witnesses. It made sense they'd talk to everyone in the area.

I texted back: *What are they asking?*

His answer was immediate: *If I have an alibi for that night.*

That wasn't a *witness* question. It was a *suspect* question. Images of the past two months flashed through my mind. Roman's laugh, his smile, his gentle touch, the warmth in his eyes when he looked at me. I shook my head. No. I'd been a public defender for seven years, so I knew anyone could do anything. But I had pretty good sociopath radar, and I'd seen nothing— not a breath, not a glimmer—of that in Roman.

I texted: *Did they tell you why?* and held my breath as I watched the bubbles on my phone screen.

Remember I told you she did a photo session at my studio that afternoon? They found my flash drive on the ground. Outside the lab.

The lab. Where they'd found her body. And I knew he didn't give those flash drives to his clients. I sat down, stunned. None of this made sense.

Is there any way someone else could've gotten it?

The bubbles started, then stopped. My heart began to pound.

That's what I'm trying to figure out.

It was the only possible explanation. Someone, probably Angela herself, must've taken the flash drive. That had to be it. Roman would remember what'd happened. The cops would realize he had nothing to do with her murder and move on.

But ten minutes later, Roman called me, frantic. "They want me to come down to the station for questioning," he whispered. "I'm afraid if I say no, they'll think I've got something to hide."

"That's what they want you to think. It's a trap. Don't fall for it."

But sweat had broken out on the back of my neck. I was really scared. But I knew—I *knew*—there was no way he could've killed that girl.

"I have to, Lauren! I didn't do it! If I talk to them, I can make them see that."

We argued back and forth, but it quickly became clear that he wasn't going to listen. "Okay, then I'm going with you."

It was exactly the wrong thing to do. Every lawyer knows that representing your significant other is a huge mistake. You lose all objectivity. But I couldn't let Roman go in for that grilling unprotected.

The relief in his voice was palpable. "You will? Oh my God. Thank you, Lauren!"

I wanted to ask him what he'd said to the cops so far, but I couldn't do it with them standing there. "I'll meet you at the station. Don't let them give you a ride, and don't say another word to anyone. Take your own car and wait for me in the parking lot."

No matter how I tried, I couldn't make sense of this. A rapist and murderer. It didn't compute. Could someone have set Roman up? But who? And why?

When I spotted Roman's car in the parking lot, I put on a confident smile. *Don't let him see you're freaking out.*

"I'm so glad you're here." Roman hugged me, then glanced at the entrance. "I've never been to a police station before."

The energy swirling around him was almost manic. If he didn't calm down, he might really do himself some harm. "Listen," I said, forcing him to meet my eyes, "you need to take a deep breath and clear your head. Are you sure you want to do this?"

His right cheek twitched, his "tell" that he was nervous. "Yes. I have to show them I've got nothing to hide."

He had no idea what he was in for. "Okay. Just remember—when they ask a question, don't answer right away. I need a chance to cut them off if I don't like where they're going."

He squared his shoulders in an effort to look confident, but his anxiety was obvious. "Got it."

I squeezed his hand, which was cold and clammy, and we headed into the station.

I'd never had a case with either of the detectives—a black woman named Dierdre and a heavyset white man named Buck—but it took me about ten seconds to see that they were convinced Roman was guilty. He wasn't going to talk them out of anything. All I could do was try to keep him from digging his own grave.

Buck took the lead. "Let's talk about that flash drive. Can you tell us how it wound up right outside that lab?"

Roman stammered. "I—I haven't really been able to think—"

Shit! I should've helped him come up with an answer to that before we came in. "Look, we don't know how that flash drive got there. But someone— maybe even Angela Morelli—must've gotten their hands on it."

Dierdre's expression showed she'd anticipated that answer. "According to your client's office manager, Mr. Stiler here is the only one who had access." She turned to Roman. "If she's wrong, please enlighten us."

Roman shook his head, his expression bewildered. "I—I can't. I don't know how it happened." He met her gaze and said in a firm but earnest voice, "I just know I didn't kill this girl. There's no way I could ever do such a thing."

Roman's plea was so sincere, so convincing, it was hard *not* to believe him, and it looked to me like Dierdre was torn. Maybe I'd been wrong. Maybe they were willing to reconsider.

But then Buck leaned forward and clasped his hands on the table in front of him. "Mr. Stiler, even if we bought the story that Angela somehow managed to ninja her way into your office and steal that flash drive, we've got your prints on the door to the lab." He tapped the slim file folder in front of Dierdre. "Would you care to explain how they got there?"

I wasn't sure they'd really found his prints on that door. Cops are allowed to lie to get a suspect to talk. Out of the corner of my eye, I saw Roman start to answer. I put a hand on his arm to stop him and noticed it was shaking.

"Assuming that's even true, you must know that Roman's at the university for events almost every week. I'm sure his prints are all over the place."

Buck looked at me. "Really? What events does he do in the lab?"

Roman said, "I—maybe I was down there for—"

I turned to him. "Stop! Don't answer that." I looked from Buck to Dierdre. "You can't say when those prints got there. My client's been doing photography for the university for years. I'm sure he had a reason to be in the lab at some point." I pushed my chair back. "We're done here. I'm not going to let him help you with your fishing expedition."

"Okay. We can't keep him...yet." Dierdre put the report back in the folder. "But I'm giving you a heads up. One of the shots on the flash drive was a selfie of Roman with the victim. He was wearing a short sleeve green Polo shirt. The lab found green fibers on the victim's chest and torso, and we intend to search his house for it."

I stood up. "Better get a warrant then."

"We already did." She glanced at her watch. "I'm giving them the 'go' signal as soon as you leave. They should be there in about fifteen minutes. If you want to observe, you'd best be on your way."

Buck looked at Roman. "I saw you drove here on your own. I'd advise you to leave your car. We've got a warrant for it, too."

Roman looked from Buck to Dierdre. "I didn't do this! There's got to be some mistake. Please! You've got to believe me!"

They stared at him, impassive. I put a hand on his shoulder. "Come on. This is a waste of time."

As we walked out of the station, I felt his whole body trembling. "Do you have anything valuable in your car?" I asked. He shook his head. "Then I'm going to ask one of the public defender investigators to come down and watch the search." I didn't necessarily think the cops would plant anything, but I never like to take chances.

When we got into my car, he leaned forward and put his head in his hands. I rubbed his back, my mind in turmoil. The flash drive, the prints…and that green shirt. There was no such thing as an actual match in fiber analysis. Even if they found a green shirt in Roman's closet, the best they could say was that a microscopic comparison showed the fibers were "consistent." But still, it was one more brick in the wall they were building around Roman.

He lifted his tear-stained face. "I'm innocent, Lauren! You've got to believe me!"

"I do. Of course I do." I started the car. "But right now, we need to get to your condo before they break down the door. You have every reason to be freaked out, but try not to let them see it, okay?"

His expression of gratitude was laced with fear. "I don't know what I'd do without you."

I tried to give him an encouraging smile. But I was scared, too.

The cops arrived just as we did. We stood in silence on the back patio and watched through the sliding glass door as they tore up the place. I didn't want to say anything to Roman until they were gone, but questions kept running through my mind: how *did* that flash drive wind up on the ground outside the lab?

And his prints on the door. People were probably in and out of that lab every day. If his prints were still detectable, that had to mean he'd been there very recently. Not good. He'd said he'd been home all night, alone. Not a great alibi.

I felt a cold stab of fear. Roman, *my* Roman…a murderer? And a rapist? I glanced at him. His face was pale; he looked numb. I didn't want to believe it; I told myself there was no way he could have done it, that he must have an innocent explanation. But I was shaken. So many things seemed to be stacking up against him.

The crime scene techs in their white jumpsuits and masks carted out bag after bag of evidence. I couldn't see what was in them, but when the detective in charge signaled to me that they were done, I asked, "Did you find the green shirt?"

He paused. "I could tell you to just wait for the evidence report. But, yeah, we did."

"Thanks. Appreciate it."

With the techs and cops cleared out, Roman and I put the place back together. It took hours. They'd left us with an ungodly mess.

When we'd finished, Roman sank down on the couch, depleted and miserable. "You were right. I shouldn't have talked to those detectives. At least, not then. I was too worked up to remember anything." He shook his head. "I wish I'd listened to you. But now I think I know what happened with the flash drive."

I searched his face. He seemed calmer, still upset, but much less frantic. He wrinkled his brow and said, "I know I went to the campus after Angela's shoot to pick up a brochure they wanted me to revamp. I don't usually take the flash drives out of the studio. But sometimes I'll put them in my pocket until I can get to my safe. It must've still been there, and it fell out somewhere along the way."

The simple answer gave me a spark of hope. "Did you pass by the lab that day?"

"I mean, maybe. The thing is, I go to that campus almost every day. Sometimes I wander around, visit the chapel or the Norris Center, just to give myself a break. So, I mean...I could have, sure."

I wished he'd remembered that when we were sitting with the detectives. But it might be better this way. I could set up another meeting—as long as he had answers to all the other questions.

"Can you think of any reason why your prints would be on the lab door?"

"You know, when they brought that up, something in the back of my mind told me I'd been there." He ran a hand through his hair, his tone aggravated. "I don't know how I could've forgotten. I had a shoot coming up for the Science Club, and I scouted the lab to see if it'd be a good location."

The spark of hope was growing. That sounded so...reasonable. "Do you remember when that was?"

He frowned. "It couldn't have been that long ago. The shoot was scheduled for next week." Roman's face contorted with pain. "Guess that won't be happening now."

Tears began to roll down his cheeks, and I pulled him close and held him. His explanations were so simple, so logical, so credible. They were the explanations of an innocent person, someone who didn't keep track of every move he made because he had no reason to think he'd need to.

"I know that talking to those detectives again is the last thing you want. But you have to do it. You have to tell them everything you just told me. I can't make any promises about what they'll do, but if they're dumb enough to file this case after that, no jury's going to convict you."

He sat back and looked at me. "What about my Polo shirt? What if they say it's a match?"

I told him about the limitations of fiber analysis. "I'm not worried. Even if they say the fibers are consistent, a million other green shirts could be, too."

What I didn't tell him was that I was *glad* the cops had found the shirt. Because if it hadn't been here, it'd mean he'd gotten rid of it after Angela's shoot—something he'd only have done if he was the murderer.

All in all, I thought we were in good shape. But just to be on the safe side, I had Roman repeat his explanations again and again for the next few days while I tried to poke holes in his story. He was rock solid.

On the day of the meeting, I stopped outside the entrance to the station and put my hands on his shoulders. "Ready to beard the lion?"

He swallowed. "I think so."

I could see he was nervous, but he was nowhere near the wreck he'd been before. "I *know* so."

And I was right. Confident but not cocky, assertive but not aggressive, Roman explained away all the evidence with a passionate sincerity that was hard to fake. When he was done, Dierdre asked the obvious question. "How come you didn't tell us all this last time?"

Roman spread his hands, his expression earnest. "I wish I had. But I couldn't think; I was freaked out. I'd never been in a...situation like that before."

Buck gave him a flinty look. He glanced at me. "Give us a minute." Then he nodded at Dierdre, and they left the room.

Roman looked stricken. "What did I do wrong?"

I shook my head. "Nothing."

But as the minutes ticked away, my doubts started to grow. I'd never advised a client to talk to the cops before. If they had something good to say, I always told them to save it for the jury. I'd thought Roman would be the exception. But maybe I was wrong. Maybe I'd just put the noose around his neck.

The steel door opened with a loud crack that made me jump in my seat. The detectives entered and stared down at Roman. Dierdre was glowering. "Your client is free to leave," she told me. "For now. But if I were you, I'd tell him to stick around. We may be in touch."

I tried to hide my relief as I stood up. "I expect you will apologize when you catch the right guy."

We walked out of the station hand in hand. It'd been the week from hell, I thought. But now, life would get back to normal.

Except it didn't.

× × ×

I WAS BUTTONING UP my coat, lost in memories I wished I could erase, when my office phone rang. I didn't recognize the number, but I'd given my card to all the kids who'd been at the party with Mia. "DA's office, Charlie Blair."

Silence. I felt a twinge of fear in my chest. "Hello? Who is this?"

The sound of heavy breathing came through the line, then a low growl. My mouth went dry as I gripped the receiver. "Who the hell is this?" I asked, my voice rising.

A weirdly deep voice said, "Who do you think?"

Oh my God! The phone grew slippery in my hand. "I'm calling the police! Do you hear me?"

Then, suddenly, I heard giggling and the high-pitched voices of little boys.

"You got her, Jake!" said a voice in the background. More giggling, then the line went dead.

I had to sit down to catch my breath. I waited for my pulse to slow to a livable speed, then pulled out my cell and checked my Ring app. All clear. But I needed a drink—and I didn't want to do it at home. Home was four walls and a television. And home wasn't safe. Maybe nowhere really was.

I drove toward the Rusty Nail, but on the way, I spotted a bar just off the main drag: The Hot Mess. How appropriate. With its shredded green awning, battered door, and blacked-out windows, it looked exactly like the type of train wreck you just couldn't resist.

As I found a parking space on the street, I realized I was already breaking the promise I'd made to myself yesterday. So I made myself another—only one drink.

Once inside, I was surprised to see that The Hot Mess was actually a step up from my usual haunt. Not a very big step, but the red maybe-leather booths were in okay shape, and the barstools actually swiveled. It smelled better, too, though I noticed a faint odor of weed floating under the usual mix of beer, sweat, and cigarette smoke. I hate that smell.

Still rattled by that damn crank call, I scanned the bar carefully. A threesome sat in a booth near the back. The light was so dim I could barely make out their gender, but I did see four and a half empty beer pitchers and a couple of trucker hats on the table. The only other customer was an older guy with· shoulder-length white hair and a chest-length beard, a glass of Rosé in hand. His eyes were fixed on the Lakers game on the TV mounted above the end of the bar.

I climbed onto a stool at the opposite end and set my purse on the seat next to me—just in case anyone decided to get friendly. Not that it looked like I was in any danger of that. No one had even bothered to look up when I walked in.

The bartender, who'd also been watching the Lakers game, walked up. At first glance, I'd thought it was a man, but now I saw she was a woman with a super short haircut. Refreshing. I was liking this place more and more.

"I'm Harley." Her voice was deep and no nonsense. She put a cocktail napkin on the bar in front of me, and I smiled to myself. *Fancy.* "What're you in the mood for?"

"How about a double shot of Ketel One on the rocks?"

"Coming up."

Thirty seconds later, she brought my drink. It looked like a very generous version of a double. The Hot Mess might just be my new home away from home, but I'd made myself a promise. I stared down at my drink, running a finger down the side of the glass. *Be smart. Don't finish it.* If I just nursed it for a change instead of slugging it down like water, I might be able to pull it off. I took a tiny, micro-sip and scrolled through my email.

Tyler's "emergency discovery motion" was probably a publicity stunt—Erika was right about that—but it didn't bode well that he was already playing spin doctor. And he'd really done a makeover on Mia. Though I thought her frightened expression was for real. It'd made *me*, a woman who knew better, wonder whether that was the face of someone who could stab her own mother to death.

The video of her interview with Skip and Erika, not to mention the testimony we'd get from people like Axel, would counteract some of that. Especially if Axel cleaned up as well as Mia.

Harley walked over to me. "You gettin' ready for another one?"

My impulse said 'yes!' But for a change, I didn't listen. And happily, I still had half my drink left. I patted myself on the back as I said, "No, thanks."

She put the tab down on the bar. "You think you might come around tomorrow?"

I definitely didn't. Tomorrow was a Friday, and I never go to bars on date nights. Too many amateur drunks. "Why? You have karaoke or something?" I fucking hate karaoke.

She rolled her eyes. "Seriously? Look at this place."

She had a point. The Hot Mess was as basic as it got. No stage, no pool table—not even a jukebox. "Then what's the deal on Fridays?"

"A nice, long stretch of Happy Hour. Five to nine." Harley flicked a glance at my glass. "But it doesn't cover that high-dollar stuff."

I put a twenty on the bar. "I'll keep it in mind."

She nodded to me. "Drive safe."

I definitely would. I wasn't even buzzed.

Outside, I stopped and scoped out the street. On my right I saw a Bank of America, a small computer repair store, and a nail salon—and no one around. To my left was an old stationery store and a yogurt place now closed. And again, no one nearby.

I'd just started to head toward my car, which was parked at the end of the block, when I heard footsteps pounding up behind me. Before I could turn, a fist slammed into my back like a battering ram. I screamed and fell face-down, my forehead banging into the pavement. The world began to spin, and I couldn't move, momentarily paralyzed in shock.

A voice snarled, "Your purse, bitch!"

A cold arrow of fear shot through me. My back screaming in pain, I rolled and saw a man in a ski mask standing over me, holding a knife. Gasping, I ripped my purse off my shoulder, struggling with the strap, and held it up, yelling, "Here! Take it!"

He grabbed my purse, then punched me in the side of the head so hard, I saw stars.

As I fell back, I heard a man behind me shout, "Hey!" The asshole who'd mugged me took off running, and as I struggled to sit up, I saw a shape run past me—the man who'd shouted, trying to catch him. But it was too late. He'd disappeared around a corner.

I'd managed to push myself up enough to lean on one elbow, but my back hurt like hell and my head felt like it'd been hit with a lead sap. Everything was blurry.

The man came back. I dimly recognized him as one of the guys who'd been sitting at the table in the bar. "Ma'am? Are you okay?" He spoke over his shoulder. "Did anybody call 9-1-1?"

I followed his gaze and saw the two other men he'd been with, standing a few feet away. One of them said, "Yeah. Ambulance should be here any second."

Ambulance? Oh hell no. Dazed as I was, I knew I didn't want that. I hate hospitals, doctors, and sick people. Every inch of my body howled in agony as I pushed myself up into a sitting position. "I don't need an ambulance. I'm okay. Just a little banged up."

The man stared at me. "Are you nuts? You probably have a concussion. Take it easy."

I wanted to say no, but I didn't seem able to get up off the ground. The wail of an approaching siren grew louder. Hunching over, I dropped my aching head into my hands. I'd gotten an awful feeling when I'd heard that jerk's voice, the anger in it, the way he'd said, "bitch." For a split second, I'd thought…

×××

As the staff at Dominican Hospital got me gowned up and IV'd, the fear lingered. Could my attacker have been him? I thought I'd sensed something when I'd looked up at him. But I didn't know how much I could trust myself. Admittedly, I was obsessed with the idea that he'd track me down. But a mugging? Why would he bother?

Luckily, I was alone with my thoughts. They'd given me my own room—pretty classy, considering my injuries were so minor. I was already feeling a lot better. I had a slamming headache, but the nausea was gone, and I thought I could probably stand up on my own.

When I told the doctor—a short, thin woman with zero bedside manner—that I was good to go, the corners of her mouth turned down. "You're not the doctor. I am, and I say you'll be staying with us at least until tomorrow morning. Maybe longer."

"What? No way." I had to be in court for Tyler's "emergency discovery motion."

"Yes, way." She tilted her head at the doorway. "And you've got company."

Two unis were waiting. Damn. Now everyone would know I'd been mugged. I'd be a topic of office conversation for days. Just what I didn't need.

I tried to answer the usual questions about the jerk who'd attacked me: height, weight, facial features. But now that I was forced to break it all down, I realized I didn't even know what race or ethnicity he was. I'd seen the knife in his hand, but I hadn't noticed the color of his skin. And I'd heard his voice, but not enough to tell whether he had an accent.

Listening to myself say "I don't know" to one question after another, I had to concede that the flash of recognition was probably all in my head; the product of paranoia, and likely, the hope that it *was* him, because at least then I'd know my family was safe. The unis snapped their notebooks closed with a sigh.

I told them about the guys at the bar, and the one who'd tried to chase the asshole down. "They might've seen more."

The unis said they'd head over, and I lay back, glad to be alone. But two minutes later, I had company again.

"Charlie, my God!" Skip hurried toward my bedside. "Are you okay?"

Just the person I *didn't* want to see. "Yeah, I'm fine. The doctor's being a pain."

He looked down at me, shaking his head. "What were you doing in a place like that, in that neighborhood? Alone? That's…I'm sorry, but that's insane."

Shit. Now Skip knew way too much about my private life. "I've never been there before," I said in a rush. "I didn't know it was such a bad area. I was driving by and thought I'd stop and have a drink. That's all."

Of course, that wasn't all. And he didn't know the half of it. I wanted him out of there ASAP, but I didn't need to give him any more reasons to wonder about me. So, when he asked me to run through the whole story again, I answered his questions for as long as I could stand it, then said, "Sorry, Skip. I'm running out of gas…"

He sighed. "Okay. Get some rest. We'll take another crack at their descriptions tomorrow." He paused at the door. "Do I need to tell you to give that dump a pass from now on?"

I shook my head, but as I watched him leave, I thought about what Pete, my bartender buddy at The Rusty Nail had said. That the way I was living almost guaranteed I'd wind up on the receiving end of exactly what'd happened tonight. Or worse.

I wanted to believe I didn't know what I'd been doing. I'd rationalized that hanging around Lower Ocean, far away from my actual neighborhood, was a way to stay safe, to make sure I didn't run into anyone I knew…or him. I'd even rented a UPS mailbox there. True, I couldn't let mail come to my apartment. But I couldn't lie to myself, either. The box didn't have to be in Lower Ocean. And now, stuck in the hospital with nothing to do but think, I picked up the memory where I'd left off: with Roman a free man.

×××

IT WAS SUPPOSED TO be a joyous time. Roman was cleared, and we could go back to our happy lives. But reality woke me with a resounding slap across the face. The cops couldn't tag him for the murder, but that didn't mean the public had to let Roman go. The keyboard warriors went after him on every social media outlet, from Twitter to Reddit to NextDoor. I got dragged mercilessly, as well, framed up as a snake who'd fabricated evidence to get her boyfriend off.

Roman and I changed our phone numbers and deleted our online accounts, but that didn't stop the truly dedicated. They just turned to snail mail. Mine only came to me at work, as the public defender's office shielded our personal addresses. But Roman didn't have that protection. Letters piled up at his condo. Someone graffitied "Rapist-Killer!" on the wall of his studio. We avoided going out in public. I would've asked for police protection, but I had a feeling that if someone did attack us, the cops would just look the other way.

My family was wary. Some of the nastier posts about Roman had shown up on my mother's Facebook page, and my father—ever the law-and-order fan—always sided with the cops. I hoped they'd come around eventually, but their skepticism was obvious.

We did our best to adjust. After Roman sold his studio to another photographer, he took to visiting his brother, Adam, in upstate New York for days at a time. I moved back into my apartment and only occasionally stayed at Roman's condo when he was home.

It was a hard time for both of us, but it really seemed to take a toll on Roman. About a month after the cops let him go, he hit a new low. He was supposed to get back from one of his many trips to see Adam on a Friday night, and as he always liked me to be there when he got home, I went to his place after work. But he didn't show, didn't answer my calls or texts; he didn't appear at all until late Saturday afternoon.

Worried—and pissed off—I snapped, "What happened to you?"

He threw down his duffel bag. "What happened to me? My life went to shit. Or haven't you noticed?"

I stared at him, stunned. "You're saying that to *me* of all people?"

But he went on as though I wasn't there. "I had to drive by *my* studio and see that fucking sign. 'New Owner'!" He jabbed a finger at his chest. "*My* studio! That asshole's got it, and I have nothing!"

"I'm so sorry." I tried to reach out to him, to comfort him. "People will forget, Roman, you'll see. We just need to give it some time."

He pulled away, his tone bitter. "For how long? Months? Years? What am I supposed to do in the meantime?" He pointed to the stack of letters that'd come while he was gone. "Frame my death threats?"

The ugliness coming off him went deeper than his words. I understood his anger and depression. I felt it, too. But there was a darkness, a tinge of menace that I'd never noticed before. Had it always been there?

Deeply unsettled, I told him to call me when he was ready to apologize and left.

Now on my guard, I forced myself to look at him without the rosy lens of our first days together. And slowly, I began to see the chinks in his golden armor. The big blowouts didn't happen often, but the little things—the small acts of cruelty—kept piling up. Like the night he told me a joke over dinner, then said abruptly, with a disgusted expression, "Has anyone ever told you how ugly you look when you laugh?" Or the day we went to the Riverwalk for a picnic. He wanted to take a photo of me but kept adjusting my pose. Finally, he threw the camera down and snapped, "I can't do this. You don't have a good side."

Like I said, little jabs. But always thrown in the middle of what seemed to be a sweet moment, as though he'd deliberately set me up so he could catch me off guard, which made it hurt even more. I became flinchy, aware that the next shot was coming but never knowing when. I'd start to laugh or smile, then catch myself, thinking, look out.

I tried to tell myself it was temporary, a reaction to the pain of being unjustly accused of a heinous murder. You only hurt the one you love and all that jazz. When the public moved on and the hate campaign ended, Roman would get back to his old self.

Well, the public did move on. But Roman only seemed to get worse, the jabs more vicious—and more frequent. I pulled back, made excuses to avoid him, let his calls go to voicemail, and kept it short when I did pick up. I knew I was just avoiding the inevitable. But I guess I didn't want to face the fact that the dream was over.

After two weeks of my ghosting him, Roman showed up at my apartment. When I saw him through the peephole, I was tempted to pretend I wasn't home. But he'd probably seen me drive into the garage.

"Hey, what's up?" I said, forcing a smile as I opened the door.

He walked past me, sat down on the couch, and patted the spot next to him. "You tell me."

I sat as far away as I dared. "Nothing to tell. I've just been busy. Work's a bitch lately."

"You're such a workaholic," he said, his tone conveying total disbelief. He held his hands out. "Here, let me rub your feet."

His jangly energy made me uneasy, and I shook my head. "Uh, that's okay."

Roman's eyes bored into mine. "Whatever's going on with you, we have to fix it, Lauren. Because I can't imagine you leaving me." He seized my hands and held them so tightly it made me wince. "You'd never do that, would you?"

A cold ripple of fear ran down my spine. The vaguely threatening tone underlying his words was all the more frightening for its ambiguity. "No, of course not."

The time had come. I had to end it. But I was afraid to do it in person. Pleading a headache, I said I needed to lie down and suggested dinner that weekend.

Two days later, I called him and dropped the hammer. "I think I…need to be on my own for a while."

There was a long silence on his end. I held the phone in a death grip, my throat tight as I waited for the explosion.

But his voice was calm, almost gentle. "Are you sure? Is that really what you want?"

Relief washed over me, and I sank down on my bed. For the first time in months, he sounded like the Roman I'd fallen in love with at the diner: kind, thoughtful, caring. I almost wished I could take it back. "Y-yes. It's been a rough time. For both of us. I—I really need to get my head together. I'm so sorry, Roman."

There was another long pause. "I'm sorry too, Lauren."

There was something in his voice. I couldn't put my finger on it. But as I hung up, my heart felt like it weighed a hundred pounds. The brief glimmer of the man I'd loved only made the loss more painful.

Hannah got teary when I told her I'd broken up with Roman. "I'm so bummed for you, L. I really thought it'd work out."

My parents didn't even try to pretend they were sorry. "It's for the best, dear," my mother said as she patted my arm.

Strangely, at times, I found myself missing Roman. On a couple of lonely nights, the sight of the tokens from our sweet, early days—the winged-pig figurine he'd given me for our first month anniversary, the photo he'd taken of the cozy Italian restaurant that'd become "our" place—even made me think about going back to him. But the ugly memories were too fresh. And slowly I managed to accept the truth that all I'd really lost was a fantasy. No one was as perfect as I'd believed Roman was, and after a while, he couldn't keep up the act.

Three weeks later, on a brilliantly sunny Sunday morning, I was lying in bed watching TV when I got a call from Hannah. My little sister was distraught. "The cops just called Uncle Steve! It's Lyra! Lauren, she's dead."

I jerked up. Our cousin, Lyra? How was that possible? She was only nineteen. I flashed on my last image of her: petite slender, a soccer ball under her arm, lips curved in a crooked grin, her long, black hair twisted into a messy bun on top of her head. "No! That can't be! What happened?"

Hannah screamed. "Some psycho killed her!"

My vision blurred as I tried to process the words. "What psycho? When?"

"Last night!" Hannah wailed. "It's all over the news!"

Numb, disbelieving, I flipped through the local channels until I saw a male reporter standing at the edge of the Northwestern University campus. "…a source has told us she was robbed and strangled. A campus patrol officer found the body near the elevator in this parking structure behind me early this morning. Lyra Claybourne, a freshman here at Northwestern, is the second victim to be found dead on campus grounds in the past four months…"

An icy fist wrapped around my heart. I couldn't breathe. I choked out, "Hannah, I—I'll call you back," then ran to the bathroom and threw up.

As I slid to the floor, the scene at our family picnic last summer flashed before my eyes. Lyra and her brother, Michael, throwing a football with Roman, all of them laughing, bathed in the glow of a late summer sun.

Roman's last words to me echoed in my ears: *I'm sorry, too.*

He'd done it. I could feel it in my bones. He'd killed Lyra, my beautiful little cousin. It was payback for me leaving him. And now I was sure he'd killed that girl, Angela Morelli, too—and God knew how many others.

I rested my head on my knees and sobbed, imagining the terror Lyra must've felt as he'd wrapped his hands around her neck, her agony as she fought for air while he tightened his grip. How the last thing she saw as she lay dying was his face. The face of a man she'd never have met if it hadn't been for me. I felt my stomach lurch again, but there was nothing left. My body convulsed with dry heaves. Revulsion filled me as I remembered the softness of Roman's gaze, the way he'd said he loved me, the warm touch of his hand as he stroked my face. It'd been an act, a way to hide the monster who was the real Roman Stiler. And I'd fallen for it. I'd wanted my fairy tale romance, and Lyra had paid the price.

I hugged my knees, rocking back and forth, sobbing until my throat was raw.

The ring of my cell phone pierced the air. Hannah. I'd forgotten to call her back.

I stumbled to my bedroom. "Hannah, I'm so—"

"This is Chicago PD, Homicide. Detective Dierdre Robinson. We met when you brought in your client—"

"I remember."

She continued in her flat, official voice. "I believe Lyra Claybourne was your cousin. I'm sorry to inform you—"

"I know, my sister told me." I couldn't bear the pain of hearing her say it.

"We need to speak to your client."

I wanted to tell Dierdre to shoot him on sight. But I gritted my teeth and said, "Roman Stiler is no longer my client."

"Then since you're not bound by the privilege," she said, her tone more aggressive, "we'd like you to come in for questioning."

I could tell she thought she'd have a fight on her hands. "I have no problem with that, but I don't know anything. I haven't had any contact with him in weeks."

"But you do know whether Stiler had met your cousin."

"I…yes. He met her." Thanks to me. I felt my stomach begin to heave again.

Dierdre drilled down. "He ever talk about her?"

"No, never." I had a question of my own. It was almost too painful to ask, but I had to know. I squeezed my eyes shut. "Was Lyra…assaulted?"

Dierdre's voice softened. "We're waiting for the autopsy, but it doesn't seem so. Her clothing was…ah, intact."

Tears began to flow again as I opened my eyes. "Th-thank you."

She ended the call saying she'd be in touch and that she was sorry for my loss. The trite words, added as an afterthought, didn't begin to account for the sheer, breathtaking scope of what had happened. I tried to call Hannah but got her voicemail. She was probably with Mom and Dad. With a trembling hand, I found their number and held my breath as I listened to the phone ring.

"Lauren? Is that you?" My mother.

I heard my father's voice in the background, saying, "I don't want to see her."

My mother stuttered, "I—ah, I—I'm sorry, but I don't think this is a good time."

I felt like I'd been socked in the stomach. Breathless, I pleaded, "Mom, I had no idea that he…that he would…" In desperation, I grasped at the only straw I could think of. "It might not be Roman. The detective said Lyra's case was…different. Please, tell Dad!"

My father yelled, "Hang up, Barbara. I don't care what she has to say!"

The line went dead. Broken in body and soul, I cried myself to sleep.

The next day, I wrote a letter to my aunt and uncle, trying to convey the depth of my sorrow. I offered to do anything I could for them. But I never got a response. And Hannah never returned my call.

The rest of the world was morbidly eager to connect. It took less than an hour after the news of Lyra's murder broke for the press to start calling. I hung up on the first two reporters then stopped answering my phone. But they still managed to find out that I was no longer Roman's lawyer or girlfriend. With our names back in the news, the trolls flooded social media again, weaving insane conspiracy theories, many of them claiming that I was responsible for Lyra's murder. Although their logic was nonexistent, at thier base I agreed with them: it was my fault. Yet, a part of me clung to the slim hope that Roman was innocent. That my only sin was a misjudgment of character.

After three weeks, I was desperate to find out where the investigation stood. Surely Dierdre and Buck had made some progress, but I didn't know whether I could trust them. If they told Roman I'd met with them (Maybe as a way of goading him into incriminating himself?), he might come for me. Or worse, for someone else in my family.

But there was one detective I thought I could trust. Brett Chapman worked homicides. We'd had a few cases together and had gotten kind of friendly—as friendly as you can be with someone who's trying to nail your clients. He'd know where the case against Roman stood. Whether he'd be willing to say anything was a different story. But we'd had coffee before, even flirted a little over drinks at The Bullshot, a courthouse hangout, so I thought there was a better than even chance he'd agree to lunch, especially since I'd be paying.

Sure enough, he accepted, and I suggested a deli a couple of miles away from the courthouse, where we wouldn't bump into anyone from my office. Or Roman. The deli wasn't close to Roman's neck of the woods, but still I was nervous. I didn't know what he'd do if he saw me with another man, especially if that other man was a homicide detective.

Before meeting, I gave myself enough time to circle the area and make sure Roman's car was nowhere in sight. As I got out of my car, I clutched my keys in my hand and wondered how long I'd have to live this way, being fearful about my every move.

Inside, I didn't have a clear view of the door, but I could tell when Brett arrived—I saw a couple of the waitress' heads turn. He *was* easy on the eyes. He had the kind of warm, masculine features and strong jaw you see on TV shows featuring firemen and Mr. Mom husbands. As he neared the table, I saw that he was wearing the sports jacket and slacks that were standard fare for detectives, but no tie.

I raised an eyebrow. "Trés casual."

He pulled a conservative navy blue tie out of his jacket pocket. "But ready for action. As always." He grew solemn. "I'm so sorry about your cousin."

I bit my lip. "Thanks. Can we keep this conversation just between us?"

He nodded, his expression curious. "Sure."

I decided to go for it. "I know you guys don't like to talk about the status of investigations, but since I'm family…"

I could see he was uncomfortable, but he finally nodded. "I'll tell you what I know. But you have to keep it to yourself."

I held up a hand. "Promise." Leaning in, my voice low, I asked, "Have they found anything to tie Roman to Lyra's murder?"

Brett's eyes flicked around the restaurant, before he said quietly, "They're trying, but it's not looking good. The coroner confirmed there was no sexual assault, and the perp stole her purse and diamond ring."

I'd known that'd be a problem. "Doesn't mean he didn't do it. He's smart enough to change his MO."

He shrugged. "True, but it doesn't help."

"What about DNA?" I could hear the strain of desperation in my voice.

My first choice was for Roman to be innocent, for the whole thing to be a tragedy, but a tragedy that wasn't my fault. Failing that, I wanted them to find the evidence that would put him away forever. The worst-case scenario was for him to remain a suspect but manage to evade conviction. Angela Morelli all over again.

I felt sick as Brett shook his head.

"None so far. The lab found traces of latex on her neck. Seems the perp wore gloves."

I pushed away the image conjured up by his words as the tiny spark of hope inside me died out. No way Lyra's murder was a random act of violence. I remembered how Roman had always wanted to talk about my cases, how he'd question me endlessly about what my clients did to screw up and get caught. DNA in particular was a fave of his. I'd been charmed, thinking he was just taking an interest in my work. What a fool I was.

My tone was bitter as I said, "Not your typical meth head looking for money."

"No, doesn't seem so." He gazed at me with concern. "I heard you dumped him?" I nodded, and he said softly, "So Lyra was payback."

Tears sprang to my eyes. I blinked them away. "Why not just kill *me*?"

He hesitated, lips pressed together. When he spoke, his voice was sorrowful. "Because he'd rather make you suffer." He gazed at me with sympathy. "And you are…"

I was. His compassion warmed me, even as it brought a lump to my throat. And now I had to face the question I'd been desperate to avoid. "How did I not see it? There had to have been signs."

"You guys weren't together all that long—"

"Three months. That's long enough," I said, miserable. How horrifying to think I'd been one of those pathetic women who fell for psychopaths but were too punch drunk with love to see the obvious.

He held up a hand. "Not sure I agree. Maybe you didn't know…what he was. But you knew something. You did break up with him."

"And now my cousin's dead." A tear escaped and rolled down my cheek. "Maybe if I get lucky, I'll be next."

His voice was gentle. "It's not your fault, Lauren." Then he frowned. "Has Roman made a move on you?"

I shook my head. "But I'm worried that he'll go after someone else in my family."

"I highly doubt it. Be too obvious. That's probably what'll keep you alive, too."

I wasn't sure I cared. "For now, anyway."

Concern deepened the lines in his forehead as he reached out and took my hand. Miserable as I was, I felt a small shiver of excitement at his touch.

"I'll do whatever I can to help you, Lauren. Keep an eye out as much as possible. But unless we manage to bust him for Lyra's murder, your best bet might be to disappear."

CHAPTER THIRTEEN

E RIKA STOOD ON THE darkened sidewalk in front of Danny's house, outside the range of his new motion detectors, and texted, *Ready for a test run?*

He texted back a thumbs up, and she walked toward the front door. When she was within ten feet, the whole perimeter of the house lit up like an airport runway.

Danny came out and scanned the area. "Looks good. What do you think?"

Erika joined him on the front walk. "It's great. They won't dare mess with you now."

He nodded, but she could see he was still anxious. She put her arm through his as they headed into the house. "What does Julia have to say about this?" she asked.

Erika had hired a shrink to deal with this problem. She knew Danny wouldn't do it. Not that Danny objected to seeing Julia. He just couldn't afford her rates. His start-up company was generous with shares, but it didn't pay all that well.

She'd been afraid his delusion was a sign of schizophrenia, and while Julia hadn't disagreed, she'd pointed out that Danny wasn't hearing voices, just sounds—a relatively mild symptom. Other than this issue, he managed his life very well, with a career that required highly disciplined, complex thinking.

They walked into the kitchen, and Danny poured them each a glass of the wine Erika had brought the night before. "Julia wants me to 'consider,'" he made air quotes, "that I might be amplifying normal sounds in the neighborhood." He rolled his eyes. "She doesn't get it."

Erika dug her nails into her palms. She'd hoped Julia might be able to prescribe some meds for him. But if she hadn't even been able to get him to see it was *possible* the so-called assholes weren't real, there was little chance of that.

Her cell phone rang. It was Skip, and what he had to say shocked her. When she ended the call, she told Danny, "Charlie just got mugged."

"No shit? How?" When Erika filled him in on the details, a look of confusion crossed his face. "She was in Lower Ocean? *Why?*"

Good question. Everyone knew the area was dangerous. And Charlie had been at a dive bar, no less. Alone. Clearly, there was a lot Erika didn't know about her. "No idea. I'd better call her, see how she's doing."

But her call went straight to voicemail. She left a message, telling Charlie to take some time off and to let her know if there was anything she could do. She knew it was shitty of her, but she was glad to have Charlie out of her hair for a while.

Danny was watching her. He took a sip of wine. "How's it going with her? She still a pain in the ass?"

Erika sighed and nodded. "Unfortunately. But not for long." She told him about the defense's demand to start trial immediately.

His eyebrows shot up. "And you're okay with that? Timing seems kind of tight."

"I'm way okay with that." He winced, and she remembered he'd said he was having trouble with his lower back. "Did you see the chiropractor today?"

Danny brightened. "I did. And it still hurts, but it helped. Larry always knows how to fix me."

"I'm so glad." But Erika had never seen him look that happy just because he got his back cracked. "He must've been really exceptional this time. You look like you just beat someone at *Fortnite*."

Smiling, he picked at the corner of the label on the wine bottle. "I...uh, I met this girl in the waiting room. Fiona Thornberg. She was there for her sciatica. Anyway, we got to talking, and...I think I might ask her to go out for coffee or...or something."

"Danny, that's great!" It'd be so nice if he had a girlfriend, or even just someone to hang out with. It might take his mind off the "assholes."

He pulled out his phone, tapped the screen, then held it out to Erika. "Pretty cute, no?"

Fiona *was* cute. Shoulder-length blonde hair, big brown eyes, and a sweet smile. "Really cute." As Erika started to hand the phone back, she accidentally touched the side of the screen and saw three more photos. "Did she send you all these?"

He took the phone back. "Oh, no. Um, she gave me her Insta."

Erika smiled. Fiona must be at least a *little* interested. "Nice."

She headed home feeling cautiously optimistic. She didn't know whether this Fiona would wind up being Danny's one and only. But maybe she'd be able to bring a little light into his world. He could really use it.

×××

THE NEXT MORNING, ERIKA tried to act confident as she walked into the courtroom. Tyler was already at counsel table, reading some paperwork in a file folder. Whatever he had up his sleeve, it'd be bad for her. The only question was how bad.

The deputy brought out Mia, now dressed in a baby blue cardigan and pale blue blouse buttoned all the way up to the neck. Erika had no doubt Tyler had scored at least a month's worth of nonthreatening pastels for Mia. He'd have stuck a halo over her head if he'd thought he could get away with it.

The bailiff called the court to order, and Judge Butler came flying out. He frowned at Tyler. "I've got another trial going, so this had better be a real emergency, counsel."

Tyler moved to the podium. "Understood, Your Honor. But I view this as an emergency because my client's life is in danger in jail. She's probably the youngest one there, and she's bound to be a target for older, more violent inmates. And I have information that I'm hoping will persuade you to at least lower her bail, if not release her on her own recognizance."

What the hell? Erika tried not to let her alarm show.

The judge leaned back with a skeptical look. "Let's hear it."

Tyler held up the lab report. "First of all, we've just received test results that show foreign DNA on the doorframe of Shelly Hansen's bedroom. Touch DNA, which makes it very likely it was deposited by the killer."

Judge Butler gave him a skeptical look. "Not sure I buy that latter part. Is that all?"

"No, Your Honor," Tyler said. "We believe there are a number of potential suspects who likely had motive to kill Shelly Hansen that the Sheriff's Department has failed to investigate. For example, we've received information from her friends that she was very sexually active, and that she frequently dated men she'd met online."

The judge interrupted, looking downright annoyed. "So? My brother met his wife online."

Tyler held up a hand. "Not done, Your Honor." He picked up his file and took out a piece of paper. "According to our sources, Ms. Hansen has dated her *clients* in the past. In fact, she spent her *own* money to help bail one of them out—Alberto Sanchez—just *two days* before her murder." Tyler paused, then said in a louder voice, "I have *never* heard of a bail bondsman putting up their own money to make a client's bail. Never. It seems likely to me that Sanchez was more than just a client. And now he's gone missing. I'm not saying that proves he killed her, but it's more than a little suspicious—and the Sheriff's Department has made no effort whatsoever to look into him."

Erika held onto her poker face with an effort, as she clasped her hands tightly in her lap. She'd known about Shelly's active dating life, but this was the first she'd heard of Shelly spending her own money on a client's bail. Erika had made a point of going through Shelly's business records. How could she have missed that?

It worried her. This whole Sanchez-as-killer argument worried her. Not that anything Tyler had said came close to proving Sanchez had committed the murder. But the fact that Shelly had put up her own money to bail him out was strange. And with the wrong jury, "strange" could turn into reasonable doubt.

Shelly's former clients were yet another worry. Erika knew that none of her clients from the past year were viable suspects. Skip had done his homework. But what if Tyler dug up someone from before then? It might sound crazy that a client she'd dated years ago would suddenly decide to hunt her down, but juries had been known to buy crazier stories. And an ex-con from Shelly's past with no alibi might be *just* persuasive enough to create reasonable doubt about Mia, even if there was no physical evidence to connect him to the murder.

The gallery started to buzz. The reporters were loving this new curveball. Erika's head began to throb.

The judge gaveled them to order. "If you can't keep still, you can leave." He turned back to Tyler. "I'm not so sure that's suspicious or at all related to the murder. It *is* unusual for a bail bondsman to put up his—or her—own money for a client, I'll grant you that. But I'd think the last thing he'd want to do is kill the hand that fed him. Whether they were having an affair or not." He looked down at Tyler. "Anything else?"

Tyler shook his head. "But we believe this evidence shows the State's case has holes big enough to drive a truck through. And we've only just begun to investigate. I'm sure we're going to find enough evidence to justify a dismissal. In light of that, I submit that Mia should be released on her own recognizance."

The judge turned to Erika. "Madam prosecutor, what do you have to say to all this?"

Erika surreptitiously wiped her sweaty palms on her thighs as she stood. Afraid her voice would shake, she forced herself to take a deep breath. *Stay calm.*

"Counsel seems to have mistaken rumors and innuendo for reasonable doubt. So what if Shelly dated men online? Counsel hasn't offered a scintilla of proof that any of them were around in the months before her death. And women do manage to survive online dating—in rather impressive numbers. The same goes for any former clients Shelly might've dated. If counsel had read the discovery we've provided, he'd know that Ms. Hansen hadn't dated any former clients in the past year. As for why Alberto Sanchez absconded—if that's even true; he might've just missed a court date—the much more obvious reason is that he didn't want to face his charges and go to jail."

Erika spread her hands. "I remind the court of Occam's Razor. The simplest explanation is the best one. When you hear hoofbeats, think horses, not zebras. Counsel's argument is awash in zebras, Your Honor. He's given you no valid reason to lower bail for this defendant. We ask that you deny the motion."

The judge nodded at Erika. "Agreed. Motion to lower bail is denied." He looked at Tyler. "While I think you're doing an admirable job of fighting for your client, and while you may—or may not—have turned up some interesting leads, this appears to me to be a ploy to spin the press. Don't pull this stunt again, counsel, or I may cite you for contempt." He banged his gavel. "Court is adjourned."

Mia would stay in jail, but Erika knew Tyler had gotten what he'd wanted out of the hearing: giving the press straw men to chase. Every story they wrote about the men Shelly had dated would sow new seeds of doubt in the minds of potential jurors.

As the reporters left the courtroom, she saw Tyler whisper something to Mia, then quickly follow them out. He was in a hurry to stoke the fire he'd started. Erika watched him with a sense of coming doom.

This hearing had been a catastrophe.

CHAPTER FOURTEEN

I OPENED MY EYES to find myself in darkness. A soft beeping sound was coming from somewhere, and I bolted up as a wave of panic filled me.

Then my throbbing head and back reminded me where I was. I was in the hospital. I'd been mugged outside that scuzzy bar, and Skip had found out about it. I groaned as I lay back down.

By the time Dr. Sunshine released me on Thursday afternoon, I was going nuts. It was too late to make it to court. Which bummed me out... not at all. One less chance to get caught on camera. And while I was curious about Tyler's "emergency," I knew I'd find out what it was soon enough.

The minute I got home, I headed for the shower. Dominion Hospital was a class operation, but still—it was a *hospital*. I had to be careful with the scrubbing, though. I was sore all over, especially my head and back, where that asshole had punched me.

Clean, but still rattled, I poured myself a drink and curled up on the couch. As I reached for the remote on the side table, I thought again about my attacker. Could it have been Roman? Lyra's killer had worn latex gloves. I tried to envision my mugger's hands, but I couldn't bring up the image. I'd been too dizzy to see anything but the knife and the ski mask.

I wished I could ask for Skip's help. He might at least be able to tell me whether Roman was in Chicago. But then I'd have to reveal who I really was. A nonstarter. There had to be another way.

×××

ON FRIDAY MORNING I was sorer, with little aches and pains to go along with the bigger ones in my head and back. I didn't have my usual fuzzy brain or acid stomach, though. This is what it's like to wake up sober, I thought, stretching. It'd be nice if I could make it happen again.

Still, I decided to call in sick. I was in better shape than I'd expected, but I still felt lousy. When I picked up my cell phone, I saw that Erika had called the night before. Skip had told her what'd happened. She'd left a nice message, telling me to take some time off. I snorted. She'd be happy if I took the next *six months* off.

I spent an uneventful weekend recuperating, my only foray into the world a visit to a sporting goods store to buy a gun. I'd never been a big fan of firearms, but I was a fan of staying alive—at least for the time being. The only problem was the ten-day waiting period. I needed protection now. So after I filled out the application for a .38 caliber Smith and Wesson, I asked the owner to show me his best self-defense knife. He'd tried to talk me out of it. "You'll just wind up cutting yourself. But…your call." I'd glared at him. Yes. Yes, it was.

The Fox folding Karambit was a black, evil-looking piece of metal with a grip that made it easier to swing, as opposed to jab. Since upper body strength wasn't my forte, I figured I'd be able to pack more power into the former. That owner might be right, I thought, looking at it. But it made me feel better. I practiced whipping it out of my purse all weekend, feeling equal parts stupid and badass.

I woke up on Monday shockingly bright-eyed. Since getting out of the hospital, I'd managed to limit my booze intake to one drink per night. The first night was pretty easy, since I was still woozy. It got harder after that, and last night I'd almost caved and poured a refill. But…I didn't. Maybe I'd try to go cold turkey tonight.

After showering, I studied the damage in the mirror. The bruise on my head was mostly under my hairline, but some interesting colors were showing at the edge. I fixed my face as best I could, slugged down a cup of coffee, and headed to work.

Erika looked surprised when I showed up at her office. "That was fast. Are you sure you're well enough to be back?"

"Kind of achy, but generally okay. And we've only got about two weeks until trial." Sixteen days, to be exact. I'd never seen a big case move this fast. I doubted Erika had either. It was nuts.

She was looking at me differently today. I thought about telling her it was my first time at The Hot Mess or saying I hadn't known Lower Ocean was such a rough area, but it would sound like I was protesting too much. So screw it. Let her think what she wanted. She would anyway.

When I asked her to catch me up on Tyler's so-called emergency hearing, she looked upset. "I think it could be real trouble."

But when she told me what Tyler had—and what he'd claimed it meant—I didn't see what the big deal was. "I mean, it's weird that Shelly chipped in her own money to bail out this Sanchez guy, but how does that make him a suspect? If anything, it's the opposite. And if Tyler dredges up some ex-con Shelly dated, it might give the press a tickle, but I can't see how it'd do much more than that. Besides, isn't Skip checking out her exes?"

Erika's expression was apprehensive. "He is, and none of them are former clients. At least, as far as we can tell."

"If Skip hasn't found any, then I doubt Tyler can." Erika's endless angsting over ridiculous shit was exhausting me. I stood up as I said, "Honestly? I can't imagine a jury'd believe that a guy who dated Shelly more than a year ago would suddenly decide she had to sleep with the fishes."

Erika gave me a dour look. "You never know what a jury's going to believe."

Lord. Whatever. "Skip was going to find out whether the men Shelly dated in the past six months had alibis, too. What's happening with that?"

"He ruled them all out."

"Then how come we don't have a report on it?"

She waved me off, her tone irritable. "I don't know. I'm sure we'll get one soon." Her cell phone dinged. "Skip has a witness he wants to bring in. Didn't say who, but he should be here in ten."

I moved to the door. "Okay, I'm going to get some coffee. Want anything?"

Erika shook her head. I wondered whether I'd come back to work too soon. Not because I wasn't feeling well, but because I was running out of patience with the Queen of Paranoia. She'd been around the block long enough to know better. Her endless worrying was really starting to get on my nerves.

And then a memory caught me off guard. Back in Chicago, my friends had claimed that when I was in trial, I agonized nonstop. And very annoyingly. But, as I told them, I had to make sure I was prepared for the worst. My clients deserved nothing less.

Erika was probably doing the same—and I was hating the part of myself that I saw in her.

×××

WHEN I GOT BACK TO her office, Skip was already there with our witness, a broad-shouldered gym-rat guy in his twenties with a tribal tattoo on the back of his neck. Erika gestured to him and said, "This is Dante Werner. He called Skip after he saw Tyler's interview with the press on Thursday."

"Hi, I'm Charlie Blair." We shook hands, and he barely met my eyes. Never a good sign. I supposed he might be shy.

Then he opened his mouth.

"When I saw that lawyer on the news, it really pissed me off. He was trying to make it sound like Mia's some poor, innocent little girl. She's not. She's a lying bitch." He set his jaw. "I don't know if she killed Shelly—but I wouldn't put it past her."

Erika asked, "I understand your father and Shelly were seeing each other?"

Dante cleared his throat. "Yeah, for around six months, and then we moved in with them."

"When was that?"

He squinted. "I was a senior in high school, so three years ago." His expression darkened. "Mia totally hated me, right from the start. She started fu—uh, messing with me on day one."

She started messing with *him*? A fifteen-year-old girl "messing" with this bigger—and probably buff back then, too—eighteen-year-old guy? I wasn't loving this dude.

Behind her desk, Erika sat back and studied him. "How so? What'd she do?"

"She stole money from me!" His tone was aggrieved. "And when I told Shelly and my dad about it, she said I was lying, that I was just trying to get her in trouble. Then she planted empty bottles of Jack Daniels under my bed and showed them to my dad and Shelly as payback."

"Did you tell them she planted the bottles?" Erika asked. Dante nodded. "What did they do?"

Dante huffed. "What they always did. Got in a fight. Dad believed me, Shelly believed Mia. My dad told Shelly over and over that she let Mia get away with too much. Mia hated my dad for that, but she couldn't get to him, so she took it out on me. And she stole money from Shelly, too."

"Did you ever catch her at it?" Erika asked.

He rolled his eyes. "Only like ten times. I caught her sneaking some cokehead loser into her room, too. But Mia said I was lying, and Shelly blew me off. As usual."

Dante struck me as a whiny punk, and I didn't get why he thought these petty squabbles made Mia a killer. Beyond that, the judge wasn't going to let any of this junk into evidence. I darted a glance at Erika, but I couldn't read her expression.

Skip said, "Tell them about the fight you guys had."

Dante's voice was heated. "One night—toward the end—I caught Mia with a baggie of Oxy. I grabbed it and said I was telling her mom. She lost it. Picked up a pair of scissors and stabbed me." He rolled up his sleeve and pointed to his shoulder. He had two deep, jagged scars, whitened with age. "Flat out tried to kill me.

Kill him? Hardly. But now I understood why Skip had been in such a rush to bring him in. I couldn't say I was shocked. The girl *was* charged with stabbing her mother to death. Still, she'd really gouged the guy.

"I assume you told your father and Shelly," Erika said.

"Yeah. And same as always, they got in a huge fight. My dad said Mia was a pathological liar and a sociopath, and that Shelly's denial was gonna get somebody hurt." Dante exhaled. "He wanted to call the police, but Shelly wouldn't let him. She broke up with him on the spot and threw us out." His hands balled into fists. "It was all Mia's fault."

Erika nodded. "Are you willing to testify?"

"Hell yeah."

Was she serious? This kid clearly had an axe to grind. Tyler would tear him a new one on the witness stand. If it were my call, I wouldn't let him anywhere near the courtroom—unless it was for his own arraignment, which I was sure would be coming someday soon.

Erika thanked him for his time, and Skip ushered him out. As the door closed behind them, I decided to be blunt.

"That guy comes off like a whiny bitch. No, correction, a whiny bitch with a giant grudge."

Erika's voice was cold. "Really? Even with those scars?"

"Yeah, even with those scars. The jury's going to hate him, Erika. You honestly think his story's worth it?"

Erika spoke with intensity. "I do. It'll show what Mia's capable of, up close and personal. She *stabbed* him, for God's sake."

I wanted to ask her whether she'd have felt the same if this were any other case. I had a very strong feeling the answer would be no.

"I guess we'll need to turn Dante's statement over to the defense."

"Yeah, and I'm going to file a motion to ask the judge for a ruling on admissibility."

Not a bad idea. Hopefully, he'd rule against us and save Erika from herself. "We'd better file it under seal." Otherwise, court filings are accessible to the public—i.e., the press. In person, Dante wasn't impressive. But in writing, where his bitchy attitude and mega-grudge wouldn't show, his statement would be a bombshell.

"Right. Do me a favor. Call Skip and tell him I need Dante's statement ASAP, so I can attach it to the motion. And if you've got any recent case law I can use, shoot it my way. I want to file the motion today."

I didn't know why the big rush, but I went back to my office and followed orders. By the time Erika sent me the finished motion, it was almost five o'clock. I barely made it to court in time.

Back at the office, I brought Erika her copy of the file-stamped motion.

"Thanks," she said, slipping it into a folder. "Now you should get out of here; get some rest."

I nodded. "How about you?"

She turned back to her computer. "Got more work to do. See you tomorrow."

×××

I DECIDED TO STOP at the UPS store and pick up my mail. I knew it'd be closed by the time I got there, but I had a key that gave me 24/7 access—part of the reason I'd chosen it. It was a drag having to rent a mailbox, but I needed to keep my home address as hidden as possible All traces of daylight were gone, and the clouds that covered the moon glowed softly in the night sky. The parking lot was nearly empty, just a few cars clustered in front of the liquor store and the Domino's Pizza next door. A homeless man was sitting on the ground with his back against a glass storefront, smoking a particularly smelly joint. I held my breath as I walked past.

Inside, I fished two credit card bills and a flier advertising the services of a local dentist with a toothy grin from my mailbox. With a sigh I started toward the door and saw a pickup truck pull into the parking space next to mine. Three drunk-ass rednecks stumbled out. As they neared the UPS store, the one wearing a black bandana around his head told the homeless guy to "get the fuck out of here and get a job." Then he saw me. He sauntered up to the glass, stuck his tongue out between two fingers, and wiggled it at me. Classy.

I waited for him to knock it off and move on. Instead, he grabbed the door handle and yanked it—hard. It rattled in the frame, and I jumped back, incredulous. Was he seriously going to break in? My heart skipped a beat as I reached into my purse. Expecting to grab my Mace, my hand grazed the handle of my new knife. I'd forgotten about it. But I didn't know whether it'd scare him off or just provoke him to pull out his own.

Before I could decide, one of his buddies grabbed him by the collar and mumbled, "Let's go. I'm hungry."

I hurried home, heart still in my throat, and poured myself a drink. So much for going cold turkey. I'd felt pretty good about buying that knife when I was in my living room. Standing face to face with a drunk redneck in Lower Ocean was a different story.

As I took a sip, my phone rang. It was Letitia, the court clerk. She cut right to the chase, her voice stern.

"Someone leaked Dante's statement. The kid's been talking to every reporter in town."

I stood rooted to the spot, unable to speak. "We filed under seal."

"Well, somebody *unsealed* it. The judge wants to see you and Erika in chambers first thing in the morning."

She hung up. I felt numb as the obvious—and ugly—answer washed over me. I'd filed the motion *one* hour ago. Only myself, Skip, and Erika could've leaked it that fast—and I knew *I* sure as hell hadn't done it.

I didn't want to believe Skip or Erika would do something so sleazy and dangerous. But Erika had been plenty tweaked by Tyler's "emergency" hearing and the press it'd generated. Leaking Dante's statement was an effective counterpunch.

I turned on the television and checked local news sources online. No one seemed to be taking quotes from our motion or the report of Dante's statement. They were just saying that a motion had been filed and running short clips of Dante saying Mia had stabbed him. Skip might've told him we were filing a motion to find out whether the judge would let him testify. In which case, Dante himself could've been the leaker. Maybe.

But I didn't like it. The thought of having to appear in chambers tomorrow filled me with dread. I poured the rest of my drink down the drain. I needed to be in shape for the thrashing we were about to get.

×××

MY STOMACH WAS A mess as we followed Tyler into chambers. I'd pounded four cups of coffee on an empty stomach and the acid was burning a hole in my gut.

The judge waited for us to sit, then fixed Erika and me with a piercing look. "I don't have to tell you how serious this is. The defendant's right to a fair trial has been placed in jeopardy by the release of this highly prejudicial material—material, I might add, that I probably never would've allowed into evidence. I'd like to hear your explanation for how this got to the press. And it had better be good."

Erika met his gaze, her tone concerned but calm. "I can't say I know for sure what happened, Your Honor. But from what I've seen, I think maybe Dante reached out to the reporter—"

The judge cut her off. "And managed to come up with exact quotes from the motion? Is that what you're trying to tell me?" He pushed a copy of a news article toward us. "Look at this." He pointed to the second paragraph. "Two of those lines came straight out of Dante's statement—the one *you* attached to your motion."

I read it along with Erika. The judge was right. Two lines were verbatim quotes. I supposed it was *possible* Dante had repeated the exact lines to the reporter. But not very likely.

It'd looked bad before. Now it looked so much worse.

Erika's face paled as she stared at the article. Finally, she stuttered, "I—d-don't know what to say."

Clearly, she hadn't seen this article, either.

But I couldn't let us go down in flames. It was my reputation on the line, too, and I was the new face in court. *I* knew I hadn't leaked the statement, but the judge didn't. And the reporter who'd written that article would never give up his source.

"Your Honor," I said, "we filed this motion under seal—as you can see from the heading. Why would we go to the trouble of doing that and then deliberately leak it to the press?"

"I don't know," Tyler cut in, his tone sarcastic, "maybe to give yourselves cover? And make the very argument you just made?"

I felt the blood rush to my face. "You have no right to accuse us. Dante could've said the exact same thing to the reporter that he said to us. After all, it was *his* statement." I scrambled for another explanation and came up with: "Or, for all we know, a reporter might've hacked our computers."

Tyler barked out a harsh, mirthless laugh. "Or a rogue CIA operative planted a camera in your office. Please." He turned to the judge. "I'm asking the court to publicly sanction the prosecution for misconduct, then issue a ruling in open court stating that Dante's statement is unreliable and untrue and will not be admitted."

Erika found her voice. "That's outrageous! Your Honor, I'm telling you as an officer of the court that we didn't leak anything. And I'm requesting that you issue a gag order so counsel won't use this opportunity to smear us in the press."

The judge held up a hand. "Enough! I'm not going to gag anyone at this point." He glanced at Tyler. "If counsel is foolish enough to draw more attention to this statement by talking to the press, he'll have to bear the consequences."

He turned back to me and Erika and gave us a hard look. "I'm going to order the sheriffs to conduct an investigation. If I find out that either of you did this, I'll report it to the State Bar. Furthermore, I'll demand that the guilty party—or par*ties*—be fired. I have no doubt Harrier will listen."

With that, he dismissed us.

A judge had never blasted me so badly in my life, and the look on Erika's face told me she was reeling too. Her hand shook as she pushed the button for the elevator. When she saw me looking, she whispered, "Thanks for jumping in."

I nodded. *As if I had a choice.* We didn't speak again until we got to her office and I'd closed the door.

"Are we going to talk to Dante about this?"

He'd be the first one the sheriff's deputies contacted. We needed to get to him before they did and find out what he was going to say. If he admitted that he was the leak, we'd be off the hook. There wasn't much the judge could do to him.

But if Dante said a reporter had reached out to him for comment on his statement, the three of us would have our necks on the chopping block.

Erika was still rattled. "I'll have Skip do it."

Of course you will. That way, I wouldn't be there to see him program Dante to tell the right story. Fury rolled through me as I headed back to my office. What about this case was sending Erika off the rails? What was she hiding?

When five o'clock rolled around, I was more than ready to go home. I took a long, hot shower, then went to my living room window and stared out at the ocean. A party yacht was anchored off the coast, and the lights from the cabin flowed out into the night. I imagined all the happy people laughing, dancing, having fun—not worrying about getting disbarred and fired.

I wished I could believe the leak of Dante's statement was the last of Erika's sleazy moves, but I had a strong feeling that it wouldn't be. And there was nothing I could do to stop her. I needed to protect myself from the fallout, but how could I do that when I'd be sitting right next to her during the trial every friggin' day?

CHAPTER FIFTEEN

Erika hadn't slept through the night in weeks, but after the beating from Judge Butler, she couldn't sleep at all, couldn't stop her brain from circling in an endless loop. What she'd have to do to win the Hansen case; how if she failed, Steers might go free. It felt like she was careening down a steep, winding road on two wheels.

By 4:30 a.m., she gave up and got out of bed. Given her mental state, she worried it might be dangerous to drive—even on surface streets, but she made it to work without a problem. A small victory, but she'd take it.

The moment she got to her office, she called Skip. "Have you spoken to Dante?"

Skip's effort to sound unconcerned didn't quite land. "He's at work. Said he'd be home by three. I'm planning to go to his place."

"Okay. See you at Georgia's."

Damn it. She'd hoped Skip would get to Dante before the interview with Shelly's sister. Erika tried to distract herself with work but found herself reading the same words over and over as she imagined all the worst-case scenarios.

Finally, it was 3:30 p.m. She called Charlie. "We should get going. I'm not coming back to the office after the interview, so you'll need to take your car."

"Got it."

Charlie's attitude had been cool—almost frosty—ever since the Dante leak. No doubt Charlie suspected her, Erika thought. But if things worked out right, Charlie wouldn't be able to do anything about it.

Fucking Harrier. Erika got into her car and slammed the door with a bang. If he hadn't forced her to take on a second chair, she wouldn't have had to deal with any of this. A wave of anger shot through her so intense it gave her a stomach cramp.

×××

UNLIKE THE LAST TIME she'd been to Georgia's house, the sun was shining in a cloudless blue sky. But the bright light only brought the battered front door and sagging roof into sharper relief.

Skip barely knocked once before Georgia opened the door. A shorter, heavier—and much less pretty—version of her sister, she was one of those women who just didn't know how to do makeup. But she did a lot of it anyway. Her cheeks sparkled with glittery blush—a bad choice even in an eighties disco, Erika thought—and her black eyeliner had been piled on in thick, wobbly strokes.

"I've been wondering when you'd get to me." She waved them in, her tone a mixture of smug satisfaction and impatience, and led them to a living room that looked like it'd been furnished by Goodwill twenty years ago. The brown plaid couch bowed in the middle; the two "leather" recliner chairs were scratched and torn, then mended with silver duct tape. Erika bet she'd been jealous of her sister. Not only had Shelly gotten the looks, but she'd married a rich man and wound up with the money, too.

"Mia was always a willful child, but she was very close to her father," Georgia said.

Just her tone of voice told Erika she was a know-it-all. She didn't so much speak as pronounce.

"He had a way with her," Georgia went on. "She'd listen to him. Mia was devastated when Shelly divorced him. And *that's* when she really went downhill." She stabbed the air with a finger to emphasize her conclusion.

"What kind of problems did Shelly have with him?" Erika asked.

Georgia pursed her lips. "Nothing bad enough to justify a divorce. He liked to gamble, took off for Vegas once or twice a week. Shelly said sometimes he'd just disappear in the middle of the night." She waved a dismissive hand. "I told her there were worse things than a man who liked to have fun, but Shelly was always hard to please."

Erika was on Shelly's side. Her ex sounded selfish and immature. "So Mia's problems started after he moved out?"

Georgia nodded. "But she really lost it when he died." She pulled a sad face as she tapped her chest. "Heart attack. The poor man had a bad ticker."

"When you say Mia 'lost it,' what do you mean, exactly?"

Erika immediately regretted the question. Georgia went on—and on—about the booze, the drugs, the boys, and of course, the endless battles with Shelly. As she spoke, Erika found herself feeling sorry for Mia. Losing a beloved parent when she was so young had to have been earth-shattering. Erika knew she'd have been destroyed if she'd lost Danny at that age. Still, she kept her voice neutral as she said, "I've heard the fighting got worse in the past year."

Georgia rocked back in her chair and held up her hands, palms out. "Oh! It *absolutely* did! Mia was out of *control*. You know she stayed with me for a few days before she got arrested?" Erika nodded. Georgia pursed her lips, said, "I did *everything* for her. Opened my *home* to her. But was she grateful? No!"

"Did Mia say anything to you about the night of the murder?"

Georgia made a sour face. "She barely spoke to me. And she stank up the whole house with her smoking. All I asked was that she get rid of those awful cigarettes and keep her room clean. Did she listen? No. She didn't listen to a word I said!"

Erika had had enough. "Did Shelly talk to you about Mia in the past couple of months?"

Georgia pointed again, her expression triumphant. "*That's* the thing I need to tell you. I spoke to Shelly two weeks before she died, and you know what she said? She said Mia threatened to *kill* her."

Erika lifted her eyebrows. "I see."

Georgia frowned, obviously disappointed she hadn't gotten the big reaction she'd expected. But to Erika, it was hardly a game-changer. Tyler would play it off as trash talk, thrown out in the heat of the moment—and it probably was. Erika might still try and get the statement into evidence, just to dirty up Mia's image with the jury, show that those pastel outfits and Peter Pan collars were just costumes.

The problem was Georgia's credibility. If Mia were found guilty, Georgia stood to inherit the whole estate, and clearly she could use the money. The sagging couch, the duct-taped lounge chairs, the stained, threadbare carpet—each represented one more reason to lie.

The question was, did Georgia know she was in Shelly's will? Erika had to find out, but carefully. "Do you think Mia knew what she'd inherit if Shelly died?"

Georgia stared off into space, then said, "Well, she certainly knew about her father's money. And she probably had some idea of how much Shelly was worth."

Erika jumped on the opening. "Which was...?"

"I'd say two or three million if you count the house. And she probably thought Shelly left it all to her," Georgia said with a smug smile.

"But she didn't?"

"Nope." She lifted her chin. "She left twenty-five percent to me."

So much for Georgia. "Do you know whether Shelly told anyone else about Mia threatening to kill her?"

Georgia sniffed, as if offended that anyone else's word mattered. "I don't. But you might ask my daughter, Alicia. She and Mia hung out sometimes."

If Alicia didn't pan out, she'd have to forget about putting any family members on the stand. Erika thanked Georgia for her time and rose. "Please, do me a favor. Don't talk to the press about any of this."

Actually, Erika would be glad if Georgia talked to reporters. She'd said that for Charlie's benefit.

Georgia gave her a knowing look. "You mean like that boy, Dante. I'm too smart to do that. They've been calling me like crazy. I don't even pick up the phone anymore."

She was loving every bit of it, Erika could tell. This wasn't the first time she'd seen family or friends enjoy the macabre limelight—*finally*, it was their turn—but she'd always thought it was gross.

She glanced at Skip and Charlie to see if they had any questions. They shook their heads. Their flat expressions told her they weren't Georgia fans either. "Great. We'll be in touch. Thanks for your time."

When they reached Erika's car, Charlie glanced back at the house. "What are you going to do with Georgia?"

"Nothing. I'm hoping Alicia knows about that death threat."

Skip said he'd set up an interview. "And I talked to Dante."

Erika knew it couldn't be bad if Skip was willing to tell her in front of Charlie. "What'd he say?"

"That after I'd had him read his statement, the words must've just stuck in his head. He didn't realize he was leaking anything."

Charlie peered up at him. "How'd he get in contact with the reporter?"

"Remember how Dante said he wanted to talk to us because he'd just seen Tyler on the news?"

Charlie nodded.

"Well, when I told him the judge might not let him testify, he got mad. He called the TV station and asked for that reporter. Or to quote Dante, 'the dumbass who was buying all that lawyer's bullshit.'"

Charlie took that in. "And that's what he's going to tell the judge's investigators?"

Skip nodded.

"Then I guess we're in the clear."

Skip shrugged, nonchalant. "Seems so."

Erika tried to mimic his casual tone. "Good. Mystery solved. Thanks, Skip." She pressed the remote to unlock her car. "Let me know when you get hold of Alicia."

"Will do."

Erika got into her car and waited for Charlie and Skip to drive off, then leaned back and closed her eyes. Catastrophe averted.

But she knew—she *knew*—that the wheels she'd set in motion were bound to keep spinning, forcing her to do more and more to keep them from flying off. And she didn't know how long she could do it without spinning out of control herself.

CHAPTER SIXTEEN

THE RUSTY NAIL WAS almost empty. A bald guy and a younger kid who looked like his son were sharing a pitcher of beer at a table near the door, but I had the bar area to myself. Sliding onto a stool, I ordered a single shot of Ketel One and congratulated myself on my restraint.

Pete brought it to me with a skeptical look. "You sure?"

I eyed the glass. It did look kind of pathetic. But I made myself nod. "Maybe a club soda, too?"

He threw his towel over his shoulder like he knew I was kidding myself. "You got it."

I pulled out my cell phone to check my Ring app. As always, I held my breath while I waited for the footage to load. And as always, I didn't see anything suspicious. But more and more, I was starting to fear that it only meant Roman was doing a good job laying low.

I scanned the area behind me again. Still just the bald guy and his kid.

When Pete came back with my club soda, I tried to sound nonchalant. "Has anyone been asking about me?"

He looked at me like I'd asked whether space aliens liked his martinis. "No, why would they?"

Self-conscious, I made up an excuse. "A witness on a case I had a few months ago has been calling the office, trying to find out where I live, acting a little nutty."

He frowned. "I'll keep an eye out." He nodded at my sad drink. "Let me know when you're ready."

I took a micro sip, hoping to make it last, and thought about Dante being able to repeat a full *two lines* of the statement word for word. Ridiculous. The judge didn't buy it, and neither did I. Erika had to have leaked his statement to that reporter. We were just damn lucky Dante was willing to go along with the coverup.

But relying on him was an insane risk. Dante wasn't some tough, street-savvy ex-con who was used to dealing with cops. He was a nasty little turd with a chip on his shoulder. If the judge's investigators went hard at him—a distinct possibility, given how thin his story was—he might crack.

Erika had to know that. Which meant she had an alternate story for Dante to fall back on. Something simple and easy to sell. A story that'd cover her and Skip—and satisfy the investigators.

And then it hit me like a frying pan to the face. The alternate story was *me*. They'd say I was the one who'd leaked the statement. Simple. Believable. And it covered Erika. If the investigators didn't seem to be buying Dante's explanation, he'd blame me and say I'd pressured him to lie. I could deny it all I wanted, but I'd never be able to prove it wasn't true.

Livid, I downed the rest of my drink in one swallow. That goddamn bitch. I'd had my doubts about her, but it had never occurred to me that she'd stoop so low. I held up my glass and signaled Pete for a refill. "Make it a double."

He brought the bottle over and poured. "You okay?"

"As okay as I can be knowing I just got fucked." I held up my glass. "Cheers."

Pete gave me a sympathetic nod as he moved back down the bar. "Life sucks."

Erika didn't *want* it to come to that, I was sure. It'd be news. And no matter which of us got blamed for leaking the statement, it'd make the whole prosecution team look unethical, not to mention desperate. Beyond that, the judge and many others might well suspect Erika was in on it. After all, she was the lead prosecutor. No, throwing me under the bus wouldn't be Erika's first choice. But it would keep the judge from taking any direct action against her.

Of course, I didn't have solid evidence to back up my theory. Unless Dante came clean, I never would. But the more I thought about it, the more it made sense, especially in light of everything else I'd seen Erika do. Hard to believe I'd considered her a role model. That felt like a century ago. All I wanted now was to get out of this quagmire. Strong-arming witnesses, leaking to the press, setting me up—I didn't know what was next. I just knew a "next" was coming, and it'd probably be even shadier. My job, my new life—my whole career—were in serious jeopardy.

But if I asked to leave, I'd have to explain why. I couldn't tell the truth. Erika would just deny everything, and I had no way to prove she was lying. Worse, if I went after her now, she'd fight back by getting Dante to say I was the leak. Not only would that shred my credibility, it'd probably end my career as a prosecutor.

I couldn't tell Harrier some innocuous lie about not being able to handle the stress, either. He'd either see right through it and try to find out what was really going on, or he'd decide I was a fainting flower who couldn't handle the pressure of a heavy case, which meant I'd get stuck prosecuting shoplifters and drunk drivers for the rest of my life. I'd blow my brains out.

No, all roads led back to the same ending: me out of a job and maybe a career. But that didn't mean I had to stand by and let myself get screwed over. If I figured out what Erika and Skip were up to, I might get enough ammunition to back them off and protect myself—and Mia.

I started to take another sip of my drink and saw there was more than half left. Given the mood I was in, I knew if I finished it, I'd just keep going. If I stopped now, I'd be okay. That meant I had to leave. I paid the tab and headed out before I could change my mind.

But as I walked to the parking lot behind the bar, the hairs on the back of my neck stood up. I could feel it. Someone out there in the dark, watching me. My breath caught in my throat as I pictured Roman waiting, ready to spring. I put my knife in my coat pocket and scanned the area with my mini flashlight. There was no one in the street, and the only vehicles other than my car were a white pickup truck and an old blue Honda Civic. I shined my flashlight into their windows. No one.

Then I saw a low, concrete wall, separating the parking lot from an old pawn shop. A perfect hiding place. Terrified, I gripped the knife in my pocket as I moved forward and peered around the edge. No one there.

I took one more glance up and down the street. Still empty. Eyes peeled for any sign of movement, I started to head for my car. But as I reached the parking lot, something scraped across the asphalt off to my right. I gasped and whirled around.

No one was there. All I saw was an empty McDonald's wrapper. I stared at it, chest heaving. Maybe the wind had blown it across the ground. Maybe that's what I'd heard. Maybe.

Was it all in my head? It seemed so. But now I was *definitely* sober enough to drive. So, there was that.

When I got home, I poured myself a shot of Cuervo Gold with a shaking hand.

Had it finally happened? Had Roman found me? The possibility left me panic-stricken, but it might mean my family was safe, and that was all that mattered. I'd been texting with Hannah every few days, checking in. But after tonight, I needed to hear her voice.

I closed my eyes and prayed she'd pick up as I listened to her phone ring once, twice, three times…

"Lauren? Hey. What's going on?"

Relief washed through me. "Nothing much. Just wanted to reach out, see how you're doing."

"I'm good. Kind of under the gun. I've got an exam in Statistics tomorrow."

Something was off. She sounded…forced. "What happened? Is it Mom and Dad?"

She sighed. "I didn't want to worry you, L, but…Mom called last night. She said Dad saw a man sitting in a car parked across the street. He stayed there for hours, and he…he looked like Roman."

"Oh, my God!" Frantic, I said, "They should call the police! Did they call the police?"

"They did. The police sent a car out right away, but he was gone. They said they'd put extra patrols in the area." She paused, then added, "It'll be okay, Lauren. They'll be fine, I'm sure."

But the quaver in her voice said she wasn't. "You haven't seen Roman, have you? Tell me the truth. Please!"

"No! I'd tell you. Really."

"Can I call you tomorrow after your exam?" I heard the note of hysteria in my own voice.

"Of course," she said. "And I'll get hold of you the moment I hear anything, 'kay?"

I was shaking as we ended the call. If anything happened to my parents...I couldn't even finish the thought. I paced the living room, hating the feeling of being so powerless.

A memory came to me: Brett, before I left Chicago, asking me to stay in touch. He might be able to find out whether Roman had left town. It was only eight o'clock his time. After hours, but not too late.

I poured myself another drink and called his cell. He answered on the first ring.

"Lauren—I mean, Charlie, are you okay?"

Just hearing his voice made me feel better. "Uh, not really," I said, and told him about my Dad's possible sighting of Roman. "The police are on it, but they can't be there twenty-four-seven. I was wondering...could you find out if Roman's left Chicago?"

"Sure." He paused, then asked, "I take it you haven't had any sightings yourself?"

Should I tell him about tonight at the Rusty Nail? After hearing about my dad, I felt kind of silly. Roman couldn't be in South Carolina and California at once. I must've imagined it. But that mugging... Taking a deep breath, I told him about getting robbed by the man in the ski mask.

"Are you fucking kidding?!" he exploded. "Why didn't you call me?"

"And tell you what?" I asked, frustrated. "That I got jacked by some guy I couldn't pick out of a lineup of one?"

He blew out a breath. "Right, I'm sorry. But you got the feeling it might be Roman?"

It sounded ridiculous to me now, like yet another product of my imagination. "Yeah, but so what? I've got Roman on the brain. Every time the wind blows, I think it's Roman."

"Who wouldn't?" he sighed. "Look, I don't know how he could've managed to find you. I did a pretty good job of burying Lauren Claybourne."

"Unfortunately, there is one way." Briefly, I told him about getting forced onto the Hansen case, then added, "We went to court for the arraignment a little while ago, and I thought I avoided the cameras, but…"

"I don't suppose you can get off the case?"

If only. For so many reasons. "Unfortunately, no. And if he already saw me in court, it won't help. But maybe I'm wrong—maybe I'm just imagining things."

"Or not. I'll get right on it." He continued, his tone urgent, "But in the meantime, change your habits. Don't take the same route to work every day, and don't go out in public alone if you can help it. Especially at night."

"Got it. Thanks, Brett. I really appreciate it." I already felt safer.

"Not a problem. I'll be in touch."

I wondered what I'd do if he found out Roman was here in Santa Cruz. I couldn't keep running forever.

And I might not even get the chance.

CHAPTER SEVENTEEN

Erika looked out her bedroom window. The wind had kicked up, forming frothy white caps out on the ocean. She touched the glass, felt the cold go through her.

As she pulled a wool jacket out of her closet, her cell phone rang. It was Skip. He didn't usually call her before work. Her heart began to pound, her mind leaping to the worst possible conclusion. "What's going on? Has he—"

Skip cut her off. "No. You know better than that."

Right. He'd never call her on her cell, or even her landline, to talk about that. Erika rubbed her temple. "Sorry. What's up?"

"Alicia said she can come in this morning. But we can go to her place if you're still worried about reporters. She has her own apartment, so we won't need to see Georgia again."

She weighed the options. "I'd rather have her come in. Just make sure nobody gets to her."

"Not a problem. We should be there by 9:30."

She had to stop living in the world of disastrous scenarios, Erika thought as she ended the call, or she'd wind up in the hospital if not a mental ward. She was halfway to the office when her cell phone rang again. Thinking it was Skip, she answered without looking at the screen. "Hey. What's going on?"

Phillip Hemingsworth's imperious baritone filled the car. "Good morning. We wanted to find out whether the defense has filed the motion for a new trial yet."

Shit! Erika wished she could say this was a bad time and put him off. But she knew he'd just talk over her. He got what he wanted and not a moment later than he'd asked for it. "No, they haven't. I doubt they'll file until we're closer to the date of the hearing." The defense wouldn't want to give her any more time to prepare than they had to.

He grunted impatiently. "But I trust you have some idea of what they're going to argue."

Erika stopped at an intersection, and as she slowed, she got that horribly familiar feeling. *Oh, God, no.* Her heart started to pound; she could feel the sweat break out in her hairline. This was going to be a bad one. She needed to pull over, but she had to wait for the light to change. *Breathe. You'll be okay. Just breathe.*

She gripped the steering wheel and fought to keep her voice steady. "I'm sure they'll argue that keeping out T. Rayne's prior arrest for assault was error. Probably bring in affidavits from some of the jurors saying they would've voted to acquit Steers if they'd known about it."

The traffic light finally turned. But she was in the left lane, and the right lane was packed. Her heart pounding like a trip hammer, she put her blinker on and tried to find space to wedge in. But a black Acura wouldn't make way. Tunnel vision began to set in and her hands were starting to feel numb. Erika could feel her panic rising. That'd never happened before. Terrified that she'd lose control of the car, she glanced at the Acura again. *Please! Let me in!*

But the driver wouldn't budge. Tears filled her eyes as her terror mounted.

On the phone, Phillip's tone was almost angry. "That ruling on the prior arrest was already litigated. How can they bring that up again? It's over. We won."

His voice was like the whine of a buzzsaw, hovering in the background while her brain kept sounding the alarm. *This time you're not going to make it.* She forced a deep breath.

"They can bring up anything they want, Phillip. It doesn't mean they'll get anywhere with it." Her heart was racing so fast it felt like it was going to burst. She had to do something. Erika rolled down her window and leaned across the passenger seat to put her arm out. But the driver didn't see her—or he ignored her. Tears rolled down her cheeks as she sat penned in, trapped and helpless.

In the background, Erika heard Phillip tell his assistant to put another call on hold. *Take the call! Please! Let me go!*

He came back on the line. "Then you're not worried about what the judge will do?"

Erika barely managed to choke out, "No."

He gave another grunt. "Let's hope you're right. Listen, Rochelle and I will be going down to Monterey Bay for a charity board meeting in a few days, and we'll be stopping by. We'll get lunch."

"Great." It was all she could to manage. *Get off the phone!*

"My assistant will set it up."

The moment he ended the call, her heart slowed, and feeling began to return to her hands. It was over. But she could feel bile rising in her throat. She managed to pull over onto a side street before she opened the door and threw up.

This couldn't be happening. Now she couldn't even take surface streets? Fresh tears sprang to her eyes.

But as her brain cleared, she realized that this time was different. This attack hadn't come out of the blue. She'd been fine before—and after—Phillip's call.

×××

ERIKA MADE IT TO work, but she felt worn thin. The attack had taken it out of her. She sat back and closed her eyes.

"Erika? Are you okay?"

Jerking up, she saw Charlie peering at her through the window. Oh shit! How much had she seen? Erika forced a smile as she got out of the car.

"I'm fine. Just tired. And I was thinking about what to ask Alicia. She's coming in this morning."

The wind picked up, and Charlie pulled the scarf more tightly around her neck. "What time?"

"Nine thirty." That'd give Erika just twenty minutes to recover. When they got upstairs, she said, "I've got a few calls to make. See you soon."

She sank into her oversized chair and managed to catnap. The brief rest helped. By the time Charlie arrived, Erika felt as close to normal as she could hope for. She thought Charlie seemed distracted, though.

"Any leads on your mugging?" Erika asked.

"Not that I've heard. Given my shitty description, I doubt the jerk will ever get caught."

Whatever was bothering her, Erika thought, that didn't seem to be it—or at least not all of it.

"Alicia and Mia are pretty close in age, aren't they?" Charlie said. "Isn't Alicia nineteen?"

Erika nodded. "But I don't know how much contact they had." A knock sounded on the door, and she raised an eyebrow. "Guess we're about to find out."

Skip ushered in a slightly plump girl dressed in jeans and a blue parka. Alicia had her mother's brown eyes, but her round face and button nose had to have come from her father's side of the family. And unlike her mother, she wore no makeup.

When Skip introduced her, she dipped her head then sat down, her shoulders hunched. Erika could tell she was scared and very nervous. That was normal. But the way Alicia cringed in her chair didn't seem like a reaction to just the immediate situation. It seemed like her reaction to life, like she'd been beaten down so often she was constantly waiting for the next blow.

Having met her mother, Erika suspected she knew why. Feeling sorry for Alicia, she gave her a warm welcome, introduced herself and Charlie, then asked about school. When Alicia seemed to have calmed, she started with some easy questions.

"How long have you known Mia?"

Alicia looked down at her hands, which were folded in her lap. "Just about all my life. But we've never been super close."

Close or not, Erika could already tell Alicia was going to be reluctant to say anything negative about her cousin. "How often did you see her?"

"Lately? Maybe once a month." She glanced up at Erika, then dropped her gaze to her lap again. "We hung out a lot more when her dad was alive."

Yet another person in Mia's life who'd seen a change after her father's death. "Why?"

"Mia was just...angry all the time." Alicia stared out the window. "I mean, she always had a temper. But after her dad died, she'd go off about the stupidest things."

And her grief had manifested as anger. Erika got that. She knew from vast personal experience that when a wellspring of rage was boiling inside you, a bent paper clip could unleash it.

"What kind of things?"

"Like, when Shelly got her Tesla, and she said I could drive it to go to dinner, Mia just lost it, had a screaming fit." Alicia tucked her hair behind her ear.

"Why? Because she was jealous?" Alicia nodded. "Anything else?"

Alicia took a deep breath. "A year ago, she asked to borrow my Doc Martens to go to a concert, and I didn't want to let her because she always wrecked the stuff I loaned her—if she even gave it back."

She stopped abruptly. Erika prompted her, "What happened when you said no?"

Alicia swallowed. "She slapped me so hard she almost broke my nose."

My God. "What did you do?"

Alicia shrugged. "I just...pushed her away and got out of there." She touched the side of her face, as though reliving the pain. "She called me later and apologized. And I...said it was okay. So..."

"You two made up?" Alicia nodded. Erika sighed. Only someone who thought they deserved to be treated that badly would've put up with Mia. "Did all that happen after Mia's father died?"

"Yeah. She was super close to him. At first, when her parents split up, it really messed with her head. But when he found a place close by and she got to see him almost every day, she seemed better."

Erika's picture of Mia was filling out—and so was her motive to kill. "Did Mia and her mother fight a lot before the divorce?"

Alicia's brow furrowed. "They fought some." She paused, then said, "But it got much more...intense and...uglier after."

It was classic. The child of a divorce almost always blames one of the parents. And it seemed to Erika that—fairly or unfairly—it was usually the mother. "What about after her father died?"

Alicia nodded. "The fighting got worse. Him dying kind of destroyed Mia." Her expression darkened as she added, "That's when she started hanging out with those other guys."

"You mean Axel and Larissa, all those kids?"

Alicia's nose wrinkled. "Yeah. They're the reason Mia got so into partying."

Erika had seen Mia as a ringleader or at least someone at the head of the pack. But now it sounded like she'd fallen in with a bad crowd to escape her misery. For the second time since Mia's arrest, Erika felt bad for her. She wished she didn't.

"I've heard that in the last year or so things really went downhill between Shelly and Mia."

Alicia chewed on her lip. "Yeah. Shelly got a lot stricter. Mia hated that."

Erika could see that Alicia would be a double-edged sword. On the upside, she'd help paint the picture of a daughter who blamed her mother for her father's death, whose festering rage had finally spilled over. But she'd also paint a sympathetic picture of a girl unhinged with grief over the loss of her father. Hopefully her next answers would help Erika decide whether the upside outweighed the downside.

"Did you ever see Mia get physical with her mother?"

"A few times. Once, Shelly told her she couldn't go to the movies, and Mia slapped her across the face. Just like...*boom*, out of nowhere."

"Did it ever get worse than that?"

Alicia sighed. "Yeah. My mom had borrowed Shelly's vacuum cleaner because ours was broken. When I brought it back, Mia and Shelly were in a big fight about Mia being out all night. When Shelly told her she was grounded for a month, Mia went nuts. Grabbed the bat Shelly kept in the foyer and swung it at her."

Jeezus. A bat? "Did she hit Shelly with it?"

Alicia sank farther down in the chair. "Yes. On the shoulder. And then she swung it at Shelly's head, but Shelly grabbed it out of her hands."

It was a miracle Shelly had survived as long as she had. "How did it end?"

"Mia ran out and drove away. I—I don't know what happened after that. I was kind of freaked out, honestly, so I went home."

Time for the final question. "Did you ever hear Mia threaten to kill Shelly?"

"I never heard that. But that's what Shelly told my mom."

Had Georgia made it up? Erika wondered. It was entirely possible. It didn't seem as though Shelly had done much confiding in her sister.

"When your mother told you about that," Erika asked, "did it surprise you?"

"N-no. Not really." Alicia bit her lip. She looked from Erika to Charlie and Skip, then asked, "Do I have to testify?"

"Maybe." Alicia's testimony was some of the strongest proof of motive—and of Mia's capacity for violence—they'd found. And unlike her mother, Alicia was a credible, relatable witness. The jury would buy every word she said.

Alicia's face crumpled, and a tear rolled down her cheek. "I just feel so bad. No one's there for her."

Erika didn't know what to say to that. It seemed to be true. She remembered Mia's terrified expression as the unis handcuffed her, how vulnerable and alone she'd seemed. "I understand."

Alicia wiped away the tear. "Do you really think she did it?"

"I do. What do you think?"

"I don't know. I don't want to believe it. But if Mia was really drunk or high...and just lost it...maybe."

That did it. The fact that even Alicia—who sympathized with Mia—thought it was possible she'd killed her mother made her a powerful witness. She couldn't testify to that opinion. But that feeling would come through on the stand.

The girl was tired; it was time to let her go. Erika thanked her for coming in, said she'd be in touch.

When Alicia and Skip left, she asked Charlie, "What do you think?"

"She's a great witness. I vote we put her on."

"Agreed."

Charlie stood up. "We still don't have Skip's report on the alibis for the men Shelly dated. We need to nail that down. And what about that guy Tyler mentioned, Alberto Sanchez?"

Erika felt a flash of anger. "I told you, Skip's got that covered. And Sanchez is a red herring."

Charlie locked eyes with her. "Probably so. But we should make sure."

Erika saw the defiance in her gaze. She'd thought Charlie had thawed after the Dante leak issue got resolved. Now she wasn't so sure.

She'd keep a closer eye on her. If Charlie got to be any more problematic, she'd have to do something about it.

CHAPTER EIGHTEEN

I TOOK BRETT'S ADVICE and found a different route to the office, driving with one eye on the rearview. But when I tried to reach Hannah later that morning to get an update on my parents, the call went to voicemail. Fear gripped me, and it was all I could do to stay focused during Alicia's interview. I left Hannah three more messages, getting more anxious by the minute, and kept checking the ringer on my cell to make sure it was working.

Finally, as I was packing up to leave, Hannah called. I was breathless as I said, "Are they okay? Please tell me—"

Hannah cut in, "They're totally fine. Sorry! I only just saw your messages. The cops picked up the guy this afternoon. It was a neighbor's brother."

I leaned against my desk, weak-kneed. "So it wasn't Roman."

"No," she said, sounding as relieved as I felt. "The guy got kicked out of the house after a fight with his brother and had to move into his car until he found a place to stay."

I almost laughed. "Mystery solved. Thank God." I remembered to ask, "How'd the exam go?"

"I'm not sure," she said. "I was a little…distracted."

By her worry about Mom and Dad. I felt a surge of guilt. "Maybe if you tell them the circumstances, they'll let you retake it?"

She said she thought they might, then told me she had to go. "My roommate's throwing a 'whatever' party. As in, no particular reason. But that works for me."

I smiled. "Rock on. Thanks for calling, H. Love you."

"Love you back, L."

After work, carrying my grocery bags to the car, I saw the wind had died down, leaving behind a gorgeous fiery sunset. I'd hit West Cliff Drive, I decided, a stretch of road along the coast with a great view of Monterey Bay. I needed to chill—and think about whether I should risk trying to figure out what Skip and Erika were hiding.

It was a relief to focus on something other than Roman, I'd been finding. Going after Skip and Erika was unquestionably dangerous, but I doubted it was life threatening.

To make sure no one was following me, I took a circuitous route to my favorite spot on the drive, a bluff that overlooked the ocean. The sea was calm, and I leaned back in my seat and stared at the ebb and flow of the waves, wondering where all this was going to leave me. And Mia, who was looking more like a girl deranged by grief than the pathologically spoiled brat I'd seen in the interview video.

What if I found out that Mia was innocent but couldn't prove it? What would I do? What *could* I do? Nothing, as far as I could see. She'd get convicted, and the real killer would get off scot-free. Would I be able to stay in the Santa Cruz DA's office, knowing I'd been a part of that? I didn't think so.

But where would I go? Santa Cruz was the only DA's office in California that'd had an opening. Even if Erika and Skip didn't catch me, I'd be out of a job—and out of California. Any other place I applied would see that I hadn't even lasted one full year in Santa Cruz. Not a great look.

And if I did find a way to prove that Mia was innocent, then what? Skip and Erika might wind up getting fired. Or worse, they might not. Unless I came up with proof that they'd knowingly framed Mia to protect someone else—or to hide something they'd done—they could just claim they'd been mistaken. It happens. In the aftermath, I'd have an enemy for life. A very powerful enemy. Erika wouldn't be able to make any direct moves against me, but who knew what she could do behind the scenes to fuck up my career?

When I first decided to move to California and become a prosecutor, all I'd wanted was to keep practicing criminal law and stay as anonymous—and alive—as possible. But now, seeing that Skip and Erika were willing to violate all ethical boundaries in the service of some unknown goal, something had become clear to me. It wasn't enough to fly under the radar and survive. I needed to do good in the world. To atone for my sins. And if Roman did come for me, at least I'd have accomplished something worthwhile.

The decision gave me a heady rush. For the first time in months, I dared to hope that a day might come when I'd be able to look in the mirror without cringing. I let myself take one last look at the waves, softly rippling in the moonlight, and headed home.

×××

I WOKE TO THE sound of someone screaming. When I opened my eyes, I realized it was me. I'd been dreaming that Roman was holding a giant butcher knife to my throat. Sweaty with terror and hoping it was time to get up anyway, I grabbed my cell phone. 3:16 a.m. Shit.

I made a drink and took it into the living room, pulled a fuzzy white throw blanket up to my chin and found a travel show host whose voice was the human equivalent of white noise. Finally, I managed to drift off.

When my alarm rang three hours later, I felt like shit—fuzzy-headed, my neck stiff from sleeping in a weird position, and shaky—but I couldn't afford to lose any time. The trial was twelve days away. Once it started, I'd be stuck in court with no way to do any private investigating.

I was on my way out the door when Brett called. I stepped back inside, my heart hammering. "Was he in Chicago?"

"Yep. And I've got surveillance footage of him driving in and out of the parking garage in his building from the day you got mugged to the day you went to the Rusty Nail."

Roman couldn't have made it to either of the bars in time, not if he were driving. "But he could've flown out here," I said, thinking aloud.

"You must think I'm one shitty detective," Brett said, chuckling. "I checked the flights, commercial and private and all the surveillance footage. There was no passenger matching Roman Stiler's description."

I was relieved but still troubled. The fear that Roman would hunt me down had receded in the past months, but it'd never gone away. Now, as much as I wanted to believe I'd just imagined someone following me, that fear had been reignited. I couldn't dismiss it so easily.

"Do you guys know what he's up to lately? Is he working?"

It was a long shot. Lyra's murder was a cold case, just like Angela's, so the detectives might not be keeping tabs on Roman anymore.

"I heard he's planning to open a sporting goods store in Naperville with his brother, Adam."

It wasn't a new idea; I'd heard Roman talk about it back when we were dating. Adam had a sporting goods store in upstate New York that had done well. "Then he's not working a steady job?"

"No, but don't worry. I'll keep monitoring the surveillance cameras at his building. FYI, as of about an hour ago, he hadn't left his condo." Brett paused, then added, "If you feel like someone's following you again, call me right away, okay?"

I thanked him and said I would.

It was 7:30 a.m. by the time I made it to my office—later than I'd planned. But Erika didn't usually come in until 8:30, so that gave me an hour to myself. I'd start by digging into Mia's past, see if there were any sources that hadn't been checked out.

A little digging, and there it was: Mia'd gone to a rehab center called Pathways two years ago, not long after Shelly broke up with Dante's father. I wondered if it was Mia's way of showing gratitude to Shelly for throwing them out.

Pathways was a half-hour drive away. No counselor would meet with me unless I got official authorization, which meant Skip or Erika would find out. But if the center did group therapy, I could try to find some of the kids who'd been in Mia's group. If I got lucky, maybe somebody had stayed in touch with her. The tricky part was figuring out how to keep my visit a secret.

At 8:30, I went to see Erika. She looked like she'd spent the night under a bridge. Her face was drawn and pale, and there were blue circles under her eyes. I blinked, surprised. Even with all the pressure she'd been under in the Steers trial, she'd always looked like she had it under control. Was it guilt, I wondered?

I stood in the doorway. "Morning. Mind if I go out for a bit? My car was making a weird sound on the way in. I think I should get it checked."

Erika peered at me, then nodded. "Just come back as soon as you can. We need to get a couple of motions filed."

She looked at me suspiciously as I left.

×××

PATHWAYS WAS A SINGLE story, three-sided rectangle. The open end faced a lush green hill awash in an early growth of bright yellow sourgrass and mustard. A nice view for the patients in good enough shape to appreciate it.

On the way, I'd figured out how to keep my visit secret. It wasn't a foolproof plan by any means, and it depended on a fair amount of luck. But I'd known when I decided to do this that every move I made would involve some degree of risk.

A young woman at the front desk took me to the administrator, Josephine. I showed her my badge and said that I was looking into Mia's background. "By any chance, do you keep in touch with the girls in Mia's group therapy sessions?"

Josephine looked at me over the top of her bifocals, which were perched on the end of her nose. "Unfortunately, they usually keep in touch with us. It's depressing how many of them wind up coming back."

She pulled up Mia's file on her monitor. I leaned in and saw a photo of Mia in the upper right corner of the screen, sitting cross-legged on a chair, her hair tucked up in a bun on top of her head. It struck me then, how much she reminded me Lyra. Not feature for feature, just...a style, a way of holding herself. And now I remembered the other photo of Mia, the one I'd seen on TV, her lopsided smile, so like Lyra's crooked little grin. At the thought that I'd never get to see it again, I felt a lump in my throat.

Josephine's voice brought me out of my reverie. "There's only one girl from Mia's group on this list." She pointed to the name, Brook Johnson. "We actually just heard from her lawyer. She got arrested last week, and he's trying to get the court to let her do her time here instead of in jail."

I wrote down the name. "That's very helpful. Thank you." Time to put my "plan" into action. "I need to ask you a favor. Do you think you could keep our visit confidential? We want to be respectful of Mia's privacy. As you know, the press has been all over this case, and if it comes out that we're looking into Mia's stint here, you'll have reporters on your doorstep for days."

She frowned. "No, of course. I'll be glad to keep this conversation between us. Do you really think she killed her mother?"

"I do." I stood up. "But if we find anything to the contrary, we'll certainly follow up on it."

× × ×

HAD THIS VISIT BEEN a bust? I wondered as I walked back to my car. If I went to see Brook Johnson, Erika would find out for sure. And what would Brook be able to tell me? She clearly wasn't in Mia's life at the time of the murder. It probably wasn't worth the risk.

I glanced at the clock. I'd only been gone for thirty-five minutes. Mechanics take longer than that to pop the hood. If I got back to the office too fast, it'd look suspicious.

Might as well go to the crime lab and kick some ass about the fingernail scrapings. I wasn't sure how Erika would feel about it. She insisted on calling all the shots, no matter how minor. But I was just checking on the status of evidence listed in the coroner's report. Surely she wouldn't get bent about that.

When I got to the lab, I showed my badge to the assistant at the front desk and told him I was handling the Hansen murder. "We haven't received the test results on the fingernail scrapings yet, and the trial's starting in less than two weeks. We need that report ASAP."

He tapped some keys on his computer, peered at the monitor, then shook his head. "I don't show any testing on scrapings."

I stared at him, speechless. "That can't be right. I'm sure they got sent over a while ago."

He stood up, said, "Hang on, let me go check," and disappeared into the lab.

When he reappeared, he was shaking his head. "We never got any fingernail scrapings from the coroner."

"What?" That was impossible. I knew the coroner had collected them. It was in the autopsy report. "Are you sure?"

"Yes, I'm sure." He glared at me, his tone impatient. "I asked the supervisor, and he showed me his list of evidence. We never got the scrapings."

Shit. The coroner's office must've screwed up and forgotten to send them. I needed to head over there and tell them to get those scrapings to the lab—*now*.

Erika would definitely want to approve that move first, but I was sick and tired of being treated like a law clerk. And someone was going to have to goose the coroner's office. It might as well be me. Feeling a little rebellious, and a lot self-righteous, I drove there thinking, *fuck her.*

But as I approached the entrance, I got that creepy feeling again—the sense that someone was watching me. I stopped and looked around. Two detectives were heading for the parking lot, deep in conversation. A burly postal worker was carrying an empty box back to his truck, and two young women wearing badges around their necks sat on a bench at the side of the building, smoking cigarettes. No one seemed to be paying me the slightest bit of attention.

Who could be following me? According to Brett, it couldn't have been Roman before. So it probably wasn't Roman now.

Erika? Or, more likely, Skip? After they'd set me up to get fired, I had to at least consider that they might have me followed to make sure I wasn't doing exactly what I *was* doing. But that was crazy. They couldn't risk my spotting them, and they sure as hell couldn't bring anyone else into their little cabal. I sighed. Maybe the whole situation had made me paranoid.

Feeling calmer, and more than a little guilty about the trouble Brett was going to on my behalf, I walked up to the receptionist. "I'm looking for your...ah...evidence custodian? I'm not sure what you call the person. But I need to see whoever's in charge of sending evidence to the crime lab for testing."

"Jared takes care of all that." She pointed down the hall. "Third door on the right."

Jared, a slender young man in a button-down shirt and knit tie, was staring intently at his monitor. I knocked on the doorframe. "Excuse me.

Jared?" He looked up at me and nodded. I introduced myself and told him I was checking on the status of the fingernail scrapings. "Apparently they never got sent to the lab."

His tone was defensive. "If the pathologist collected it, then I promise you, we sent it out for testing."

The last thing I needed was a pissing match. I had to cool him down.

"I'm sure you're right, but would you mind checking? That evidence is crucial for us."

Jared still seemed hostile, but he asked me for the case number, typed it in, and nodded at the screen. "As I thought. Our records show they went out to the crime lab three weeks ago."

That couldn't be right. "Can I take a look?"

Jared gave an irritable huff as he turned the monitor toward me. "See for yourself."

I read the log. Sure enough, it listed the scrapings, the date, and the notation, *"Sent out for testing."* My eyes moved down, searching for the name of the person who'd transported them to the crime lab. Whenever evidence is moved from one place to another, a record has to be kept of who moved it, when, and where they took it. It's known as maintaining a "chain of custody," and it's done to prove that evidence has been handled properly. But the space where the name should've been was blank. I pointed to it. "How come it's not filled out?"

Jared turned the monitor back and frowned. "I—I don't know. My assistant must've forgotten."

I was starting to get worried. "Don't you make everyone sign for evidence before it's released?"

"Of course, I do. A hundred percent of the time." He took a stack of forms out of his inbox. I watched as he went through them, one by one. "Here it is."

But as he read it, a look of shock spread across his face. My heart began to pound. "What?"

After a long beat, he slid the form over to me. The box where the transporting party's signature was supposed to be was an illegible smear. I stared at it, stunned. What was going on here?

"Don't *you* remember who it was?" I snapped at Jared. "I mean, aren't you the one who makes the person sign for the evidence?"

Jared blanched, then swallowed. "Not necessarily, no. I leave the forms next to the evidence locker. Everyone who removes evidence is supposed to fill one out and leave it for me. It's kind of an honor system."

Shit. This was a fuck-up of epic proportions. Someone had lost—or gotten rid of—key evidence, and I had a strong feeling it was the latter. The illegible signature was a tipoff. At a glance, it made it look like the person had signed his or her name. If I was right, I knew who'd done it. Which meant I had to keep Erika from finding out what I'd learned.

"Listen, Jared. We don't need to sound any alarms yet. Let me look into this. It might just be a mix-up. Maybe the scrapings accidentally got put with the wrong case." I silently prayed that Jared's fear of getting fired for using his stupid "honor system" would make him willing to keep this quiet. Lord knows, it should.

He cleared his throat. "I...uh, yeah. No problem. And I'm sure you're right. The scrapings will turn up at some point."

I very much doubted that. Even if they did, they'd be useless. After having been bounced around to who knows where, there'd be no way to ensure they hadn't been contaminated. No judge would let that evidence in now.

I stared at the piece of paper. Was there any chance I'd find prints on it? Probably not. But there was one thing I could do. I pointed to the form. "Would you mind giving me a copy of that?"

×××

BACK IN MY CAR, the enormity of what I'd discovered hit me. Cops were in charge of the chain of custody. And the only cop who would have handled such critical evidence was Skip.

I supposed it was possible that this was just a screw-up, that the crime lab had lost the scrapings. But given what I'd seen so far, it seemed far more likely Skip had gotten rid of them. Which was why I'd been pretty sure I wouldn't find any prints on that form. No way Skip would've let that happen.

If I was right, he'd obviously been careful not to let anyone see him take the evidence. How he'd managed that, I didn't know. But Jared's super high-tech "honor system" had surely played a part. Fucking Jared.

More important than *how* Skip had done it, though, was *why*. You don't dump key evidence if you think it'll help prove the case against your suspect. Not if you know you've got the right one.

Skip either knew Mia was innocent, or he was afraid she might be. Either way, he didn't care. He and Erika were covering for someone, hiding something. Or both. And they were setting Mia up to take the fall.

CHAPTER NINETEEN

Erika was looking forward to dinner at Skip's. It'd be good to get out of the house and think about something other than her impending doom. And Danny had seemed better since they'd had the motion detectors installed, though she knew it might just be a temporary fix.

Her office phone rang. She frowned at the screen. "Letitia? What's up?"

"Can you come down at three o'clock? Steers' lawyers just called. They're asking for a court order to let him talk to some reporter on camera."

Erika felt the blood rush to her face. "You've got to be kidding! The judge isn't going to go for that, is he?"

As a matter of policy, and safety, inmates weren't allowed to do on-camera interviews. But a judge could override it for specific cases.

Letitia's voice was weary. "I sincerely doubt it. But we've had a lot of calls from Steers' groupies—I mean, supporters. Most likely the judge just wants to let them say their piece before he shuts them down."

"Yeah, I'm sure you're right."

As Erika ended the call, burning rage spread through her body. That scum-sucking pig! Camera time? For that sociopath? It was outrageous! She kicked the metal trash can next to her desk as hard as she could. It flew across the room and hit the wall under the window with a loud *bang*. "Goddamnit!"

She was shaking as she pulled out her cell phone and called Skip. "You won't believe this!" She told him what Letitia'd said.

"Jeezus H. Christ. But I do believe it. It's fucking par for the course with them. Don't worry, the judge will nix it."

Skip said he'd swing by to pick her up. Erika was glad he'd be there—someone needed to keep her from stroking out. She began to pace. By the time Skip got there, she was a nervous wreck. He looked pointedly at the trash can, which was still lying on its side next to the wall.

"Can't say I blame you. But honestly, I don't think there's a chance in hell of the judge going along with it." He picked up the trash can and set it next to her desk.

"Thanks." Erika shook her head. "I got...overheated. But tell me, how does this asshole still have groupies?"

Skip sighed. "For the same reason Charles Manson did. And Ted Bundy. And Richard Ramirez."

"Seriously, what is wrong with my gender?"

"I'm gonna walk away from that one." He glanced at his watch. "We'd better head over."

She checked the mirror on her desk to make sure she didn't look as frazzled as she felt. "What do you want to bet they've packed the courtroom with reporters?"

"That's a sucker bet. Of *course* they did."

×××

THEY WERE RIGHT, OF course. It wasn't SRO in the courtroom but it was close, and almost every single person in the gallery was press. Steers' lawyers filled his side of counsel table, all of them coiffed and suited up for their turn in front of the cameras.

As Erika moved up the aisle, Steers emerged from lockup. He made a point of smirking at her as the bailiff uncuffed him. She deliberately looked away.

But now it was so clear. Danny was right: He *was* her foster father. Not physically, of course. Steers was fair-skinned and blond, her foster father dark-haired and olive complected. But they had the same smooth confidence and charisma. And every fiber of her being wanted to wrap her hands around Steers' neck and choke him till his eyes popped out.

Skip glanced at Steers as he sat down. "Tom Ford would not be happy to see that asshole wearing his suit."

In spite of her fury, the comment almost made her smile. "All spiffed up for his star turn." She shook her head. "Fucking reporters. They'd give airtime to Beelzebub if it got them ratings."

He raised an eyebrow. "Isn't that what they *are* doing?"

Judge Butler took the bench and trained a skeptical eye on the defense lawyers. "I understand the defense is requesting that I make a special order allowing Mr. Steers to give an on-camera interview to a reporter for KNSC. Please enlighten me as to why your client thinks he deserves special treatment."

The lead lawyer, Dick Stanton, a tall, combative pit bull of a man with thinning blond hair moved to the podium. "I'd like to start by saying we appreciate Your Honor granting us this hearing." He angled his body toward Steers as he said, "As you know, the press has been very anxious to talk to Mr. Steers throughout this case. That wasn't possible while the trial was pending. But now that it's over, we think he should be allowed to speak, and tell his side of the story."

The judge said, "Counsel, you've been telling his side of the story since you were retained. And I remind you that the case is not concluded. Your motion for a new trial is still pending."

Stanton nodded. "Yes, of course, Your Honor. But Mr. Steers wants the chance to tell his story himself, and when I said that the case was done, I merely meant that we don't have to worry about jurors being unduly influenced anymore. So, there's no real reason not to allow it."

"We'll see." Judge Butler turned to Erika. "Prosecution?"

Erika rose, her heart beating fast—too fast. *Don't lose it.*

"I'd like to point out that if Mr. Steers wanted to tell his side of the story himself, he had the chance to take the witness stand and testify at the trial. He chose not to, and we all know that was his choice to make. It's very obvious that the only reason he wants to do this interview is so he can tell his lies without being cross-examined—"

The pit bull jumped to his feet. "Objection!"

The judge nodded. "Sustained. Ms. Lorman, anything else? Beyond the *ad hominem* attacks?"

Shit! She knew the judge hated personal jabs. Why had she said that? "Counsel's only argument is 'Why not?' But that's not a reason to bend the rules for a convicted murderer. I ask that this transparent effort to garner public sympathy be denied."

The judge frowned. "While I agree counsel hasn't given a particularly compelling reason to allow it, I don't see the harm. He's right about that, isn't he? It's not like we have a jury to worry about."

Erika stared at the judge in disbelief. Was he really going to let them get away with this? She controlled her voice with an effort. "The harm is in allowing a convicted murderer and rapist to freely spin public opinion without fear of being challenged."

Stanton jumped up again. "Who says he won't be challenged? I'm sure the reporter will push him for answers."

Erika couldn't help herself. "Oh, come on, counsel. Are you seriously trying to say you'd ever allow him to talk to a reporter who'd hold his feet to the fire? Because I find that impossible to—"

"Stop!" Judge Butler thundered. "Both of you!" He glared at Erika, then at the defense lawyer. "I'm going to grant the request. I don't see a significant downside. And while there is still a motion pending, I feel very confident in my ability to avoid being influenced—either by what Mr. Steers might say or by any expression of public opinion." He rapped his gavel. "So ordered. This court is adjourned."

Erika stood rooted to the spot as she watched the judge leave the bench. She heard the defense high fiving, saw Steers turn to her with a look of triumph. Her eyes burned with fury. She wanted to go over to that gloating piece of garbage and beat him to death.

In that instant, a terrible feeling came over her. The feeling that she'd left her body and entered a surreal world where she could only watch but not control the Erika puppet standing at counsel table. She didn't know how to move, how to make her body do anything. And she didn't know how to find her way back.

What the hell was going on?! What if she was stuck out here in this nightmare place? What if she never got back into her body?!

Skip took her arm, giving her a look of concern. "Come on, let's get out of here."

But she couldn't move. Skip's voice seemed to come from another dimension. Erika was afraid to speak, afraid to hear what strange sound might come out of her mouth.

"Erika. Let's go." He squeezed her arm. "Don't give him this."

Go! Just get to your office.

Erika let him guide her out of the courtroom. She couldn't feel herself moving. Reporters swarmed around her, clamoring for her reaction to the ruling. She managed to say, "No comment," but the voice didn't sound like hers.

She saw her body move to the elevator and down the hall to her office. Inside, she was screaming, horrified. *Please let me get back. Please.*

Skip closed the door and put his hands on her shoulders. "Are you okay?"

She couldn't let him know. No one could know. She saw herself nod, go over to her chair, and sit down. Skip offered to get her water. She heard her voice say, "Thanks." The word seemed to echo.

When he left, she closed her eyes, but that made her dizzy. She sat up, frantic. If she could just make her body *feel* something. She made her hand grip the edge of her desk and squeeze it as hard as she could. She looked down at herself, saw her fingers pressed against the wood. At first, she felt nothing. Her panic grew.

But finally, it worked. She felt her hand! And with that, the surreality began to fade. Like a fogbank that melts in the sun, it slowly but steadily receded until at last it was gone. She was back inside her body, clinging to the edge of the desk.

She tried to grapple with the shock. What the hell *was* that? And how was she going to keep it from happening again? Erika felt battered, as though her psyche was being flung against one wall after another by some unseen force.

But she couldn't dwell on that. She had to pull herself together, show Skip nothing was wrong. When he came back with two bottles of water, she told him she'd just been upset by the ruling. "Why would he let him do this? It makes no sense."

Skip shook his head. "It's ridiculous. But I also don't think it matters all that much. The judge is the only one we have to worry about, and he isn't going to give a shit what that jerk says to some reporter."

Erika stared at him. "Doesn't matter? Are you kidding?! He's trying to spin the next jury!"

He looked her in the eye. "There won't be a next jury."

But Erika couldn't be so sure.

A knock on the door made her jump. She was still shaky. "Yeah?"

A voice said, "It's me."

Charlie. The last person she needed to see right now. Erika leaned back in her chair and tried to look relaxed. Skip opened the door. "Hey, come on in."

"I heard about the ruling," Charlie said after the door closed behind her. "Why the fuck did the judge do that?"

Erika gave her a flat look. "No clue."

Skip was nonchalant. "We'll survive." With a glance at Erika, he said, "We were just talking about those reports we got from the unis."

Charlie asked, "You mean about the kids not seeing scratches on Mia's arms?"

It was hardly news. They'd had those reports for over a week. Skip was just trying to get off the subject of the ruling in case Erika flamed out again. "Great stuff for us."

"Yeah." Charlie paused, then said, "About that. It looks like we still don't have the test results on the fingernail scrapings they took from Shelly. I know the lab's been kind of slow, but shouldn't that've been done by now?"

Skip frowned. "Yeah, definitely. I'll give them a call."

"Thanks." Charlie started to leave, then turned back to Skip. "About those guys Shelly was dating. Do you know when we'll get a report on that?"

Skip looked surprised. "You should have it already. A uni checked out all the guys she'd been seeing in the last six months."

"How many were there?" Charlie asked.

"Four. We alibi'd them all."

Charlie took that in. "Mind if I talk to the uni?"

"Not a bit. Matter of fact, I'll have him give you a call—right after I rip him a new one for not getting that report to you." He moved to the door. "I'd better get going."

Skip left, and Erika fixed Charlie with a cold glare. Charlie's endless pushing about Shelly's exes was riding her last nerve. "You have your answer now. Happy?"

Charlie lifted an eyebrow. "Aren't you? We don't want Tyler to ambush us by coming up with some other dude in the middle of the trial."

It annoyed her that Charlie never let anything go, but okay, she'd gotten too hot. Erika softened her tone. "Sorry. I'm still pissed about Steers' interview."

Charlie nodded and left. Erika tried to work on her opening statement, but couldn't make herself focus. Her mind kept drifting back to her out-of-body experience. What if it happened during trial? Or while she was driving? What if it didn't pass?

The thought was so terrifying, her mind recoiled. She pushed the questions away and forced herself to go back to work, but by six o'clock, she'd only written a page and a half. She decided to admit defeat and quit for the day. Maybe she'd check in with Danny, see how he was doing.

It was a little early for him, but surprisingly, he answered.

"Hey, want some company? I'll bring dinner."

His voice was still thick with sleep. "I'm not in the mood for Italian."

Erika rolled her eyes. He was such a grump when he first woke up. She told him to decide, and he chose pho.

Nervously, she got into her car and tapped the jazz playlist on her phone. Miles Davis's "Kinda Blue" came on. She took a deep breath and pulled out of the parking lot. *It's going to be okay*, she told herself. *You're fine.*

And miraculously, she was. Maybe it was the music, or maybe— she almost didn't dare to hope—the surreal thing had been a one-time occurrence. Either way, she made it to Danny's with no problem and rang his doorbell, feeling downright triumphant, cartons of pho in hand.

Danny was still in his pajamas. Through a yawn, he mumbled, "Sorry. Had a really late night."

Meaning, he'd gotten to bed around ten in the morning. "Work?"

"And *Fortnight*. Got way into it with some of the guys at the office. I'll go put on some clothes."

That was good. Normal. She could do with more of that.

Danny changed into his usual uniform of navy sweats and a long T-shirt. As he sat down, he asked, "So, is it going any better with Charlie?"

"Not really. I feel like she's constantly looking over my shoulder."

Danny made a face. "I couldn't stand that. There's no way you can tell her to back off?"

Erika sighed. "I wish." She tasted the soup. It was better than she'd remembered.

Across from her, Danny put down his spoon. "You know what? We should go for a sail. Do you realize we haven't done that since you caught the Steers case?"

Erika blinked. He was right. Sailing was their favorite escape. Danny had joined the club his freshman year at the University of California in Los Angeles. When Erika flew down to visit—she'd graduated college early and was in her first year at Stanford Law School—he'd taken her out on a catamaran. Her little brother always had a "need for speed." Driving with him was a white-knuckle experience, and he was an equally wild sailor. They didn't just sail, they flew. Danny had the boat heeling until they were practically parallel with the water. As they laughed into the wind, the sun on their faces, they were, for a few golden hours, just two normal siblings, their dark childhood forgotten.

It'd become their ritual. And after Danny moved up to Santa Cruz, they'd made a point of going at least twice a month. But then the Steers case had sucked up Erika's life. And now, with the Hansen trial less than two weeks away...

"I wish I could, but..."

Danny shook his head. "I know you're under the gun, but you need this." He put a hand to his heart with a mock serious expression. "And I am willing to take a hit for the team."

"Your sacrifice is much appreciated." Erika grinned, gazing at him with affection. Surely a day off wouldn't kill her. "How about Sunday?"

"Sold. I'll rent a day-sailor."

"Perfect." The very thought lifted her spirits. "How's it going with your new CEO?"

"Not bad, actually." He launched into a story about some of the improvements they'd made at the company and how much he was loving his new project. It was good to see him so relaxed. She wouldn't mention the "assholes," Erika decided. If he'd moved past it, she didn't want to stir things up.

And seeing her brother in such fine form made her feel better about her own issues. If he could get past his problems, maybe she could, too.

Danny stood up. "'Scuse me. Nature calls." He pointed to his empty bowl. "All that liquid."

She raised an eyebrow. "You know you can spare me the details, right?"

He laughed. "Just didn't want you to struggle with the mystery."

Danny left, and Erika wandered into the family room, where his computer was set up. It was an elaborate arrangement, three monitors and a state-of-the-art sound system. He liked to work to music. She tapped a key so she could see his latest screen saver. But a photo popped up instead, and Erika's eyes widened.

It was a picture of Charlie. It looked like it'd been taken in the hallway of the courthouse. Erika could see a sliver of her own shoulder at the edge of the frame. The original photo would barely have shown Charlie—she was off to the side, a few feet away from Erika. But it'd been cropped and enlarged to focus on her.

Danny must've done it. But why would he go to the trouble?

A deep sense of foreboding filled Erika. As she reached for the mouse, her hand trembled.

CHAPTER TWENTY

I HAD TO HAND it to Skip. He was smooth. I'd brought up the fingernail scrapings to see if there might be a hitch in his voice, a slight hesitation, and he hadn't missed a beat. Of course, he had to have known it was going to come up sooner or later. He'd been prepared.

I packed up my iPad and considered hitting The Rusty Nail on my way home. I wanted to go back to the scene of the crime—so to speak—and prove to myself there was nothing to be afraid of. Roman was in Chicago; he wasn't stalking me or my family. But I was on a mission. This was no time to risk a drunk driving bust. In fact, maybe I'd double down and make it an alcohol-free night.

When I got home, I popped my Trader Joe's chicken enchilada dinner into the microwave and thought about Skip. I'd seen prosecutors and cops do a lot of questionable things in my time, but deliberately destroy critical evidence? Never.

It made one thing clear: I couldn't let my fear of getting caught stop me or slow me down. I wouldn't throw all caution to the wind, but I had to explore all leads, and if I couldn't find a way to cover my tracks then to hell with it. I'd deal with the consequences.

Which meant I was definitely going to see Brook Johnson. She might be worth the risk, she might not. But I couldn't ignore any potential source of information.

As I ate, I thought of a way to make it look less suspicious. And tomorrow was Saturday—perfect timing. But I needed someone on the inside, someone who worked at the Blaine Street Facility where Brook was housed, who'd be willing to keep a secret. A tall order. I wracked my brain for any friendly contacts I'd had with the deputies there. No one came to mind.

Then it hit me. Monique Lafayette. I'd prosecuted an inmate who'd shanked her and gotten him sentenced to ten years in state prison. We'd stayed in touch after the trial; she'd emailed a month ago to tell me she'd been transferred to Blaine Street. I might be overstepping, I knew that. It was a big ask, and we were work-friendly—not take-a-bullet-for-me friendly. Still, if I told her that I thought something shady was going on, she might want to help. Even if she didn't, I could trust her not to tell anyone.

I opened the freezer to pull out my bottle of vodka—then stopped. I slammed it shut, went to the living room to get away from my booze, and called Monique.

She sounded surprised, but not unpleasantly so. "Charlie Blair. What the hell are you up to?"

"No good, as usual." I asked her how she was doing at Blaine Street, and after we caught up, I got to the point. "Look, I need your help. It's about the Hansen case. I don't want to say much right now, but I think something's going on that's not…kosher."

She paused. "Not kosher as in…illegal?"

I didn't want to sound overly dramatic, but destruction of evidence *was* a crime. "Yeah. I can tell you all about it when I see you." Not on a phone. "But right now, there's someone at Blaine Street I have to see, and I need some cover."

She gave a *hmph*. "I'm listening."

"Before I tell you, I need you to promise that, either way—whether you'll do it or not—you'll keep this to yourself."

Her voice was wary. "I can keep a secret. Long as your plan doesn't involve a felony."

"Not even a misdemeanor." I told her what I needed, then closed my eyes. *Please say yes.*

There was a long beat of silence. "Okay, I got your back."

I exhaled slowly. "I really appreciate this, Monique."

"No problem. But watch yourself. You're walking one hell of a tightrope."

×××

THANKS TO MY PLEDGE of sobriety, one cup of coffee was all it took to kickstart my engine Saturday morning. Still, it'd been a tough night; I'd had the dream again, the one where Roman pinned me down on the bed and pressed a butcher knife to my throat. I woke up screaming then tossed and turned for hours. The good news? I wasn't hung over. I had to admit, not having to hide from the sunlight like a vampire was kind of nice.

As I drove, I braced myself for a short, hostile interview. Pathways wasn't some fancy rich kid retreat. It was a county-run facility that treated a fair number of lower-income patients. Between Mia's entitled attitude, abrasive personality, and inexperience with kids from less tony zip codes, I imagined she hadn't exactly been beloved.

Brook Johnson gave me a wary look as she sat down. Her jail-issue jumpsuit was stretched tight over her stocky frame, and her braided hair was laced with silver beads that clacked as she moved. When we picked up the phones, her tone was hostile.

"They told me you were the DA on Mia's case. If that's why you're here, you may as well leave. All I know is what I saw on the news."

I shook my head. "I'm not here to talk about the case, and I'm not looking for dirt. You were in Mia's group when you were in rehab last time. I just want to know more about her."

She tilted her head and studied me. "If I talk to you, are you gonna help me get into Pathways?"

I wasn't sure how much weight my vote would carry, but I didn't mind trying. "I'll do whatever I can."

Brook leaned back in her chair. "Go on, then. Ask your questions."

"From what I understand, Mia's mother sent her to Pathways because she was doing coke and meth. How'd she feel about going to rehab?"

Brook gave me a deadpan look. "Like the rest of us. Better than jail, not as good as home."

That didn't tell me much. I tried a more direct approach. "Did she ever talk about her mother?"

Brook's eyes narrowed. "No more than most of us."

Her attitude more than her words told me what I needed to know: Brook was a friend. She might not out-and-out lie to me, but she wasn't about to offer up anything negative if she didn't have to. "How bad was her drug problem?"

She shrugged. "I've seen worse. Her problem wasn't drugs so much as…other stuff."

"What other stuff?"

Her nostrils flared. "Her father dying, for one. Her asshole stepbrother and his low-class dad, for another."

Stepbrother? "You mean Dante?"

"Yeah." Her expression was sour. "Started hitting on Mia almost the day they moved in."

That would've been horrible for a girl at any age, but Mia was just fourteen. "Did she tell anyone about it?"

"Who was she gonna tell? Her mom?" Brook's expression radiated sad futility. "Mia never liked him or his dad. She pitched a fit when her mom said they were moving in. Didn't matter. So Mia figured if she told her mom about Dante, she'd just think she was lying to get them kicked out."

And Mia might've been right. "How'd she deal with the situation?"

"Booze, coke, meth." Brook sighed. "Look, I'm not saying Mia was an angel. She was already getting high because of her dad dying. But when her mom hooked up with that loser just six months later?" She raised her palm. "That's when she got into the heavy stuff, like meth."

Much as I sympathized with Mia, I had to admit, it painted a vivid picture of a girl with plenty of reasons—both logical and illogical—to hate her mother. Maybe enough to kill her. "Mia must've been pretty pissed off."

"She was, but then, you know, when it all blew up, Shelly did the right thing."

"By 'blew up,' I assume you mean when Mia stabbed Dante because he found her stash?"

Brook nodded. "Dante's dad wanted to call the police, but Mia finally told them about Dante moving on her all the time."

So *that's* why they hadn't called the police. Dante had lied. Shocking. "I assume Dante denied it."

Her tone was sarcastic. "Of course. But Shelly took Mia's side, so his dad backed down."

The whole Dante story sounded very different now. "Have you been in touch with Mia since Pathways?"

"No. Which is a drag because we got kind of tight. But Pathways isn't the real world." She tapped the plexiglass between us. "This is."

It was true. And I was sorry about that. "Was Mia tight with anyone else in your group?"

She thought, then shook her head. "Not that I saw."

Damn. I hadn't gotten much out of this interview. "Has Mia's lawyer spoken to you?"

Brook shook her head. Which meant Tyler might not know about her. I'd make sure he did.

Brook leaned forward, her tone firm. "I know it doesn't matter what I think. But I don't believe she did it. She and her mom had their shit. And believe me, Mia could lose it like no other. But I never got the feeling she hated on her mother like that." She paused, her expression thoughtful. "Not like that."

It wasn't evidence, and I knew all too well that anyone could be capable of anything, given the right circumstances. Still, Brook struck me as someone who saw things pretty clearly, for better and for worse.

I thanked her and promised to put in a good word with the judge. "I just need one thing from you."

When I explained what it was, she nodded. "No problem. You gonna help Mia?"

Great question. I gave her an honest answer. "If I can."

As the deputy came in to take her back to her cell, she said, "You better talk to the judge soon. I go to court next week."

"You got it."

I headed for the exit, but before I could leave, I saw Monique's curvaceous figure hurrying toward me. She grabbed my arm. "Hold up. I've got to tell you something."

She led me down the hallway and stopped at a metal door that led to a stairway. After she looked through the small glass window, she pulled me inside and let the door slam behind us with a loud *clang*. In an urgent whisper, she said, "You're right. Something funky's going on. Your girl, Mia Hansen? They just gave her a new cellie. Tanya Wilson."

She said the name as though I should recognize it. "Who's that?"

"She's a snitch. Testified against her cellies twice last year. Look her up." She glanced at the door. "Could be a coincidence. Everyone's got to be somewhere, right? But…"

But my scalp was tingling. "Can you find out who put in the request to get her transferred into Mia's cell?"

She looked at me like I'd asked where my lap went when I stood up. "I can look at the file, and it'll show me a name. But your cop would be stupid to do it himself."

Yeah, he would. Damn. "Does her lawyer know?"

"If he does, it didn't come from me. I can't be spouting off to defense attorneys when I don't have proof of anything."

Neither could I. "Thanks for the heads up."

"What heads up? This conversation never happened." She yanked open the door and walked out.

I could feel my outrage building. There was no way Tanya'd landed in Mia's cell by chance. She had to be a "fisherman," an inmate the cops use to "fish" for incriminating statements from their cellmates. In return for their services, fishermen usually got a sweetheart deal on their own case, like a nice chunk of time off their sentence. It's not illegal. Cops are allowed to plant an informant in a jail cell in the hope that the inmate will spill. And informants aren't allowed to pressure an inmate to confess. The problem is, you can't know for sure *how* they get an inmate to talk. Informants don't necessarily wear a wire, which means they can squeeze their cellmate like a juice box. And sometimes they just lie and make up a confession. It's easy to do. Lawyers give their clients the police reports and witness statements so they can help prepare their defense. All the fisherman has to do is sneak a look at that paperwork.

If Tanya made up a lie, she'd have an easy time selling it. Mia was young and naïve. It was entirely believable that she'd spill her guts to her cellmate. But that brought me back to the question that kept plaguing me:

Why? Why would Skip and Erika stoop to using a jailhouse snitch? The case against Mia was strong and getting stronger. Framing a guilty person; it didn't add up.

The answer—the only one that made sense—was the one I kept bumping up against: They had something to hide. Something they were afraid would come out as long as this case stayed open. Which was why Mia had to get convicted, fast. I'd been right to predict that Erika—and Skip, because this one was his bailiwick—would step further and further over the line. And now I had another prediction: There'd be no such thing for them as too far.

CHAPTER TWENTY-ONE

E RIKA TILTED HER FACE up to the sun and inhaled the crisp, salty air.

"Coming about!" Danny shouted.

The boom swung toward her head, giving her mere seconds to scramble to the other side of the boat. "Hey! You trying to kill me?"

He grinned as he trimmed the sail and picked up speed. "Just keeping it interesting."

Erika laughed, a full-throated, joyous laugh—her first in months. Skimming across the water, the wind whipping through her hair, she felt cleansed, free. Danny was right. A day out on the ocean was just what she needed.

She held up a hand to shield her eyes as she called, "So what's your big news?"

He pulled the tiller toward him and sent the boat flying even faster. "CQT just picked up another round of funding. The CEO said I might be in for a raise pretty soon." With a rueful smile, he added, "Probably still won't be enough to pay my own freight but better than nothing."

Erika knew he hated to lean on her for financial help, though she'd made it clear she didn't mind. "That's great! They *should* show you some love, given how much you bring to the party."

"I'll tell 'em you said so."

"Give me the number," she said, setting her jaw. "I'll tell 'em myself."

"No way," he chuckled, "You'll scare the shit out of those guys."

A lull in the wind slowed them to a standstill, and Erika leaned over the side to trail a hand in the water, gazing down at the St. Christopher medal that dangled from her necklace.

Danny shook his head. "I wouldn't do that if I were you."

No sooner had the words left his mouth than a heavy gust blew in, filling the sails. The boat lurched forward, nearly sending Erika overboard. "Yikes!"

She jerked back, clutching her necklace. It was a gift from Skip's mother, Loretta, and the only piece of jewelry Erika had ever cared about. She and Loretta had hit it off right from the start, but within just three months of that meeting, Loretta had suffered a stroke that left her partially paralyzed, unable to walk and barely able to speak. Skip had reluctantly, and tearfully, moved her into a nursing home. But not long after, he noticed that she'd become fearful and withdrawn. The director of the home agreed to have Loretta examined by the staff doctor. His diagnosis: early-stage dementia.

Erika had asked if she could visit, though she worried it might upset Loretta if she didn't remember her. But Skip thought it was a good idea. Though it'd been hard to communicate, Loretta had no problem recognizing her, and Erika had had a feeling about what'd caused her to change. She told Skip to find a doctor outside the facility, get a second opinion.

Sure enough, that doctor ruled out dementia—and confirmed the likelihood that the staff had been abusive. Erika had helped Skip find a good home for his mother and launched an investigation that eventually shut the place down. In the process, she and Loretta grew close. Although speech was hard for her, her mind was as sharp as ever, and Erika made up for the sparse conversation by reading to her, playing games—Risk and Scrabble were big faves—and watching TV. Loretta loved cooking shows; they'd give thumbs up or thumbs down votes on the dishes.

Caring for Loretta, Erika found, was like a balm to her soul. No matter how tired or anxious or upset she was, their visits always made her feel better. In Loretta, she'd found the mother figure she'd dreamed of as a child.

But the stroke had taken its toll, and Loretta began to decline, slowly at first, then rapidly. Erika watched in helpless agony as she lost all speech, then all movement. Though she didn't know how much Loretta could hear or understand, she still spent hours sitting next to her bed, talking or reading to her, playing her favorite cooking shows on TV. Until finally, her last day came. Skip had been called out on a case—to his bitter regret—but Erika had been by her side. She'd been filled with grief as she watched Loretta take her last breath. She'd never feel a love like that again.

The loss was still so painful. And yet, Erika thought, as she tucked the St. Christopher medal into her shirt, she was grateful to have had Loretta in her life—no matter how briefly.

×××

DANNY PULLED UP TO the curb in front of her house. Erika said, "That was so much fun." She raised an eyebrow. "The near drowning aside."

Danny gave her a mock incredulous look. "What are you talking about? I had it totally under control the whole time."

She looked at him fondly. For the first time in weeks, the knots in her neck and shoulders had loosened. The smile she gave him was relaxed, genuinely happy. "Thanks for a great day."

He returned her smile. "Let's not wait that long to do it again."

As Danny drove off, Erika stared up at the bright, blue sky, smiling, then moved up the walk to her small, Spanish-style house. Between dinner with Skip and Carson and a day on the ocean, it'd been a fantastic weekend.

But it almost hadn't happened.

Finding Charlie's photo on Danny's monitor had rocked her. Worse, he'd caught her. Privacy was an obsession for her brother, but Erika had known she had to ask. Making her voice as gentle as she could, she'd said, "Danny, why do you have Charlie's picture?"

"I was curious about the person who's been grieving you. But she never gives any interviews and that," he'd pointed to the photo on his monitor, frowning, "is the only picture of her I could find. What's the problem?"

"No problem. I was just surprised. And I didn't mean to pry."

His expression turned to one of understanding. "You don't have to worry about me, Erika. I'm seeing my shrink; I'm taking my meds. I'm good. Really."

He did seem okay, and given her endless complaints about Charlie, why wouldn't he be curious? "I'm sorry. I'm such a putz."

He'd laughed. "No, you're not. But let me put your mind at ease." He'd gone over to the computer and deleted the photo. "There. Now you have one less thing to worry about."

So, crisis averted. But the concern that something was happening with Danny lingered in the back of Erika's mind. Her intuition wasn't always spot-on, but it was right often enough to keep her from dismissing it.

As she headed to the shower, she saw that she'd gotten some sun. She almost looked healthy. A day like today made her realize what her life might be like once the Hansen trial was over and Steers had lost the new trial motion.

It couldn't happen soon enough.

×××

ERIKA'S THOUGHTS TURNED TO Charlie on her Monday drive to work. So many puzzle pieces in the picture of her didn't seem to fit together. She'd been a superstar defense attorney in Chicago, then chucked it all to be a prosecutor in a small-ish city in California? She didn't have any friends or family out here, so what was she hiding—or running from?

Time to find out. If Charlie had a secret, it'd give Erika the leverage to make sure she kept quiet about what she'd seen. She called Skip the moment she got to her office and asked him to stop by. As they ended the call, her intercom buzzed. "I've got a woman here to see you. Name's Fiona Thornberg."

Erika paused. The name was familiar, but why? Then she remembered. That was the woman Danny had met at the chiropractor's office. Erika blinked, puzzled and a little concerned. "Thanks. You can send her in."

A few seconds later, Fiona appeared in her doorway. Tall and long-limbed, her sun-streaked hair swept over one shoulder, she looked like the prototypical California girl. "You're Danny Lorman's sister?"

"Yes, come on in."

Fiona stepped in and gestured to the door. "Okay if I close it?"

"Sure," Erika said, but her stomach tightened.

Fiona sat down and tucked her feet under the chair. "I wanted to talk to you because I don't want to call the police if I can avoid it."

Erika sat up, her heart giving a heavy thud. "Why? What happened?"

Fiona gripped the arms of the chair. Her words tumbled out rapidly. "I don't know if Danny told you, but we met at the chiropractor's office? We talked for a few minutes, just waiting room chitchat. I didn't even tell him my last name! But that night, he started sending me pictures and notes on Instagram. I don't even know him!" She paused to catch her breath, then said, "I asked him to stop, but he just kept sending me all this...stuff. So I blocked him, and he started texting me on my cell phone. I never even gave him my number!"

Erika was momentarily speechless. This wasn't Danny. Was Fiona delusional or...or lying? But she didn't seem unstable. And what reason would she have to make something like this up?

"What was he saying?" Erika asked.

Fiona's expression was anguished. "That we're perfect for each other, that we were going to be so happy together." Her voice got higher. "When I blocked his texts, he started sending me emails! All these romantic letters about us, saying that we should move in together. I begged him to stop, but he just kept sending them. So I blocked *those*."

She teared up, her voice pitching even higher. "And *then* he started leaving letters and notes in my mailbox, on my car—he even put one under my door! And the other night, he parked in front of my house and sat there almost all night! How did he find out where I live?" She wrung her hands and gave Erika a pleading look. "I need you to make him stop. Because if he doesn't, I'll have to call the police."

"But he only met you ten days ago—"

"That makes it even scarier! It's like he just tore into my life!"

Erika's brain fought against Fiona's words even as it registered their truth. She remembered how Danny had made it sound so sweet, so innocent, so...normal. But he'd been *stalking* her.

Her little brother—a *criminal*?

Erika was shocked and frightened. For him and Fiona.

As the wall of feeling hit her, to her horror, it started again—some unseen force, knocking her out of her body, trapping her in an alternate universe. *Oh God, not now!* But even as she desperately tried to stop it, she felt herself floating away.

Through her rising panic, she forced herself to say, "I'm so sorry. But please believe me, my brother would *never* harm you. Never!" Her voice sounded tinny and far away.

Fiona's lips trembled. "What he's doing *is* harming me. He hasn't threatened me or...or anything. But he's obviously sick, and I'm scared to death. I'm always worried he might be following me. I have nightmares about him grabbing me off the street!" A tear rolled down her cheek. "I don't know what else I can do..." she trailed off, swiping at her face with her sweater sleeve. "I just can't stand it anymore."

Erika's pulse raced as the waves of panic grew higher. This was worse than before. But she had to focus. Fiona was suffering, and Danny was in grave danger.

She couldn't feel her lips move as the tinny voice said, "I'll get him to stop. I promise."

Fiona's eyes welled up again. "I really hope so. The guy needs serious help."

Erika's voice echoed as she said, "Thank you for giving me the chance to take care of this." She saw her body stand up and give Fiona her card. "If he shows up again, or—or leaves any more letters, please call me."

Fiona left, and Erika saw herself close the door, then lean against it and begin to cry. Her body moved to a chair and perched on the edge of the seat like a stick figure. She saw tears running down her face, but she couldn't feel them. She'd never be able to get back, she thought; she was going to completely lose control. Some distant part of her brain told her to breathe. She made her body slide back in the chair and watched herself take deep breaths.

The next thing she knew, she was curled up in the chair, her head on the armrest. She'd fallen asleep. And as she opened her eyes, she realized the spell had passed. She was okay. Freaked the hell out, but okay.

Then her brain kicked into gear. She had to do something about Danny, and fast. She'd go see him tonight, but she couldn't handle this alone. She needed to talk to his shrink, Julia.

As she picked up her cell phone, she saw that it was almost 9:30. Skip would be there at any minute. Erika checked the mirror on her wall.

Her hair was a mess, her face pale, and her mascara smeared. She did what she could to fix the damage and left a message for Julia.

For a moment, she considered telling Skip about Fiona's visit. If Danny didn't stop what he was doing, she might need Skip's help. But Danny would be furious. If Julia could pull him through, no one would ever need to know.

When Skip arrived, he was smiling. "I have a bit of good news." His voice dropped low. "Mia's new cellie is already hitting paydirt. Mia told her she thinks she might've done it."

Erika frowned. "'Thinks'? 'Might have'? So she's still saying she doesn't remember."

"She remembers more, but yeah, she's still claiming she doesn't have a memory of the actual murder. I know it's not perfect, but we're moving in the right direction."

True. But if that was as good as it got, it wouldn't be enough. "Tanya's going to get slammed as a professional snitch. No one's going to believe her unless she gets Mia to give up some details." Something that showed the kind of first-hand knowledge only the killer would have. How the confrontation started, or how Mia cleaned up afterward—that'd be all they needed to sell it.

"You're sure no one can trace Tanya back to you?"

"A hundred percent. I've got a guard who owes me big time. He's the one who's talking to her. She's never seen me, and she never will."

Using a jailhouse snitch was a first for them. It was a practice they both deplored. That they were using one now only drove home how desperate their situation was.

Which brought Erika to her other idea. "I've been thinking about Charlie. There're things about her that just don't add up." She described the inconsistencies she'd noticed, then added, "And I checked out her personnel file. The address she listed as her home? It's a mailbox at a UPS store. In Lower Ocean, of all places. It might not mean anything, but…"

Skip nodded. "She might not want people to know where she lives."

"We should see if she's got something to hide. It'd be good to have some leverage. Just in case things go south."

"I'll see what I can find out."

There was a knock on the door. "It's me."

As Erika called her in, she saw that Charlie wore a look of concern.

Charlie said, "Something happened over the weekend."

Erika sat back, wary. "With the case?"

"Yeah." Charlie took a seat, looked down at her folded hands. "Monique, a friend of mine who works at the Blaine Street jail, called to tell me that an inmate had information on Mia Hansen. Monique said the inmate would talk to us if we promised to ask the judge to let her do her time at a rehab center."

Erika frowned. "Who is she? And what's she in for?"

"Brook Johnson. Possession of meth. No strikes on her record. She was in rehab with Mia a couple of years ago."

Skip said, "I could go talk to her, see if she's got something worth trading."

"The thing is, she only wanted to talk to a prosecutor," Charlie said. "And according to Monique, she was kind of iffy about it. She thought Brook might change her mind if we didn't act fast. So I decided to just do it myself. I figured whatever she had to say couldn't be all that great, or you'd have heard it already."

Erika's upbeat mood was shattered. The little bitch! How dare she?! Her tone was icy cold as she said, "You should've called me. Do I need to remind you that I'm the lead on this case?"

Charlie stared at Erika for a beat but remained calm. "I thought I was doing you a favor. Saving you from wasting your time on a useless—"

Erika snapped, "But it wasn't useless, was it?"

Then she caught herself. This was no time to lock horns with Charlie.

Luckily, Charlie seemed unfazed. "I...no. As it turned out, it wasn't."

Erika took a deep breath. "Charlie, I'm just worried. You took a statement on your own without backup. If this Brook girl decides to hitch up on the stand—"

"I do have backup. Monique was there. But you're not going to want to put Brook on the stand."

Whatever Charlie was about to tell her couldn't be good. "Because?"

Charlie recounted what Brook had said about Dante. Erika wasn't happy to hear it, but the news could've been worse. Much worse. "I take it you think it's all true."

"Yeah, I do. More importantly, I think a jury will believe it."

Skip said, "I'd better go take Brook's statement."

Erika agreed. "Make sure to tell her we'll be happy to help her get into Pathways." They'd have to turn the statement over to Tyler and permanently scratch Dante off the witness list. But she didn't mind. He'd served his purpose. It was probably better this way.

As Skip left, Erika said, "I don't love that you took it upon yourself to see Brook without telling me. But I have to admit, you helped us dodge a bullet."

Charlie gave her a grim smile. "Well, I never was much of a Dante fan."

"Obviously with good reason. So, thanks."

Charlie stood up. "Sure."

Erika thought she'd managed to calm the waters.

She waited for the door to close, then took out her phone and texted Skip. *Pls talk to Monique and Brook. See if C's story checks out.*

Skip texted her a thumbs up. Erika leaned back in her chair. Maybe Monique really had called Charlie. But if not—if Charlie had lied and found Brook on her own—that meant trouble. Real trouble. Because it meant Charlie was taking matters into her own hands.

CHAPTER TWENTY-TWO

THE DOOR CLOSED BEHIND the last person to decamp for the day, leaving a silence so abrupt it felt like all sound had been sucked out of the air. My ears rang; my head ached. I wanted to get out of there. I really needed a drink. I supposed I could work at home. I was using my personal iPad for my private investigation; I couldn't use my desktop because Erika's computer and mine were networked. But given the mood I was in, if I went home, I'd start pouring, and I had no faith in my ability to stop. And I couldn't lose more time. We were due to start picking a jury in just nine days.

Having exhausted my only lead on Mia, I'd shifted my focus to Shelly. I'd spoken to the uni who'd checked out the men she'd dated in the six months before her death, but Skip had been right. There'd only been four, and they all had alibis.

For a minute—stuck as I was in a world where everyone seemed to be lying about something—I'd wondered whether the uni was telling the truth. But his report had been turned over to the defense. If he was lying, Tyler would've busted our chops by now. So I moved on to Shelly's phone records. I was zeroing in on the last three months when my cell phone rang.

It was Brett. My breath caught in my throat. "What's going on?"

"Nothing, everything's okay. I just wanted to reach out and see how you're doing."

The relief left me dizzy. "I'm okay. Still a little nervous, obviously. But I think maybe it's all in my head. I've been dealing with a weird situation on this case, and it's making me…jumpy. No one's following me."

"What kind of weird situation?"

Only then did it occur to me that I could talk to Brett about Skip and Erika. But not here, in the office. "This isn't a good time."

"Understood." After a brief pause, he said, "You know, my sister lives pretty close to you, in Monterey. She's been bugging me to come out for a visit. I could fly out this weekend if you're not too busy."

A rush of excitement flooded through me. "That'd be perfect."

Brett said he'd text me when he figured out his schedule. I couldn't wait to unburden myself. And to be honest, I was stoked at the prospect of seeing him. I remembered our meeting at the deli back in Chicago, the way he took my hand. I'd felt the chemistry. But did he? Suddenly nervous, I guessed I'd find out soon enough.

What the hell was I thinking? I didn't have time for this. I told myself to snap out of it and went back to Shelly's phone records. In each of the three months, she'd reached out to the police department. Which made sense. Bail bondsmen would want to verify all kinds of client information—arrest records, contact info, any past failures to appear in court. Bailing people out of jail was always a gamble. It paid to know what kind of risk you were taking.

But when I got to the month before Shelly's murder, I saw she'd called the station four times, all in the week before her death. She'd made the last call the day before. Four phone calls in less than a week. More than she'd made in the last three *months*. This had to mean something.

Tyler's argument from the "emergency discovery" hearing about a client she'd bailed out a few days before the murder came back to me. She'd used her own money to help him make bail. He'd been due to appear on his case shortly after the murder. But, according to Tyler, he'd failed to show up and had "mysteriously disappeared."

I pulled up the paperwork and read the client's name: Alberto Sanchez. Right. Moving faster now, I compared the dates on the paperwork with Shelly's calls to the Sheriff's Department. She'd made two calls to the station on the day she bailed Sanchez out. The first at 2:35 p.m., the second at 4:27. I scrolled down to the second page and saw a printout of a court docket dated three days later. It listed all the defendants who had appearances that day and the activity on each of their cases.

Alberto Sanchez was at the bottom of the list. He'd been busted for carrying an unregistered loaded gun. That's a "wobbler," i.e., a crime that can be charged as a misdemeanor or a felony. They'd charged it as a felony.

The entry next to his name said: *FTA: BWI.*

Failure to Appear: Bench Warrant Issued.

I went back to Shelly's phone records. She'd called the station for the third time on the day Sanchez failed to appear in court. Then she'd called a *fourth* time the day after. By that time, the bench warrant had already been issued. There was nothing for her to do, no reason for her to call.

Maybe she'd wanted to give the cops some more information to help them find Sanchez. She'd put up her own money for this guy. If bail got forfeited, she'd be on the hook for a chunk of change.

I sat back and drummed fingers on the desk. Was there anything worth exploring here? Tyler claimed that Sanchez absconded because he'd killed Shelly. I didn't think even Tyler bought that bullshit. Most likely Sanchez hit the road because—as Erika had said—he just didn't want to face the charges.

But what intrigued me was how Shelly seemed to have taken a particular interest in Sanchez. To put up her own money to help him make bail, to repeatedly call the cops…

And now one other thing came to mind. When I'd mentioned to Erika that I thought we ought to at least look at Sanchez, she'd dismissed the idea out of hand. Wouldn't even discuss it. That might've been because Skip had checked him out and found no connection to Shelly's murder. But Erika hadn't said that. She'd just said it was a "red herring." Maybe she'd wanted to shut me down because there *was* a connection between Sanchez and what they were hiding.

What I needed to do was talk to the cop—or cops—Shelly had spoken to. But any move I made, even just asking who those cops were, would get right back to Skip.

I'd have to tackle it from the other end and talk to Sanchez. It'd be great if he'd been picked up on the bench warrant, because he'd most likely be in custody. No one would bail him out now that he'd jumped. The problem was, in order to find out, I needed to get access to the police or court database. I knew just the person to ask, but I didn't want to make that call in the office.

I closed down my iPad, pulled on my coat, and headed out to my car. As I crossed the lot, I felt my skin crawling. *Again.* I didn't know whether to be scared or worried about my sanity. I looked around. There was no one nearby, just a forest green Land Rover and two security patrol carts in the parking lot to my right. I peered into the windows of the Land Rover. No one inside. To my left were a white Lexus and a Sheriff deputy's patrol car; I didn't see anyone in either, but I was glad to know a deputy might be close by. I turned and scanned the entrance to see if there was someone behind me. Nope. No one in the side entrance either.

But that feeling, it was so strong. Frustrated and nervous, I put my knife in my coat pocket, and with one hand on the can of Mace in my purse, I picked up my pace. I'd almost managed to convince myself I was being paranoid. But now I was forced to admit that I'd never been the type to think there were monsters in the closet—not after sitting next to so many in court. The fact that I kept getting this feeling had to mean something.

Brett had pretty much ruled out Roman. But if it wasn't him, then who? And why?

×××

MONIQUE ANSWERED MY CALL on the third ring. "What, are you my new BFF now?"

As stressed as I was, I had to smile. "It wouldn't hurt you to do a little slumming every once in a while."

She *hmph*ed. "You calling to find out what happened with your…ah, buddy?"

She meant Skip. "That, and one other thing."

Her tone was suspicious. "What other thing?"

"It's not a big deal." I looked at the car clock. Almost seven. She should be off duty by now. "Maybe I can tell you about it over a drink? I'm buying."

"You sure are."

Fifteen minutes later, she walked into The Rusty Nail. Monique was gorgeous and well aware of it. So was every male in the place, including

Pete. I watched all the heads—well, there were only three, but still—turn to stare. As she looked around, her expression said, *what the fuck?* She eyed my booth like it was a moldy urinal, then pulled a Kleenex out of her purse and wiped down the seat.

"How the hell did you find this place? Or better question, why?"

Lately, I'd been asking myself the same thing. But right now, the bar served my purpose. No one would walk in on us here.

Pete came over then and asked what we were drinking. That was a first. If you wanted a drink in the Rusty Nail, you went to the bar and ordered one. I raised an eyebrow at him, but he ignored it and asked Monique, "What can I get for you, ma'am?"

Seriously? Ma'am? Since fucking when?

"I'll have Ketel One and soda, with a slice of lime."

Pete nodded and, for the first time ever, actually smiled. "Coming up."

I held up a hand. "Not that you asked, but I'll have the same." As he headed back to the bar, I turned to Monique. "Must be fun to watch 'em get up on their hind legs and beg all the time."

She gave me a faux weary look. "Honestly, it can be a burden."

I'd forgotten how much fun she was—and what it was like to have drinks with a friend. But this wasn't a hangout. This was business. "Did Skip talk to you?"

Her expression turned serious. "Yeah. And he was pretty slick about it. Thanked me for reaching out to you."

"He's no dummy. Did Brook talk to him?" I'd primed Brook to say she'd asked Monique to get one of the Hansen prosecutors.

Monique nodded. "I saw her afterward. She's cool. You're covered."

"She really is." I hoped my letter to her judge would help. Even if it didn't, I was sure Erika's would.

Pete brought our drinks and gave Monique a glass—the cleanest one I'd ever seen in the joint—full of extra limes. "Just in case."

I could tell he wanted a reason to linger, but Monique thanked him in a way that said, *Move on, buddy.* She squeezed one of the limes into her drink and said, "FYI, he told me if there's a next time, I should call Erika. Not you." She peered at me, her expression troubled. "What the hell is going on here?"

"I have a guess, but I don't have any proof yet." I looked around, then leaned toward her. "This has to stay between us, right?"

She frowned. "Of course."

I told her what I'd been seeing and why I suspected they were either framing Mia to protect someone else or hiding something. Maybe both. Monique shook her head, her expression troubled. "That's some gnarly shit. How are you gonna figure it out?"

"I'm thinking this Alberto Sanchez guy might have some answers. That's why I need your help." I explained what I needed, and she frowned at me.

"It'll be easy enough to find out whether he got picked up on the warrant. But, Charlie, you're dealing with a couple of people who'll fuck you up hard if they find out what you're doing. How're you going to pull this off?"

I sighed. "One step at a time."

We sipped our drinks in silence, that lame answer hanging in the air between us.

CHAPTER TWENTY-THREE

Erika glanced at the digital clock on her monitor for the hundredth time. It was 6:30. Julia should have called by now. Erika was trying to get some work done while she waited, but she couldn't stop thinking about Fiona and her brother. He'd never done anything like this before. Or had he? What had happened to him? Finally, at a quarter to seven, Julia called her on Facetime. Erika hated Facetime even more than she hated talking on the phone. Her irritation must've shown –exactly why Erika hated it— because Julia said, "I know you don't love this, but if I'm doing a session via telephone, I have to be able to see as well as hear. Now what's going on, dear?"

Julia's characteristically warm, grandmotherly tone calmed Erika. It was no mystery why Danny had stuck with her all these years.

"Danny's been…" Erika had to close her eyes. The words were almost too painful to say out loud. "Stalking a woman." She could hear the mounting hysteria in her voice as she described his behavior. "I can't believe he'd ever hurt her. But I never thought he'd stalk anyone, either. And if he doesn't stop, she'll call the police."

Julia's expression was concerned. "I take it you believe this woman is telling the truth?"

Erika swallowed, squeezing her eyes shut to hold back the tears. "I—yes. I do."

Julia nodded. "I know this is very upsetting. Obviously, I'll need to see Danny right away. Can you get him to come in tomorrow around this time?"

"Yes." Erika had never gotten involved in Danny's sessions before. But this was an emergency. She'd drug him and carry him there in a wheelbarrow if she had to. "I'm planning to go see him tonight. Is there anything I can say or do to get him to stop?"

Julia sighed. "The only thing you can do is try to make him see how his behavior is impacting Fiona. Explain that it frightens her, that she doesn't reciprocate his feelings—and that he's in danger of getting arrested. I'll take it from there."

"Do you—" Erika had to force herself to ask the next question. "Do you think he might turn violent?"

Julia gazed at her with sadness. "I don't know. The fact that he's never shown a propensity for violence is certainly a good sign. And not all stalkers assault their victims. The data indicates that more than half never go that far. But that won't keep him from being arrested if he continues to behave this way."

A part of Erika couldn't believe she was having this conversation. She didn't *want* to believe it. And in that moment, the surreal feeling began to creep over her. Her heart began to race. *No! Not again!*

Julia frowned and leaned forward. "Erika? Are you all right?"

But she was gone, out of her body. She had to make herself speak, tell Julia what was happening. Her voice sounded thin and distant.

"I keep having these...spells. I feel like I'm not in my body. Like I'm watching myself from somewhere up above. And I...I'm scared that I..."

"You're afraid you'll never be able to come back."

She knew. Erika nodded, too frightened to speak.

Julia's tone was firm. "That's extremely unlikely. What you're experiencing is called dissociation. It's a known symptom of extreme anxiety."

Just hearing that made her feel better. The episode was already starting to pass. "What can I do to keep it from happening again?" Erika asked weakly.

"I can prescribe some anti-anxiety meds for you. But they tend to make you sleepy, and they won't necessarily stop the attacks from coming. They'll just take the edge off when it happens." Julia studied her, then said, "The situation with your brother is obviously very stressful, and I know you're prosecuting the Hansen case. Maybe the combination is too much."

Erika wished that was all it was. "You think I'll keep getting these episodes until everything's resolved?"

"Or until you figure out a way to deal with the stress. I assume you don't want to take anything?"

Erika shook her head. "It doesn't really sound like it'll help."

"Then the only other thing I can recommend are self-relaxation techniques like deep breathing and meditation. You can find some very good ones online."

Erika wasn't optimistic. But she had nothing to lose. "I'll give it a try. Thanks, Julia."

"My pleasure, dear. Will you be coming with Danny tomorrow?"

"I think I'd better." Erika needed to see how he responded to the session.

Julia gave Erika a sympathetic smile. "Hang in there. We can work through this."

Erika hoped Julia was right, but she'd handled stalking cases, and from what she'd seen, the perpetrators were like addicts. Even if they went to jail, they'd go right back to it the moment they got out.

She texted Danny.

I need to come by. Want me to get dinner?

Erika felt a knot form in the pit of her stomach as she waited for his answer. No matter what she did, it was going to be awful. And if he shut her out, refused to listen, well, what then?

Finally, his reply: *I already ate.*

Okay. Be there in twenty.

The knot in her stomach tightened.

×××

WHEN DANNY LET HER in, he gave her a puzzled look. "Are you okay?"

"I…yeah. Want to go sit in the living room?"

Erika loved her little brother like she'd never loved anyone in the world. It killed her to have to say what she was about to say.

"I had a visitor today. Fiona Thornberg."

He was alarmed. "She went to your office?"

Erika nodded.

"Why?"

Erika took a deep breath. "Because she didn't want to call the police on you." She met his gaze. "She said you've been stalking her, and she's scared. Really scared."

Danny's face flushed, his tone pitched up defensively. "Scared? Why? I didn't do anything to her. I just sent her some photos and a few emails. And a couple of nice cards. What's so wrong with that?"

Erika stared at him, at a loss for words. Then, gathering herself, she blurted, "She asked you to stop! What you're doing, it's a crime. She's terrified of you, Danny."

"Terrified? Why? I just told her I loved her! That she's beautiful, that—"

Erika was incredulous. "Love her? You don't even *know* her. When you wrote to her, what did she write back?"

He stared at the floor. The silence hung between them. "Nothing," he said reluctantly.

Erika spoke softly. "She did, Danny. She told you over and over again to stop contacting her. Are you saying you don't remember that?"

His voice dropped to a whisper, his gaze still on the floor. "No, I do. I just thought she'd…change her mind. She'd see how much I loved her…"

Erika had a lump in her throat. "Danny, that's not love. That's obsession. If you loved her, you'd listen to her. You'd leave her be when she said to stop contacting her. You wouldn't sit in front of her house all night or send her texts and emails and…and notes. Don't you see that?"

He looked up at her, his expression wounded. "But I don't get why she's afraid of me. I'd never do anything to hurt her. She knows that." He added in a quiet voice. "I mean, she *should* know that."

The pain in his expression made Erika's heart ache. "But she doesn't, Danny. How can she? She doesn't know you at all, and she doesn't want to. She doesn't want…you. And if you don't leave her alone, she *will* call the cops. If that happens, you'll lose your job, your career…everything."

She looked into his eyes, searching for some sign that she was getting through to him. He hung his head and said, "Okay, I get it."

Did he? Or was he just capitulating so he wouldn't have to listen to any more? Had he always been this person and she just hadn't seen it? Or were his gears slipping? If so, she might be fighting a losing battle. But she'd never give up. She'd do anything to save him.

"I've made an appointment for you to see Julia tomorrow, and I'm going with you."

He gave an exasperated sigh. "I know you're just looking out for me, but you don't have to hold my hand. I'm not a little kid."

Erika waited for him to meet her gaze, then said, "Danny, you're standing on the edge of a cliff. I'm going to do everything I can to keep you from taking that last step."

CHAPTER TWENTY-FOUR

WHEN I GOT TO THE office the next morning, I found that Tyler had hit us with a batch of motions asking to exclude all kinds of evidence, including testimony about Mia's drinking, drugging, and all-around bad behavior. We'd known it was coming, but the hearing on the motions was set for Monday, and dealing with it would take up all the time we had left before trial started.

Which meant I only had five days to figure out whether Mia was guilty. And Erika—uncharacteristically—had decided to delegate and asked me to split the motions with her. So I was really under the gun.

I worked through lunch, painfully aware that every minute counted. By 4:30, I'd managed to make a good dent in my half of the motions. Monique must've found time to get to a computer by now, I figured, and I was about to pick up my cell phone when she called.

"Hey. I'd love some good news."

"And I'd love some diamond earrings so big they'd blind a person if I turned my head just right. Looks like we're both shit out of luck."

Damn it. Sanchez hadn't been picked up. "So the warrant's still outstanding?"

"Yep. He's in the wind."

I sighed. "Okay, thanks."

I'd have to find Sanchez myself, which meant I had to get on it right now. I decided to sneak out, so Erika wouldn't know I'd left early, and pulled up Sanchez's last known address on my iPad. At the time he got busted, he'd been renting a room in a house on Raymond Street in Beach Flats.

×××

Beach Flats was just ten minutes away. I pulled to the curb in front of Sanchez's house, a small yellow ranch-style fronted by a chain link fence. As I got out of the car and headed toward the gate, that creepy feeling came over me again. I held my breath as I took in my surroundings: an ancient white pickup truck loaded with bags of something that smelled like manure parked in the driveway of the house on the right, a battered-looking bicycle chained to a tree down the street. Across the road, a red Ford Fiesta with a crucifix hanging from the rearview mirror was parked in front of a house with bars on the windows and a rusty old blue Razor on the lawn. And as usual, not a soul to be seen.

I tried to shake it off, but it was really starting to get to me. If I *was* being followed—and I had to allow for the slight possibility that I wasn't—he or she was very good. I wanted to call Brett, just to make sure he still had Roman in his sights. But I worried about being a pest—or worse, coming off like some paranoid nutcase.

When I knocked on the door of Sanchez's old house, I saw the front windows were covered with cardboard. No one answered. I knocked again and leaned in to listen for any movements. Silence.

Next door, a short woman with a braid down to her waist answered my knock. I told her in my not-ready-for-primetime Spanish that I was a friend of Alberto's, that I was worried about him, and asked if she'd seen him lately.

She shook her head. "I just live here one week. *Pero*, I never see nobody in that house."

Assuming she was right and the house was vacant, that killed any chance of talking to Sanchez's housemates. I thanked her and moved down the street. Only two other neighbors answered their doors, and both claimed not to have seen Sanchez recently. They said they didn't know anything about his housemates, either, but I wasn't buying it. The houses were small, flimsy, and tightly packed. If someone was yelling in their living room, the people three houses down could probably hear every word.

But I couldn't blame them. I was just some *gringa* who claimed to be Sanchez's friend. For all they knew, I might be from ICE.

It was starting to get dark. I decided to call it quits, but as I headed back to my car, the prickling between my shoulder blades got stronger than ever. I tried to stay calm as I surreptitiously looked into the cars parked along the street. Was that a man, slouched down in a black SUV up ahead?

Barely breathing, I walked past, straining to see out of the corner of my eye—and ready at any second to break into a run and yell for help.

But I didn't see anyone. Had I been mistaken? Or had he been hiding? The prickling between my shoulder blades spread across my back as I pictured Roman jumping out and coming after me. *Screw the calm act.* No one was around to appreciate it anyway. I ran the rest of the way to my car. I'd just pushed the buttons to turn on the engine and lock the doors when someone rapped on my window. I shot up in my seat, about to scream, then saw it was a young Latina woman, holding her hands together, prayer-like.

"Please, I hear you're looking for Alberto."

I swallowed and tried to catch my breath as I turned off the engine. My heart was still pounding as I got out. I told her my name was Katie and gave her my cover story. "I'm worried about him. I was hoping maybe someone in the neighborhood had been in touch."

She said her name was Laura and that Sanchez was a good friend of hers, too. "He got deported a few months ago, so he was gone for a while. But then he came back. When I saw him, he told me they arrested him, like, a day or so after he got here." She paused, her expression concerned. "He was acting all scared and nervous, you know? Not, like, normal."

He might've just been afraid of facing charges. Between felony possession of a gun and illegal entry, he might do some real prison time before he got deported again. "When did you last talk to Alberto?"

She knitted her brow. "I think it was just, like, maybe a week ago?"

So he was still in town—*after* Tyler claimed he'd disappeared. To my mind, the fact that Sanchez had stuck around after Shelly's murder eliminated any possibility that he'd killed her. I pointed to the yellow house. "Was he living there at the time?"

Laura shook her head. "He said he was staying with friends. He didn't say where, but it had to be close by because I ran into him on this street."

The yellow house was the address he'd given Shelly and the police. So he'd moved without telling anyone. That told me Laura was right about him being scared. And it might mean Sanchez was worried about more than just doing time.

I gave Laura my number. "Please call me if you hear anything, okay? And thanks for talking to me. You're the only one around here who would."

She lifted her hands. "People are...nervous these days. You know?"

I did. We promised to stay in touch and as she left, I decided to try and canvass the next street over. But as I started the car, I saw a black and white police cruiser drive by at the end of the block. Shit! If the cops spotted me here, they might tell Skip. I'd have to find another way.

× × ×

SINCE I WAS CLOSE TO Lower Ocean, I decided to treat myself to some tacos from Lupe's. It was completely dark by the time I got there. As I walked up to the window, a lowered, metallic green car blasting Spanish rap pulled into the parking lot. Lupe glanced at it with a guarded look as she took my order, and when I finished, I saw her reach under the counter before moving to the grill. Probably making sure her gun was at the ready.

I stepped back and took out my phone. A beefy white guy with stretchers and a nose ring got out of the car. Two others rolled out behind him: a tattooed wonder with a cigarette hanging out of his mouth and a skinny, long-haired Latino kid.

I went back to my email as they walked over to the stand and gave their orders. When they finished, the beefy white guy shuffled toward me. "Hey, *chica*. What's good? Wanna have some fun?"

The tattooed guy swaggered over and blew out a smoke ring as he looked me up and down. "You seem like the kind of girl who can party *hard*."

I knew I should ignore them and go wait in my car. But I was in a lousy mood, frustrated by the slow progress I was making and rattled by the nonstop feeling that someone was following me. "You seem like the kind of guy who can only fuck something that has an air valve."

The beefy one moved in close and glared down at me. "Bitch, what'd you say?"

A bolt of red-hot anger shot through me. "Yeah, I don't think so." I jammed my three-inch heel into his instep as hard as I could and twisted it.

He screamed in pain and started to raise his fist, but Lupe shouted. "I got a gun, *pendejo*!"

Over his shoulder, I saw her pointing her .45 caliber. He turned and threw up his hands. "It's cool. I'm cool." He backed up but glared at me over his shoulder as he hissed, "You better hope I never catch you alone."

I was still shaking with rage as he limped away. Lupe waved me over and shoved my order toward me. As I took the bag, I saw that she'd left the gun on top of the counter. "Thanks."

"Why you always gotta get into it with *cabrons* like that? You jus' askin' for it. Don't come back here! You gonna get me killed." After she spat out this last, she slammed the window shut.

When I got to my car, I looked over the roof at the three amigos. They were mad dogging me. I laughed and held up a middle finger, then took off.

But as the adrenalin ebbed away, I stopped laughing. It'd felt good to stomp that jerkweed, but it wasn't smart. If Lupe hadn't been there, I'd have wound up in the hospital—if I was lucky.

And now, her words came back to me. *Was* I asking for it? I'd brushed it off when Pete said something similar. Skip, too. But they were right. If I kept it up, one of these days, I'd get what I was asking for. I just didn't know whether that felt like a threat or a promise.

I tabled the existential question and focused on the more immediate issue. Sanchez was a possible lead, but I had no idea how to find him, and I only had five days. Even if Laura did get a line on his whereabouts, it might be too late.

My other source of intel was even harder to tap: the cops Shelly had spoken to, ostensibly about Sanchez. But I couldn't think of a way to find out who they were—let alone talk to them—without tipping Skip off.

For the first time, I considered giving up my crusade. Maybe I should just dump it all in Harrier's lap and let him run with it. Problem was, I didn't have any faith that he would. All I had were suspicions with zero solid evidence. It'd come down to my word against Skip and Erika's—and they'd just lie. And frame me up for the Dante leak. Harrier would be happy to let them bury me. If Erika, the veteran he'd entrusted with the biggest cases in the county for years, went down, he'd go down with her. Me? I was a relative nobody. If I got called out for unethical conduct, there'd be no fallout for him. No, I had to keep going. It was the only shot I had at finding the evidence that'd break it all open—or shut it all down.

CHAPTER TWENTY-FIVE

A s Erika got dressed for her lunch with Phillip and Rochelle, she got a text from Skip asking her to stop by the station. Her spirits lifted. Maybe he'd dug up some dirt on Charlie.

In the car, she took deep breaths and gave herself a pep talk. *If it happens again, just remember that it'll pass, you'll come out of it.* She decided to try listening to a podcast. Something to keep her mind off of everything. She'd heard of one that featured self-made business success stories. It sounded interesting—and safe.

She found it on her phone, then hit the road. Driving surface streets was already getting old. Especially when she seemed to get stuck at every red light. But the podcast helped, let her think about something different, and she got to the Sheriff's Department without a hitch.

Skip led her to an interrogation room and made sure the cameras and mics were turned off. "One of my unis spotted Charlie in Beach Flats."

"I thought you weren't going to get anyone else involved in this," Erika said, alarmed.

"I didn't. It was a lucky break. He happened to be driving by yesterday and noticed her standing on the sidewalk, talking to some Latina woman."

This might be the worst-case scenario. "Beach Flats? Isn't that where Sanchez was staying?"

He nodded. "The uni didn't remember what street she was on. He wasn't making a big thing of it, just thought it was weird seeing her there, in that neighborhood. I couldn't press him too hard for specifics without sounding a little *too* interested."

"No, you're right. But what the hell was she doing?"

He shrugged. "She might've been asking for directions. I guess we'll have to wait and see. I did make some progress on her background check. Got two hits on the Illinois State Bar records for a Charlotte Blair. One was a woman in her eighties. The other was a woman who got admitted the same year as Charlie. The thing is, her status shows she's been inactive for the past year—"

Erika sat up. According to Charlie's résumé, she'd been active and practicing right up until she left Chicago a few months ago. "That doesn't jive."

"Exactly. I have to warn you, the state bar website doesn't list date of birth, so I can't be a hundred percent sure the woman I found on the website *isn't* her. But her profile doesn't show she worked at Charlie's law firm. And it should, shouldn't it? Don't you guys have to keep the state bar up to date with things like that?"

"Yeah, definitely."

Skip put his hands on his knees. "I'm thinking our girl Charlie *isn't*... Charlie."

Erika stared, at a loss for words. She hadn't known what Skip would find, but she hadn't expected anything like this. "If you're right, her old boss lied for her."

"Assuming he even *was* her old boss. He might just be a friend who was willing to do her a favor."

"What about the law firm's website? Does it show her having been an associate?"

"No. But it didn't show any of their past associates. Just current ones. I did some superficial checking on the boss, and he seems to be clean, apart from maybe lying for her. I guess I could try and use that to strong-arm, but—"

Erika held up a hand. "No, don't do that. We want leverage, not a lawsuit."

"Agreed. I'd like to try and social engineer some information out of the associates. See if I can get someone to chat about who the boss's friends are. If I get lucky, I might find out which one of them left town around the time Charlie showed up in Santa Cruz."

Erika played that out, then nodded. "As long as you keep it general—and make sure you don't slip up and say the name Charlie." They couldn't risk him warning her and giving her a chance to cover up whatever it was she was hiding.

"Don't worry. I'll be smooth as glass. But if she did all that—changed her name, dummied up her résumé, *and* moved across the country to join the other side—there had to be a damn good reason."

"Just be careful, Skip. No one can know about this." To investigate one of their own, he'd need authorization from the top. If it came out he'd done it on the sly, he'd be in big trouble. And opening an official investigation was exactly what they *didn't* want.

"Definitely not. But it's going to limit what I can do."

"Understood." Erika felt like she'd sunk to a new low, even though it had been her idea. "Somehow, this feels even worse than setting her up for the whole Dante thing."

Skip lowered his gaze. "Yeah. But look, even if I find something on her, we won't necessarily have to use it."

Erika's expression was one of sad resignation. "Unless we do."

×××

SHE DROVE TO THE office, emotions warring within her. Charlie hadn't asked for any of this. The opposite, in fact. But she was smart and savvy. Whoever she'd been in her past life, it was clear to Erika that she not only knew her way around a murder case, she knew how to investigate one. If her appearance in Beach Flats meant she'd decided to find out what was going on in the Hansen case, she might succeed. And that would be catastrophic.

Like it or not, they had to get dirt on her to protect themselves. It was yet another in the long series of consequences Erika hadn't foreseen and certainly hadn't intended.

She pulled into the parking lot and stared at the building where she'd spent the happiest years of her life. If someone had told her just two months ago that she'd be in the middle of a horrible predicament—of her *own* making, no less—she'd have called them crazy. She'd always tried to do the right thing. To be the good guy.

Going so far astray made her question everything about herself. She didn't know who she was anymore, didn't recognize this person who did what she'd done. What she *was* doing. But this part of her must've been lurking inside all along. She just hadn't known it was there. And now that she did, she'd never be able to see herself as that good guy again.

Erika headed to her office. She was worried about Skip's plan. It'd only take one wrong word for someone at Charlie's old firm to get suspicious and sound the alarm. And if Skip got caught, he might get fired. One more thing Erika would never forgive herself for.

She worked steadily until it was time for her lunch with the Hemingsworths, then reluctantly shut down her computer and left. The only good news was that it wouldn't take long. Phillip didn't do leisurely.

The sun was drifting in and out from behind fluffy white clouds, which hung in a rich powder blue sky. Erika actually found herself enjoying the drive as she listened to her podcast. And the restaurant, Shadowbrook, was perfect for a day like this. It had seven dining rooms, each with a different view. Phillip always asked for—demanded—the one looking out on Soquel Creek. It would've been a nice peaceful break if she was with anyone else.

She found Phillip and Rochelle already enjoying a glass of white wine. Erika shook hands with Phillip and hugged Rochelle, who looked pale and drawn. And way too thin.

Phillip held up his glass. "You really should try this Pinot Grigio. It's excellent."

Erika wouldn't dream of having a drink with Phillip under any circumstances, but especially not now, when she knew he'd spend the next hour throwing questions and hypotheticals at her like she was a human dartboard. "Thanks, but I have to go back to work."

The waiter came over to take their orders. Erika decided on the creamy artichoke soup. She thought it might be easy enough on her stomach to go down and stay down. Phillip ordered shrimp scampi for himself and Rochelle, who ordered another glass of wine. Phillip gave her a disapproving look, but Rochelle shrugged him off with an, "I'll be fine."

Her voice was brittle, strained. Erika looked at her, then at Phillip. Did he see that his wife was suffering? Maybe. But in all fairness, he was, too. In his own bullying, obnoxious way.

The waiter had barely stepped away from the table before Phillip started in. "I was thinking about what you said the other day. How the defense would probably bring in statements from jurors saying they would've voted to acquit if they'd known about T. Rayne's prior arrest. Based on my research, it doesn't seem they can get away with that."

Here we go. "No, the affidavits aren't admissible. But that doesn't mean they won't try."

As she'd predicted, it went on and on all through lunch. She barely had a chance to taste her soup. Which was okay, because she'd lost her appetite. She made her answers as lengthy as possible so Phillip would shut up and eat his shrimp. When they'd finished, she mentally breathed a sigh of relief.

Phillip stood up. "Excuse me, I'm going to use the restroom." He looked down at Rochelle. "Get the waiter to bring us the check. We need to leave, or we'll be late."

As soon as he was out of the room, Rochelle leaned over and put a hand on Erika's forearm, her expression tense but weary. "I'm so sorry for… everything."

Erika looked into her eyes. "I know."

"I wish he'd stop obsessing about the new trial motion," Rochelle sighed. "You've made it perfectly clear there's no reason to worry."

Her words pierced Erika's heart. She might very well lose that motion, and she was painfully aware that if she did, it'd be her fault. Rochelle's worn features, the sorrow in her eyes—it was all a visceral reminder of the horrifying impact that loss would have on the Hemingsworths. Erika didn't know if she could live with the guilt. But she couldn't let Rochelle see any hint of doubt.

She forced a confident tone. "No, there's nothing to worry about."

CHAPTER TWENTY-SIX

A<small>S I FINISHED THE LAST</small> of my responses to Tyler's motions, I saw that it was after six o'clock. I made sure my iPad was in my briefcase and headed out, wondering whether Erika's little fisherman, Tanya, had squeezed anything out of Mia yet. I wouldn't find out until they were done using her—which might not happen until the very end of the trial.

Distracted by my disgust, I didn't notice the envelope tucked under the windshield wiper of my car until I reached for the door handle. I tried to see if it had my name on it, but from what I could tell, it seemed to be blank. I looked around to see if there were similar envelopes on the other cars. No. Only mine.

Alarm bells ringing in my head, I spun around, hoping to catch sight of the person who'd put it there. But all I saw were two women on the cleaning crew moving toward the building, and a kid racing down the street on a mountain bike. I tried to tell myself it was probably no big deal, but my heart was pounding. Grasping the envelope by a corner, I carefully pulled it out and turned it over. It was blank. My foreboding mounted.

At home, I locked the door with the deadbolt and put the envelope on the kitchen table. I wiped my sweaty palms on my jacket and, using a knife, pried open the flap.

I shook the envelope and a greeting card fell out. It showed a drawing of two hands holding a vase of flowers. I held my breath as I flipped it open. No signature, just the preprinted words, "Thinking of You" in flowery script.

I backed away from the card, shaking, as its menacing import became clear. No more room for doubt. Someone was definitely following me, watching me. And they wanted to make sure I knew it. It had to be Roman. No one else would gaslight me like this.

Panicked, I called Brett but got his voicemail. He would've told me if Roman had left Chicago. And yet I couldn't imagine who else it could be.

The piercing sound of a car alarm broke into my thoughts, the noise rattling my already-frayed nerves. *Someone turn that thing off*, I prayed, but it kept going and going. Wait. Was it *my* car alarm? Had Roman followed me home?! I picked up my phone to call 9-1-1, then, belatedly, sanity kicked in, reminding me that, A) It might *not* be my car, and B) even if it was, my alarm went off every time the damn Escalade in apartment 4B drove past it. Still, before I headed downstairs to the garage, I put my knife in my pocket and grabbed my can of Mace.

The apartment building only had twenty units, so the garage was relatively small, and the owner kept it well lit. There didn't seem to be anyone around. And the offending car alarm was definitely mine.

I moved toward my car, remote in hand, and hit the button. But as the alarm stopped, a short, wiry Latino man stepped out from behind the rear bumper. I gasped and jumped back as I held up my can of Mace and shouted, "Who the hell are you?"

He recoiled and raised his hands. "I'm Carlos Sanchez! Laura give me *su numero*. She say you look for *mi hermano*."

His brother. "Alberto Sanchez?"

He nodded. This was just what I'd hoped for, but it seemed too good to be true.

"Why didn't you just call me?" I asked.

His gaze was fixed on the can of Mace. "I try, *pero* you no answer. Maybe *porque* you don't know *mi numero*."

I still wasn't sure. Roman could've sent him to track me down. But I did religiously screen my calls. And if I didn't recognize the number, I let it go to voicemail. I was starting to think he might be legit. "Why not leave a message?"

"*Su telefono* say mailbox *lleno*."

That was fair. My voicemail box probably *was* full. I'd blocked about a million spam callers, but that didn't stop them from leaving messages.

His tone was earnest. "*Y ayer* I see you in Alberto's *barrio*. I try to talk to you, but you go away *muy rapido*. So I follow you *a su casa*. I wait *por* you come out. But I make alarm…sorry."

Slowly, I lowered the can of Mace. If he was telling the truth—and I thought he was—Carlos obviously hadn't been the one following me. I didn't love the idea of bringing him up to my apartment, but we couldn't talk here. And going out in public, where a cop or the guy who *was* following me could see us, was even worse.

"We shouldn't talk here. Come on."

I led him upstairs and offered him a bottle of water, but he declined. "Do you live in that *barrio* where you saw me?" I asked.

He shook his head. "I went there to look for Alberto. No one knows nothing."

So those neighbors I'd talked to weren't dusting me off. If *Carlos* couldn't get intel on Sanchez's whereabouts, then they really didn't know. "When did you last hear from your brother?"

"*La semana pasada.*"

Last week. Not that long. I took in his worried expression. "What makes you think something's wrong?"

He swallowed hard. "*De ordinario*, I don't worry. *Pero* he was very scared. I tell him to come stay with me. He say he coming. But he don't come. And he don't answer his *telefono*."

Scared. That's what Laura had said, too. "Did he say what he was afraid of?"

Carlos gripped the edge of the seat. "He…no. *Pero* he say after he talk to *la abogada del gobeirno*—"

The whoop of a police siren came screaming through the window. I held up a hand to stop him and went over to shut it. "I'm sorry, can you repeat that?"

"He say after he talk to *la abogada del gobeirno*, bad things happen to him."

The government lawyer. *Abogada*. A woman. "Did he tell you her name?"

He shook his head. "No."

"What did he say to her?"

Carlos leaned in and spoke rapidly, his English now almost completely gone. I had to ask him to slow down and repeat it all twice. As I translated what he said, my brain struggled to make sense of it.

Sanchez had told this prosecutor that he saw "the chef on the night the woman got killed." It sounded like Sanchez had been talking about the Steers case. But how could that be?

"What else did he tell her, *la abogada*?"

Carlos began to rub his knees as his speech grew in intensity.

He said Sanchez had been a dishwasher in the restaurant across the street, so he saw the chef every day. Sanchez told the lawyer he'd been working late on the night of the murder. He remembered that he'd seen the chef leaving the restaurant around midnight.

I stared at Carlos, unable to breathe as I realized what this meant.

Midnight was well after Natalie had been killed. And Steers' restaurant was an hour away from her house.

Alberto Sanchez had given Steers *a complete alibi*. Holy mother of God.

There was only one female prosecutor who could've spoken to him: Erika. I felt like the top of my head was about to blow off.

"Did he tell you what *la abogada* said when he gave his statement?" I was almost breathless.

He wrinkled his brow, then said, "He see that she don't like what he say. She ask if he is *seguro...muchas veces.*"

She asked if he was sure, over and over again. A very ugly picture was beginning to emerge. As I asked the next question, I felt like I was running toward an oncoming train. "How long after he spoke to *la abogada* did he get deported?"

Carlos looked at me, his expression angry and sad. "Two days."

I fought to come up with an innocent explanation. "Did Alberto get arrested for anything?"

"No, he don't do nothing. They just...take him. Á Guatemala."

"Did he think *la abogada* got him deported?"

Carlos nodded. *"Esta claro, no?"*

Yeah, it was clear. In any language. He pissed off the prosecutor and two days later he's on a plane to Mexico. The connection was hard to miss. But one thing puzzled me. "If Alberto was so scared, why did he come back?"

Carlos gave a heavy sigh as he explained that Sanchez had money hidden somewhere, and he'd come back to get it. He'd planned to return to Guatemala, but then he'd gotten arrested.

"Why didn't he just ask you to pick it up and send it to him?" Carlos said he hadn't been living here. He'd been staying with his girlfriend in San Diego. Sanchez only called him after he got arrested, to ask for help—probably with bail money. But my guess was, by the time Carlos arrived, Shelly had kicked in some of her own funds.

"Did Alberto tell you the name of the cop who arrested him?"

Carlos paused, then shook his head.

Could it have been Skip? It was one of a thousand questions flying around in my head. I needed some time to absorb all this. Carefully, I said, "Did Alberto tell anyone else about that prosecutor getting him deported?"

His tone was emphatic. "No. *El tenia miedo. Muy peligroso.*"

He was too scared to tell anyone. I'll bet. I took Carlos' phone number, walked him out to his car, and watched him drive away, thinking he was right. It would've been *muy peligroso*—very dangerous—for Sanchez to talk. And it still was—assuming he was alive.

But I could think of one person he might've felt safe enough to tell: his bail bondsman, Shelly Hansen.

CHAPTER TWENTY-SEVEN

I GOT BACK TO my apartment, mind whirling.

Sanchez had alibi'd Blake Steers. And Erika had lost her shit. She buried his statement and got him deported so the defense wouldn't be able to find him.

I got why she'd done it. She didn't want to risk that sociopathic piece-of-shit getting off. There was no doubt in my mind that Steers was guilty. Sanchez was just wrong.

But what Erika had done was un-fucking-believable. Morally. Ethically. And of course, legally. Hiding Sanchez's exculpatory statement was bad enough. Getting him thrown out of the country was downright dangerous. ICE wasn't careful where they dumped deportees. For all Erika knew, Sanchez had fled gang turf because his life was in danger—and ICE had tossed him right back into the thick of it. She should've turned over Sanchez's statement and shredded him on cross.

How could he be so sure he'd seen Steers on the night of the murder? Did he write it down? *No.* Why would he? Did something unusual happen to Sanchez that night? *Probably not.* When he saw Steers, did he tell any of his coworkers, "Hey, there's Blake Steers"? *No, of course not.*

Thanks, Mr. Sanchez. No further questions.

But then Erika would've had to let the jury make the call. And she knew they might not make the right one. The case had been a hard-fought battle, and if any of us doubted just how close it'd been, the jurors' comments to reporters had squashed those doubts but good. It'd been hard to believe

Steers had killed "that girl," they said. They'd talked about how difficult the decision was, how some of them "worried" they hadn't done the right thing. And that was *without* an alibi witness like Sanchez. If he'd testified, it was entirely possible the jury would've walked Steers out the door.

Erika couldn't let that happen. So she—or maybe Skip—had gotten Sanchez deported. They were both in on it, that seemed clear to me. Although Sanchez hadn't mentioned Skip, he had to have been with Erika during the interview. And Sanchez's statement had never surfaced, so they must both have agreed to shred it.

I turned the call to ICE over in my mind. The agency didn't have the manpower to act on every tip they got. And Skip and Erika had needed to make sure they got Sanchez out of the country fast. They would've had to flash their badges to make sure they got action. And no doubt they'd asked the agent to keep it quiet, which meant there wouldn't be any record of their contact. No help for me there. I supposed Sanchez might've been picked up in a sweep, but that would've been a hell of a coincidence. Didn't pass the smell test.

So what must've happened after Sanchez got deported? I sat back and crossed my arms. He manages to get back into the country to pick up his money but winds up in jail. He's scared—and pretty damn sure Erika got him deported. He figures she'll try to do it again, and he turns to the only person he can think of who might be able to help: Shelly.

Who maybe doesn't believe him right off the bat. With over twenty years of experience in the bail bonds business, Shelly would have known that getting a witness deported was a horrible—and highly illegal—thing to do. But Sanchez's story is hard to dismiss. Shelly's convinced enough to put up her own money to help him make bail. And she decides to check it out. That scenario explained the unusual number of calls Shelly had made to the cops. She'd called to tell them what Sanchez was saying.

During my conversation with Carlos, I'd wondered whether Skip had been the one who'd arrested Sanchez. But now I realized that the last thing Skip or Erika would've wanted was to keep him around. Steers' new trial motion was still pending. And one of the best ways for the defense to get a retrial was to show they had newly discovered evidence that might've made a difference in the verdict. Sanchez's testimony was a defense attorney's dream come true.

Shelly would have known that. Steers' defense had been doing every cable and network talk show they could get. It was just limelight-sucking, saber-rattling bullshit. But if they heard Sanchez's story, they'd have the real deal. And now, as I put it all together, I realized what it meant: Shelly had been killed to keep her from talking about Sanchez. The Steers case and the Hansen case were connected. And Sanchez was the link.

I went to my iPad and opened the file with Shelly's phone records. I was right. Shelly was killed the day after she made her fourth, and last, call to the Sheriff's station. For all I knew Sanchez might be dead, too. The thought gave me chills.

But Shelly and Sanchez didn't just pose a serious threat to Steers' conviction. They also posed a huge personal threat to Erika and Skip. Getting Sanchez deported to keep him from testifying was felony-level witness tampering and obstruction of justice. They'd be fired, Erika would be disbarred, and they'd both face criminal charges and prison time.

Even if Sanchez wasn't around to make the claim himself, Shelly's report of what he'd said would most certainly get action. She had credibility. She was a successful businesswoman, well known and liked in the community. And although her statement about what Sanchez had told her was hearsay, it'd be enough to persuade a judge to order an investigation. The defense would pull out all the stops to find Sanchez—assuming he was alive—and with Steers' money, they'd probably succeed.

Then it hit me. Of course Sanchez was alive. That's why Erika was in a big hot hurry to get Shelly's case done. She was afraid he'd show up and the whole story would come rolling out. She wouldn't be so scared if he were dead.

What would happen if he did surface? If Shelly's murder trial was still pending, he'd make the defense—and the judge—take a closer look at the suspicious timing of the date he made his statement to Erika, the date of his deportation, and the timing of Shelly's phone calls and her date of death.

That was why Mia had to get convicted fast. Because once she was found guilty, Sanchez's story would carry a lot less weight. A jury would've already ruled that a drugged-out girl with a big grudge killed her mother in a fit of rage. Case closed.

But if I was right, Mia was innocent.

There was just one big problem with my theory: it seemed to point to Skip or Erika as Shelly's murderer. I leaned back, rubbing my temples. Dumping evidence and strong-arming witnesses was one thing. Murder, especially a brutal murder like Shelly's, was a bridge too far. I didn't buy it. And if they hadn't killed Sanchez, the source of the damning evidence—which clearly, they hadn't—then why kill Shelly, who was just a second-hand witness?

But that begged the question: if it wasn't them, then who? I couldn't think of anyone else with the motive and the means.

I had to consider the possibility that I was wrong.

And if I was wrong, then Mia *had* to be guilty.

But no. I shook my head, sat forward. To me it seemed far more likely that Erika and Skip knew Mia was innocent, and they needed her to take the fall so they could cover for the real killer.

It all…fit.

So say I was right. Then what? I began to pace, wishing I could talk to Brett. But when I'd called earlier, it had gone to voice mail. I circled the living room my body so tense, every muscle ached. I had no clue who might've killed Shelly and no idea how to figure it out. All I had going for me was Carlos. But even if he were willing to come forward—by no means a guarantee—his statement wouldn't be enough to prove what Erika and Skip had done. It'd help if I could find Sanchez, but if he was dodging his own brother, I didn't like my chances.

The only other avenue was the one that posed the biggest risk of exposure: find the cop Shelly had spoken to and get him to tell me what she'd said. But that was sure to alert Skip.

Feeling like a huge weight had settled on me, I went to the kitchen and made a drink. It was one thing to question whether Mia was guilty. It was a vastly different thing to know she might well be innocent but not have a clue what to do about it.

I stared down at my glass, filled with self-loathing. Someone else probably would've known what to do, but I didn't. I wasn't good enough.

Just like I hadn't been good enough to spot Roman, missing every sign that should've clued me in to what he was. I'd failed to save Lyra, and now I was failing to save Mia. Clearly the only thing I did know how to do was get drunk. Mia deserved so much better.

I finished my drink and poured myself another. I was halfway through it and starting to feel the buzz when my cell phone rang.

Brett.

My encounter with Carlos had momentarily eclipsed the discovery of that greeting card. I'd left it on the kitchen table, unwilling to touch it again. As I glanced at it now the terror came rushing back. I sat up abruptly and painfully sober and told him what had happened.

"I've got to ask. Are you sure Roman's still in Chicago?"

"From what I've seen, he's been home the whole time," Brett said, perplexed. "I check the surveillance footage at his condo every day, and I've seen him driving in and out. He's got a black Mercedes sports coupe, right?"

"Right." My head throbbed. This made no sense.

"I was going to fly out to you tomorrow, but I think I'd better stick around and do some more digging."

Already in a miserable frame of mind, my spirits sank even lower. I hadn't realized just how much I'd been looking forward to seeing Brett. But I wanted to stay alive. My stomach dropped. I thanked him, then poured myself another drink—and prayed he'd find something soon.

CHAPTER TWENTY-EIGHT

D ANNY SAID ALL THE right things during his session with Julia. That he realized he'd let his imagination run wild; that he'd built a fantasy out of a few minutes of conversation with a stranger. But did he believe it? As children, he and Erika had both learned to say what people wanted to hear.

Erika's gaze drifted to her desk, to the framed selfie of her and Danny at Magic Mountain. It'd been taken a few months after she'd left for college. When she'd moved out, she'd sworn never to set foot in that house of horrors again. But leaving Danny behind had filled her with guilt—he was just fourteen—so they found ways to meet in different places. She smiled as she remembered how they'd made themselves sick, riding Goliath over and over, the hamburgers they'd had for lunch not making it past ride seven.

For Erika, those trips were more than just a way to stay in contact. They were a way to reassure Danny that she'd always be there to take care of him. From the day he was born, Erika had been as much a mother to him as a sister. She'd never questioned her role before. But now, for the first time, she worried about her ability to do it. She could only hope that with Julia's help, he'd pull through this.

She turned back to her computer with a sigh. Their responses to Tyler's motions were due in just three days, and they'd start jury selection right after that. She'd have to work through lunch *and* dinner to make sure she was ready. But that was fine by her. The trial couldn't come soon enough.

×××

THAT AFTERNOON, SKIP SHOWED up unexpectedly. "I know you're busy, but I wanted to pass on some good news."

"I'm never too busy for that."

He closed the door. "One of the unis on the case got a call from a neighbor who lives around the corner from Shelly. Said he saw a person who looked small enough to be female running away from the crime scene at around one thirty in the morning."

"Might be Mia?"

Skip nodded. That *did* sound good.

"So she was probably getting rid of the murder weapon."

"That's my take."

"Any description?"

"Only that she must've had dark hair because he would've noticed if she was blonde." He added, "You'll get more out of him, I'm sure."

"Hopefully." But dark hair was a good start. It was one hell of a windfall if it played out. "Where's this guy been? Why didn't he tell the unis when they door knocked?"

"He was up in Toronto. His wife was home, but she didn't know he'd seen anything. He told the uni that by the time he got back, Mia was already in custody, so he figured the cops didn't need him. He only came forward now because his wife guilted him into it."

"Is anyone searching the area she was headed toward?" If they could find the murder weapon there, the case would be a solid winner.

"Sent a team of unis out, and I've got a call in to the guy. I'll let you know as soon as he gets back to me."

Skip stood up, but Erika held up a hand. "Wait. Did you manage to talk to anyone at Charlie's law firm?"

"Yeah, sorry. I meant to tell you." He sat back down, mouth twisted sourly. "I didn't get diddly squat. I posed as a PR person for a law school alumni association. Said we were looking to do hero pieces on some of the best grads, like their boss, so we were trying to round up his friends, past and present, to get some quotes."

Erika was impressed. "Nice. And really? Nothing?"

He shook his head. "They just didn't know anything about the boss's social life—past or present."

"Is that the end of the line, then?"

"Until I can think of another way to go."

A part of her was relieved, Erika had to admit.

Skip called her an hour later, saying that the man could meet with them today. "And we'd better go now, because he said he has to catch a six o'clock flight."

It was 4:30. "I'm ready. You mind driving?" Erika hadn't had one of her episodes since her FaceTime call with Julia, but she didn't want to risk it happening again in front of Skip.

He said he'd pick her up in ten minutes. Erika finished the last lines of the response, pulled on her coat and headed downstairs, where Skip's car was idling at the curb. "Thanks for being the chauffeur. What's this guy's name again?"

"Lewis Argonian."

Hopefully he was as good as he seemed. Witnesses sometimes backed off when it was time to give their official statement. If he changed his tune and gave a description that eliminated Mia, it'd be big trouble.

Which was why Erika had decided not to bring Charlie.

× × ×

Lewis answered the door with an irritable expression, his tone brusque. "Come in. But you'll have to make this quick. Like I said, I've got a flight."

He led them into a small living room and waved them over to the blue chenille sofa. Lewis took the wingback chair across from them as he straightened the collar of his plaid button-down shirt.

Erika was glad he didn't want to waste time on small talk. "I understand it was about one thirty in the morning when you saw this person running?"

He folded his arms across his chest. "I never said the person was running. Just moving fast."

"Understood." Erika took in his body language and the defiant note in his voice. Lewis was definitely the prickly type, which meant he'd be tough to bend. Hopefully she wouldn't need to. "Did something wake you up? Or were you just up that late?"

"I'm always up late. So, no. Nothing woke me."

Then he'd been fairly alert. She didn't know whether that was a good thing or a bad thing. "Where were you when you saw her?"

He wagged a finger at her. "Don't you go putting words in my mouth. I didn't say it was a female. All I said was the person *could've* been a woman. But it might've been a man."

Not great, but at least he hadn't eliminated Mia. Yet. "Sorry. Could you tell the approximate height or weight of this person? Heavy-set? Thin? Medium?"

His brow furrowed. "I...no, not really. I mean, the person wasn't heavy. I'm sure of that. But they could've been medium or thin. And height?" He shook his head. "Not my strong suit. All I can say is, I'm sure they weren't as tall as me."

Erika took in his lanky frame. "You're about six foot one or two?"

"Six foot. Used to be six foot one, but you know...old age."

This was all pretty vague, but so far, they were safe. "Did you notice this person's hair?"

Lewis sighed. "Like I told that patrol officer, I thought the person might have dark hair because I would've noticed if it were blonde. And if you're going to ask me whether I noticed what they were wearing, the answer's no."

Erika could tell he was out of patience. "Can you show us where you were when you saw this person?"

"Yeah." He led them into the kitchen and nodded toward the window over the sink. "I was standing right there."

The window had an unobstructed view of the street. "Where did you see the person?"

Lewis moved in next to Erika and pointed to the corner. "Right there. They were heading up that way, to the left."

Erika had seen photos of the neighborhood. There were several houses and a vacant lot in that direction. Unfortunately, the unis had already canvassed them and come up empty-handed. Lewis was all she had.

As she took in the view, she noticed there weren't any streetlights nearby. No wonder his description was so loose. "One last question. Did the person appear to be holding anything in either hand?"

He frowned. "Could've been, I guess. I only saw them from the side."

"So you didn't see them from behind?" Erika asked.

"No." He glanced at his watch. "We about done here? I've got to finish packing."

Erika looked at Skip. He said, "We are," and held out his hand. "Thanks for your time."

Lewis reluctantly shook hands, then led them to the door. "When do I have to come to court?"

"We start picking a jury next week," Erika said. "So probably around ten days. We'll call you with an update when we know more."

As Skip pulled away from the curb, Erika gave voice to her thoughts. "He won't hurt us. In fact, he might even do us some good."

Skip agreed, and they rode in silence back to the office. "Look, about Charlie's past. I'm gonna keep trying. There's got to be something there."

Erika thanked him, though she wasn't optimistic, and headed up to her office. She'd just booted up her computer when Charlie stopped by. "So how'd it go with the neighbor?"

"Pretty well. Argonian's description's a little loose, but it sounds like Mia." She told Charlie what he'd said.

Charlie's tone was dismissive. "Not exactly a game-changer. Sounds to me like it could be anyone."

That seemed awfully negative. Erika pushed back, just to see what Charlie might do. "Maybe, standing alone. But it won't be. When we add it to the rest of the evidence, I think it'll be pretty compelling."

Charlie shrugged. "I guess we'll see soon enough. But I've got to give you some bad news." She stepped inside and closed the door. "I've been hounding the crime lab to get the test results on Shelly's fingernail scrapings. They claimed they never got them, so I called the coroner's office. The coroner's office said someone signed them out to take them to the lab a while ago, but they don't know who that was."

Erika stared at her, incredulous. "So what are you saying? They just... disappeared?"

She looked Erika in the eye. "Basically, yeah. They're gone."

"And they don't know who picked them up?" Erika put a hand to her forehead, her mind swimming. "How can that be?"

Charlie lifted her palms. "The signature was illegible. Just an ink smear."

Those scrapings were crucial evidence. They couldn't have just vanished. "There must be some mistake. I'll call the crime lab. Maybe they put the scrapings in with someone else's case."

Charlie's tone was sarcastic. "Yeah, good luck with that. Even if they do find them, the chain of custody's broken. Tyler's going to raise holy hell about contamination."

This was a disaster. "Skip must know who picked them up from the coroner's office. He'll figure this out."

Charlie shook her head. "I can already hear the champagne corks popping in Tyler's office."

Erika gave her a hard look. "Thanks for the vote of confidence."

"Sorry. Just being a realist." She left.

That was one hell of an attitude, but Erika didn't have time to ponder it. She needed to talk to Skip. She reached for the phone, then stopped.

A bad feeling washed over her. She and Skip had talked early on about how those fingernail scrapings could make or break the case. No way he'd let anyone else handle evidence that important. Erika knew what that meant. Skip hadn't wanted to take a chance that the scrapings might have come from someone other than Mia. So he'd dumped them. And now she'd have to make sure he got away with it. Because she was the reason he was in this mess to begin with.

CHAPTER TWENTY-NINE

I'D WOKEN UP WITH a bad case of the shakes and a truly spectacular headache. I'd really dived into the bottle after talking to Brett, and I'd been well on my way to blitz land even before that. I gritted my teeth. Admittedly, I had good reason to be depressed and scared. But getting drunk and freaking out was useless. There was nothing more I could do about Roman—or whomever was following me. The only thing I had any power over was Mia's case. And time was running out. We'd start the hearing on Tyler's motions on Monday, and then we'd roll right into trial. All I had was today and the weekend to figure out once and for all whether Mia was guilty or innocent.

I went to my office with a renewed sense of purpose and worked as fast as I could. The light from my monitor burned my eyes; the sound of my fingers hitting the keys reverberated in my head. But I had to buy myself time to get on with my investigation, and by 2:30, I'd made enough progress to take my first step. I pulled out my iPad and checked all the records and news articles I could find to see if there'd been any ICE sweeps in the months between Natalie's murder and Steers' trial. *Nada.* Sanchez's claim was checking out.

Which meant I had to confront the thorny problem of figuring out who Shelly had spoken to at the cop shop. I spent the rest of the day pacing my office, trying to force my soggy brain to come up with a plan. Finally, an idea started to take shape. On edge, I walked to my car, scanning the parking lot with a nervous eye. But there were plenty of people around, a virtue of leaving early. My mind drifted back to Erika's reaction to the missing fingernail scrapings. The look of shock on her face was real—which floored me.

Why hadn't Skip told her? To give her plausible deniability? Or was it—could it possibly be—that he hadn't dumped them? I guessed it might be a case of human error, but I didn't believe it. Still, Erika's reaction made me rethink my belief that she and Skip knew Mia was innocent. I tried to play devil's advocate. Both things could be true. They did think Mia was guilty, but just in case the scrapings turned out to be a problem, Skip decided to buy a little insurance and get rid of them.

If so, maybe their goal was just to get the case done before Sanchez surfaced, not to frame an innocent girl.

×××

THE MOMENT I WALKED INTO my apartment, I knew something was wrong. I'd been so distracted I'd forgotten to check my Ring app. I stopped dead in my tracks and looked around at the kitchen and living room. Something felt off. Like someone had been here. Or maybe was *still* here? Was it Roman? I pictured him hiding behind a door, a piano wire stretched tightly between his gloved hands.

My stomach see-sawed as I stood there frozen, listening for any signs of movement. *Was that a faint rustling coming from my bedroom?* I had to strain to hear over my thumping heartbeat.

Barely breathing, I started to reach for my knife...then stopped. I couldn't afford to swing and miss. I pulled out my can of Mace and held it at the ready as I tiptoed to the bedroom doorway. I didn't see anyone. I stepped in and quickly bent to check under the bed. Nothing. I crept to the closet, my heart beating so hard it was painful, my finger on the trigger of the can. I took a deep breath and threw the door open. Again, no one.

I moved to the bathroom and peered into the shower and tub.

Nobody there.

Now that I at least knew no one was crouched behind a door waiting to spring, I checked my Ring app. A FedEx delivery guy walked by, my next-door neighbor shuffled down the walkway in her robe and slippers—as usual—and a man in a hard hat and work boots moved toward the stairs. No one even stopped at my door.

I checked my bedroom window. It was closed, but not locked. Had I left it that way? Maybe. I didn't see any sign that it'd been forced. And I liked to leave it open whenever possible. The tiny room could get awfully stuffy. But I didn't know how anyone could reach it. My apartment was on the second floor, and there was no balcony, just a sheer drop down the back of the building.

Was there some way to get up here that I didn't know about? I looked outside. My bedroom window offered a (not very) charming view of a barren hill and a small road that ran along the length of the building. On the side of the road near the building, I saw a couple of pizza boxes and some empty beer cans—signs of a party, or maybe just lunch. No way to scale the wall.

But someone *had* been in my apartment. I was sure of it. I took a moment to catch my breath, then went back out to check the living room window. Locked. The pillows on the couch, the throw blanket on the chair, the sad little cactus on the coffee table—everything seemed to be where it belonged. Nothing looked out of place in the kitchen, either, so I went back to my bedroom and scanned it inch by inch. The bed was made, the lamp and the clock on my nightstand where they should be. My desk, though…

The photo of Hannah was sitting on top of my daily planner. Had it been there this morning? I couldn't be sure. My memory was unreliable at best.

Something seemed to hover in the air, something unfamiliar. I tilted my head back and inhaled. It smelled like…men's cologne. Was it—could it be—Roman's? I inhaled again, more deeply. But it was so faint. My paranoia might be conjuring it up.

Frustrated, I rubbed the back of my neck. It was such an eerie vibe. I couldn't really say anything was wrong; it just didn't feel right.

But that was Roman's style. Breaking in, leaving enough of a trace to let me sense he'd been here—but not enough evidence to be sure—was just the kind of crazy-making thing he would do. The thought of him in my bedroom made me feel violated.

Suddenly nauseated, I sank down on my bed and forced myself to take deep breaths. I wanted to call Brett, but he'd *just* reassured me Roman was still in Chicago. It was too soon to call him again. And even if I did, what would I say? That I got a weird vibe? He'd run for the hills, and I wouldn't blame him. I'd been jumpy lately—especially after finding that greeting card. I might be going crazy, overdoing the whole *look-out-behind-you* thing. People moved up and down the hallways in this building at all hours. It'd be so easy to get caught. The more I thought about it, the less I believed Roman would risk it.

Get up, I told myself. I couldn't afford to sit here and weep into my hands. I needed to put my plan into action. The first step was finding out how the station would have handled Shelly's calls. Using the burner phone I'd bought as a backup, I called them and said I worked for Speedy Bail Bonds and needed to verify some client information. The woman said she'd connect me to the deputy on the desk, and I hung up. I had what I needed. The deputy I had to find was the one who'd been "on the desk" when Shelly called.

The next part of my plan—to find any bail bondsmen who'd called the station on the same day as Shelly—had a few points of weakness. All of them could leave me in Fucked City.

1) I didn't know whether bail bondsmen kept a record of which deputy they spoke to.

2) I'd have to talk to those bondsmen in person—as myself. If I called them on the phone and pretended to be a reporter or a writer, they'd dust me off. If I wanted them to go to the trouble of searching through their records, I'd need to use the case as my cover, tell them it was part of our investigation into Shelly's murder.

But if one of those bail bondsmen happened to be friendly with Skip and decided to tell him I'd been asking questions…

And there was another problem. I'd looked up the bail bonds companies in the area and found that, as usual, they were clustered around the main county jail. Which meant there'd be cops all over the place, and lots of them would be sheriff's deputies who worked with Skip. Again, more roads straight to Fucked City. My plan might be hopeless, I thought, but hey, at least it was absurdly dangerous.

Still, it was the best I could come up with, and I was out of time. If I went through with this, there was a pretty decent chance I'd get caught—and then fired. The thought of losing everything and having to start over, *again*— probably in another state—was overwhelming. Not to mention depressing.

As I moved to the kitchen and made a drink, I noticed I'd left my iPad open. I refreshed the screen and saw the notes from my trip to Pathways. It brought to mind the photo I'd seen of Mia. The one that so reminded me of my cousin. I'd just finished helping her pack for her freshman year in college when she confided she was more than a little nervous. She'd looked up at me, "Do I sound like a wimp?" I'd smiled, "Oh, hell no. Everybody gets nervous. I did, too." I'd hugged her and told her she was about to have so much fun she'd never want to come home. She'd brightened, "Then let's start now." She played one of her favorite songs, "Call Me Maybe," and we laughed as we danced around the room. My heart ached at the memory. Lyra. Dead, because of me. This might be my only chance to make up for it.

Any lingering doubt about what I was going to do vanished. I didn't care how many cops I had to dodge or bail bondsmen I had to throttle, I was going to get the name of the deputy Shelly talked to.

I started to take another sip of my drink, then stopped. I'd sworn off this shit. I took my glass to the sink, poured it out, and headed for the shower. For the first time in months, I fell asleep before midnight.

CHAPTER THIRTY

ERIKA COULD FEEL HER anxiety mounting as she headed to her car. She tried to listen to a podcast, but the host's voice sounded robotic and tinny— the way her own voice sounded during one of her episodes. She turned it off, rolled down the window, took a few deep breaths, and managed to make it home. The one good thing about this new wrinkle in her mental health situation was that driving no longer seemed to be a trigger. Of course, she was still taking surface streets everywhere. But it was *something*.

All she wanted was to veg out on the couch with some old *Friends* reruns, but she had to check in on Danny. Just to be safe.

No answer on his landline.

She called his cell. His voice was soft. "Hi. What's up?"

Erika's breath caught in her throat. That's how he'd sounded when the so-called assholes were "fucking with" him. "Just wanted to see how you're doing."

Danny whispered. "I'm fine. Can we maybe talk later?"

Wait a minute. He hadn't answered his landline, so he wasn't at home. Why would he be whispering? The assholes only came for him at his house. Not outside.

"Danny, what's going on? Are you having any...trouble?"

He was silent for so long Erika thought the connection had dropped. Finally, he whispered, "No. I'm...I'm just on my way to the store."

But she knew the route he took to the store. He never deviated. Ever. It took him down streets that would still be busy, and she didn't hear any sounds of traffic.

Then it hit her. *Oh, God.* He was sitting outside Fiona's house.

"Danny, you need to get out of there. Now! She's going to call the cops."

He didn't answer. Erika sat up, gripping the phone. "Danny, you *know* how dangerous this is!"

He continued speaking in that low voice. "It's a public street, and I'm not doing anything. What are they going to bust me for? Sitting?"

Erika wanted to pull her hair out. He could be so rational, and so crazy. It was like dealing with two different people. She closed her eyes and took a deep breath. "Just get out of there and come over. We'll talk about it, okay? But please trust me. You're going to wind up in jail."

Danny's tone was exasperated. "Fine. I'm leaving. But I'm not coming over."

"Okay." Erika heard the engine turn over and, a minute later, the squealing brakes of a bus. She let out a sigh of relief. "Are you taking your meds?" Julia had prescribed Ativan.

A beat. Then another. "They're too strong."

He was probably cutting his pills in half, like he'd done with the Zoloft. "Then ask Julia for a different prescription. When's your next appointment?"

His voice was normal now. "Tomorrow. And I'll talk to her about it. Not *you*."

Erika would call Julia tomorrow. She couldn't trust him. For now, she kept him on the phone until she heard him walk into his house.

By the time they ended the call, Erika felt like her whole body had been wrung out. She could barely keep her eyes open. The hearing on Tyler's motion was in just three days and the trial would start right after. She wouldn't be able to keep tabs on Danny. She'd hoped to avoid it, but she had to talk to Skip.

How would he react when he heard that her brother was a stalker? The thought brought tears to Erika's eyes. Skip and Carson knew about Danny's quirks: his upside-down hours, his obsession with security, but this was a whole different world of crazy. Genuine, for real, dangerous crazy. And Danny would go ballistic if he learned she'd told Skip.

×××

WHEN SKIP ARRIVED, ERIKA brought him into the living room. "Anything to drink? I think I've still got a bottle of that Cabernet you guys like."

"No, thanks. I'm good." He sat down on the couch and looked at Erika with concern. "What's going on?"

Erika took the rocking chair across from him. "Danny's been…stalking someone." She told him the whole story. As she spoke, she gripped the arms of her chair to keep from crying.

Skip's brow furrowed. "He hasn't actually made contact with her, right? It does seem like deep down he knows that what he's doing isn't okay."

"Maybe. But we *just* had that session with his shrink, and he said he'd stop. What's so scary about this is that it might mean he can't control himself. If he takes things further…" She couldn't bear to say it out loud. "I—I just can't let that happen."

Skip gave her a look of sympathy. "I understand. And I don't want to pile on, but there's another issue for you to consider. When the trial gets going next week, you'll be back in the spotlight again. If Danny gets busted, the press will go nuts."

She hadn't even thought of that, but Skip was right. It couldn't help but spill over onto her. And Harrier hated a scandal of any kind. He might take her off the case—God forbid!—or even fire her. If she lost her job, Danny would probably get evicted. He couldn't afford to pay the rent on his salary.

Something else occurred to her then. "If Danny gets arrested," she said softly, meeting Skip's eyes, "CQT will fire him in a heartbeat." CQT was a relatively new company. They couldn't afford to keep an employee who spooked their investors, not even one as brilliant as Danny. "Honestly, I'm afraid of what it'll do to him if he goes to jail, even for a night. He might really…fall apart." Tears filled her eyes again.

"I'm so sorry. I can't imagine how hard this must be," Skip said gently. "We can't stop him from calling this woman. The only thing I can do is try to keep him from going to her house. How would you feel about putting spyware on his phone? It'll let me see what he's doing. Where he goes, who he calls, all his text messages."

Could she do that to her brother? It was such a violation, especially for someone as obsessively private as Danny. But if she didn't, he might wind up in handcuffs. "I feel shitty about it. But I can't think of anything else."

"I should probably put a tracker on his car, too."

Erika was uneasy. "How are we going to do all this?"

"You'll have to install the spyware. It requires physical access to the phone. And I'll need you to get him out of the house so I can install the tracker. You have the remote for his garage, right?"

Erika nodded. "When do you think you'll be able to get everything?"

"I can probably have it by tomorrow. Can you get Danny to go out with you tomorrow night?"

"He's pretty pissed off at me. But I'll try."

Then she remembered something else: that photo of Charlie on Danny's computer. She told Skip about it, said, "It bothered me at the time, but he claimed he was just curious and then he deleted it, so I let it go. But now…"

Skip frowned. "You think he's getting…wrapped up with her, too?"

Erika almost wished that was it. "Maybe, but not because he thinks he's in love with her. The opposite. I told him she was a pain in the ass and that I wished I didn't have to work with her." She paused, not wanting to say the next words. "I'm probably overreacting, but what if he…hurts her?"

His eyebrows went up. "To get her off the case?"

Erika nodded, miserable at even having to think that of Danny. It was a crazy rationale, but…it was possible. "I don't want to believe it. But I'd never have thought he'd actually stalk someone either."

"I hear you. But so far it doesn't look like he's inclined to get physical. We'll just have to hope it stays that way. And look, Erika, from what I know of him, he's definitely not the type."

"Thanks so much, Skip." Erika never liked to ask for help—for anything. But she had no choice. And at least it was Skip, who'd always been her safe haven. "I'm so sorry to hassle you with this. I just…didn't know what else to do."

Skip stood up. "I'm always glad to be there for you. You know that."

As she walked him to the door, she asked, "By the way, has he…?"

"No. He still hasn't turned up. Not as far as I can tell." He squeezed her arm. "Don't worry. It'll all work out somehow."

Erika nodded without much conviction. She hoped so. Because it had to.

CHAPTER THIRTY-ONE

I DECIDED TO TRY a little camouflage for my visit to Bail Bonds Village. Jeans, a denim jacket and a dark knit cap so my blonde hair wouldn't stand out like a neon sign. It probably wouldn't throw off my stalker, but I'd be out in public and well within screaming distance of an army of cops. The very definition of a good news/bad news situation. Before I left, I made sure all the windows were locked and my Ring camera was working.

As I drove, I mentally charted my course: I'd start at the end of the block and with a little luck I wouldn't have to move down to the last bail bond companies—the ones right next to the jail—to get my answers.

I parked in a public lot a quarter mile away so no one would spot my car, then hiked to my first target: AAA Bonds. All those "A's" probably helped pull in business back when people used telephone books. The sign over the front window looked like it'd been made that long ago.

A bell rang when I opened the door. Very old-school—like the beefy man with a fringe of brown hair talking on the phone and rocking back and forth in a large swivel chair. I figured he was the owner.

He held up two fingers when he saw me. I nodded, surreptitiously checking the place out. His battered wooden desk was covered with paperwork in no discernible order. If that was any indication of his record-keeping habits, this was going to be a bust.

When he finished the call, he said, "I'm Fred Eggleston, CEO of this fine establishment. Who're you looking to bail out?"

"No one." I told him who I was and showed him my badge. "I'm working on Shelly Hansen's murder—"

"Terrible thing." He shook his head. "And by her own kid! Jesus!"

Maybe there *was* solidarity in the bail bonds community. The thought gave me hope. "We're looking into everyone Shelly contacted during her last week. Her records show she called the Sheriff's Department a few times. We need to figure out which deputy she spoke to." Now, I had to lie and hope he bought it. "For some reason, the station doesn't keep a record of who has desk duty."

He seemed unfazed. Excellent. I listed the dates, and asked, "Did you happen to call in on any of those days?"

He pursed his lips. "Wouldn't surprise me." He set a dusty laptop on his desk and fired it up. "I don't usually keep track of who I talk to, but you never know." He typed and peered at the screen. "Seems I did call."

I put my hand in my jacket pocket and crossed my fingers. "And?"

He shook his head and closed the laptop. "No names. Sorry. Anything else I can help you with?"

Damn it. If Fred was any indication, I was screwed. "No. But thanks for trying."

His expression was sad. "Shelly was a real good woman. Good at the business, too. Ethical, decent." He sighed. "Anyway, I wish you luck."

As I walked out, I scanned the area for cops. I didn't see any, but I picked up my pace anyway.

The next company, Instant Bail, had a fresher sign, and when I walked in, the owner—a short man with a heavy gold chain around his neck—was actually working on a computer. When I introduced myself, he got almost as choked up as Fred. But when I told him what I needed, he didn't bother to check his records, just shook his head.

"I never write down their names. Maybe I should. Might come in handy—sure woulda been good for you, huh?"

Yeah, huh? I hit three more places and got the same result. And each company brought me closer to the jail.

As I left the last bail bond office, I saw two sheriff's deputies walk out of the jail and head for the parking lot. This was truly suicidal. I had to pull the plug. But then the image of Mia's face, her smile, came back to me. Fuck it. This was my only lead. I had to play it out.

There were two companies left. The next one, Uncle Bernie's Bail Bonds, seemed like a lost cause. Old Uncle Bernie wouldn't bother with recordkeeping. He probably used a typewriter. I skipped it and went to the last company, Duncan's Bail Bonds. But it was closed. Shit.

Uncle Bernie's it was.

I'd expected an old man in corduroy pants and a cardigan. Instead, I found a guy in his twenties, tatted from wrist to neck, his ears pierced with black stretchers, typing away on a laptop. I stared at him, jarred by the gap between my expectations and reality.

He looked up. "Can I help you?"

"I really hope so." I introduced myself, told him I was prosecuting the Hansen case. He was a mouth-breather, and the mention of Shelly's case made his jaw drop even further.

"Gnarly ass murder, man. You really think the girl did it?"

Less and less. "Seems so." I told him what I was looking for. "Any chance you called the sheriffs to get information about a client on any of those dates?"

"Tell you in two secs." His fingers flew over the keys. "Yep, I did. The first and the last."

The date when Sanchez was bailed out, and the day before Shelly died. I steeled myself for another disappointment as I watched him scroll through his records. "I guess you don't have the names of the deputies, though. Right?"

He gave me a mildly exasperated look. "Yeah, I do. How else would I be able to sue if I got bad info?"

I felt like kissing his litigious face and decided not to tell him he'd never get to first base with a lawsuit. "Who were they?"

"Looks like I got the same cop on both dates. Reggie Maynard."

I hadn't expected that, but it sure made things easier. "Thanks, Bernie. Appreciate it."

He blew a raspberry. "Bernie's my granddad."

Of course.

×××

I TROTTED BACK TO my car victorious. I had my name, now I just needed to figure out how to get him to talk without making him suspicious. As I started the engine, I checked my Ring app. Everything looked normal. Relieved, I headed for home.

I'd just reached the onramp to the freeway when Brett called. "Hey, Charlie," he said. In the background, I heard a woman's voice come over a PA system. "Are you home?"

"On my way there. Where are you?"

"Burbank Airport," he said. "Mind if I meet you at your place?"

I wondered why he hadn't told me he was coming, but with all that'd been going on, I was glad—*very* glad—he was here. "Not at all, come on over."

I was about to ask if he had any news, but he said "Thanks" and ended the call before I could get the words out.

×××

WHEN I GOT HOME, I FOUND Brett sitting on his backpack at the top of the stairs. His hair—thick and dark brown—was longer than I remembered it, but otherwise he looked the same: gorgeous dark eyes, clean shaven, and tastefully buff.

His lips curled in a little smile as he stood up. "I think this is the first time I've seen you in jeans."

I took in his black jeans and leather bomber jacket. "Same," I said.

But I could tell this was no pleasure visit. Something was on his mind. As soon as I unlocked the door, I went to check the windows. Still locked. At Brett's puzzled look, I said, "Someone might've broken in yesterday."

His eyes widened with alarm. "Why didn't you—"

I held up a hand. "I wasn't sure. I'm still not."

Brett raked a hand through his hair. "Sorry, I didn't mean to jump your shit like that."

"I'll tell you about it. But you first." I was nervous; I could see he was distressed. I got us each a bottle of water, then gestured to the couch.

Brett sat and clasped his hands together, his expression somber. "I staked out Roman's condo. It took a couple of days, but finally, last night, I caught him driving out. I didn't want him to know that I was surveilling him, so I had a patrol unit make a traffic stop." He met my eyes, his expression dark. "It wasn't him. It was his brother, Adam."

I felt the blood drain from my face. So it'd been Roman all along. Of course. Who else would go to the trouble of torturing me, gaslighting me this way? "Did the uni get any information on Roman?"

"She tried. Asked him where the owner of the car was. He claimed Roman was at home. Obviously, I didn't have probable cause to search the condo, but I'm sure he's lying."

I swallowed. "To give Roman cover."

Brett nodded. "Which doesn't necessarily mean he knows what Roman's up to. Dierdre and Buck said they'd follow up."

A cold comfort. Adam and Roman were tight. I said, "He won't tell them anything."

"It is a long shot," Brett said, and sighed, his expression bleak. "I've been trying to track Roman down, but so far: nothing." He glanced at the front door. "Now, what happened with you?"

I told him about my sense that someone had been in my apartment. "But my Ring app didn't show anyone breaking in, and there's no way he could've gotten in through the bedroom window. So I figured I'd just imagined it."

"I think we both know better now," Brett said. "Can I see your footage from that day?"

"Sure." I found the date on my Ring app and hit play.

Brett watched, then pointed to the man in the hard hat and work boots. "Was a construction company doing work on the building?"

I frowned. "Not that I know of. But I can find out." I called the manager, then told Brett, "She said they were fixing the rain spout on the third floor." My mouth went dry. "But the crew wouldn't just let some stranger—"

"I don't think they did," he said as he headed to the door. "I'm going to have a look."

I followed him outside, toward the thick brush that covered the ground behind the building. He moved to the area below my window and pushed through a tall clump of weeds. Seconds later, he reached down and hoisted up a ladder.

My head swam; I had to put a hand on the wall to steady myself. "He swiped it?"

Brett dropped the ladder as he dusted off his hands. "No. I'm guessing the crew left it there. Roman just got lucky."

But that meant he'd been here, watching, waiting...

My legs felt like rubber as we walked back to my apartment.

Inside, his expression grim, Brett asked, "Mind if I take a look at that greeting card?"

I pointed to the kitchen table, where I'd left it. "I tried not to destroy any prints, but I seriously doubt he was dumb enough to leave any."

Using a napkin, Brett picked it up by the edges. As he opened the card, something fell out. I froze. "What the hell?"

He dropped the card and leaned down to get a closer look. When he turned to me, his eyes were wide with shock. "It's a photo of you."

I moved to the table, heart racing. It was a closeup that captured me in profile, unposed, obviously taken surreptitiously as I left the office. "So that's what he did when he broke in." He'd left the photo, to make sure I knew he'd been here. I swayed as the room began to spin.

Brett put an arm around me. "Come on," he said, as he led me to the couch.

He had me lay back and put cushions under my legs, then knelt down next to me. After a few minutes, he said, "Any better?"

I nodded, but glad as I was that this proved my family was safe, I was badly shaken. "He's escalating."

Brett was grim as he said, "And I'd bet he'll make another move soon."

"What kind of move?" The moment I uttered the words, I wanted to snatch them back.

"I don't know, but he's taking bigger risks. Seems like he's getting more and more unhinged." He pressed his lips together as he gazed down at me. "Look, I don't want to impose, but would it be okay if I hang around for a little while?"

Okay with it? I was so grateful I was almost speechless. "Yes, sure."

But as I gave it some thought, I realized I couldn't just hole up in my apartment and wait for Roman to come for me. I had a possibly innocent girl to clear.

"Don't worry, I wasn't expecting to stay here," Brett hurried to reassure me, mistaking the reason for my worry. "I'm sure I can find a hotel that's close by."

"That's not it." I shook my head and sighed. "I'd better catch you up."

CHAPTER THIRTY-TWO

ERIKA DRESSED FOR HER dinner with Danny, hoping the restaurant wouldn't be packed. They were meeting at Oswald, one of his favorites, but a lot of people loved the place and it was a Saturday.

Skip, as promised, had gotten the tracker and the spyware, and Erika had called Danny to make amends. A fight like that—any kind of fight, really—would've been unthinkable when they were kids. Life in their foster home was too dangerous. And although Erika took the majority of the physical abuse, Danny occasionally wound up on the wrong side of Vincent Brogan's fists, too. They were constantly on the alert—for themselves, and for each other.

They'd developed their own ways of dealing with Brogan. Danny figured out how to make him laugh, and on occasion it'd work to distract him. Later, Erika had discovered that Danny's new skill wasn't just a lucky break. She'd seen the book in his backpack—a collection of jokes and funny stories—and realized it was purposeful, his way of protecting them.

Erika couldn't make Brogan laugh, but she could provoke him when he was gunning for Danny. To save her brother, she'd take the beating. That loyalty lingered. Even as adults, their friction points were small: her annoyance at him always being late; his irritation with her forgetting to return his calls.

The argument they'd had Thursday night was bigger. When Erika had called, she didn't even know if he'd pick up. That he had was a victory in itself.

She kept her tone light and casual. "Hi. How're you doing?"

In contrast, Danny sounded subdued, flat. "I'm okay. Just playing *Minecraft*."

"I'm sorry if I got a little...pushy last night."

There'd been a long beat of silence. Long enough for Erika to worry that he might hang up on her.

Then he said, "No, you were right. I shouldn't have gone there. It's just...I went out grocery shopping, and I...I found myself driving to her place." He'd sighed. "Don't worry. It won't happen again. I promise. I'm on top of it now."

Erika had quietly let out the breath she'd been holding. He wasn't angry anymore, and he sounded good. Rational. Maybe they didn't need to bug his phone and his car; maybe he was over it.

But he'd said all that before—to her and to Julia. She couldn't afford to be in denial. "I don't want to interfere in your life. I just want you to be safe."

His voice had gotten warmer. "Yeah, I know. So, how's it going with you?"

"We start trial on Wednesday. Want to do dinner tomorrow night, while I still have a semi-life? I was thinking Oswald. I'm buying."

"Oh man, then I'm ordering everything on the right side of the menu!"

×××

DANNY WAS AT THE bar when she got there. She slid onto the stool next to him and nodded at his wine glass. "What's that?"

"A really good Pinot Noir." He slid it over to her. "Have a taste."

She took a sip, though she wasn't in the mood to drink. "It *is* good. I don't know how you always manage to find the best...everything." Whether it was bed sheets or pepper grinders, Danny always chose the top-of-the-line.

"Research. Lots and lots of research. Mostly on the company's dime." He smiled. "Which makes it even sweeter. So, catch me up. How's the case going?"

It was the perfect opening. "Pretty well. Believe it or not, I'm really glad to have Charlie. We got hit with a boatload of motions by the defense. I would've been in big trouble if it wasn't for her."

Maybe she was laying it on thick, but her worry about that photo of Charlie had lingered. She'd decided to talk her up, let him know there was no reason to do…anything to her. Although now, seeing how together he was, she felt ridiculous for even considering that.

"That's awesome," he said, grinning. "Maybe she can save you from the all-nighters, too."

"I wouldn't mind." Erika had barely slept during the Steers trial. This one wouldn't be any easier. In fact, it'd be even worse—ironically, in part because of Charlie. "What's new with you?"

"I did talk to Julia about…the other night." He bit the inside of his cheek, an old childhood habit.

Erika had wanted to ask him about Fiona, but she hadn't been sure it was a good idea to bring it up so soon. Now Danny had given her an opening. After the hostess took them to their table, she framed it gently. "Is it okay if I ask you something about Fiona?"

He gazed at her with sadness. "I'm sorry for putting you through all this. You've got so much on your plate already."

Erika's throat tightened as she reached out and took his hand. "I'm happy to be there for you. You're the most important person in the world to me."

He gave her a grateful smile. "Likewise." He squeezed her hand. "Ask whatever you want."

"I just wondered, why Fiona? What was it about her?"

He slowly nodded. "I've been wondering that myself. I think it's because she reminds me of Lisa."

So many things fell into place with that answer. In high school, Lisa Solomon had been the love of Danny's life. But she was one of the popular girls, a shiny, pretty blonde who ran with the in-crowd. To her, a brilliant loner like Danny was good for help with her calculus homework, but when he finally got up the courage to tell her how he felt, she shot him down—cruelly. Laughed in his face at the idea of going out with him.

Any teenage boy would suffer. But Danny wasn't just any teenage boy. He was never the same with girls after that. Fiona was his chance to rewrite history, Erika thought. To finally win Lisa over. It made her want to cry—and gut Lisa with a rusty butter knife. But that didn't explain why this was happening now, after more than twenty years. It made her think that something in him was changing and not for the better. "Have you told Julia about Lisa?"

"Not yet. But I will." He stared down at his wine glass. "She just got divorced, you know. She's living in Santa Barbara now. Has a daughter in eighth grade. Tammy. She's a real soccer star."

Alarm bells started ringing in Erika's head. "How do you know all that?"

"Oh, uh…we're Facebook friends." He took a sip of wine and glanced around the restaurant. "What happened to our waiter?"

"I'll go ask the hostess."

He stood up. "No, that's okay. I have to use the restroom anyway."

As he left the table, Erika eyed his cell phone. She'd almost talked herself out of downloading the spyware—until he'd mentioned Lisa. She glanced toward the restroom to make sure he was gone, then grabbed his phone.

×××

It was her last Saturday before the trial. Erika had hoped to sleep in, but her eyes flew open at seven o'clock and all her fears started to swirl in her head. She got up, just to give herself something to do besides dwell on all the ways her life could fall apart. At nine o'clock, she called Skip. "Did it work?"

"Yep. You did good." Skip paused, then said, "Mind if I come over? I have a couple things to tell you, and I need to get hold of your phone so I can give you access to the tracker and spyware apps."

"Sure, I'll make you some tea."

His tone was disdainful. "That nasty herbal stuff? No thanks. I'll stop at Coffee Bean."

Erika had forgotten he didn't like chamomile tea. It was practically the only thing she could drink without getting the jitters these days. "It happens to be good for you."

"So's exercise. See you in ten," he said.

Erika cleaned up the kitchen, and eight minutes later, Skip showed up. She could tell by his expression that whatever he had to say, she wasn't going to like it. They sat at the kitchen table, and Skip asked for her phone. He downloaded the apps, then handed it back to her. "How was he?"

"He seemed fine, but…" Erika told him about Lisa and how much Danny seemed to know about her. "So now I'm worried he might go after *her*."

"Don't borrow trouble, Erika. Nothing's happened yet. Maybe it never will."

She hoped he was right, but with every passing day it felt more and more like her world had turned into a ticking time bomb. "Anyway, what's the news?"

"We won't be starting trial on Wednesday. Mia got sick. Some nasty virus is running through the jail. Bunch of inmates went down for the count. She'll be okay, but she's going to need some time to recuperate."

"Damn it." Erika so wanted to put this trial to bed. But that wasn't big news. "What else?"

Skip met her gaze. "My contact just told me that our informant's gone south. She's saying she lied. Claims the only thing Mia's ever really said is that she didn't do it."

"Oh, shit." Erika slumped in her chair. She'd been counting on that testimony. "What made her turn?"

Skip shook his head. "No idea. But all of this'll set the trial back a week or so."

"I have bad news of my own." She tried to keep her tone neutral. "Charlie said the crime lab never got Shelly's fingernail scrapings, but the coroner's office has proof that someone picked them up. Apparently, they don't have a record of who it was. Was it you?"

Skip looked stricken. "No." He rubbed his forehead. "I think a deputy told me he was going to make the run to the coroner's office, but I can't remember who it was." He fell silent, his expression worried. "What happened to them? They can't just be gone."

Erika studied his reaction. He seemed completely sincere. It was odd that Skip had let some other deputy handle the evidence and not even made a note of who it was, but the stress they were under was relentless. It'd thrown Erika off her game—badly. Skip had to be going through his own version of hell.

And the crime lab had screwed up before, had actually lost evidence in past cases. They'd just been dope charges, and it had happened a few years ago. But it was impossible to say it couldn't have happened again. True or not, she'd go along with his explanation and pray no one would ever be able to prove otherwise.

"They might turn up in some other case, but even if they do…"

He nodded, his expression grim. "They'll be useless. Jeezus. I fucked up. I'm so sorry."

"I'm really worried, Skip. Tanya's gone, and now this…"

"I know. But we've got a ton of other evidence. Motive, DNA, that statement Mia gave. And snitches can backfire on you. We're probably better off without Tanya."

Maybe so, but Erika felt like she was losing control, that anything might happen.

Skip said, "There's this, though. I remembered that an old partner of mine moved out to Chicago a while ago. I emailed him to ask if he could do some digging for me."

Erika wasn't thrilled with the idea of bringing someone else into this. "Did you tell him what you wanted?"

He nodded. "And I sent him a color copy of Charlie's driver's license. Don't worry. We can trust him."

She sure hoped so. "I assume you told him to be careful who he talks to."

"Of course."

It was a risky move, but now that they'd lost Tanya and the trial would be delayed *and* Charlie had been spotted in Beach Flats—Erika desperately needed the leverage.

"Just tell him to make it fast," she said, and felt her chest tighten with a sense of impending doom.

CHAPTER THIRTY-THREE

WHEN I FINISHED FILLING BRETT in on the Hansen case and what I'd discovered, he looked impressed. "Nice work—for an amateur."

I shot him a mock dagger of a glare. "You mean someone who has to do it all secretly, without handcuffs and a badge?"

He chuckled as he held up his hands in surrender. "Seriously, you did good. So now that you know which deputy Shelly spoke to, you need to get him to tell you whether she was calling about Alberto Sanchez?"

"Right." If Deputy Maynard confirmed that Shelly had called the station to report Sanchez's story, that probably *would* be enough to bust Erika for burying Sanchez's statement and getting him deported. Not enough to get her charged with the actual crimes she'd committed but enough to trigger an investigation. And that'd shut down the Hansen trial. They'd have to explore the possibility that Shelly had been killed to keep her from talking—which, if true, would mean Mia was innocent.

Brett looked at me skeptically. "Aren't you worried the deputy will get suspicious and tell Skip what you're up to?"

"Not if I do it right." And figuring out how was going to be crucial. But for now, all I needed to do was find out when the deputy was on duty.

I called the station, told a plausible lie, and learned he was due back tomorrow afternoon. Perfect. To Brett, I said, "I'll have to go in to the office tomorrow." Calling the deputy on a Sunday would look better if I did it from work. "How do you want to do this? Want to ride with me?"

Brett shook his head. "It'll be better if I tail you." His gaze was sympathetic when he saw my expression. "I know. I don't like it either. But the only way to bust him is to catch him in the act, and he won't make a move if he sees I'm with you."

That was, unfortunately, true. Beyond that, I knew seeing me with another man would enrage Roman. I didn't know how his fury might manifest, and I didn't want to find out. I needed it to end. I couldn't live like this, constantly looking over my shoulder, waiting for the other shoe to drop.

"You mentioned a hotel, but wouldn't it be easier for you to stay here?" I asked Brett.

"It would." He gave me a searching look. "If you're okay with that."

As I returned his gaze, I thought I might be a little too okay with it and marveled at the insanity of my even *thinking* about a hookup at a time like this. But to Brett I just shrugged and said, "Sure," with as much nonchalance as I could.

It'd taken a while to spool out the whole story about Shelly's murder, and as I looked out the window, I saw that it was dark and probably way past Brett's dinner time. "You must be starving."

He nodded. "A little bit."

Surprisingly, after all I'd been through, I was hungry, too.

We decided we were in the mood for pizza, and Brett ordered a bottle of red to go with it. Wine's okay; I like the taste. It's just usually too wimpy for my purposes. But tonight, my purposes didn't include getting blotto, so it was probably for the best.

We'd finished eating and were sipping our second glass when Brett asked, "If you'd been in Erika's shoes, would you have done it? Buried Sanchez's statement and called ICE?"

I had to take a minute to think. "I don't think so."

Brett's eyebrows lifted. "You don't sound sure."

I wasn't. Not a hundred percent.

Because truth be told, I didn't give two shits about Blake Steers' right to a fair trial. He was the kind of vermin that needed to be put in a cage for life—by any and all means necessary.

But present moment aside, I wasn't Erika. Why Steers got to her the way he did I'd never know. What I did know was that if Mia hadn't been in the mix, I probably would've let the whole thing go. I didn't agree with what Erika had done, but I did sympathize with her. And it was possible she really believed Mia was guilty. Sure, it was probably confirmation bias. But I thought it might be genuine.

"What about you?" I asked. "Would you have done it?"

Brett traced the stem of his wine glass, then said, "No. But I'm sitting here, sharing a bottle of wine with you. Not sitting in court, facing the serious risk that a maniac like Steers might go free. If I were," he lifted his eyebrows, "I might feel differently."

"Fair point." It's a lot easier to say you wouldn't cross a line when there's nothing at stake. Brett yawned, and I realized I was starting to fade myself. I stood up. "We should probably call it."

As we made up the couch, something occurred to me. "Roman's bound to notice that you're hanging around. Won't that make you a target, too?"

"Maybe." Brett saw my face fall and said, "This is my choice, Charlie. It's on me, not you." He nodded toward his backpack. "Remember, I *do* have a badge and handcuffs—and a gun."

And on that cheery note, I trundled off to bed.

×××

THE NEXT MORNING, BRETT followed me to work. I was glad to have him watching as I walked into the near-deserted building—the only other soul the lone security guard in the lobby. I'd forgotten how empty the office was on the weekends. Ordinarily, I liked the solitude. Today, even with Brett somewhere behind me, I wanted to get out as fast as possible.

He joined me when I reached my office. I sat down at my desk and practiced the question I planned to ask Deputy Maynard. "Does that sound okay? Just business as usual?"

"Did to me." He took in my tense expression. "You should try breathing, though."

"Breathing's for pussies," I joked. But I was nervous as hell. This was it. If I got the wrong answer, it was over. I could feel my heart thumping against my ribcage as I called the station and waited for him to come to the phone.

Finally, I heard the line click over. "Deputy Maynard."

I tried to sound casual. "Do you happen to know whether Shelly Hansen made any calls about domestic violence complaints within a couple days of the murder?"

It wasn't my real question. But it was a safe one that'd give me the answer I was looking for.

"I took a couple of calls from her just before she died, yeah. But she didn't tell me what it was about. Just asked for the lead investigator on the Steers case, so I put her through to Skip."

I thanked him and let him go, then lay back in my chair, weak with relief.

Brett asked, "I'm guessing he gave the right answer?"

"Sure did." I told him what the deputy had said. "And Skip never wrote it up."

"Seriously?" He shook his head. "Wow."

Wow indeed. *Any* kind of contact with a murder victim in the days before their death had to be written up. Even if Shelly had called with a routine request for client information, Skip would've had to write a report about it. In the beginning of an investigation, you simply don't know what might turn out to be important.

But Skip had spoken to Shelly at least *twice* in the three days before her murder, and not only had he not written a report, he'd never even *mentioned* any calls. Moreover, the fact that Shelly had asked for the lead investigator on the Steers case made it very clear she'd called the station to talk about Sanchez. She had no connection to the Steers case *other* than Sanchez.

"So now it's not just a theory," I told Brett, trying to wrap my mind around it. "It's a fact. Skip—which also means Erika—knew Sanchez was claiming he'd been deported because of his statement."

Brett nodded. "But that doesn't completely clear Mia—"

"No, but it sure points to the possibility that someone else killed Shelly to keep her from talking. They'll at least have to investigate."

"Definitely," he said. "Anything else you need to do here?"

"I'm done."

But as we moved past the reception area on our way out, I heard one of the receptionist's phone lines ringing. Strange. I paused and looked at the screen. No name, just a number. "That's Erika's line." I frowned. "Who'd be calling her at the office on a Sunday?"

Brett shrugged and tipped his head toward the phone with a devious look. "One way to find out."

"I like your style." I picked up the receiver and put it between us so Brett could hear. "DA's office, Erika Lorman."

A harried female voice said, "You're the one handling the Mia Hansen case, right?" I said I was. "Good, because I need to give you this thing. My son was walking the dog and the dog got stuck on this spot, and he just kept digging and digging. He came up with some bones—"

Wait, what? Another murder? "Human bones?"

She sounded impatient. "No, no. Probably a rabbit or something. But right next to them was this cell phone. The battery was dead, so I plugged it in to see if I could figure out who it belonged to. There was a text on the screen to a boy named Axel. I've been following the case in the news. That's that girl's boyfriend, isn't it? The girl who...who did it?"

"Maybe." If she was right... "I assume you want to turn it in."

"I...yes. Please. But I don't want to be a witness and get all balled up in this thing."

Too late, but I wasn't about to tell her that. "Tell me where you are, and I'll send my assistant to pick it up." She gave me an address close to Mia's house. "Great. My assistant will be there in fifteen minutes."

Brett smiled. "Nice work, counselor. But from what you've told me, Erika's going to have a fit if she finds out you did this on your own."

"Let her. With all the dirt I've got on her now, she can't touch me."

×××

I'D ASKED BRETT TO stay in the car. As he'd pointed out, I wasn't supposed to be doing this, let alone doing it with a cop from out of state. Besides, I told myself, there was no way Roman would make a move in front of an audience in broad daylight. Still, I scanned the area carefully before I got out of my car and made sure my can of Mace and knife were within easy reach in my purse.

The woman's house was next to a vacant lot, not far from George Argonian's place. That must've been where the dog dug up the cell phone. I wondered why the unis had missed it. But it wouldn't be the first time a dog had succeeded where humans had failed.

I opened the trunk and searched for something to put the phone in so I wouldn't get my prints all over it. The only thing I could find was an old paper grocery bag. It'd have to do.

The woman who answered the door looked exactly like she'd sounded on the phone. She seemed to be in the middle of baking something; I saw smears of flour and buttery grease on her apron, and her bushy, dark blonde hair fell across her eyes. She brushed it off with the back of her hand. "Are you the assistant?"

I said yes and held out my badge. "And your name is?"

She examined the badge. "Nancy Holmes. I'll go get it."

I thought about asking her to slide the phone onto a piece of paper, but she'd already manhandled it to death. There was no point. I pulled my notepad and a pen out of my purse and wrote up a receipt. When she came back, I held out the bag, and she dropped the phone in as though it was radioactive.

"Do you know where your son found it?"

She pointed to the vacant lot. "Not exactly. Somewhere in there."

I gave her my pen and notepad. "Would you please write your name down on the receipt?"

She did so, reluctantly. "This doesn't make me a witness, does it?"

I couldn't tell her a total lie. "It's not really up to me. But I'll do my best to keep you out of it."

Thanking her, I hurried to my car and texted Brett that I was heading home.

How had the phone wound up in that vacant lot? I wondered, as I waited for a light to change. Then I remembered Mia had taken off her hoodie when she broke the window. It could've fallen out of her pocket and been dragged away by some animal, a coyote or a raccoon.

Anxious to see what was on the phone, I parked and ran upstairs. By the time I got to my apartment, I was wheezing like a ninety-year-old smoker.

262 × Marcia Clark

I bent over, hands on my knees, and tried to catch my breath. I really needed to start working out.

When Brett walked in and saw me, he laughed. "Should I get the oxygen?"

I barely managed to eke out, "Yes, please."

In the kitchen, I spread out a paper towel and slid the phone out of the bag. The screen was cracked and caked with dirt. It'd obviously been out in the elements for a while. Probably hopeless to think there'd be any prints or DNA left on it.

I used a pen to refresh the screen. The text popped up. *I'm at the house. Mom locked me out. !!! Can I crash at your place?*

The meaning hit me all in a rush. It was Mia's phone, all right. And that was the text she'd insisted she'd written to Axel when she got home on the night of the murder. But no one had believed her because Axel had never received it. And it hadn't shown up on any of the cell phone records.

Because Mia had forgotten to hit send.

If that was true, then the front door *had* been locked with the deadbolt when she got home. Mia did have to break in through her bedroom window, and Shelly *had* to have been dead already when she got home. Otherwise, the sound of breaking glass—so loud even the neighbors heard it—would have woken her up. And no way in hell could a drunken, stoned Mia have taken Shelly down if she were awake.

Mia had told the truth.

I was breathless as I laid it all out for Brett. "This is it. Solid evidence that Mia's innocent."

Brett's eyes widened. "Then who *did* kill Shelly?"

I sank down at the kitchen table, thoughts swirling. It was the question I'd been pondering all along. The only other person I'd considered seemed so unlikely I'd rejected the notion as impossible. But with no other suspects in view, I had to revisit that idea—and think of a way to find out whether the impossible was possible.

I talked it over with Brett, examining the idea from every angle I could imagine, just to make sure I hadn't missed anything.

By the end of the night, I knew what I had to do.

CHAPTER THIRTY-FOUR

Erika had just finished unloading the dishwasher when her doorbell rang. Danny. He was on the porch, facing the street, his back to her. She glanced at her watch. 6:30 a.m.? Early for him to be out and about. She pulled the door open, smiling. "Well, color me shocked."

But when he turned, his expression was cold. "Mind if I come in?"

Erika stood back, alarmed by the anger in his voice. "What's wrong?"

He marched past her into the living room, then spun around, glaring. "Did you really think I wouldn't notice you put spyware on my cell? Or a tracker on my car? How fucking stupid do you think I am?!"

Erika stood rooted to the spot, unable to speak. Only then did it dawn on her that Danny—a genius-level coder and paranoid privacy freak—would *of course* know how to tell whether his phone was bugged. And once he'd found that bug, *of course* he'd checked his car. Why hadn't she thought of that? The pain of her stupid mistake spread over her body like a fusillade of a thousand tiny needles.

Danny went on, his voice rising. "At first, I thought it was the assholes who're always fucking with me. But they wouldn't be able to get to my phone or my car." He was breathing hard, his speech getting faster. "Then I realized that the spyware showed up right after our dinner." His eyes bored into hers. "Tell me I'm wrong."

Erika was too stunned to speak. When she found her voice, her words trickled out, weak and thin. "I—I was worried. You went back to Fiona's house the day after we saw Julia. I thought you might not be able to..."

Now his voice was louder, his face turning red. "To what? To stop? But I *promised* you I would!"

"But, Danny, that's what you said before—"

He cut her off, his expression incredulous. "Do you really not see the difference? When we had dinner, I made the promise to *you*."

Erika gazed at him with sadness. She knew he thought it was that simple. "I know you'd never mean to break a promise to me. But you might…slip again. You said you hadn't intended to go back to Fiona's house. Remember? And then when you talked about Lisa…" She trailed off.

His stare was hard and steady. "I told you we were just Facebook friends. Or did you decide I was lying about that, too?"

Erika looked away. "I'm so sorry, Danny—"

"Is that what you think of me?" His body was shaking with rage. "That I'm some nutjob who goes around stalking women all the time?"

His fury hit her like a pile driver, and Erika backed up, frightened. She'd never seen him like this. "No! I was just afraid for you!" She had to pause to catch her breath. "Maybe I—I overreacted, but I was only trying to protect you. After the situation with Fiona—"

"The situation with Fiona?! What 'situation'?" he made air quotes. "You call falling in love with someone a 'situation'? *Now* who's the crazy one?"

Erika looked at him with despair. It was a lost cause. "I never meant to hurt you."

He spoke quietly, his voice filled with pain and disappointment. "You were the one person in the world I knew I could trust. And I thought you knew you could always trust me." He looked away. "But I was wrong. You never trusted me. And now I can't trust you either."

He turned and walked out.

×××

Erika didn't know how long she sat sobbing on the couch. Her little brother, her only family, was gone. Danny was the keeper of her past, the one person in the world who understood her. Memories of him playing the clown as he tried to protect her from their foster father seared her heart. As young and vulnerable as he was, he'd been there for her. And she'd repaid him by stabbing him in the back.

It felt like her whole world was crumbling. She lay slumped, too weary and broken to move. Engulfed in misery, she lost track of time.

But at some point she noticed moonlight shining through the sliding glass door, and Erika went out to the balcony. The crisp, cold air burned her lungs as she took long, deep breaths.

She couldn't let herself fall apart. If she did, Blake Steers would go free. That could not happen. She'd find a way to make up with Danny. She'd keep reaching out until he came around.

As Erika watched clouds glide across the moon, she wondered how all this would end. Certainly not with a happily ever after.

Half an hour later, Skip called. "I have some…interesting things to tell you. You in the mood for company?"

She really wasn't. But it must be important, or he wouldn't have asked. "Sure."

There was a pause. His voice dropped lower, concerned. "Are you okay?"

Erika sighed. She could never hide anything from Skip. "I'll tell you when you get here."

"I'm on my way."

Though Erika did what she could to make herself presentable, her eyes were red and swollen when Skip showed up. He greeted her with a, "What's wrong?"

"Danny found the tracker and the spyware, and he lost it. We had a huge fight."

Skip's expression was stricken. "Oh, my God. Erika, I'm so sorry. Let me talk to him. It's my fault. That stuff was all my idea."

"But I was completely on board with it, and he knows that. At this point, he's too worked up to listen to either of us."

Skip sighed. "Okay, but let me know if you change your mind. I'll do anything."

She knew he would. "Thanks, Skip. Anyway, what's going on?"

He leaned forward. "I heard from my buddy in Chicago. About Charlie."

CHAPTER THIRTY-FIVE

As Erika had expected, Tyler sent her an email on Monday morning saying Mia needed a week—possibly two—to get well enough to come to court. Since Erika was fully prepped for trial, she called in sick and went back to bed.

A long, empty day stretched out in front of her. Plenty of time to suffer over her fight with Danny and everything else that'd gone wrong in her life in the past few months.

After Skip left, she'd written to Danny three times. As of midnight, he hadn't responded. Erika couldn't get back to sleep. She went to her laptop, hoping he'd emailed. Her heart sank when she saw he hadn't.

Maybe she should give it a rest, she thought. Give him time to cool down. But she worried that if she didn't keep showing him she cared, he'd go on persuading himself that he'd been right to be angry, to break it off with her—until he literally reached a point of no return.

No, it was better to continue making contact. She'd show him he wasn't the only one who could obsess. Erika had started to write him again when a knock on the door made her jump.

Her heart lifted. Danny. It had to be Danny.

But it wasn't. It was Charlie—with an expression that told Erika this was no social call. "We need to talk," she said, holding up a brown paper bag.

Erika stepped back and gestured toward the living room. "Have a seat. Want some tea? I have chamomile and mint."

"No, thanks." Charlie was silent as Erika sat down in the rocking chair across from her. "I'm here to tell you what you've probably known all along. Mia's innocent. And I can prove it."

Erika frowned. "What the hell are you talking about?"

Charlie pulled a cell phone out of the paper bag. "Check out the text."

Erika stared down at the screen shocked. "How did you get this?"

Charlie told her about the call from the neighbor. "If Mia was really locked out, then the rest of her story checks out, too. Shelly was already dead by the time she got home." She paused, her eyes fixed on Erika's. "She was killed to keep her from telling anyone that you got Alberto Sanchez deported so he couldn't testify in the Steers case."

Erika froze, her mind reeling, spooling out and away. It was happening—she was outside her body, looking down. She heard her voice say, "That's bullshit." But it sounded like a recording. Could Charlie tell?

Charlie drilled her with a fierce look. "Shelly tells Skip that Sanchez thinks you got him deported. The day after Shelly talks to Skip for the last time, she's dead. The timing alone speaks volumes."

Erika tried to think of something to say, but she was drifting further and further away. She looked down at herself, a rigid stick figure in a rocking chair. *This is your life! You've got to fight!*

"You can't prove I got anyone deported," said her tinny voice.

Charlie sat back and folded her arms. "Yes, I can. I've got a witness. Alberto's brother, Carlos. Sanchez told him everything."

Erika's vision was darkening.

Think! Push back!

Charlie was going to ruin everything. She had to stop her.

Somehow, her lips began to move. "You think anyone's going to believe the brother of a felon who jumped bail over a prosecutor and a detective who've worked every major case in this city for years?"

Charlie's chin jutted forward. "They'll believe him because it all fits. If Shelly had kept talking, Steers' defense team would've found out about Sanchez. They'd win the new trial motion, and you'd be hosed." She glared at Erika. "No wonder you were in such a hurry to get Mia convicted. You had to shut it all down before anyone figured out what you did."

Her vision was fading, Charlie's body just an outline now, and her heart was pounding so loud and hard the sound filled her head, blocking out all other thoughts. She needed air. *Get up! Go outside!* But she couldn't move, and Charlie was staring at her. *Say something!*

"All you've got is Sanchez's brother. The rest is just speculation. No judge is going to buy it."

"It'll be enough to throw out Steers' conviction and grant him a new trial."

A roaring sound filled the room, drowning out Charlie's voice.

She's going to destroy you! Do something!

Fresh air had helped before. Erika saw her body move to the sliding glass door. As she opened it, a gust of icy wind blew in. She tilted her face up to the sky, let the air fill her lungs…and it worked! The episode began to fade. Erika closed the door and leaned against it, nearly faint with relief. But the spell had drained her. It took everything she had to pull herself together.

Charlie was probably right. The evidence she'd found might be good enough to get Steers a new trial. And if that happened, the defense would go to the ends of the earth to find Sanchez. That'd be the end of…everything.

But Erika had one card left to play. She turned back to Charlie. "I know that text you found on her phone makes it seem…less likely. But Mia has to be guilty. So, if you want to try and take me down, I guess I can't stop you…Lauren."

A look of shock spread across Charlie's face. Then her features hardened. "So I changed my name. Big deal. It's not a crime. You, on the other hand, are on the hook for quite a few."

Erika was well aware of her jeopardy. She'd spent too many sleepless nights lying in bed in a cold sweat, terrified of exactly this scenario. But she trained a steady gaze on Charlie and said, "Without Sanchez, you've got nothing. And I sincerely doubt that even Steers' lawyers will be able to find him. Clearly, his own brother doesn't know where he is, or you'd have tracked him down by now."

Erika could see that Charlie was trying to tough it out, but she wasn't done. "And at least I didn't get my own cousin killed. How do you live with that? Or with the fact that you literally got in bed with a serial killer? If I give this story to the press, your cover will be blown. And you'll get to live through it all again. It'll make a lot of people wonder about you. 'How did she—of all people, a criminal lawyer—not know?' Harrier won't even wonder. He can't tolerate the tiniest scandal. It'll take him about ten seconds to fire you."

Erika sat down in the rocking chair. "So here's the deal: you shut up about Sanchez and let Mia's case go to trial—and I'll keep your secret. Or you can push your story, and I'll call one of my friends at Channel Four."

Charlie's face flushed red. "Go ahead. Out me. You can't possibly punish me any more than I punish myself." She looked Erika in the eye. "You think I changed my name because I was worried about bad PR? I could give a shit. I had to get a new identity because if I didn't, I was pretty sure Lauren Claybourne would be next."

Only in that moment did the cruelty of her own threat hit Erika. For the love of God, Charlie had lost her cousin so tragically, and here she was, threatening to use that painful secret as...as leverage? She couldn't believe she'd stooped so low.

Who was this monster she'd become? Strong-arming witnesses, leaking to the press, setting up Charlie to take the fall. This wasn't her. Erika was the good guy who went to the mat to fight for victims—tough, but always fair. She was someone people trusted to do the right thing. That she could fall so far as to use Charlie's tragic past to pressure her was beyond comprehension. In trying to save herself, Erika had lost sight of the fact that she'd become someone who was no longer worth saving.

Enough, she thought. This has to stop.

Her voice was raw with emotion. "Fuck. I'm sorry. Forget what I said. I won't tell anyone about you, no matter what you decide to do."

Charlie blinked, speechless, then gave her a skeptical look. "Really?" Erika nodded. Charlie fell silent as she studied her, then said, "But...don't you care that Mia's innocent?"

Still reeling, it took Erika a moment to get her bearings. Her brow furrowed. "Of course I care. I mean, I would. *If* she was innocent, but she's not. She can't be." It was Erika's turn to search Charlie's face. Clearly, Charlie was convinced she was right. "If you're so sure it's not Mia, then who do you think killed Shelly?"

Charlie's voice was firm. "Natalie's father. Phillip Hemingsworth. He and his wife were in your office every day. Everyone knew he had a temper, that he lost his shit if a witness said 'yeah' instead of 'yes.' I think he and his wife found out what Shelly was saying, probably from you, and Phillip knew that if Shelly got to the defense, the Steers conviction had a good chance of getting thrown out." Charlie gave her an accusatory look. "That's why you set Mia up. To cover for him. Because if Phillip Hemingsworth got busted, so would you."

Erika saw the logic, but she shook her head. "I'm not covering for Phillip. In fact, we suspected him right from the start."

Charlie's eyes were still narrowed, her lips stretched thin with doubt. *Might as well put my cards on the table*, Erika thought. She said, "Because you're right. They did know about Shelly. We had to warn them that she'd probably give the defense some serious ammunition for the motion for a new trial."

There was a long beat of silence. When Charlie spoke, her tone was suspicious. "Then how come I never heard about it?"

"Are you kidding? If he found out we were looking into him, there'd be hell to pay. We checked him first thing, we just did it…quietly."

Erika had known they couldn't stop Shelly from talking. They'd decided they'd just have to bluff, deny having taken a statement from Sanchez, have him deported, and hope the judge believed them. It might've worked. No one at ICE would talk, and no one could prove they'd ever made contact with Sanchez. As long as he stayed gone, they'd probably have been okay.

Charlie folded her arms. "Then Phillip knew you got Sanchez deported."

Erika gave her a hard look. "No. He didn't. And neither do you. All he knew was that Sanchez told Shelly he could give Steers an alibi."

Charlie was defiant. "Even if I can't prove you got him deported, I can prove you hid the statement of a key witness. Carlos's testimony will bury you."

Erika wasn't so sure about that. But it wasn't impossible, and she couldn't afford to take the chance. "I'm not saying I'm in the clear. But what would you have done? You saw what that trial was like. And if the judge grants the motion, it'll be even harder the next time—whether they find Sanchez or not."

If Erika didn't find a way to make Charlie back off, all the outrageous risks she'd taken to convict Steers would be for nothing. She leaned forward, fists clenched. "If Steers gets out, he'll go on raping and torturing—and maybe killing—more women. He will. You know it as well as I do. I told you about Melody."

Charlie stared out through the sliding glass doors, her expression troubled. "But why didn't you charge Phillip with the murder?"

"Because he had an alibi. Phillip and Rochelle were at a fundraiser up in San Francisco that night."

"That...can't be right," Charlie said, shaking her head. "Was he there all night?"

"According to about a hundred people at the event, yeah. But how about this? I'll get Skip to take another look. See if there's any evidence that Phillip dropped out of sight for a while."

Erika watched Charlie for her reaction. Slowly, Charlie nodded. "That'll work. I have one other idea, too." After a beat, she added, "And...I need to tell you about Roman. There's something you should know."

×××

CHARLIE LEFT AN HOUR later, and Erika sank down on the couch, her hands over her eyes. She had to tell Skip about their confrontation—and about that psychopath, Roman, Charlie's ex. She'd been stunned to hear that in spite of all Charlie's efforts to hide, he'd found her. Afraid for Charlie, Erika had insisted she let Skip do what he could to help.

She couldn't deny that Charlie was right: the text on Mia's phone proved she'd told the truth—about the deadbolt anyway. But if Mia was innocent, that raised harrowing questions. She thought they'd done a good job checking out Phillip's alibi. But what if they'd missed something? Maybe they'd been too willing to dismiss him as a suspect. It was an awful—but real—possibility.

And Erika had to face facts: if it turned out to be Phillip, she was to blame for Shelly's death. By getting Sanchez deported, she'd set in motion the wheels that had led inexorably to Shelly's murder.

The realization was soul-crushing. She didn't know how she'd live with the guilt. Or whether she should even try.

CHAPTER THIRTY-SIX

I STARTED TO SHUFFLE out to the kitchen to get my morning caffeine fix—then stopped just in time. I was half-naked and not alone. I pulled on sweatpants and a hoodie and did my best to smooth down my palm tree of hair. Having Brett here was comforting, no question, but it was also a little awkward. My apartment was fine for one person, but a tight squeeze for two, especially two who weren't intimate.

Still, having Brett camp out on my couch did keep me on the straight and narrow. Getting wasted in front of him was out of the question. I didn't know how I looked when I was blitzed—I only got drunk when I was alone—but I had a feeling it wasn't pretty. With Brett here, I could have one drink, maybe two, but that was it. Of course, the upside was that my mornings no longer felt like a struggle for survival.

Today, Brett was at the kitchen table working on his laptop, already dressed and ready to go. Self-conscious—I definitely wasn't ready for my closeup—I hurried to the coffeemaker. "Hey, sleep okay?"

Fortunately, he was focused on the computer. "Just fine. I assume you'll be at the office all day?"

"Yeah," I said as I filled my travel mug.

I'd told Brett about my encounter with Erika, and how I'd thought of one last thing that might conclusively prove who'd killed Shelly. The problem was, with my dicey memory, I wasn't sure it existed. Another reason to be glad I was barely drinking.

He stood up and pointed out the window to the street below. "I take it you didn't hear the alarm go off last night. Someone backed into my car. I didn't want to leave you alone too long, so I just stopped the noise. I need to go check it and make sure it'll drive."

Squinting down, I saw that the grill was pretty well bashed in. My heart gave a hard thump. "Do you think it was Roman? Letting us know he's onto you?"

"It was my first guess," he said, dour. "I'll see what I can find out."

I swallowed hard. "If it *was* Roman, then he knows you're staying here."

He nodded as he moved to the door, saying, "But it might have been a random thing. It's a busy street." He paused, then asked, "Will Skip be at the office today? Just in case?"

"Yeah, I talked to Erika. He'll keep an eye on me and try to help find Roman." At the look of concern on Brett's face, I added, "Come on, you don't seriously think Roman would try anything at the office? There must be a hundred people in and out of there all day—and a bunch of them are cops."

"No," he said with a sigh. "But I feel better knowing Skip's there."

"Don't worry. I'll be okay."

Brett left, and as I got ready for work, I found myself taking more time than usual with the hair and makeup routine. I felt a little ridiculous. All the mascara in the world wouldn't matter if Roman caught up with me, and Brett probably wouldn't notice if my nose fell off.

But, surprise, when I went back out to the kitchen, he gave me an appreciative smile and said, "Car's running fine. Ready?"

"As I'll ever be." His smile felt good, but I was anxious. If the report I thought I remembered didn't really exist, I didn't know what I'd do.

×××

I CLOSED THE DOOR to my office and wiped my sweaty palms on my thighs as I sat down at my computer. *Please, let me be right. Please let it be there.*

As I pored over page after page, my anxiety mounted. I kept thinking it had to be here…or here…or here. It wasn't, though, and as the day wore on, my heart sank. Maybe I was wrong. Or I'd imagined it. Eyes burning with fatigue, head aching, I reached the end of the last batch. Nothing. I must've wished it into existence.

But as I was about to concede defeat, there it was. And not just the report, the photograph, too. I thanked the Gods of Evidence as I printed it and headed to Erika's office. I knocked, then held out the pages, hand trembling. "Found it."

Erika seemed subdued and distracted. I got that. She'd seen a side of herself she'd probably never known was there, and it'd shaken her to the core. I was betting she'd never let that side emerge again.

As I watched, she read the report and eyed the photograph. "You think this'll pan out?"

"I guess we'll see." If it didn't give us the proof I hoped for—much as I now believed in Mia's innocence—I'd have to admit I might be wrong. But if it did…

Looking past her, I saw that Steers' motion for a new trial on her monitor. "You know, I want that asshole to die in prison just as much as you do."

Erika rubbed her eyes. "Yeah, well. I don't know how I'm going to do that, if…"

If Phillip got arrested. In that case, the whole story about Sanchez would come out. I wasn't sure what would happen to Skip, but Erika would be in deep shit. Hiding exculpatory evidence was a huge ethical violation. She could get fired—or even disbarred.

So she had plenty of reasons to say she'd stick with Mia and dare me to talk. I thought it said a lot about her that she was willing to suffer the consequences instead of duking it out. "I know. And it'll be hideous if Steers wins. But he might not. At this point, we don't really have a choice."

She gave a weary nod. "I agree."

I studied her. "Why'd you do it? Bury his statement, I mean."

She stared out the window, her expression tortured. "I was afraid Steers might beat the case, and I…lost it." She paused. "He brought up some old demons I thought I'd dealt with. I didn't realize that at the time."

I could relate. "Well, I don't know if it helps, but if I were in your shoes, I'd have been tempted to do the same."

She looked at me. "It kind of does, actually."

Ours was a weird détente, one that had only emerged after the threat of mutual destruction, but I was okay with it. Even though I was sure she'd set me up to take the fall for the Dante leak. As they say, desperate times call for desperate measures. At base, her cause—to put away a violent sociopath—was noble.

I nodded at the new trial motion. "I'll give you a hand with that if you want."

She raised her eyebrows, then shrugged. "Sure. I'll send you what I've done so far. Thanks."

I didn't try to reassure her that everything would be okay because I didn't think it would be. If the evidence I'd found proved Phillip was the killer, Erika would be hosed. If the evidence didn't pan out, if Skip couldn't punch a hole in Phillip's alibi, we'd have to go forward with the trial, even though I didn't believe Mia was guilty. I went back to my office, glad to have the motion to distract me.

The Steers case was a complex web of circumstantial evidence; it forced me to focus. By the time I'd finished taking notes, it was after six and I was ready to call it a night. I texted Brett that he could meet me any time for the drive home, and he said he was on his way.

I headed to Erika's office and found Skip there. My hopes soared. "Hey, any news?"

But he shook his head. "Not so far. I have to be careful. If Phillip gets wind of what I'm doing, he might dummy up an alibi."

"Don't worry," Erika reassured me. "We won't stop until we have a definitive answer. It's just going to take a little longer."

Brett showed up a short time later, and I made the introductions. After chatting briefly, I said, "We're taking off. You guys staying?"

Erika nodded. "I've still got a lot of work to do on the motion."

×××

BRETT CAREFULLY SCANNED THE parking lot as he walked me to my car. "This place empties out fast, doesn't it?"

"County workers don't get paid overtime. When the clock says five, they say goodnight."

Brett smiled as he gave me a pointed look. "Clearly not all of them."
As I got in, he said, "Try not to drive so fast this time, okay?"

"And make it easy for you? Where's your sense of adventure?"

"In my high school locker," he said, as he closed my door.

I headed home, one eye trained on the speedometer, the other on my
rearview to make sure Brett was keeping up with me.

I'd stopped at a red light when he called.

I answered, surprised. "Hi, what's—"

The *whoop whoop* of a police siren blared on his end. Brett shouted,
"Don't go home! Something's—"

A voice on a bullhorn cut him off. "Put your hands where we can see
them! Now!"

"Brett? Brett!"

But his cell went dead. I stared at the phone, uncomprehending. A car
horn blasted behind me, and I jumped in my seat, then saw that the light
had turned green. I hit the gas, my heart beginning to pound. The way that
cop was yelling, it didn't sound like an ordinary traffic stop. Why had they
pulled him over? Could this be Roman's doing?

Frightened and confused, my brain kept looping through the questions
as it groped for answers that wouldn't come. I didn't know what to do.
My whole body shaking, I drove aimlessly, eyes darting to the rearview
every few seconds, terrified that I'd see Roman following me.

Should I drive to the police station? What would I tell them? Frantic,
I began to force deep breaths. I couldn't just drive around all night. And then
I saw that I'd unconsciously circled back toward the office. That was it!
Erika and Skip were there! I grabbed my cell phone and tried to find Erika's
number, but my hands were slippery with sweat. The phone slid out of my
grasp and fell to the floor on the passenger side. Afraid to pull over or try
to reach for it with only one sweaty hand on the steering wheel, I picked up
speed, and almost cried with relief when I saw the building up ahead. The
light streaming through the windows felt like a beacon guiding me to safety.

I hit the driveway so fast I caught air. The lot was empty, save for a few
security patrol carts. Good. I drove to the side entrance, where I could park
closest to the doors.

My heart hammering painfully in my chest, I grabbed my purse and keys and jumped out. But as I headed toward the steps, I heard the roar of an engine. A white Cadillac flew past me, then came to a screeching stop ten yards away. The driver's door flew open, and I stared in mute horror as Roman leaped out—a Roman I'd never seen before, with long, stringy hair and a patchy beard. But what chilled me to the bone was the way his eyes blazed with fury as they fixed on me.

I screamed and ran up the steps. But just as I reached the door, he grabbed the collar of my jacket and yanked me backward. I screamed again as I fell, tumbling down the steps, my head slamming into the concrete. Dazed, I reached for the handrail to try and pull myself up, but he pushed me down and grabbed me by the throat with both hands.

I struggled to breathe as I stared up at the twisted mask that was Roman's true face. Eyes fiery with bloodlust, teeth bared in a feral grimace, he was like a demon escaped from hell. I tried to twist out of his grasp, but as he tightened his grip, I could feel myself losing consciousness.

I tried to pry off his hands, but lack of oxygen made me weak. Desperate, I twisted my head and bit his fingers as hard as I could. He let go with a yelp of pain. I pulled away and threw a wild kick that caught him in the stomach, knocking him back.

I began to stagger away, but my head was swimming. Behind me, Roman was already pushing himself up. My heart sank. There was no hope. I couldn't outrun him; I could barely walk. I was dead.

But in that moment, I heard the screech of tires. Headlights lit up Roman's face. I threw myself onto the stairs as the car zoomed past me and heard Roman yell, then the dull thud of metal on flesh. When I turned to look, I saw his body lying a few yards away.

I peered into the darkness. Was he breathing? I couldn't tell. But he wasn't moving, and his right leg was bent at an odd angle. Dizzy and numb with shock, I lay back on the cold ground, wondering who my savior had been.

It was Erika. She was ghostly pale, her expression panicked, as she ran over and put a hand on my shoulder. Her voice shook as she said, "Charlie? Are you okay?"

I looked up at her worried face and managed a half-smile, though my head was throbbing and my throat was on fire. I croaked out, "How did you know...?"

"I heard you scream." She pulled her cell phone out of her coat. "Skip was gone, and I—I didn't know what else to do."

I gazed at her, overwhelmed with gratitude. And then, the irony of it all hit me: The woman who'd threatened to ruin me had just saved my life.

Erika called 9-1-1, and seconds later, the shriek of sirens pierced the air. My stomach turned over, and I threw up until there was nothing left.

Then the patrol cars were there, lights flashing, sirens blasting, the ambulance right behind them. The cops jumped out, and Erika pointed to Roman and said, "He was about to kill her."

×××

ERIKA RODE TO THE emergency room with me. I kept fading in and out of consciousness, but I managed to tell her about Brett. "Roman must've set him up somehow. Can Skip—"

"Already on it." She refilled my water and held the cup to my lips. "Drink."

I took a sip, then let my head drop back on the pillow. "Erika, I—I don't know how I'll ever be able to thank you. I can't begin to find the words—"

She raised an eyebrow. "I kind of owed you one, don't you think?"

I knew she was referring to the ways she'd been prepared to screw me. I couldn't help but smile. "Well, since you put it that way."

She held up a hand. "Just tell me you don't have any other homicidal ex-boyfriends lurking around."

"I'd like to say no." I sighed, "But given my track record, I wouldn't put money on it."

A nurse trotted in and said, "Let's get those X-rays done, shall we?", then rolled me out. I felt like I'd been put through a meat grinder, and I thought for sure something was broken. But it turned out I was basically okay. Banged all to hell, but in the end, I didn't even need stitches.

When I got back to my room, Erika was waiting. "I haven't heard anything yet."

"What about Roman? Is he...?" I knew what I hoped the answer would be.

She peered at me. "Dead? Unfortunately, no. The doctor said he's got internal injuries, some broken bones. But he'll live."

Angry and bitterly disappointed, my hands balled into fists. I wanted to punch a hole in the wall. "Why do the assholes always make it?"

Erika nodded sadly. "It does seem that way. But look at the bright side. He won't skate on this one."

That was true. And this was *premeditated* attempted murder. He'd get life. I flashed on the bone-chilling memory of his face as he'd strangled me. That was the last thing poor Lyra saw. The guilt lay on my chest like an anvil. Nothing could make up for her death. But at least he'd never get to kill again.

×××

I'D SENT ERIKA HOME and turned on the TV when Brett came rushing into my hospital room, fear and worry etched on his face.

"Charlie! Oh my God, I'm so sorry!" He swallowed hard as he took in my bruised neck and forehead, the cold white room.

I pushed myself up to a sitting position, every part of my body shrieking in protest. "What happened? I've been so worried."

He was grim as he said, "A homeless man got killed in a hit and run last night. Someone phoned in a tip that my car was involved."

An icy fist clutched my heart. "Roman. He killed him. And then he backed into your car to make it look like you." As Brett nodded, I closed my eyes. "Jeezus."

He said, "When the cops finally let me know what they'd arrested me for, I told them to check the surveillance cameras on your street. The security camera on your building cleared me...eventually." He shook his head, irritated. "Took them forever to get the footage."

Roman had to have known Brett would get cleared sooner or later. But he'd only needed to peel him off long enough to get to me. "Are they going after Roman for the hit and run?"

"Now that they've heard about you, yes," he said, upset all over again. His eyes scanned my face and neck. "And if they can find the car he used, they might be able to tag him for it."

Roman could wind up with two life sentences—a lovely thought. It sank in then, looking up at Brett. Roman's reign of terror had ended. I could stop looking over my shoulder, stop worrying about what he'd do next, stop living in fear that my next breath might be my last. Most importantly, I could stop fearing for my family. At last, they were safe.

But as I looked up at Brett, I realized it also meant he would go back to Chicago—and I was surprised by how sad that made me feel.

×××

THEY LET ME GO home the following day, and I decided to take the rest of the week off. I was a mass of aches and pains. Luckily, the story of my near-demise—and Erika's heroism—wasn't a major headline, and we'd managed to play it close to the vest, saying only that Erika had saved me from a "deranged attacker." The press hadn't found out about my past. Yet. But I knew they would.

I felt guilty about calling in sick. I was supposed to help Erika with the new trial motion on Steers. When I told her I wasn't coming into the office, I offered, "But I can work from home. If you just send me my notes, I can—"

"Don't be ridiculous! I'll be fine. Take it easy; get some rest."

I said I would. Not that I had a choice. Brett—who'd insisted on staying until I was on my feet—wouldn't even let me get my own coffee.

So I had plenty of time on my hands. And I spent almost all of it worrying about the Hansen case: what that report would yield, what progress Skip had made on Phillip's alibi. Waiting has never been a strong suit of mine. But now, with nothing else to do? Sheer torture.

By the end of the week, I was dying to get back to work, technicolor face notwithstanding. But that night, Erika called. I stared at the phone, afraid to pick up, knowing she was going to give me answers—and that they might not be what I wanted.

I looked at Brett. "This could be it." I tried to keep the apprehension out of my voice as I answered, "What's up?"

Erika said she wanted to pay me a visit, and I agreed. I told Brett she was coming over, then went to put on concealer and change into real clothes.

Fifteen minutes later, she knocked on the door. When I let her in, I tried to read her expression, but her face gave nothing away.

As we moved into the living room, I had no idea what was coming.

CHAPTER THIRTY-SEVEN

Erika's intercom buzzed. It was the receptionist. She glanced at Skip and Charlie, who sat in front of her desk. "They're here."

Skip nodded and left. Erika gazed at Charlie. She looked pale in spite of the layers of makeup she'd used to try and cover her bruises. "You sure you're up for this?"

Charlie nodded. "I look worse than I feel."

Skip ushered Rochelle and a glowering Phillip Hemingsworth into the office. As they sat down, Phillip snapped, "I'd like to know why we couldn't hear about this update on the phone."

Skip took the lead. "I have some...unexpected news. Foreign DNA was found on the doorframe of Shelly's bedroom."

Erika had worried about that finding when she'd first seen the report. The doorframe was a place the killer might've inadvertently touched and not thought to wipe down—unlike a doorknob or the deadbolt lock. But she'd eventually decided it was no big deal, and when Charlie had suggested they compare it to the DNA samples taken from the Hemingsworths during the Steers case, she'd been skeptical about the likelihood of finding a match.

She watched their reactions as Skip said, "That DNA belongs to you."

Phillip's face flamed red. After a stunned pause, he shouted, "That's impossible. I've never been anywhere near that house!"

Erika let his words hang in the air as the heat of his outburst filled the room. Then she shook her head. "Not you, Phillip." She turned to Rochelle.

Phillip pointed a finger at Erika. "That's outrageous! How dare you?" He looked at his wife. "Tell them!"

Rochelle clutched the arms of her chair, her gaze fixed straight ahead.

They should've realized long ago. In San Francisco, Skip had found out that, although Phillip and Rochelle had been at that fundraiser together, Rochelle had left early, pleading a migraine. Armed with that information, he'd found a closed-circuit camera that showed Rochelle driving toward the freeway at 10:30 p.m.

Plenty of time to make it to Santa Cruz by midnight.

If only they'd dug harder to begin with. Mia, instead of being thrown in jail, would've been allowed to grieve the tragic loss of her mother in peace. But they'd been hellbent on locking down the case before Sanchez could resurface. And so they'd blown right by key evidence that would've proven Rochelle was the killer.

In a trembling voice, Rochelle said, "I only meant to talk to her. I needed to make her understand—"

Phillip drew back, incredulous. "No! You can't be serious."

But Rochelle continued, her voice filled with anguish, "She had her daughter. I lost mine! I had to make her see. If that man's statement came out, it'd ruin everything. My baby's killer would just…walk out the door. But she wouldn't listen. She said the defense had the right to know—"

Phillip put a hand on her shoulder. "Rochelle, stop! Stop talking! Now!"

She pressed on, her eyes fixed on a distant point. "Everybody has rights—except Natalie! It was like she thought my Natalie's life was nothing! I asked her what if it were *her* daughter? How would *she* feel? But she just said she was sorry, she had to do it. I—I was going to leave, but then—"

Phillip was beside himself. "I said *stop*! Do you hear me? Stop!"

But Erika could see the dam that'd held all the pent-up rage and torment of the months since Natalie's murder had finally burst.

"Then I saw the photos on the kitchen counter. Shelly with her daughter." Rochelle teared up, her face crumpling. "My Natalie…I'll never get to take any more photos with her." Her voice became ragged and harsh. "And that…woman was going to destroy my only chance to make that bastard pay for killing her."

She began to cry heavy, mournful sobs that wracked her body. Phillip sagged in his chair, shaking his head back and forth in disbelief.

Skip waited for her tears to subside, then advised Rochelle of her rights. But her glazed, vacant eyes said she wasn't processing any of it. She was an empty shell.

Charlie opened the door to let in the backup officers. As Skip gently escorted Rochelle out, one of them offered Phillip a ride to the station. He looked up, his eyes wide and staring, his face pale. As he laboriously pushed himself out of the chair, he looked like he'd aged a hundred years.

After they left, Erika's eyes filled with tears, the weight of her guilt so heavy it was hard to speak. "It's my fault. All of it."

Charlie frowned. "You didn't tell her to kill Shelly."

"I might as well have." Erika looked around her office. The view of the ocean, the framed diplomas on the wall, the photos of herself and Skip at a fundraiser, a selfie taken during a day-cruise she and Carson had chartered for Skip's birthday. This office had been her home, her sanctuary for the better part of fourteen years.

But not for much longer. Her career was over.

She might go to jail. And she richly deserved it.

Charlie sighed. "So, what now?"

"Now I call Tyler."

×××

IN THE COURTROOM THAT afternoon, Erika scanned the gallery for reporters. To her relief, there were only two people who looked like they might be press—probably because they'd scheduled the hearing on such short notice.

Tyler approached Erika. "Thank you. Not many prosecutors would be willing to pull back from the ledge like this."

Erika gestured to Charlie. "She's the one you should thank."

He turned to Charlie with a smile. "I guess you can take the girl out of the defense firm ..."

Charlie just shrugged.

The bailiff brought Mia out of lockup, and Tyler headed over to her. She looked thinner and very pale. But she wore a wide, slightly dazed smile.

As Erika watched her, she thought, *You almost put her away for life.* She knew then, with a cold certainty, that she'd never forgive herself.

Judge Butler took the bench at exactly 2:30. "My clerk said you *both* asked for an emergency hearing. I'm assuming this time it's a real one."

Erika stood. "It is. The People move to dismiss all charges against Mia Hansen."

The judge stared at her. "On what grounds?"

Erika took a deep breath. "On the grounds that she did not commit the murder of Shelly Hansen. We've apprehended the suspect, who's being booked as we speak."

The judge raised an eyebrow. "Since I'm sure the whole city will know very shortly, would you care to tell me who that suspect is?"

Erika gave him a grim look. He'd presided over the Steers case too. This was going to be a shock. "Rochelle Hemingsworth."

The judge wrinkled his brow. "Natalie's mother?"

Erika nodded.

He was silent as he absorbed the news. Then he sighed and said, "I assume I'll learn more about this at the new trial motion tomorrow."

"You will." Erika's stomach clenched at the thought of what lay in store. The judge gave her a searching look, then picked up his gavel.

"The People's motion to dismiss is granted. The defendant is to be released from custody forthwith. Bail is exonerated." The judge banged his gavel and looked down at Mia. "Good luck to you, young lady. I'm sorry for what you've been through." He nodded at Tyler and left the bench.

Mia and Tyler hugged until the bailiff came to take her back into lockup. As she turned to go, she glanced over her shoulder at Erika and Charlie and gave them a tentative smile.

Mia seemed different now, Erika thought. Older, in a way. She could only hope the experience wouldn't leave her permanently scarred.

×××

By the time Erika and Charlie got back to the office, the local news stations had the story on blast. "CASE DISMISSED! WILD CHILD GOES FREE!" "MOTHER OF STEERS VICTIM ARRESTED FOR MURDER!"

Erika's phone was ringing nonstop. She stared at the blinking lights, wishing she could throw it out the window. The last thing she felt like doing was talking to reporters.

Then it occurred to her: she didn't have to. When Harrier found out about Sanchez, he'd fire her on the spot. She didn't need to keep him happy anymore.

Charlie gave Erika a puzzled look. "Aren't you going to answer?"

Erika was defiant. "No. You want to talk to those jackals, have at it. I don't have much time left here, and I don't want to waste it giving soundbites."

Charlie's tone was sympathetic. "Want to come hang out in my office? It'll be quieter there."

Erika appreciated the gesture, but she shook her head. She wondered whether Charlie would still be in her life once she left the office. She knew Charlie was grateful to her, but that didn't necessarily mean she'd want a real friendship. The thought made her feel more than a little blue. She'd wound up really liking Charlie.

"Skip should be back any time now. We have to write up the report on Sanchez."

The new trial motion was tomorrow. She needed to get it to the defense tonight.

Charlie nodded, her expression glum. "I really wish there was a way out of that."

Erika did, too. As she settled behind her desk, Skip walked in and glanced at the ringing phone. "I take it you dismissed on Mia?"

"It'll slow down when they realize I'm not talking."

"I've got the Hemingsworth arrest report." He opened the file folder he was carrying, took out a pen, and signed it. "I'll leave you a copy." He frowned at the signature, then at the side of his left hand, which was smeared with ink. "Damn it."

Charlie leaned in and looked at the report. "Never knew you were a lefty."

He sighed. "I usually manage to avoid making such a mess." He grabbed a Kleenex and wiped off his hand. "Anyway, I bumped into Mia at the jail."

Erika gave him a pained look. "Please don't tell me she thanked us." Mia didn't owe her anything close to thanks.

"Okay, I won't tell you. But she said she's sober now. Plans to go to college, get a degree—the whole nine yards."

"Huh. Did not see that coming," Charlie said. "But good for her. Where's she going to stay?"

"With her aunt," Skip said. "But not for long. As soon as her mother's will gets sorted out, she'll be able to get her own place."

Charlie *hmphed*. "Her own mansion, you mean. She's gonna be one rich kid."

If Erika had been able to smile, that would have done it. "Good. Maybe it'll help her get over the hell she's been through." She turned to her computer. "Shall we?"

Skip pressed his lips together. "Listen, Erika. You don't have to take the rap for Sanchez. I can tell the defense I hid the statement, that you never knew about it."

He glanced at Charlie, who shrugged. "Works for me."

He was the best friend she'd ever had, Erika thought, meeting his eyes across her desk. "Thanks, Skip. That means a lot. But I'm the one who made this mess, and I'm the one who's got to pay."

She meant it. This was her cross to bear—and hers alone.

But Charlie gave a frustrated sigh. "At least say you took the statement after the verdict, when Shelly called. No one's ever going to know you spoke to him before the trial. Not unless you tell them."

"She's right," Skip said. "The uni who gave me the heads up about Sanchez doesn't know we ever made contact. And we're the only ones who know what Shelly said. It's going to be bad enough to admit we hid the statement for about a month. Especially since Sanchez jumped bail."

Erika looked from Skip to Charlie. They were right. And Skip was going to get some flak for burying the statement, too. She owed it to him to minimize his exposure. "Okay, I guess we can do that."

There was such a heaviness in her heart, Erika felt like she might never be able to laugh again.

But in that moment, she realized something else: she hadn't had a dissociative episode or panic attack since Charlie had confronted her at her apartment. And she thought she knew why. The worst had happened.

There were no more bombs left to explode, no more secrets left to hide. In a strange way, she was free.

She tapped a key on her computer to wake it up. "Let's get this thing done."

×××

ERIKA TOOK THE FREEWAY home to test her theory. No panic attack, not even a hint of one. It might be her only good news.

She'd changed her mind about turning over the Sanchez report tonight. The defense would've gone straight to the press. The moment they did, Harrier would fire her—and forbid her from going to court. Erika couldn't let that happen. There was still a chance she'd win the motion, and she was determined to take it. She wanted to go down swinging. It'd be her last act as a prosecutor.

At home, she put on a can of chicken noodle soup and opened her laptop to check her email. When her inbox appeared on the screen, she saw what she'd been hoping for—and dreading: an email from Danny.

She was afraid to open it. But she had to know if her brother was lost to her. She moved the cursor, clicked, and read.

Hey. Just saw the news about the Hansen case. What a bummer. You must be wrecked. Call me whenever. D.

CHAPTER THIRTY-EIGHT

I WOKE UP THE next morning even angrier than I'd been last night. I hadn't gotten more than two hours of unbroken sleep. Ordinarily, I'd have cured that problem with a deep dive into the bottle, but I couldn't do that with Brett here. Besides, I needed to be in shape for the hearing on the new trial motion.

But that meant there was no hangover to blunt my fury. I was actually shaking with anger as I tried to fill my travel cup and wound up spilling hot coffee on my hand. "Ow! Damn it!"

Brett knew how I was feeling. "I'd be hella pissed off, too. But Erika might win. Stranger things have happened."

I shook my head as I picked up my purse and moved to the door. "Not much stranger. And if she loses, she won't be around to do the retrial. Which means that motherfucker probably walks."

He gestured to my scarf; I'd taken to wearing it to cover the still very visible bruises on my neck. "Here, let me fix that."

He came over and adjusted it. Our eyes locked and for a moment, I thought he was going to kiss me. But at the last second, he pulled back. I tried to hide my disappointment as he said, "Look, if you want me to stick around for moral—"

He was finally leaving to spend a couple of days with his sister in Monterey. "Absolutely not," I said, firmly. "I know what I'll be like after that hearing, and believe me, you don't want to see it."

He raised an eyebrow. "Now I want to stick around, see what you've got. I can get pretty…special myself." He put a hand on my shoulder. "You sure?"

"I'm sure." But the truth was, I already missed him.

After he left, I headed out to what promised to be the shittiest day I'd had since moving to Santa Cruz. Considering one of those days had almost ended with me dead, that was saying something.

The courthouse lot was packed with news vans, and the line of people waiting for a seat stretched around the block. Today's hearing was always going to be a draw. But now that the news of Rochelle Hemingsworth's arrest had exploded across the airwaves and internet, I knew it'd be ten times bigger.

I kept my head down as I hurried into the office, just in case any reporters were lurking. A text from Skip pinged on my cell phone: *E wanted to get to court early. I'll come get you. Press is crazy.*

I paced, my stomach in knots—angry, scared, and worried about Erika. This day was going to be absolute hell for her, even if she won the motion.

When Skip showed up, he said, "I don't know if it helps, but Erika doesn't look any better than you."

I shot him a dagger. "It doesn't."

Luckily, he knew a route to the courthouse that skirted the crowds. As he guided me to the freight elevator, I thought of the moment yesterday when he'd signed Rochelle's arrest report. It was the same smeared signature I'd seen on the coroner's evidence form.

I didn't see any need to bust him. Mia was free. And somehow, I was a hundred percent sure he'd never done anything like that before—or ever would again.

×××

THE COURTROOM WAS ALREADY packed. I moved to counsel table and sat down next to Erika. Skip was right, she was a wreck. "Anything I can do?"

She glanced behind me at the front row of the gallery and said in a low voice, "Maybe give Melody Newman a little support. She's the one I told you about. She's freaking out."

I followed her gaze to a willowy blonde, who looked like she might fall apart at any minute. Her arms were wrapped around her body, which was shaking so hard it looked like she was sitting in a freezer.

"Just say I told you she was a friend of Natalie's."

I hurried over and introduced myself to Melody. In a wobbly whisper, she said, "He can't get out. The judge won't let him, will he?"

"I very much doubt it." Even if Steers won a new trial, I didn't think the judge would let him make bail. "Erika's going to fight very hard to win this motion."

Her head bobbed up and down, a series of trembling nods. "I know. She did such a great job before. But the defense has been saying that they—"

At that moment, the bailiff called the court to order. I reached over the rail and squeezed Melody's shoulder. "Hang in there."

She bit her lip and slid a glance toward the defense side of counsel table, where Steers was sitting. He was looking over his shoulder in her direction, but I couldn't tell whether he'd seen her.

I moved back to counsel table to stand next to Erika as Judge Butler came striding out. He took the bench and said, "Be seated." Scanning the crowded gallery, he said, "I'm issuing a warning right now. Any outburst, any talking, any sound other than breathing, you're out." He turned to the defense lawyers. "Counsel—"

Erika interrupted. "Your Honor, I have to advise the court of a new development." She swallowed hard, then said, "Early this morning, I turned over a witness statement to the defense from a Mr. Alberto Sanchez. I…I actually took this statement over a month ago. Shortly before Shelly Hansen was murdered. The statement purports to give Blake Steers an alibi for the night of Natalie Hemingsworth's murder."

A ripple ran through the gallery; I heard a few muted gasps. Although Rochelle's arrest was public knowledge, the facts underlying it were not. The judge threw an angry glance at the crowd. A heavy silence fell as he stared down at Erika. "Why did it take you a month to turn over this discovery?"

I stared at the table, my heart in my mouth. I knew Erika had to be quaking inside.

Erika's voice was low but steady. "I have no excuse, Your Honor."

Dirk Stanton, the lead lawyer for the defense, jumped to his feet and shouted, "I can tell you why, Judge! She hid the statement so we wouldn't be able to find the witness! Sanchez jumped bail. No one knows where he is. And we believe the prosecution had something to do with that!"

Judge Butler frowned at him. "Be seated, counsel. And you'll keep a civil tone in my court." He gave Erika a dour look. "Ordinarily, I wouldn't dignify that accusation by asking for a response. But the fact that you waited a month to turn over this statement leaves me no choice: Did you have a hand in this witness's disappearance?"

"No, Your Honor. I had nothing to do with Mr. Sanchez absconding."

"But your inexcusable delay in turning over the statement certainly makes it harder for the defense to contact him."

Erika clasped her hands together. "I agree. I'm sorry, Your Honor." Her voice was strained as she added, "And I apologize to the defense."

I couldn't begin to fathom what it'd cost her to say that to those scumbag bloodsuckers. Their gloating expressions left me seething.

Judge Butler's tone was somber as he sat back in his chair. "However, that does not resolve the question as to whether this witness statement is sufficiently material and credible to justify a new trial. I assume it's fairly brief?"

Dirk Stanton said, "Just a couple of paragraphs. I can give the court my copy."

He handed a piece of paper to Letitia, who passed it to the judge. The judge read it, then said, "It certainly does appear to give the defendant an alibi." He nodded at Stanton. "You have the floor, counsel."

Stanton moved to the podium as though he were taking center stage at a rock concert. "As you can see from that statement, Mr. Sanchez knew Blake Steers very well. Saw him almost every day. So there's no chance he was mistaken about his identification of Mr. Steers. Beyond that, by placing Mr. Steers at his restaurant at midnight, this witness completely eliminates any chance that my client could've committed the murder. There can be no more compelling reason to grant a motion for a new trial than the discovery of such profoundly important exculpatory evidence—evidence we could not have uncovered before this." He turned to point a finger at Erika. "Because this prosecutor willfully hid it from us!"

The judge interrupted. "Stop with the histrionics, counsel. Anything else?"

Stanton's neck turned red. "No, Your Honor."

I didn't think Judge Butler cared much for the defense team. That could be good for us. Or not.

Erika moved to the podium. She spoke slowly at first. "I don't need to tell the court about the powerful case we presented at trial. Blake Steers was the only one who had a motive to kill Natalie, and the physical evidence established his guilt well beyond a reasonable doubt. As for Sanchez's statement…I won't call him a liar. He's simply wrong. When I asked him how he could be sure he saw Blake Steers on that particular day, he had no answer. Given the overwhelming evidence presented against Blake Steers, there is every reason to believe he saw Steers on a different night. Therefore, Sanchez's testimony would not have changed the outcome. The People ask this Court to deny the motion for a new trial."

When she sat down, she was shaking. I leaned over and whispered, "You did great."

Her expression was worried. "I don't know."

Honestly, I didn't either. Just because Sanchez couldn't explain how he knew he'd seen Steers on the night of the murder didn't mean he was wrong. What made him wrong was—as Erika had said—the mountain of evidence that proved Steers' guilt.

The heavyset defense lawyer, Hugh Worthen, stood up. "The evidence against my client was hardly overwhelming, Your Honor. If you recall—"

The judge interrupted. "Of course, I recall. And if all you intend to do is talk about the evidence in a trial *I* conducted, then you can sit down, counsel."

Stanton leaned toward the lawyer and shook his head. Worthen said, "Very well, Your Honor. Thank you."

The judge said, "I'm ready to rule."

The air was so thick with tension I felt like I was breathing underwater.

"I agree that the evidence of Mr. Steers' motive was strong, as was the physical evidence tying him to the crime scene—though questions were raised by the fact that he frequently visited the victim's home. I also agree that Mr. Sanchez might very well be mistaken." The judge paused as he glanced at the statement.

That sounded good. Beside me, Erika was picking at the cuticle on her thumb so hard she was making it bleed.

He continued, "But he has no particular axe to grind. He and Mr. Steers didn't know each other. And his testimony is crucial. It goes to the very crux of the defense. For all these reasons, the importance of a witness like Mr. Sanchez cannot be overstated. I believe that if the jury had heard his testimony, the outcome might well have been different. Therefore, the motion for a new trial is granted. The conviction is vacated."

Gasps spread through the gallery, and some of the reporters ran out. Stanton jumped to his feet. "Your Honor, since we'll need time to look for Mr. Sanchez—thanks to the prosecution's malfeasance—we request that Mr. Steers be released on bail. I'm prepared to surrender his passport right now."

Erika stood up. "Your Honor—"

The judge shook his head. "Ms. Lorman, you've willfully violated the defendant's right to timely discovery, and you may have made it impossible to locate this witness. So, I'm going to grant that request. Bail will be set at one million dollars." He banged his gavel. "Court is in recess." As he stood, he looked down at Erika. "I'll see you in chambers, counsel."

The moment the judge left the bench, the gallery erupted. Angry shouts competed with cheers of triumph.

Erika sank into her chair, stunned. I was enraged. I'd known we might lose, but I never expected the judge to let that monster make bail.

I whispered, "What the actual fuck?"

Erika didn't answer.

At the other end of counsel table, the defense lawyers were laughing and backslapping, and Steers was beaming—that smug, shit-eating grin. Exactly as I'd pictured it. I wanted to smash my fist into his face. He glanced at the gallery, toward Melody, and, unbelievably, *winked* at her.

I turned to see that she was cowering in her seat, her hand over her mouth, eyes wide with shock. I touched Erika's arm. "I think Melody's going to have a breakdown."

Erika spoke with effort. "Can you take care of her? I don't know how long I'll be."

I looked at her with sympathy. The judge was probably going to tell her he intended to report her to the State Bar. "Sure. I'll bring her back to the office."

As she headed for the judge's chambers, Skip offered to help me get past the reporters. "Great." I nodded toward Melody. "She's coming with us."

Melody was practically doubled over, her face a mask of fear. I leaned down and put a hand on her shoulder. "Come on. Let's get you out of here."

Skip got us to my office using back channels, then said he had to take care of some business at the station. "Let me know how Erika's doing, okay? I'm worried about her. It's already been a bitch of a day, and it's not over."

I was, too. I nodded, then closed the door after him and sat down next to Melody, who was crying. Handing her a box of Kleenex, I said, "It's terrible. I'm upset, too. But we'll win the retrial. Especially if you testify."

She shook her head. "I—I can't. Besides, the judge said the jury might believe that guy, Sanchez. That means Blake's going to get out. It'll never be over!"

I was confused. "What're you talking about?"

She wadded up the tissue in her hand. "I never told Erika, but the night Blake roofied me, he—he raped me, and he took pictures of me. Of...of everything. He texted them to me after I broke up with him."

He was *still* abusing her after the breakup? Rage surged through me; I clenched my fists. "How long after?"

"Like, a month later—when he was with Natalie." A fresh wave of tears coursed down her face.

She broke down again. It was so ugly, so...sadistic. I was almost speechless.

"And you're afraid he'll go public with them?"

"I *know* he will! He saw me in court today! Now he knows I told Erika what he did to me, and he's going to pay me back! He'll post them online. My whole family will see them! My mother, my father...all my friends! My *boss*! My life will be ruined!"

That didn't make any sense. "He'd be insane to do anything to you now. If he so much as sends you a text with a happy face, the judge will toss his ass back in jail."

But she wasn't listening. She stood up, wild-eyed. "No, he won't! Blake gets away with everything! Don't you understand that? He just did it again! He always does!"

She opened the door and flew out. I called after her, "Melody, wait!" But she kept going. By the time I ran into the hallway, she was gone.

This was trouble—big trouble. Melody might be suicidal. I had to get her help. But I didn't know where she'd gone or how to reach her. I went to Erika's office, hoping she'd have Melody's contact information. But when I told her what'd happened, she said, "I don't have it. I'll text Skip."

"What'd the judge say?" I asked, trying to read her face.

"Pretty much what you'd expect about my ethical duties as a prosecutor, and what a serious breach this was." She paused. "But he said this was an uncharacteristic lapse for me. So…he's thinking he might not report me to the State Bar."

I was relieved. "Well, at least one good thing happened today."

Erika sighed. "Stand by for Harrier. The worst is yet to come." A look of fear crossed her face. "Actually, that might not be the worst. The judge said he'd give the defense at least a couple of months to look for Sanchez. If they find him, and he decides to talk…"

Now that Erika had admitted she'd held back his statement, Sanchez's claim that she'd gotten him deported would have a lot more credibility. It'd certainly get her disbarred—no matter what Judge Butler did.

But I thought she might be spared that particular ring of hell. "I have a feeling they won't find him."

Erika looked at me with alarm. "Oh, God. Please tell me he's okay."

"I'm pretty sure he is."

"The brother…Carlos?"

I nodded. I'd been keeping in touch with him. The last time we'd spoken, he *claimed* he hadn't heard from Alberto. But he'd sounded relaxed and upbeat—nothing like the anxious wreck he'd been every other time.

"One other thing…" I told her that the reason Sanchez had come back was to get the money he'd hidden. "So I asked Skip to find out how much money he had on him when he got busted. Only twelve bucks."

Erika's brows lifted. "So…he'd already sent the money home?"

"That's what I'm thinking. And after that one call, Carlos dumped me. Changed his phone number, even. No way he'd do that if he were still worried about his brother."

Our cell phones pinged with a text. Skip had sent us Melody's number and address, but my call went straight to voicemail. I left her a message, then asked Erika, "Should we tell Skip to send a uni to her place? I'm really worried."

Erika frowned. "I don't know. That might just make matters worse."

"Right." Finding a cop on your doorstep isn't exactly reassuring. But I was having visions of Melody searching for a razor blade. "We've got to do *something*."

"Maybe I'll drop by. She knows me. And she trusted me with *most* of her story—other than those photos." Erika shook her head. "I wonder why she didn't tell me about that."

"Honestly, she seemed incredibly traumatized." I thought about what she'd said, then asked, "Do you think she's right? That he'd be stupid enough to put those photos online—or come after her?"

Erika looked uncertain. "You wouldn't think so. But who knows? The guy's a psycho. A real one. And now he probably thinks he's invincible."

"Let's go see her. I'll drive." Erika had been through so much already. She shouldn't have to deal with this on her own.

×××

But when we got to Melody's house, no one answered the door. All the blinds were down, so we couldn't see through the windows, and there didn't seem to be any signs of life. "Should we get a uni to force entry?" I asked, squinting at the upstairs.

"They won't do it, not unless we have evidence that something's really wrong." Erika stood back and surveyed the house. "There's no indication of any problem here. It just looks like she's not home. And she didn't *say* she was going to…hurt herself, right?"

I replayed the scene in my office. "No. She was just acting kind of crazy. Any idea where else she might be?" Erika shook her head. I exhaled, frustrated. "I guess we'll just have to wait and hope she returns my call."

As I pulled into the office parking lot, I asked, "Do you mind if I bail?"

"No, not at all." Erika stared at the building. "Matter of fact, I may, too. Harrier will be happy to fire me over the phone."

"Maybe he won't. You never know."

"Except I do." She opened the door, then turned back to me. "Give me a call when you hear from her. I'll keep trying to reach her too."

I said I would and headed home, trying to block out the nauseating images of Steers' grinning face.

Worried about Melody, I poured myself a double shot of tequila and turned on the TV, hoping to distract myself. A lame reality competition did the trick—people competing to build the fanciest doghouse. Seriously. They had way too much time on their hands. But since I was watching them, I guessed I did, too. And now I was thinking about getting a dog. And a tricked-out doghouse.

I must've dozed off, because at 10:30 I woke up on the couch to the sound of my cell phone ringing. I squinted at the number—had I seen it before?

"Hello?"

I heard high-pitched, rapid breathing on the other end. Then a woman's voice: "I don't know what to do! I screwed up! Please, you have to help me!"

It was Melody. I moved into the bedroom as I asked, "What happened?"

Her voice was a shrill whisper. "Promise me you won't tell! Please!"

I had a bad feeling about this. But I had no choice. "Promise."

Her words tumbled out on top of each other. "I—I went to his house and pretended I wanted to…to hook up. I brought a bottle of wine. I put a bunch of…" she had to pause to catch her breath. "Visine in his glass. He was supposed to die! But he didn't. He's still breathing! He's still alive! What do I do now?!"

Melody had tried to kill *Steers*? By poisoning him with Visine? It took a few seconds for it all to sink in. She wasn't crazy: Visine is lethal, in large enough quantities. And it actually makes the cause of death look like a heart attack. Melody must've spent some time researching. No way this was spur-of-the-moment.

But Melody? The delicate little flower? I'd thought suicide, maybe, not…this.

I needed to focus. "Where are you right now?"

The hysteria in her voice was rising. "Upstairs, in his bedroom. He's on the floor."

I tried to remember the photos I'd seen of his house during the trial. "Okay. Let me think."

We spoke for a few minutes. When we were done, I texted Erika to tell her Melody was okay, that she was at her mother's place in Soquel. Erika texted back to say *"Thanks"* and *"Whew."*

Tossing my phone aside, I refilled my drink and settled in for a long, sleepless night of worrying about what Melody was doing and what might happen to her.

×××

By the time the local morning news came on, I was wide awake and hungover as hell. I watched for an hour but saw nothing about Steers or Melody. Not knowing what to think, I went to the kitchen to make coffee. While I waited for it to brew, I checked the news on my laptop. Nothing there, either.

After all that booze and no sleep, I'd thought I'd be able to slow down, but I was a jittery mess—exhausted and wired at the same time. Good thing Brett had gone to see his sister. Given the state I was in, no way I'd have been able to act normal. I decided to skip work, too, figured I was in no shape to go to the office.

By 9:30, I decided it was safe to take a shower. But as I turned on the water, I heard an excited voice say, "Shocking development!" I ran out to the living room and saw a BREAKING NEWS banner flash across the top of the screen.

A young reporter with long blonde hair stood at the bottom of a steep driveway framed by massive acacia trees. I turned up the volume in time to hear her say, "...as reported yesterday, famed chef and accused murderer, Blake Steers, had won at least temporary freedom after his legal team persuaded the judge to grant him a new trial. But now, that retrial will never happen. We've just learned that Blake Steers' housekeeper found him dead at the foot of the stairs in his mansion this morning. We're hearing the apparent cause of death was a heart attack. We'll update you throughout the day as we get more information. Back to you—"

I was about to change the channel to see what the other networks were reporting when my cell phone rang. It was Erika.

"I don't want to sound insensitive," I said, muting the TV, "but do you have an alibi?"

"You're not funny." She sounded nervous. "You know how they say that when something seems too good to be true, it probably is?"

Hopefully, she'd be the only doubter. "They also say, don't look a gift horse in the mouth. Maybe this is one of those rare times in life when you get lucky. You are due."

She didn't sound convinced. "I guess so."

I told her I wasn't going to work. "I'm not feeling great."

"I won't be going in either—or ever. Harrier fired me last night."

It was expected, but my heart sank regardless. "I'm sorry. What're you going to do?"

After a brief silence, she sighed and said, "I don't know. I guess see if another DA's office wants me. Or maybe give private practice a try? Might be interesting to go over to the dark side and do defense work for a change. You used to like it."

"Yeah." Until Lyra's murder soured me on just about everything. The idea of private practice had never appealed to me before, but now... "You know, there's a kind of freedom in hanging out your own shingle. And not having any John Harriers to answer to."

"Amen to that. Sounds like you're considering it yourself."

"I might be. If I had a partner."

There was a beat of silence. "Really? Given my...criminally poor judgement?"

"At least you didn't fall for a serial killer."

She sighed. "Well, yeah. There's that."

Actually, I thought we'd make one hell of a team. And I'd have to go into private practice anyway. Once the press started sniffing around Roman's case, my true story would break in all its macabre glory. And then Harrier would fire me, too.

We made plans to talk about it over dinner tomorrow night.

I couldn't be sure Melody was out of the woods yet. But Steers' autopsy would show he'd been drinking—a very logical reason for him to accidentally fall down the stairs. And the fact that no one had called Erika or me about her meant she was okay so far. I lay down on the couch, wiped out after my nightlong vigil, and finally went to sleep.

×××

IT WAS AFTER SIX, and I'd just finished setting the table for dinner when Brett got back. He shrugged off his backpack as he said, "I take off for one night, and all hell breaks loose. Blake Steers is dead?"

I went to the refrigerator and took out the champagne I'd picked up that afternoon. "Want me to open it now? Or wait until after dinner?"

He smiled. "By all means, crack that sucker open."

We drank a toast to justice, and he asked me for the details. "I don't know any more than you do," I lied. "I just saw it on the news."

He took another sip of champagne. "I bet Erika's ecstatic."

"Well, yes and no." I told him she'd been fired. "And I won't be far behind, once my story goes public. We're talking about setting up a practice together."

He blinked. "Really?" Then, he slowly smiled, said, "Actually, now that I think about it, that sounds like a great idea."

"Thanks." I stood up. "Ready to eat?" I'd decided to make dinner since I'd taken the day off, but my culinary skills being what they were—extremely limited—I kept it simple: roast chicken, baked potatoes, and asparagus. A six-year-old couldn't screw that up.

"Definitely," he said. "Whatever it is, it smells terrific."

"It bodes well for me that you're so easily pleased." I opened a bottle of white wine to go with dinner. Last night's sojourn with tequila had convinced me once and for all to lighten up on the eighty proof. When we finished, we took our wine glasses and sat on the couch.

Brett raised his glass. "Does it hold up to the standards of your usual hang, The Rusty Nail?"

I rolled my eyes. "It's not my usual hang."

"Oh, I know exactly what it is." His voice gentle, he said, "When are you going to stop beating yourself up?"

"I don't know," I sighed, then looked away. The dive bars, the dicey neighborhoods…I knew I was asking for someone to punish me. In a strange way, it all gave me a way to feel like I was paying for the unforgiveable sin of failing to see what Roman was.

"Have you considered the fact that he managed to fool everyone his entire life?" He looked into my eyes. "There's no way Angela Morelli was his first victim. Serial killers don't wait until they're in their forties to get started."

I knew that was generally true. "Roman might be the exception."

"But he's not. You know he lived in upstate New York before he moved to Chicago?" I nodded, and he continued. "After Angela's murder, we contacted the police departments out there and asked to see their unsolveds. I heard they found three homicides he might be good for." He looked into my eyes. "The first one happened over twenty years ago."

I'd suspected there were other victims, but now, to hear it confirmed…I was shocked. "So I was dating Ted Bundy?"

"Nowhere near as prolific," he said, sympathetic. "But every bit as slick—probably more so."

It did change things somewhat, recognizing that Roman had been able to deceive so many people for so long. But, Lyra. I'd introduced them. And for that there could be no forgiveness.

Brett studied my face with concern. "You need to let this go, let yourself have a life." He took my hand. "I've been thinking…maybe I should stick around and help you with that."

My heart lifted. "You—you're staying?"

"Well, not on this couch. But…yeah." With a smile, he said, "You and Erika are going to need an investigator." He gave me a searching look. "How do you feel about that?"

"I feel…like this." I put my arms around his neck and kissed him.

I'd found something I thought I'd lost forever, something I hadn't even hoped for: a chance at happiness.

ACKNOWLEDGMENTS

Dan Conaway, the best agent there ever was, I will never be able to find the words to thank you for all you've done for me. Your support, your advice, your brilliance, and your all-around wonderfulness are unparalleled. Believe me, I know how lucky I am to have you.

And thanks to Dan, I had the tremendous privilege of getting to work with editor extraordinaire Genevieve Gagne-Hawes. It's so rare to have the opportunity to work with someone who is not only phenomenally talented—truly there is no one better in the business—but is also a delight. It was such a wonderful experience, I looked forward to every round of notes and was more than a little sorry when the manuscript was done.

Thank you to Chaim Lipskar, who is one terrific assistant and a pleasure to work with.

Many, many thanks to Tyson Cornell and all the great people at Rare Bird for putting *The Fall Girl* out in the world. You guys are terrific. And a big thank you to Brian Sweany of Recorded Books, who put us together.

Last, but certainly not least, my undying gratitude goes to Catherine LePard, for her great ideas and for her unwavering support that gave me the courage to reach for my childhood dream of writing novels. And who somehow puts up with my endless, "Did you really like it?" angst-ing.